W9-BUQ-493

SOUTH KINGSTOWN PUBLIC LIBRARY

Katherine Towler

EVENING FERRY

MacAdam/Cage
155 Sansome Street, Suite 550
San Francisco, CA 94104
www.macadamcage.com

Copyright © 2005 by Katherine Towler
ALL RIGHTS RESERVED.

Library of Congress Cataloging-in-Publication Data

   Towler, Katherine
Evening ferry / by Katherine Towler.
   p. cm.
ISBN 1-59692-124-2 (hardcover : alk. paper)
1. Young women–Fiction. 2. Parent and adult child–Fiction.
3. Fathers and daughters–Fiction. 4. Diaries–Authorship–Fiction.
5. Mothers–Death–Fiction. 6. New England–Fiction. 7. Islands–Fiction.
I. Title.
PS3620.O94E95 2005
813'.6–dc22

                                    2005003689

Manufactured in the United States of America.

10 9 8 7 6 5 4 3 2 1

Book and jacket design by Dorothy Carico Smith.

Publisher's Note: This is a work of fiction. Names, characters, places, and incidents
either are the product of the author's imagination or are used fictitiously. Any resemblance to actual events, locales, or persons, living or dead, is entirely coincidental.

Katherine Towler

EVENING FERRY

MacAdam/Cage

KINGSTON FREE LIBRARY

For my parents,
Jane Kellogg and Lewis Towler,
who never wavered in their belief
and encouragement

PART I

Return

Chapter One

The bells in the church steeple tolled the hour. Rachel Shattuck turned off Front Street, toward the docks, just in time to see the ferry pulling away for the run to Snow Island. Behind the window of the wheelhouse, she could make out Captain Guido, adjusting the brim of his hat. A wake of white foam fanned out behind the boat as it swung into the channel, the horn sounding a single blast. Rachel paused for a moment to watch the ferry go, before crossing the broken cobblestones to Frank's.

The bar, dark inside, smelled of French fries. Two fishermen sat at the table by the front window in their work clothes with a pitcher of beer between them. Behind the cash register, Frank swabbed at a wet glass with a towel, his head inclined toward the transistor radio set on the shelf between bottles of scotch and gin. The muffled sound of the Red Sox game carried across the room. Rachel caught only the urgent tone of the announcer's voice, followed by a collective groan from the stadium crowd.

"What's the score?" she called as she threaded her way through the tables to the pay phone in the back.

"Five–one, Orioles. They should have taken the pitcher out two innings ago." Frank raised the towel in a gesture of hopelessness. "I think Billy Herman's brain has been fried by the heat."

"I know my brain's been fried by the heat." Rachel fished in her shorts' pockets for change and waved to May, Frank's wife, in the kitchen.

May stood behind the prep table, a cigarette hanging from her mouth and a mound of hamburger meat in front of her.

Rachel slipped a dime in the slot and waited for the operator to ask for more money to connect the call. After eight rings, a small voice said hello.

"Lizzie? Is that you?"

"Yes," the girl squeaked. "My mother's waiting on a customer."

"Well, tell her I'm on the phone. It's Rachel."

"I know who you are," Lizzie said proudly.

In the silence that followed, Rachel imagined the island's pay phone, the receiver dangling by its cord in the booth by the store. After a couple of minutes, she heard Alice on the other end. "Rachel," she said breathlessly. "I was thinking it was about time you called. Has the ferry left?"

"It just pulled out."

"Guido's been late all week. The engine keeps stalling out. He doesn't take care of that thing."

"I guess Guido's not like his father."

"No, he's not, but we're stuck with him. Is it hot over there?"

"Beastly."

"I hope we're not in for another month of this. Your father's working again. He and Eddie are putting on a new roof at the Farnwells', but when it's this hot, they knock off in the middle of the day."

"So he's got some money?"

"I guess. They got paid for half the job in advance."

"Did he give you anything toward his bill?"

"He gave me something. He pays me when he has work. Don't worry about it, Rachel."

Rachel felt, as she had before, the implication behind Alice's words. The islanders had their own way of handling things, and she shouldn't interfere. Neither of them said anything for a moment, until Alice broke the silence. "The box you sent for your father came last week. Brock took it up to the house."

"Tell him thanks."

"Sure. You know Brock. He loves hauling things around. Sometimes I think he was a pack mule in an earlier life. So when are you coming for a visit?"

"Babs and I are going up to Maine. Maybe after that."

"Plenty of people over here would like to see you."

"I know." After a pause, Rachel thanked Alice for the update on her father and said goodbye.

The greasy receiver slipped from between her fingers as she set it on the hook. She stared at the restroom doors on either side of the phone, one marked with a silhouette of a woman in a hoop skirt, the other with a man in tails and a top hat. It did not seem likely that a woman in a hoop skirt had ever entered Frank's or ever would.

Rachel went down the hallway to the kitchen and took a seat on a stool by the prep table. May's ashtray overflowed with cigarette butts. "How's your father?" May asked.

"Okay. He's doing some construction work."

A rotating fan swept back and forth at the end of the table, but it did little more than move the hot air from one side of the room to the other. May's forehead glistened with sweat. She had stacked the hamburger patties on a plate, separated by pieces of waxed paper. Flattened into thin circles, they looked like flying saucers, something out of a science fiction fantasy.

"You know I've never been over to the island," May said as she covered the pile of patties with a last square of wax paper. "I always said I was going to go."

"There's not a whole lot to see on Snow."

Shuffling across the floor in a worn pair of flip-flops, May carried the plate to the refrigerator and set it inside. "It's just you imagine something for years and it keeps getting bigger in your mind."

Rachel could have offered to take May over, but she had not been back to the island since she made the trip for her mother's funeral. "Sometimes I think it was a curse, growing up on the island."

May took another cigarette from the pack in the pocket of her apron and lit it. "It's a curse growing up anywhere, honey. You just got to make the best of it. Look at you—beautiful, young, skinny. You could get married again."

"Not in the Catholic church."

May rolled her eyes. "Go talk to the priest. They can get you an annulment if they want to."

Rachel smiled. May had made this suggestion before. "I haven't met the right man."

"You've got to leave that apartment of yours. Old Mr. Right isn't going to find you hiding up there." May scooped the scraps of hamburger from the table and dropped them in the trash. "But stay away from this dump. There's nobody worth your time in here."

Rachel laughed and told May she would see her later. On her way out of the bar, she waved goodbye to Frank, who was sliding a glass of beer toward a customer. Outside, the heat rose from the pavement in waves.

Walking up the hill from the docks, she passed the Episcopal church. The stone walls gave off an aura of coolness and quiet. It had been over a year since May climbed the stairs to her apartment to deliver the message that her mother had died. April 22, 1964—the date marked the time between before and after. She had expected that with the passage of more than a year, she would move on, but her mother's death still followed her through the days. There were times when she actually felt she was being trailed. As she made the walk to work or went up the street to the butcher's, she sensed the presence of someone behind her, though the sidewalk was empty. Today it was too hot for such illusions. She felt nothing besides the soles of her feet stuck to her leather sandals and the damp cotton of her blouse pressed to her armpits.

Rachel crossed the street and headed for the two-story building where she lived. Inside her apartment, she raised the shade over the living room window, switched on the fan, and fell into a chair. The pigeons sat on the roof of the movie theater, bobbing their heads and cooing, their feathers a sheen of purple in the sun. Through the floorboards, she could feel the vibration of Bernie Goshen's sewing machine downstairs, humming away. Sometimes he did not leave his tailor shop until long after dark. She could have found another place to live, as her friend Babs frequently pointed out, where she didn't have to listen to that "infernal" sewing machine, and she would have a phone like any other normal person, but Rachel liked her three rooms and the view of the main street below, and found the constant reminder that Bernie was downstairs, shortening hems and tapering sleeves, oddly reassuring.

Reaching inside a canvas bag on the floor beside the chair, she removed a spool of white thread and a needle. She held the needle to the light and threaded it, then spread squares of patterned cotton across her lap—calicos and plaids, splashes of white and yellow flowers on pale blue. Choosing two pieces, she turned them over and began sewing them together, linking them with a narrow seam. Later, she would arrange the strips of fabric on the floor, matching them to the design in her book of quilt patterns, but for now this was work that asked only a blank attention to the size of stitches and the straightness of lines. She liked to think of Bernie as a partner of sorts, bent over his table downstairs, deftly pushing the cloth under the needle.

Pulling the thread taut, Rachel watched as the pigeons lifted off the roof of the theater in a mass of beating wings. They hung in the air, darting at each other, their breasts puffed out, and settled back into a row on the edge of the roof. She had left Snow Island, where fewer than fifty people struggled through winters, as soon as she could pack a trunk and board the ferry on her own. She had gone to live in the city, as the islanders called Providence, but now she found herself back in Barton, just a half hour ride from the island, across a stretch of water she knew the way other people knew trails in the woods or the boundaries of their own fields. On clear days, she could see the island as she walked home from her job at the elementary school, a green shadow on the horizon that looked more like a dream someone had gone on dreaming than land. May was right. Growing up on Snow was no more of a curse than growing up anywhere else. Yet Rachel often wondered how her life might have been different if she had not spent the first eighteen years of it confined to a sliver of land six miles long and two miles wide.

She had become a person she never expected to be, thirty-three years old and no longer married, living a nun-like existence above the tailor shop, searching for her mother's face among those that passed in the street below. It was, she had discovered in the two years since she left her husband and came to live in Barton, an existence that suited her. What had mattered in the past fell away. Here in her apartment, with the shouts of children from the playground down the street sounding over the whirring fan, life was stripped down to the essentials. This was the state in which all human beings would find themselves if they admitted the truth, but they could not admit the truth. They surrounded themselves with husbands and wives, children and houses, cars and washing machines, all designed to keep any sense of uncertainty at bay. She had none of these things—a husband or a house, a car or a washing machine. Sometimes she imagined herself as a bird perched on a bare limb hanging over open space. May and Babs went on about how she had to find a man, but it was not a man she needed. No, it was precisely this—the view of the bay in the distance and the hum of traffic going by.

Chapter Two

The cries of the gulls did not greet her the next morning, or the slow ringing of the bell buoy out on the bay. There was only the rhythmic sweeping of Mrs. Santos' broom, moving over the sidewalk in front of the Priscilla Alden Hotel. Rachel raised herself on one elbow and pulled back the curtain covering the window by the bed. Mrs. Santos wore a floral print housedress, the same one she wore every morning, and a pair of pink mule slippers that slapped the pavement as she moved toward the curb, pushing spirals of dust before her. It had not rained in weeks. Even the cracked surface of the sidewalk appeared parched. Mrs. Santos reached the curb and shook the broom vigorously over the gutter, before disappearing through the hotel's main entrance.

When a knock sounded at the door, Rachel stepped from the bed and pulled on her bathrobe. Crossing the living room, she found May standing in the hallway, an apron stretched over her plump waist.

"I'm sorry," May said. "Did I wake you?"

"No. I was about to get up."

"Alice just called. Frank answered it. I didn't talk to her, but she wanted us to go get you. It's your father. He was in an accident. I don't know what happened. Frank says they're bringing him over in the boat, to the hospital."

They hadn't waited for the ferry. Probably they were coming over in Will Daggett's boat. Rachel knew this meant it must be bad.

"You want Frank to give you a ride to the hospital?"

Rachel shook her head. "I'll walk."

"Give me a call, all right?" May patted Rachel's arm. "If you need anything, I can come over. Just let me know."

It wasn't until May was halfway down the stairs that Rachel thought to say, "Thanks."

Dressing quickly, Rachel calculated how long it would take to get to Barton from the island in a motorboat. Forty minutes. They might not have reached the mainland yet. She grabbed her purse, locked the door, and descended the stairs. Through the window of the tailor shop, she caught a glimpse of Bernie. He sat at the sewing machine with a collection of straight pins between his lips and a man's suit coat spread before him. He did not look up.

Rachel made her way down Front Street, away from the theater and the hotel, following the route she took to work when school was in session. It might have been an ordinary morning, except that in the heavy air all sound and life seemed to have vanished, and she was not reviewing lesson plans in her mind, seeing the day laid out in half-hour segments devoted to spelling tests and math problems and stories of the Pilgrims. Past the library, she turned away from the center of town and the ribbon of water visible beyond the rooftops. She climbed the hill to the hospital and went through the glass doors. The smell of disinfectant and floor wax met her inside, where the stale air was at least cooler. She followed the signs for the emergency room, passing the registration desk and a collection of older women in the red smocks of volunteers. At the end of a hallway, the word *emergency* was emblazoned over a set of double doors. The doors opened as she approached, and she saw Eddie Brovelli and Will Daggett seated next to each other on a couch with their elbows balanced on their knees, leaning forward, as though the floor they stared at might be about to answer some crucial question. The image brought back the boys she once knew, when she and Eddie and Will sat in the same row of desks at the schoolhouse on Snow. Eddie held a battered baseball cap in his hand, which he turned in nervous circles. He stood up as she came toward him.

"The doctors are working on him." Eddie inclined his head toward another set of doors off the waiting area. "He wasn't conscious when we put him in the boat, but then he came to. He was pretty dazed."

"What happened?" Rachel asked.

"We were working on the Farnwells' roof. Nate was up there by himself. He'd just started hammering on the shingles, and the next thing we knew, he was on the ground."

"Was he drunk?"

"At seven in the morning? No." Eddie gave her a withering look.

"Was he hung over?"

"He doesn't drink anymore, Rachel, not since your mother…" He trailed off, without finishing the sentence. "He has one or two beers. That's it."

Rachel glanced at Will, who remained on the couch, eyes downcast.

"We're always careful," Eddie said. "I was getting some more shingles. He hadn't been on the roof ten minutes. It's so frigging hot, but you know how he is. He wasn't going to let a little heat stop him." He held her gaze, a mix of defiance and guilt in his look. "I'm sorry, Rachel. I just hope to God he's okay."

Rachel went to the chair beside the couch and sat down. The conversation felt familiar, like one they must have had in the past, though this wasn't possible. Eddie stood there for a few moments, before returning to his place on the couch. Will looked up. He spoke softly, as if talking to himself. "He's gonna be all right."

Rachel studied a painting of a sailboat on the opposite wall, aware that beside her Eddie was doing the same. At last the door swung open and a man in a white coat approached. Rachel stood and extended her hand.

The doctor's hand was cool and damp. He explained that Nate's right leg was broken. It was a clean fracture, but because of the location of the break, they had put the leg in a full cast. It appeared that Nate had also suffered a mild concussion. He was confused and didn't remember what had happened. They would keep him at least overnight to see if there was any brain injury. The doctor delivered these words with clipped precision and pivoted, disappearing behind the swinging doors before Rachel could begin to think of questions she might want to ask.

A nurse arrived in a flurry of white efficiency and led them to the elevator. When the doors opened on the second floor, they followed her down the hallway. Eddie and Will lagged behind, letting Rachel enter the room ahead of them. What she noticed first was the thinness of her father's face and the lack of color to his skin. He seemed to have shrunk in the past year. His hands lay outside the sheets. The nurse circled the bed and said in a low voice, "He fell asleep when we were bringing him up. We'll wake him up in a little while to make sure he doesn't lose consciousness, but it's best to let him sleep for a bit." She placed her fingers on his wrist and gazed at her watch. Nate's hand twitched, but he did not wake.

Rachel fell into the chair beside the bed. It occurred to her that she should get something to eat, but she wasn't hungry.

"He doesn't look bad," Will said.

"Yeah," Eddie agreed, "he looks okay." He put his hand on the back of Rachel's chair. "Look, we better get going. We left the boat down at somebody's dock. I don't even know whose. We better go take care of that."

Rachel nodded.

"He's gonna be okay." Eddie patted the back of the chair.

The men said goodbye, telling her they would call or come by later. In the silence that filled the room once they were gone, she heard her father's gruff voice reverberating through the small house on the island, and the heavy tread of his footsteps. There were times when his return home at the end of the day had filled her with delight, and times when it had filled her with dread. Now, keeping an eye on the rising and falling of his chest beneath the sheet, she could not separate the memories of one time from another.

Closing her eyes, Rachel leaned back in the chair. The sound of rustling roused her. Nate's hand was moving over the sheet as though trying to grasp something. A moment later, he opened his eyes and blinked repeatedly. Regarding her with a puzzled expression, his features scrunched up like a child's, he rubbed his cracked lips together and said, "I didn't expect to be seeing you."

"You're lucky to be seeing me at all."

"I'm always lucky to be seeing you." He raised one hand as though he were going to touch her, then let it drop.

"You fell off the roof. At the Farnwells'. You could have killed yourself."

He smiled wanly and sank back on the pillow. "But I ain't dead yet, huh?" He glanced at the window. "Is it summer?"

"It's August."

"Did I come over on the ferry?"

"No. Eddie and Will brought you over, in Will's boat."

Nate nodded slowly, though it was not clear he understood what she was saying. "Phoebe didn't come with us in the boat?"

Rachel shook her head, blinking back tears at the mention of her mother's name.

The squeak of rubber-soled shoes sounded out in the hallway, and the nurse entered the room. "We're awake, I see. How are we feeling?"

"Oh, just terrific," Nate responded.

"Mr. Shattuck, I meant that question seriously."

"I feel like hell. My head's all dizzy."

The nurse pursed her lips and went to write on the chart. "Just stay still and rest, and maybe the dizziness will go away. I'll be back to check on you in a little while."

Rachel followed the nurse out into the hall. "He's very confused," she said.

"Sometimes it takes a while to get the memory back—a day or two. I'll tell the doctor." The nurse smiled reassuringly and went off down the hallway.

When Rachel returned to the room, she found that her father had fallen asleep again. She left the number of the pay phone at Frank's with the nurses at the desk by the elevator. Downstairs, she made her way to the front entrance and out into the heat. The whole way to the hospital that morning, she realized, she had been rehearsing her reaction to her father's death, testing what it would be like to be alone in the world, with both parents gone. The story would end at last, or move on to a new phase. Chastising herself for such a sinful thought, or was it a wish, she mumbled a quick Hail Mary under her breath.

Back at her apartment, Rachel drew water for a bath. She took off the rumpled blouse and skirt, the bra and panties already clinging to her in the heat, and watched the water fill the yellowed basin of the tub. Through the floor, the hum of Bernie's sewing machine sounded. She untied the ribbon that held her hair together at her neck and stepped into the tepid water. The window, open a crack, let in humid air that made her limbs feel heavy. She leaned against the tub's sloped back and closed her eyes. Covering her breasts and shoulders, the water moved over her. Her skin felt strange, as though it had become thicker in the airless hospital room. She sank lower, until the water reached her collarbone.

Reaching for the bar of soap in the dish, she rubbed the waxy square between her hands and ran the lather down her arms. The water smelled metallic, stale with traces of the old pipes it had traveled through. She scooped it up and let it run over her face, thinking of the bath back home on Snow Island, how she and her brothers would line up to take turns in the tin tub that sat in the center of the small house's main room. In the winter, it was so cold that they stripped off their clothes as fast as they could and scrambled over the side of the tub, sloshing water onto the floor. Afterwards they clustered around the stove while their mother rubbed them dry with a towel.

Through the window, she listened to the distant rumble of traffic. Strange as it seemed, people were going to work, running errands, heading to the beach. The drivers of these cars knew nothing about her father falling from a roof and becoming a confused old man. The size of the world and the number of people in it was impossible to comprehend, even here in a backwater like Barton. How could she believe in a God who listened to the thoughts of millions, when those going past in station wagons did not know her name?

The water grew cool. She lay with her eyes closed, seeing her mother seated at the piano, her fingers poised over the keys. This is how she remembered her, in an eternal state of watchfulness, playing her music while she kept one eye on the door, alert to the possibility of Nate's return. If there was a God, it seemed inconceivable that he could take her mother and leave her father on earth.

Pulling the plug, Rachel stepped from the tub, wrapped herself in a towel, and crossed the living room. Through the window, she watched Hazel Blanton on the other side of the street, flipping through the pages of a magazine as she leaned against her taxi. A white sign with "Hazel's

Cab" and the phone number painted in red was fixed to a door.

In the bedroom, Rachel took a fresh blouse from the closet and a pair of shorts from the dresser. She would wear shorts, even though she was "going downtown," as Babs would say. Retrieving her purse from the back of the kitchen chair, she set off to call Alice with the news that her father was going to live.

Chapter Three

He regarded her narrowly, holding a spoon to his lips. Neither of them spoke. Thick orange Band-Aids covered the backs of his hands. She lowered herself into the chair and watched as Nate ate from a bowl of Jell-O, his knobby Adam's apple rising and falling, his fingers shaking. She followed the repeated motion until the bowl was empty.

Rousing himself, he set the bowl on a tray perched on the bedside table. "Think you could take that away?" he asked.

Rachel reached for the tray and carried it to a table by the door. "You've got an appetite," she said.

"I ain't eaten anything for more than a day, and all they'll give me is that shit. Goddamned hospitals."

It appeared that he was his old self again. Rachel returned to the chair.

Nate fingered the edge of the sheet and stared at her. "Haven't seen you over on the island in a while."

"I was going to come –"

"Like hell you were. You heard from Junior?"

"He's working on some new television show. I got a card at Christmas."

Nate snorted. "I guess he's doing okay. Won't give any of us the time of day anyway. You call him since –" He waved his arm over the bed in a sweeping motion. "Since this?"

"I left a message at his office. I don't think he ever goes back to that house of his. There's no point calling him at home."

Junior, the middle of Rachel's three brothers, had not been back east for almost ten years, since he headed out to California, as far as he could go while still remaining on American soil. He lived in Los Angeles and called himself Nathaniel now. He sent a huge bouquet of roses when Phoebe died, and with his Christmas card he included photographs of himself in slim-fitting suits standing next to fancy cars. Rachel had a hard time recognizing the person in these photos as the brother she had once known.

"I don't know how the hell I fell off that roof. Pretty damn stupid." Nate leaned toward her, lowering his voice. "They ain't doing a damn thing for me here. I'm going home."

"Don't be ridiculous. You haven't finished your treatment."

"Treatment? You call this treatment? Shooting you full of drugs they won't tell you what they are and giving you nothing to eat but Jell-O. If I'm about to die, I'm gonna do it in my own goddamned bed and then you're gonna bury me in the cemetery next to your mother. We'll take the morning ferry."

"You can't leave the hospital until they say you can."

"Like hell. You watch." Nate gestured toward a pair of crutches propped against the wall. "I went all the way to the nurses' station and back this morning. Anybody tries to stop me getting out of here, I'll hit them over the head with those things." He spread his hands in front of him and began cracking the knuckles, one at a time.

Rachel said she would try to find the doctor. She felt her father's eyes on her back as she left the room. Nothing had changed. Nate could still get her, or anyone else, to do what he wanted.

The doctor was leaning on the counter at the nurse's station, shuffling through papers. Rachel asked if she could speak with him. He led her down the hall to a lounge, where they sat in upholstered chairs that made the place feel like a living room.

"My father wants to go home," Rachel said.

"Well, he probably can, tomorrow or the next day. He's still complaining of some dizziness, but he seems to have regained his memory, and he's getting around on the crutches. Do you see any changes? I mean, changes in personality? We look for that with a head injury."

"No. Just that he was confused yesterday."

"Then he's always been rather…" The doctor paused, searching for the right word. "Contrary?"

Rachel smiled. "Yes. I'm sorry if he's being difficult."

The doctor waved his hand in the air, as though sweeping aside any such concerns. "Sometimes after a concussion people are irritable and excitable, when they weren't that way before. We'll see how he does, but I don't think we'll keep him more than another day."

Rachel thanked the doctor and went back to her father's room. He was asleep again. She watched him for a few minutes, wishing he could remain in this state, quiet and agreeable. Why couldn't his personality have been altered for the better by the accident? He could have become docile instead of contrary, as the doctor put it. Gathering up her sewing bag and purse, she stood by the bed. His face was relaxed, even peaceful. She wondered what he dreamed about, if he dreamed. Rachel gave him one last probing look and headed out of the room for the elevator.

She walked home and climbed the stairs to her apartment to find two pieces of paper tacked to her door, folded notes with her name written on the outside. One was from Babs, suggesting they meet for dinner at Anthony's. The other was from May. "Your brother called from California," it read. "I told him your father was doing better. He said to leave him a message if he can help."

Rachel held May's note, examining the old-fashioned handwriting, as she turned the key in the lock and let herself inside. She could not imagine how Junior could help her. She refused to call him Nathaniel, even though on the rare occasions when they did speak on the phone, he kept saying, "My name is *not* Junior. Please, Rachel. Can you get that through your head?" She knew very little about her brother's life, beyond the fact that he had money, and he was not married. They were like single stars floating in space—Junior off in Los Angeles, and Phil dead in Korea, and Andy shut away at the state school. She was the only one left. She thought of Junior and Andy the way she thought of Phil; they were absent in the same profound sense, as if they, too, had died in a war on the other side of the world. This is what had become of the Shattuck family. Nothing had turned out as anyone thought it would.

Rachel changed into a dress and went to meet Babs. The evening light fell slantwise down Front Street, and the leaves of the linden trees shimmered overhead. What made a collection of people a family anyway, beyond the common blood? Even as a child, she felt that she had stumbled into her family by accident. The father she had adored sent Andy away to the state school when he was just four years old. Andy was, as they called it then, a mongoloid. Now they had a more seemly name for what was wrong with him—Down syndrome. After Andy was taken to the state school, everything she had known and loved was cast in a new light of uncertainty and betrayal. Her father was no longer the person she had thought him to be, someone incapable of doing such a thing.

From half a block away, she could smell the grilled steak at Anthony's. Babs was waiting in front of the restaurant. She shifted her black patent leather purse from one shoulder to the other as Rachel approached.

"There's a line already," Babs said. "God, you look washed out."

Babs held the door open, and Rachel followed her inside. They stood with a press of other people beneath an air conditioner that hummed loudly. "How's your father?" Babs asked.

"He says he's ready to go home. If they try to stop him, he'll hit them over the head with his crutches."

"He's a piece of work, that man."

"It looks like I'm going to have to go with him."

"You are?" Babs' voice took on a tone of alarm.

"I don't see what choice I have. He's not in much of a condition to take care of himself."

"But we're leaving for Maine on Sunday."

Rachel had been thinking about the planned vacation ever since she returned from the hospital, wondering how she could tell Babs that she could not go. "There's no one besides me."

"What about that stupid brother of yours in California? He's about as much use as a dishrag."

The arrival of the hostess put an end to the conversation. She walked briskly toward them, pressing a stack of menus to her chest. "Two?" she called. She waved Babs and Rachel around a party of five and led them to a table in the rear. Rachel took the seat facing the kitchen's swinging door. The hostess set the menus on the table and filled the water glasses.

"I mean it. Why can't your brother get out here and do something for a change?" Babs said when the hostess had gone.

"I can't even get him on the phone. When my mother died, I had four conversations with his secretary. I never even spoke to Junior. How do you think I'm going to get him to come out here now?"

"I just don't see why you have to do everything." Babs unfurled her napkin and placed it on her lap.

"I keep thinking of my mother," Rachel said quietly. "She would want me to make sure my father's all right."

This silenced Babs. She took two long gulps of water and kept her eyes on a spot over Rachel's shoulder. After a pause, she said, "Did you hear about Sheila's son? He's been drafted."

"No. How'd you hear that?"

"I ran into her in the supermarket."

Sheila, the receptionist at their school, was universally acknowledged as the one person in the place they could not do without, more necessary than the principal.

"Didn't he just get married?"

"Yeah, and he got a job finally, assistant manager at the hardware store. I feel sorry for Sheila. She looked terrible. He has to report in a couple of weeks. Then it's Vietnam probably."

They had just started calling up soldiers, though President Johnson, and Kennedy before him, insisted that the Americans were taking an advisory role in Vietnam and would not send in ground troops. Rachel thought of her brother, Phil, and the months when they waited for his letters from Korea. The sense of dread was a constant presence, a backdrop against which everything else played out. She had tried to ignore her fear, to will it away. He would come home, she told herself. Entertaining the possibility of anything else, even as a vague threat, was not admissible, but she could not shake the dread, and when word of his death arrived, she knew that she had not believed hard enough.

"We should invite Sheila to do something," Rachel said. "Take her out to dinner or a movie."

Babs nodded. "She needs to get out of the house. She said she's just sitting there driving herself crazy."

The waitress arrived, and Babs ordered the fried clams, Rachel the spaghetti and meatballs. When the waitress left, Babs said, "Maybe I can get my sister to go to Maine. We don't want to lose our two weeks at the cottage. If we cancel this time, we might never get it back again."

"I know. I thought of that."

"You've got your new bathing suit and everything."

"I know."

Laughter sounded from the table beside theirs. A group of beefy, middle-aged men with flushed faces sat in a cloud of cigar smoke.

"Son of a gun," one of them said loudly, "she was a peach. Prettiest little thing I ever saw. Jail bait, of course. Ain't that always the way?"

Someone else let out a low whistle, and they all laughed again.

"God, you can hardly see in here with all that cigar smoke," Babs said.

When the food came, they ate in silence. The meatballs were dry. Rachel chewed them without relish and swallowed heavily. Of course she did not want to spend her vacation on Snow with her father, but the truth was she had been having second thoughts about going to Maine. She watched Babs dip the clams in ketchup and drop them into her mouth with the guilty awareness of her own failings as a friend. It sometimes seemed to Rachel that the difference in the grades they taught defined all the other differences between them. A seventh grade teacher whose students were old enough to be aware of the wider world, Babs knew what she wanted, whether she was choosing from a menu in a restaurant or making summer plans; while Rachel spent her days trying to contain the darting impulses of third graders, who often had the barest grasp of what she was trying to teach them, a confusion that seemed to be mirrored in her own life.

"Do you want dessert?" Rachel asked when the waitress had taken their plates away.

Babs shook her head. "I've lost three pounds. I don't want to blow it now."

"Three pounds? That's great."

Babs grimaced. "Three pounds is hardly going to make a difference when I put on a bathing suit."

The men at the next table rose to go, stubbing out their cigars in a platter piled with the carcasses of dismembered lobsters.

The waitress brought the check for Rachel and Babs, and they fished in their purses, each setting a ten dollar bill on the table. When the waitress delivered the change, Babs counted out the tip, and they made their way out of the restaurant.

A blast of warm air met them on the sidewalk. Darkness was falling, but it felt no cooler. Two boys went riding by on bicycles and called out to Babs, "Hi, Miss Driscoll." They were gone before she could do more than wave.

"Students," she said. "They're everywhere. That's why I've got to get out of this town."

"I'll call you tomorrow," Rachel said, "when I know what's happening."

Babs tightened her hold on her purse strap. "I'll call my sister and see what she says."

Turning away, Babs went up the hill, toward her small house on the edge of town. Rachel went back down Front Street, taking comfort in the lit windows of the apartments above the storefronts and the white curtains that moved ever so slightly in the breeze. A line of people waited for ice cream at the walk-up window in front of the drugstore. She crossed the street, noting that Bernie had pulled the shade over the door of the tailor shop and gone home.

Inside her apartment, she sat by the window without turning on the lamp and watched the teenagers gathered in front of the movie theater. Their muffled voices hung on the hot air, filled with a laconic boredom. There were things she loved about going to Maine—the feel of the warped planks of the dock beneath her feet, sleeping on the screen porch, the silence of the lake—but these memories felt stolen, hoarded against what the rest of vacation entailed. Babs insisted that they walk into town each night and sit at the bar. They might meet men. You never know. This year Rachel felt she could see the entire two weeks before they happened, as if she and Babs had become caricatures of themselves, like animated figures in a cartoon. It was easy to turn people into caricatures, she reflected, if it was not in fact the basic nature of who we all were, a collection of clichés. Still, she preferred to see herself as unique, unlike anyone else. She knew that she did not need to be with a man, that she did not need to be with anyone. Babs—and the rest of the world—thought such sentiments were unnatural. So she went along, grudgingly, putting on mascara and lipstick and sitting beside Babs at the bar, when she would have liked to be back at the cottage, reading a book.

It was too hot to turn on the lights. Rachel crossed the room in the dark, undressed, and climbed into bed. The rain came with a flash of lightning and the rumble of thunder after midnight. She woke to air moving through the bedroom. Walking through the apartment naked, she went from window to window, closing them against the rain that fell in long, driving lines. The marquee of the movie theater was dark now, and the street deserted, Hazel and her taxi gone. The pigeons had disappeared to wherever it was they roosted for the night. She thought of the birds who flocked around her when she visited Andy at the state school. In good weather she carried a bag of bread crumbs with her on the bus ride to Providence. She took Andy out to the benches by the front entrance and tossed crumbs to the birds. The sparrows came in a great mob, surrounding her, until she had to flap her arms to make them fly off. Pigeons came, too, and an occasional seagull. Andy would sit on the bench, his mouth hanging open, and stare at the branches of the tree overhead. He never gave any sign that he noticed the birds, though he seemed aware of Rachel, understanding that she was not one of the orderlies in white, that she was someone different, the dark-haired angel who took him outside.

Rachel left the window in the kitchen open a crack and returned to the bedroom. She took her nightgown from a hook on the back of the door and slipped it over her head. Nestling beneath the sheet, she thought of Andy, wondering if the storm would wake him up there in Providence, if he understood the fact of rain. She fell back to sleep, as she did so many nights, holding him in her mind, rocking his awkward body and whispering to him softly.

Chapter Four

Wind gusted over the deck as the ferry pulled away from the dock and swung into the channel. The surface of the water shone in the sunlight. Rachel gripped the warm metal of the railing, watching for the place on the horizon where the island would appear. Behind her, Nate sat on a bench, leaning back, the leg encased in the cast stretched in front of him. The crutches they had given him at the hospital were propped against the cabin wall. When the ferry was under full speed, Guido came down from the wheelhouse and handed Nate a cigarette. He struck a match, lighting the cigarette Nate held to his lips with a shaking hand.

"How long you gonna have that thing on?" Guido asked.

"I don't know. Damn doctors don't tell you anything."

"That was a close call."

Nate shrugged. "If your time is up, your time is up. My time wasn't up yet."

The men went on talking, going over Nate's accident and his good luck. Up in the wheelhouse, Keith, Guido's assistant, guided the ferry into open water, scanning the bay. Tony Mendoza, the old captain, had died in January and his son, Guido, had taken over the business. It was strange to see someone else up in the wheelhouse. For Rachel's entire life, Captain Tony had been the one to steer the ferry across the bay from

Barton to Snow Island, peering through the clouded glass, his hat pulled down on his forehead.

Gradually the island came into view. As the ferry chugged closer, trees became distinct, rising on the hills, and the shapes of houses dotted the shoreline. Rachel found the white square of her family's house above the dock, surprised to discover, as always, that the place had gone on existing without her.

She spotted Eddie as the ferry pulled alongside the dock. She did not recognize most of the people gathered in the parking lot. Summer people, she assumed. Eddie stood behind them, next to his brother, Joe. He pulled on the brim of his baseball cap and gave her a long look, as if to say *so you came*. Rachel retrieved her father's crutches and held them for him. He labored to get them beneath his arms, raising himself from the bench.

Rachel and Nate let the other passengers disembark. Nate crossed the deck hesitantly, heaving his body forward beneath the crutches. He swung the cast in front of him, took a step with his good leg, and swung the cast again in an awkward rhythm. Guido came behind him, watching closely. When he reached the gangplank, Rachel went in front, walking backwards, ready to catch him if he fell.

"Blasted things," Nate muttered, gripping the crutches more tightly with his hands.

"Small steps," Rachel said. "Take it easy."

In the crowd below, there was silence. Rachel felt people watching the slow descent and heard the collective sigh as she reached the parking lot, and Nate swung off the gangplank. Eddie pushed his way through the crowd. "Hey, Nate, you're looking good. I've got the truck here. I'll give you a ride."

Eddie helped to steady Nate and walked beside him. Nate inched the crutches over the uneven ground. "You can really move on those things," Eddie said.

Nate grunted. "You call this moving?"

Eddie laughed.

Rachel followed them through the crowd. Eddie opened the passenger door of his old Chevy and took Nate's crutches. Rachel stood back, watching her father struggle up onto the seat. "You okay?" Eddie asked.

"I'm a frigging cripple. Other than that, I'm fine."

Eddie propped the crutches against the seat and turned away from the truck. "Good to see you again, Rachel."

"It's good to see you, too, someplace besides a hospital."

As soon as Rachel had spoken, she regretted her tone. She hadn't meant to suggest she blamed Eddie for her father's accident. "It doesn't look like there's room in the truck. I'll walk up to the house," she said, trying to sound conciliatory.

Eddie went around to the driver's side, slammed the door, and called, "You can put your suitcase in the back."

She hoisted the suitcase onto the flatbed and made her way through the groups of summer people. In front of her, a woman pulled a child's wagon full of cases of beer and bags of groceries. A man came behind her with a poodle on a leash. The people looked different. They wore more casual clothing and less of it, but everything else was the same—the unloading of the ferry, the strange conveyances the summer people used to get their provisions up to their houses, the backfiring of the old cars they left parked by the dock as they started them up, Joe Brovelli watching over the scene in his policeman's uniform with a holstered gun on his hip.

Rachel crossed Bay Avenue, the single road that circled the island, and climbed the hill, passing the Union Church and then Alice's house on the opposite side of the road. She was no longer Alice Daggett, the girl Rachel had known growing up. She was Alice McGarrell now, though everyone still referred to the shingled house, where Alice lived with her husband, Brock, and their three children and her mother, as the Daggett place.

Eddie passed Rachel in the truck and pulled in front of her family's house, the next one up the hill. Peeling scraps of white paint clung to the clapboards, giving the squat structure a diseased appearance.

"I ain't supposed to put weight on it," Nate was saying as Rachel came alongside the truck. He sat sideways in the seat, the cast dangling in front of him out the open door.

"Just swing down," Eddie said. "I'll catch you."

Nate frowned, then did as Eddie said. Eddie placed his hands under Nate's armpits and held him steady. "You want to get me those crutches?" he said to Rachel.

Embarrassed that she had not thought to get the crutches before he asked, Rachel retrieved them and handed them to Eddie.

"I'm too old for this crap," Nate said.

"You just have to get the hang of it. We'll have you running down Bay Avenue in a couple of days." Eddie watched as Nate swung across the dead grass and reached the porch steps. "Take them one at a time, Nate."

Rachel expected Eddie to step forward and help her father. When he didn't, she remained beside him, frozen. Nate placed his good foot on the first step and pulled himself up with the crutches. Leaning back precariously for a moment, he hopped up to the next step. Eddie tipped the brim of his baseball hat forward, squinting into the hard light. "Piece of cake. I'll see you later, Nate."

Rachel had hoped Eddie would stay and help get her father into the house, but he was already in the truck, starting the engine. "So long, Rachel," he called.

Hands balled in the pockets of her shorts, she watched the truck pull away. Eddie swung around and headed back down the hill. She saw the shape of his hat through the cab's window, the square set of his shoulders, and wished, for one stupid moment, that they were children again, crouched together on a rock by the tide pool, trailing lines in the water to catch crabs. At the foot of the hill, he turned left onto Bay Avenue, and the truck chugged away into the sunlight. Nate waited at the door of the house, propped unsteadily on the crutches. Rachel reached for the overnight bag at her feet.

The house was filled with the rotting scent of garbage. Once Rachel's eyes adjusted to the dark interior, she spotted a pile of dirty cans next to the sink, edges crusted with the dried remains of soup and beans. Beer bottles stood on the floor by an overflowing trash can, flies hovering above them in the yellow light. Nate thumped across the floor on the crutches and fell onto the couch, the color drained from his face.

The small space had served as the living room, kitchen, and dining area when she was growing up. On the coldest nights in the winter, they even slept here by the stove, on mattresses dragged from the two bedrooms that made up the rest of the house. The furniture remained as it had been when her mother died, yet the house was a different place, dirty and disordered. Stuffing showed through the bald spots in the couch's plaid upholstery. Shoved against the wall in one corner, the spinet piano was covered in a layer of dust, and pieces of a dismantled carburetor lay strewn on the kitchen table, giving off the pungent odor of gasoline.

Nate switched on the transistor radio on the table and fell asleep almost instantly, his mouth hanging open, the breath coming and going in wheezed breaths, his leg in the cast propped on a throw pillow. She studied the labored rising and falling of his chest and felt revulsion for what he had done to the house since her mother was gone. She left him and went out to the porch, where she had a clear view of the rocky shoreline and the hazy outline of the mainland in the distance. Two women sat on beach chairs by the water, watching a group of children splashing over the rocks. The children's shrieks carried up the hill.

Taking the road back down to the dock, Rachel almost expected to find Owen Pierce seated on one of the porch benches, where he had spent most of the years of her childhood, smoking his pipe, but Owen was gone now, too. He had died at the age of ninety-two, just after she graduated from the schoolhouse.

She tugged open the screen door and peered into the gloom of the store's interior. The aisles were crowded with knots of people, groceries piled in their arms. Two small girls in wet bathing suits clutched wrapped ice cream sandwiches. Alice worked the cash register while a tall young man beside her bagged groceries. Rachel realized with a start that he was Nick, Alice's son. He had grown so much that she barely recognized him. Rachel waved to Alice and made her way to the back, collecting paper towels and plastic gloves and a can of cleanser and a bottle of Murphy's soap in a wire handbasket. Making a sweep of the next aisle and the cooler, she added a bottle of milk, a carton of eggs, butter, and bread.

People chatted as they waited in line. One woman said she couldn't remember a hotter summer. Everyone was afraid their wells would go dry. A man in plaid shorts said maybe they should do a rain dance. "That's not a bad idea," the woman responded. "Know any Indians?" The man laughed.

Rachel reached the counter and took her groceries from the basket. Arthur, the store cat, lay pressed against the cash register.

"Aren't you about a foot taller than the last time I saw you?" Rachel said to Nick.

He smiled and unfurled a paper bag. "How tall was I the last time you saw me? I'm six feet now."

"I don't know. I'm still thinking of you as a fifth grader." Rachel knew this was a stupid thing to say, but she couldn't stop herself from voicing the first thought that had come into her mind when she saw Nick behind the counter.

"That was a while ago. I'll be a senior this year."

"A senior," Alice said. "I don't know how that happened." She nudged Nick in the ribs with her elbow, glancing up at him.

The resemblance between Alice and Nick was startling. Though he was taller than his mother, his shoulders were narrow like hers, his arms and wrists thin. He had the same dark eyes and wistful mouth. He was remarkably handsome, transformed from the gawky boy Rachel remembered.

"So how's Nate?" Alice asked.

"Better. He seems pretty much like himself."

"Feisty as ever?"

"Feisty as ever. The doctor wanted to know if he was always like that or if it was brain damage."

"That's our Nate." Alice reached for the bottle of milk, penciling the price on the back of a paper bag.

"I'm just worried about whether he'll be able to work. The doctor said with somebody his age, it can take a while to recover from a concussion."

"He's tough. He's got that on his side."

"I guess. The house is a wreck."

"I haven't been in there recently," Alice said apologetically, as though she owed Rachel an explanation for the state of the house.

"Eddie's not exactly a good influence. The kitchen table's covered with car parts."

Alice totaled the column of figures and opened the old cash register, taking the ten dollar bill Rachel handed her and making change. Rachel felt that no time had passed. She was still the girl who had skipped down the hill at her mother's side and helped carry the groceries back to the house.

Nick slid two bags across the counter. "Welcome back."

Rachel thanked him and scooped up the bags, one under each arm.

Outside, Joe Brovelli was leaning against the side of his car in his police uniform, talking to Will Daggett. The men waved. Rachel nodded, pressing the bags to her chest, and climbed the hill.

Up at the house, she began by cleaning the refrigerator, discarding a milk bottle whose yellow contents were clearly bad and a couple of opened cans of beans, half-full. After she had wiped down the shelves, giving the refrigerator the medicinal smell of cleanser, she turned to the piles of cans and bottles, depositing them in paper bags she found under the sink. Nate slept while she piled the bags out on the porch. She stood over him for a moment, checking for signs of life. He let out a gentle snore.

On the table by the couch sat a small, framed photo of her brother, Phil, in his Army uniform. His hat was set squarely on his head, so that almost no hair showed. The eyes staring straight at the camera did not look like his. All humor and gentleness were gone from his face, replaced by a stiff attention to duty. He had become a soldier, every inch of him. She took the photo and wiped the dusty glass on her sleeve.

Pulling on the plastic gloves, she went to the sink and, after filling it with water, extracted plates and crusted pots from the heap of dirty dishes. When the dishes were dried and put away in the cupboards, Rachel swept the floor with an old broom she found propped in the corner by the bathroom door and then tackled the bathroom, washing the floor and scrubbing out the toilet. As she worked, she listened to the radio announcer, broadcasting the news in a tinny voice. The toll of ten dead in Vietnam that week put the total of American causalities at five hundred and six. The Vietcong's losses for the last month were estimated at three thousand, the highest number of communist guerilla causalities in a month yet. The Marines were continuing to fight the Vietcong in hill camps near the Danang Air Base. The announcer went from the news overseas to an update on the forest fires burning in New Hampshire. The drought conditions were worsening all over New England. Rachel crossed the room and turned off the radio. She understood that the war in Vietnam was inevitable, even necessary, like the war her brother had gone off to fight, but she did not like to be reminded of it.

In the bedroom she had shared with her brothers, the bunk beds and the crib where Andy had slept until he was four were gone. All that remained was Rachel's narrow bed with the metal frame, where she had found her mother the last time she came home. May had climbed the stairs to Rachel's apartment to deliver the news about her mother that day in April. Alice had called from the island, May told her. A heart attack. Rachel heard the words *heart attack* and saw her father crumpled on the floor of the garage beyond the house, where he repaired cars. It was minutes, minutes that felt like hours, before May could make her understand that her mother, not her father, was dead. I killed her, Rachel thought. She walked down to the docks and waited for the afternoon ferry, thinking again and again *I killed her.* The divorce was more than Phoebe could bear. Phoebe had prayed daily for Rachel's soul, for her redemption from this sin, the breaking of a vow that could not be broken. The divorce, Rachel knew, took away the one hope which had sustained her mother, that at least one of her children would have something like a normal life, safely married in the Catholic faith.

When Rachel had stepped from the ferry that day, the islanders assembled in front of the store parted for her, giving her uneasy glances and whispering their condolences. She climbed the hill to the house and found her father in the yard, his head beneath the open hood of a two-tone Chevy Bel Air. Rachel guessed it was a '56 from the shape of the grille, though it could have been an earlier model. She did not remember now when the full-width grille was introduced, one of many features of car styles on which her father had quizzed her over the years.

Nate brought his head out from under the hood at her approach. She had not seen him since Christmas. Grease covered his work pants and hands, his chin was dotted with stubble, and a cigarette hung from his mouth. He dropped a wrench onto a pile of other tools on the ground. "She's inside," he said.

Rachel expected him to follow her up the steps, but he wiped his hands on a rag, pressed his lips tightly together, and walked off.

Phoebe lay on the bed with her hands at her side. She was wearing a dark blue dress with a high collar, the one she had bought for Easter. He had even done her hair. It was coiled on top of her head the way she had always worn it, the thin hairpins set in a circle against the scalp. Rachel had to stop herself from pulling the hairpins out, one by one, and doing it over again herself. The face was Phoebe's, just the same, and yet it had the stillness of something unnatural, inhuman. She was no longer human. What was she then, what had she become? There was a smudge of grease on her forehead, Nate's mark. Rachel placed her hand on the spot and drew back, frightened by the coldness of the skin. She took a tissue from her pocket and wiped the black grit away. She would have to call the funeral home in Barton. The newspaper, too. They would need an obituary and an announcement about the funeral. She toyed with these thoughts, stray details, while she sat on a straight-backed chair beside her mother's body and watched darkness fall.

"She ain't leaving this island," Nate said when he returned.

Rachel regarded him warily.

"I already dug the grave."

"Where?"

"In the cemetery."

Rachel had to think for a minute what he meant, to realize he was referring to the old cemetery in the woods at the island's center. No one had been buried there in years. She told him they could not bury Phoebe in the cemetery because it was closed.

"Says who?"

"I don't know. The police in Barton. It's closed—everybody knows that. It's got that historical marker on it."

"She ain't leaving this island, that's all I know."

Rachel wondered where she could turn. In the past, there was always her mother to make him see reason. "That's not a Catholic cemetery. She has to be buried in a Catholic cemetery."

"I don't think it makes any difference to God."

"Where are you going to have the funeral?"

"Our Lady of Snow. I called Father Slade. He said he'll come over."

Rachel hadn't heard the priest's name in a long time and was surprised. She thought Father Slade had been sent to a parish in Chicago, but her father informed her that he lived just a half hour from Barton, in Havendale.

"Father Slade will do this? He'll bury her in a cemetery that's not Catholic?" Rachel asked.

"That's right," Nate answered.

So it was settled, as most things were settled with Nate. He built the coffin himself and helped the undertaker, who came over on the ferry to finish the preparations, slide the body from the bed into the wood box. Father Slade conducted the funeral Mass at Our Lady, the island's Catholic church. He did not look the way Rachel remembered him. White hairs lay across his forehead like forgotten pieces of string, and a bulging stomach shook gently up and down beneath the robes as he recited the prayers. After the Mass, Nate loaded the coffin into the store's old delivery truck with the help of Eddie and Joe and Brock McGarrell. Rachel rode beside her father in the front seat, leading a procession down the dirt road.

The grave was off in the far corner of the cemetery, surrounded by chipped slate markers dating back to the 1700s that leaned precariously forward or tipped over on the ground, the names and dates barely visible.

The men carried the coffin through the crowded plot, making their way uneasily between the stones. Rachel stood back. They lowered the coffin into the ground, and she wondered if her father had made the hole deep enough. Afterwards there was a reception at the Improvement Center, organized by Gina Brovelli, Joe's wife, who had made meatballs in gravy and egg salad sandwiches. To Rachel's surprise, the Brovellis said nothing about the irregularity of burying Phoebe in the island cemetery and having Father Slade consecrate the ground. Perhaps they thought such details didn't matter because none of them saw her mother, a convert, as truly Catholic. Rachel clutched a paper cup full of lemonade and nodded as people mumbled "I'm so sorry" and moved away. Later that afternoon, she boarded the ferry with Father Slade. The old priest stood outside on the deck throughout the crossing. When they reached Barton, he took Rachel's hand, tears in his eyes, and said, "Your mother was an extraordinary woman."

Rachel reached beneath the bed now, dragging the broom over the uneven floor boards. She was rewarded with a pile of mouse droppings and shredded paper, which she swept into the dustpan before going on to her father's room. Empty beer bottles sat by the double bed, next to a disorderly stack of newspapers and magazines. Gray sheets which might have been white once lay in a wadded pile in the middle of the mattress, and a plaid blanket with unraveling hems hung over the bedpost. She retrieved another paper bag from beneath the sink and loaded the beer bottles into it, holding them gingerly, trying to keep the stale beer from spilling onto her fingers.

Chapter Five

"There ain't much to this stuff," Nate said.

They sat at the table together, facing each other, eating chicken soup.

"The doctor said to take it easy, not to eat anything too heavy."

"Christ, this isn't even food."

"I'm just telling you what the doctor said."

"What else did he say? That I should piss in a pot because it's too far to walk to the bathroom?"

Rachel ignored this remark and buttered a piece of toast. "You had a fairly serious accident."

Nate shrugged. "Serious. What's serious? Death is serious. Everything else is just the crap we go through."

"Fine. I'm just trying to see that you get better."

Nate laughed. "You always were my guardian angel. You used to scare me when you were a kid the way you looked at me. Nobody had eyes like that."

Rachel ate her toast, thinking that she was the one who had been scared, constantly watching for signs of the next disaster in their lives.

Nate finished the soup and pushed the bowl toward her.

"I was supposed to go up to Maine with Babs this weekend, for our vacation," she said as she carried the dirty dishes to the sink.

"And now you're stuck here with me?"

"No, I'm not stuck here, but if I'm going to give up my vacation, the least you could do is cooperate."

"Go on your vacation if you want. I ain't raining on anybody's parade. Eddie and Brock and Alice can get me anything I need."

Rachel kept her back to him and rinsed the bowls, swabbing them with a dishcloth. "You're not going to be able to work, at least until you get the cast off. Have you thought about that?"

"I can still repair cars. You just gotta prop me up on a stool or something."

Before she could think of a suitable response, a vehicle pulled up outside. A door slammed, footsteps sounded on the porch, and Eddie entered the house without knocking, a six-pack of Narragansetts under his arm. He took a seat at the table as though it were a nightly routine and offered Nate a beer. Rachel draped the dishcloth over the edge of the sink, watching as Eddie pulled a bottle opener from his pocket, uncapped the beer, and slid it toward Nate.

"Guess who's leaving for her vacation in Maine in a couple of days?" Nate said.

Eddie swung his gaze across the room. "We thought you might hang around for a while."

Rachel folded her arms across her chest. "I don't think he should be drinking."

"Nate, the doctor say anything to you about beer?" Eddie asked.

"Not that I can remember."

The men exchanged glances, like teenagers caught sneaking out of the house.

"A bottle of beer won't kill him," Eddie said to Rachel. "Want one?" Eddie slipped a bottle from the carton and held it toward her.

"No, thank you." Rachel crossed the room and tugged on the screen door. It stuck, resisting her effort to open it. She felt the men behind her, watching. She gave the door another pull, hard, and it came free, nearly hitting her in the face. The door slammed shut as she stepped into the warm darkness. The air was thick, the stars just visible overhead in a hazy sky. She stood on the top step, wondering where she could go. There were people assembled on the porch at the store, and a car drove by on Bay Avenue. She sank into the lawn chair on the porch and listened to the murmur of voices from inside the house, furious with Eddie, though she knew there was nothing she could do about it. He was thirty years younger than Nate, but they might as well both have been sixteen, sitting around drinking beer and playing cards all night, and tinkering with car engines all day.

Cigarette smoke drifted through the screen door. Their voices remained barely audible. She heard the sound of cards being shuffled and dealt. Across the still space of the bay, the lights of the bridge that connected Barton with the road to Newport glittered. On clearer nights, you could make out the headlights of the tiny cars moving over the mainland, but tonight the air was too heavy. The mainland hovered on the horizon like an uneasy apparition.

Inside, they played one hand of cribbage and then another. Her father had taught her the game when she was fourteen, after he came home from the war, and she would follow him with an awed reverence from the house to the shack where he had his fix-it shop. He had been to Italy. He had crossed the ocean on a troop ship and fought the Germans. Before he left for the war, Nate was the father who made her wooden toys and tossed an old baseball to Phil and Junior out in the yard and gave her a rough kiss goodnight. On his return, he became a hero who had seen the world. He knew what lay beyond the island. This was one of the bonds he shared with Eddie. She had never heard the men trade stories of their wars, World War II in her father's case and Korea in

Eddie's, but she had always sensed that the time they spent away from Snow had marked them in ways they believed only another soldier could understand.

The clink of bottles carried from inside. The cards were dealt again, and she heard Eddie, talking more loudly. "So she's really going to Maine?"

"I don't know. She said she wasn't going, and I said she should."

"Who's she going with?"

"That friend of hers, Babs. Somebody from the school."

"Is she divorced? I mean officially?"

"Yeah, the divorce came through a while ago. I never liked that guy."

"Neither did I."

"Phoebe thought he was the cat's meow, all educated and everything, always going on about music. I thought he was just stuck up. I could never see why Rachel wanted to be with somebody that much older than her—and a frigging librarian."

"I was surprised... " Eddie trailed off.

"What?"

"I don't know. When she and Kevin split up, I was surprised she came back to Barton. I thought she might go someplace else."

"Hell, she's about the only family I got left. Don't go wishing her on the other side of the country."

Their voices dropped again, and then there was silence, broken by the sound of cards shuffled.

Rachel eased herself out of the chair and descended the porch steps as quietly as possible. She took the road down the hill, toward the water. It was not news to her that her father disliked Kevin. When she and Kevin had come to the island for their annual visits, he and Nate could find nothing to say to each other. Kevin spent the whole time talking with Phoebe at the kitchen table, going through her sheet music and choosing pieces for her to play on the piano. Rachel supposed that her father was right. She was the only family he had left, but he saw this state of affairs as something imposed on him by an unjust fate or an angry God, while she saw it as the reaping of what he himself had sown. It all began when he sent Andy to the state school. From then on, they lived with the awareness that any one of them could be banished without warning, that what held them together was fickle and tenuous.

Moving over the dirt road, Rachel felt the worn path through the soles of her sandals. Living in Barton, she forgot about the luminous quality of nights on Snow. The darkness had its own light, a muted glow that emanated from deserted patches of lawn. The years after her father came home from the war and before he sent Andy away hung suspended like ornaments on a Christmas tree, separate from what came before and after. They were years that remained untouched, in a pool of goodness, and yet she did not want to linger there, because each polished memory contained a hint of what would follow. Still that time haunted her, pulling her back whether she wanted to return or not. They were a family then, and in her childish way, she had felt a fierce pride in her brothers and her father and her mother. They were remarkable people, each one of them, even Andy. They were not like everyone else.

Rachel crossed Bay Avenue and took the path to the store. The porch was empty now, though a car waited in the parking lot with the engine running. A boy, or young man, sat behind the wheel, his arm hanging out the open window. He tapped his fingers against the side of the car, in time to the beat of a Supremes song playing on the radio.

Inside the store, Rachel waited while Nick sold a bottle of Coke to a teen-aged girl with blonde hair. He counted out the change, and she slipped the coins into the pocket of her denim shorts and turned to go. Her bare feet were tanned a deep brown. Rachel studied her feet as the girl went to the door, remembering how she had spent afternoons in the sun when she was that age, hoping for a tan while her skin turned bright red and peeled and peeled again. This is what had separated her from the summer people. They seemed to tan effortlessly while she looked like a boiled lobster from June to September.

She stepped up to the counter as the girl swung out the door. "You've got the night shift, huh?"

"Day shift, night shift, I'm always here."

"That's not much of a vacation for you."

Nick shrugged. "My mother works hard. I try to help her out."

"The summer people need their sodas and ice cream, right?"

"Right. What can I get you?"

"I just need to use the phone. Is it working?"

"It was the last time I checked. You never know."

"I'll take my chances." Rachel set two dollar bills on the counter.

Nick opened the cash register and counted out two piles of dimes. "How long are you planning on talking?" he asked with a smile.

"Hard to say." Rachel scooped up the dimes.

The screen door swung open, and new customers arrived, three younger boys in shorts and tee shirts and bare feet. They went straight to the rack of magazines and comic books, all talking at once about what they planned to buy. Rachel thanked Nick and went out to the phone booth with the warm dimes in her hand.

She inserted a coin and dialed zero. The operator came on and asked for the number, then told her to deposit thirty cents for the first three minutes.

Babs answered on the second ring. "How's the patient?" she asked.

"Ornery. Cantankerous."

"What a surprise."

"He's driving me crazy, but I don't see how I can leave. He's still sleeping a lot, and he makes me a nervous wreck going around on those crutches. Then Eddie shows up with beer tonight."

"Great. You can baby-sit the two of them."

"I just left, I was so disgusted. Did you talk to your sister?"

"Yeah, she said she'll come up with me, and she'll pay your share of the rent, so you don't have to worry about it."

"That's nice of her. Thanks, Babs. I'm really sorry. You know I've been looking forward to this vacation for months."

"Yeah, I know." Babs made a strange sound which Rachel identified after a moment as gum snapping. "Next year. I'll make that clear to my sister. I don't want her to think she can come again next year."

"Say hello to Mrs. Anderson. And the Hershels."

"Yeah, I'll do the whole beach tour for you. We'll send a postcard."

"I'm sure it will be cooler up there."

Babs agreed that it probably would be cooler, and they said goodbye. Rachel hung up the phone, dropping the unused dimes in her pocket, and followed the path away from the store, over the rocks to the beach. A faint breeze carried off the water, warm and sultry. She crossed the rocks to the packed sand at the water's edge. The tide was low, and the waves lapped at the rocks in ripples of white foam. Up on the road, light shone from the windows of the summer houses. A door slammed, and a woman's voice sounded, calling someone's name.

Rachel walked on, toward the lighthouse, remembering how she used to pull Andy over the bumpy road in the wagon. They would sit on the beach by the lighthouse, searching for shells and rocks. Andy clutched them in his fists, exuberant over each find. In his world, every experience, no matter how large or small, fell into one of two categories—those that filled him with joy and wonder, and those that crushed him with disappointment and frustration. She had spent most of her time, it seemed, trying to protect him from the sudden arrival of despair. A cookie dropped on the floor, a toy taken from his hands, a voice raised in anger—any of these things could make his face shift in an instant from glee to heart-wrenching hurt. Perhaps, she sometimes thought, his abrupt mood swings were not that different from what "normal" people felt. It was just that Andy couldn't hide his emotions.

The afternoon when her mother had brought Andy home, Rachel stood by the dock with her brothers, waiting for the ferry. The gulls wheeled overhead, as though they were waiting, too. At last the ferry came into view, moving slowly toward them. They had stayed with Mrs. Cunningham at the lighthouse while their mother went to the mainland to have the baby. Rachel made her brothers take a bath in Mrs. Cunningham's tub that morning and dress in their Sunday clothes. Junior stayed beside her, anxious for the first sight of their mother, but Phil ran back and forth between the summer people's cars that had been left in the gravel lot for the winter. Rachel held Junior's hand tightly, her eyes fixed on the ferry. Her mother was bringing back the sister she had prayed for. Her father, who was off fighting the war, would not know about the birth of his child for weeks.

Phoebe came down the gangplank with a small bundle in her arms. Rachel ran toward her, her heart beating hard. "Let me see her," she said, tugging at the edge of the blanket.

Her mother smiled tiredly. "It's a boy."

From the start, they called the baby Andy. A longer name would not have suited him because he would always be a child. Rachel did not understand this until Joe Brovelli leaned over her desk at the school-house and blurted, "Your brother's retarded." "No, he's not," she snapped back. When she told her mother what Joe had said, expecting her to deny it, Phoebe drew her lips together and said yes, Andy was *different*. Had she done something, Rachel wondered, to make her brother turn out this way? She had not wanted a brother or a sister, really. God knew this. God had heard the awful thoughts in her mind and punished her for them. She remembered thinking how sorry she was for making her brother turn out wrong, though she stood in front of her mother, staring at the baby, and said nothing.

His face had always been strange. Rachel saw it the moment she peered beneath the blanket at the tiny bundle in her mother's arms. The eyes were too big, the mouth too slack. She told herself this was just how babies looked. He would outgrow it. She was eleven when Andy was born, old enough to ask questions, but she didn't. She went on trying to believe he was normal until Joe named what was wrong.

Andy could say a few words when her father took him away—cat, eat, truck. Rachel was the only one who was able to understand him most of the time. She sensed what he wanted before he began pointing and moaning. She could tell the difference between hunger and simple frustration, being cold and fear. Her mother would turn to Rachel, a panicked expression on her face, and ask, "What is it? What does he want?"

Rachel carried on entire conversations with Andy, following the trail of his garbled sounds and gestures. "The sun feels warm, doesn't it?" she would say. He would break into laughter and point at the sky. In good weather, he waited for her on the porch to come home from school and made his happy, chirping sound when she came into sight. He jumped up and down, his mouth open in a lopsided grin. She would pick him up and twirl him around. His laughter sounded like hiccoughs. Her mother would come out, saying in alarm, "Rachel, he's going to choke." But Rachel knew he wasn't going to choke; she knew he was just laughing. They sat on the porch on spring afternoons, Andy on Rachel's lap, and she read to him. He followed the lines on the page when she held her finger beneath them, and she imagined that one day she could get him to read if she just kept at it. Andy cooed when he was held, like a dove.

They did not tell her that he was going away. Rachel returned from school one afternoon to find that he was gone. Her mother's face was bloated from crying. "Your father took Andy to the state school in Providence," she said. When Nate returned, he muttered, "It's best this way. They know how to take care of him there."

Once a year, they went to visit Andy, taking the ferry over and riding the bus to Providence. The visits lasted an hour at most. Afterwards they went to eat at a diner and boarded the bus back to Barton. Sometimes they spent the night at the Priscilla Alden Hotel. The first time they went to the state school, Rachel saw in an instant that Andy had changed. He did not call out or speak the words he had used at home. He did not seem to understand who they were. As time went by, the sounds he made became less and less articulate. He moaned and rolled his head. Rachel could no longer tell what prompted his outbursts, though she was certain that inside his clouded mind was a person who felt what she felt, who wanted the basic things that anyone wanted, affection and belonging and knowing that he mattered.

Her parents and her brothers never spoke of Andy. They did not even mention his name when they planned and carried out the annual visits, which they referred to simply as "going to Providence." Andy became a phantom, a memory Rachel clung to while everyone else pretended there was nothing to remember. When Rachel moved to Providence, she went to see Andy once a week. She held his hand and talked to him the way she had back at home. She learned about what it meant to have Down syndrome. Even if he had not been sent away, if they had known how to help him more when he was young, Andy would never have been a "high functioning" Down syndrome patient, as the doctors termed it, yet she was determined to undo at least some of the neglect. She tried to coax him to speak. He stared at her without responding. She read to him from the newspaper and children's books, but no matter what she tried, he looked vacantly past her, head bobbing. She stopped going to see him so frequently. When she married Kevin and went to work at an elementary school in Providence, the visits fell off to once a month. She felt sick and ashamed at not going to see him more often, but she could not bear it. Trapped behind his uncomprehending eyes, she saw the boy she remembered, the glimmers of understanding he used to display. It took days after each visit to shake the sense of longing for that other Andy, the one who might have learned to talk and live a semblance of a life if he had not been locked away, exiled from everything he loved and knew.

Rachel passed the old inn and came to the lighthouse. The inn was empty, its rows of windows dark. The Gibersons still owned the place, but they no longer operated it as a public inn and only came once or twice a year. A row of rocking chairs sat on the long porch as though waiting for someone to fill them. Turning from the shore, she climbed the path to the road. She tried to ease her guilt over Andy by sewing, making a new quilt each year to give him at Christmas. It took her most of the year to complete the quilt, and then she would start on a new one for the next year. He kept the quilt with him all day, wrapped around his shoulders, and slept with it at night. By the time she brought the replacement each year, the old one was covered with food stains and worn at the edges.

When she reached the house, Eddie's truck was gone. Inside, the lamp burned by the kitchen table, and three empty beer bottles sat beside the deck of cards. From her father's room came the sound of snoring. She stood in the open doorway. He lay on his back, still dressed, on top of the covers, his hands hanging palms up at his sides. She crossed the floor, trying not to make the boards creak. Unlacing the boot on his good foot, she pulled it off and set it by the bed. He stirred, exhaling heavily and shaking his head, as if bothered by the buzzing of a fly, but he did not wake.

Chapter Six

Rachel lay listening for the sewing machine downstairs, thinking that she was back in Barton. Instead, the low undertone of the foghorn sounded in the distance. Opening her eyes, she found a wet swirl of fog beyond the window.

Stepping from the bed, she pulled on her underwear and shorts and blouse, and eased open the door, gliding past her father's room. He had managed to turn onto his side, the cast awkwardly stretched along the edge of the bed. His raspy breathing had the roughness of sandpaper. She hurried to the bathroom and latched the door behind her. She used the toilet and washed herself as quickly as possible, running the water in a quiet trickle, not wanting to wake him.

The wet air clung to her face as she let herself out of the house and started down the hill. Rachel could see people on the porch of the store, though she could not make out who they were. She crossed the road and took the gravel path toward the dock. "Morning," Joe Brovelli called as she approached. Will Daggett sat beside him on a packing crate.

Rachel returned Joe's greeting and stepped through the screen door. Inside, the small space was thick with the smell of coffee. Alice was seated on the stool behind the counter.

"You can't see a thing out there," Rachel said.

Alice looked up from the ledger book. "It's going to burn off and be hot as hell again."

"When did you start serving coffee?"

"We've always served coffee. Except during the war, when we couldn't get it."

"I don't remember coffee when I was a kid."

"My mother always kept a pot going in the morning for the quahoggers."

"Guess I better have some then."

Alice took the coffee pot from a hot plate on a shelf behind the counter and poured Rachel a cup. Rachel paid and carried the cup over to a small table by the door holding a pitcher of milk and a bowl of sugar.

The door swung open, and Lizzie went darting toward the counter. She eyed Rachel warily. "Lizzie, say hello to Miss Shattuck," Alice said.

Lizzie stuck a finger in her mouth. Like Nick, she resembled her mother in so many ways—her small frame and thin arms, her unruly brown hair, her pensive eyes. Rachel thought of Alice all those years ago, when they were students together at the schoolhouse. Alice, who was eight years older, had filled Rachel with awe when she went to the blackboard and solved math problems. Now Alice did not look like she had ever been that girl, with her thick waist and long hair, her worn blue jeans and plaid shirts.

"You're the one on the phone," Lizzie said, removing her finger from her mouth.

"Right," Rachel responded. "Now I don't have to call. I'm here."

Lizzie gave her a look that suggested this was a rather obvious statement. Alice ran her hand over the girl's head. "Didn't Grammy brush your hair?" she asked.

Lizzie shook her head.

Rachel left Alice smoothing the tangles from her daughter's hair and carried the coffee out to the porch, where she sat on the bench. Joe stood, leaning against the railing with his back to the water. "The fog will break by noon. You can still get some quahogging in today."

Will extracted a cigarette from the pack in his breast pocket and lit it, cupping one hand around the end. "Yeah, but I don't like losing the morning. Screws up everything."

"That's the weather for you," Joe said, as though he took pride in the freakish nature of the seasons in New England. "The clams will still be there. How's your father doing, Rachel?"

"Okay."

"Since your mother's been gone, we watch out for him, you know. You probably remember what it's like. If you live on this island year-round, you're family. It's not like the mainland."

"I appreciate the help you all give him." Rachel sipped the coffee and kept her eyes on the shrouded surface of the water beyond the dock.

"We're not looking for appreciation. That's just the way it is. Your father's part of the family."

Rachel supposed he was suggesting that they treated her father like family when she didn't, but she continued to drink the coffee without responding.

"You have anything to do with that school board over in Barton?" Joe asked.

"Not really."

"I guess you heard they want to shut us down and send all the kids to the mainland. Budget stuff. They say it's too expensive to keep the schoolhouse open. I don't know who they think they are, telling us to send kids seven, eight years old over on the ferry every day. And what about in the winter? We get iced in, and the ferry doesn't run. I'll be damned if I'm going to let my kids live with somebody on the mainland for the winter. That's what I told the school board. You can't take kids away from their parents. I don't care who you are."

Rachel had read about the conflict in the Barton paper. The school board had agreed to keep the schoolhouse open for another year. After that there would be more budget reviews and no doubt more battles.

"They scheduled the hearing on a Monday in March," Joe went on. "They thought none of us would make it. We rounded up every motorboat and quahog skiff on the island and took everybody, even the kids. They thought we were gonna roll over and play dead, but they had another thing coming. There they are building a new high school, and they won't give us a measly few thousand dollars for a teacher and some books. It ain't like we're asking for much. Just give us a teacher and some pencils."

Rachel knew that this simple request was not so easily filled, budget or no budget. Since Miss Weeden retired, it had been a challenge to find and keep a teacher on the island. "What about sending the older kids over to the mainland for high school?" she asked.

"If we make one concession, that's it. We send the high school kids over, and they'll say there's no reason to keep the elementary school kids here, either. Besides, it's better to keep them together. The younger ones do better with the older ones at the schoolhouse. Miss Hopkins was okay last year. She's young, right out of college, but that means she knows all the new stuff about teaching. We got Owen Pierce's house fixed up for her. He left it to Miss Weeden, you know. She lets the schoolteacher live there in the winter, and she rents it out in the summer. We all pitched in and did some work on it. There's a nice little wood stove and plumbing and electricity—all the amenities. We give her a car, too. Your father lets her have that Ford coupe of his. I don't know what else anybody could want."

Rachel thought this last statement was a joke, but she saw by the expression on his face that he was serious. She refrained from suggesting that young women just out of college might want more of a life than the island offered, with someone to talk to besides Joe Brovelli and his children.

"Sounds like you've got her set up pretty good," Rachel said. She finished the coffee and dropped the cup in the trash can by the door. "I better be getting back. See you later."

Joe said goodbye, and Will gave a slight nod of his head. She climbed the path to the road and turned onto Bay Avenue. She could just make out Joe's voice, amplified by the fog. "Guess she's staying for a few days, anyway," he said. Will's response, if he made one, was lost in the thick air.

Rachel walked away from the dock, toward the dump. The fog brought an eerie silence to the island. The sound of her footsteps came back from the pavement, distant and muffled. Only the foghorn broke through, the long cry sounding once every sixty seconds like a voice searching for itself.

Joe Brovelli had never liked her, and she had never liked him. Sometimes she found it hard to believe he was Eddie's brother. Eddie didn't swagger the way Joe did. Will Daggett was different, quiet and kind, the way she remembered him as a boy, when he helped his mother and Alice at the store. He lived with his wife and two sons down near the old Navy base.

She passed the Improvement Center, a long white building that served as the island library and community center, and went on by the dump. A car came out of the mist and went past. She raised her hand in a wave, and the driver, a man wearing a squat cloth hat, waved back. She did not recognize him. Once she had known all the summer people, at least by sight. The year-round population of less than fifty islanders swelled to five hundred in the summer. Rachel had prided herself on keeping track of the comings and goings of the summer people, who was renting which house and for how long.

A pebble rolled beneath the thin sole of her sandal, sharp and hard.

She flinched and kicked it away. Past the dump, where the road forked, she took the turn toward the far end of the island, out to Gooseneck Cove. She was almost to the sandy beach when she heard the sound of a vehicle approaching. Eddie's truck appeared in the white light, chugging toward her, and came to a stop. "Nice day for a walk," he said.

"They say the fog will burn off."

"Who's 'they'?"

"Your brother, Alice, Will."

"You've consulted the weather forecasters at the store, I see. Want a ride?"

"Where are you going?" Rachel asked.

"No place." Eddie leaned across the seat and opened the passenger door.

Rachel circled the front of the truck and climbed up into the cab. Empty potato chip bags and candy bar wrappers littered the floor. Eddie backed up, a cigarette between his lips, and turned around. He went down the stretch of dirt road, driving fast, outrunning the dust that swirled behind the truck. At the cut-off for the sandy beach, he turned the wheel hard and pulled to a stop at the head of the path that wound through the beach grass.

"Remember that winter the fox sat outside the schoolhouse every day, and you and me and Phil tried to catch it?" he said as he shut off the engine.

Rachel saw the long-legged fox sprint across the snow, and the three of them chasing after it, struggling to run in their cumbersome boots. "What made us think we could catch a fox?"

"We were kids."

"It used to watch us through the windows at the schoolhouse, like it wanted to get in. I thought that fox was the most beautiful thing."

"It wasn't so beautiful when it got my grandmother's chickens."

"Did your grandfather shoot it?"

"Probably. He was always shooting something." Eddie drummed one finger on the steering wheel and turned to look at her. "What I told you at the hospital was the truth. Your father doesn't drink like he used to."

"So why are you bringing beer over?"

"I told you—he has a beer, two beers. It's when he can't get the stuff that he goes on a binge. I figure it's better for him to drink a couple of beers than that."

"So you're doing him a favor by drinking with him?"

"Jesus, Rachel, don't get all holier than thou on me. I'm trying to tell you I look out for him. He's been pretty lonely since your mother died."

Rachel studied a crack that ran along the bottom of the windshield. "I couldn't bring myself to come over."

"Did I say you should have?"

"No."

There was another long silence, until Rachel said, "It's a strange thing, how when somebody is dead they can seem to be more *there* than when they were alive. I kept telling myself I had to come over here. I even packed a bag and went down to the ferry once, but I couldn't get on. All I could think about was how when I got off the ferry, she wouldn't be here."

Eddie took a drag on the cigarette and stubbed it out in the ashtray. "That's how it was when I came back from Korea. I couldn't get up in the morning, I couldn't drive over to the store, I couldn't buy a pack of cigarettes without thinking about Phil."

"And then it stopped? You didn't think about him so much?"

"No, I still think about him all the time. I just got used to it."

Beyond the rounded hood of the truck, tendrils of fog clung to the low bushes of the beach roses, turning the pink flowers to indistinct blots of color. "I dream about him," she said. "I wake up thinking he's alive, and then I remember."

Eddie tapped his finger on the steering wheel again.

"He's always the same age in the dreams. He doesn't get any older. Sometimes that makes me really sad, and sometimes I think, isn't that wonderful? He's still nineteen."

"Phil should be here. I can't stop thinking that. He should be here. I remember my grandfather and grandmother a lot, but it doesn't seem like they should be here. They had decent lives, they had kids and grandkids. I would have liked them to stay around longer, but I couldn't argue with it when they went. But Phil should be here."

"My mother should be here, too."

After a moment, Eddie said, "Yeah, she should." He shifted his weight against the seat. "I better get going. I've got to pick up some stuff down at the store and get to work."

"You don't want to take a walk on the beach?"

"Nah, I've got to get over to the Farnwells'."

Rachel pushed open the door and stepped out. "I'll see you then."

Eddie nodded. She slammed the door, and he started up the truck, giving a quick wave as he gunned the engine and backed up to the road.

Rachel followed the path to the beach. She could just make out the shoreline down below when she reached the sand. The beach grass brushed her bare legs as she cleared the path, and she saw herself at twenty, drying dishes and placing them in the cupboard. She could even remember what she had been wearing that night, a blue cotton skirt that swirled around her knees, and a white blouse, and the saddle shoes that made her feel so sophisticated. She was home from Providence for the weekend. Phil and Eddie pulled up outside in another Brovelli truck and came bounding through the door. They stood side by side, smiling, as though they believed the momentous news they had to deliver could be discerned simply by looking at their faces, and then Phil announced that he and Eddie were leaving for the mainland in the morning to enlist. The sun had just set, and the sky was full of a suffused light that gave the still water down below the appearance of glass. Phil stood there with his fingers curled through the belt loops of his pants, radiating pride. Nate jumped to his feet and shook Phil's hand and then Eddie's, and slapped them on their backs. They were going to follow in his footsteps and serve their country. He could think of nothing finer, nothing that could make him happier.

Rachel crossed the beach to the water, her feet sinking in the sand. Eddie had not returned from Korea until six months after they buried Phil in the Catholic cemetery in Barton. He arrived home at the end of the summer, days before she was due back at college. They spent those days together, walking the paths in the woods without speaking, staring mutely at each other across the table at the Brovellis while Eddie's mother filled their plates with food. Rachel could not look at Eddie without seeing Phil. He brought her brother back with an aching vividness that she wanted both to escape and savor. On the night before she left for school, Eddie came to say goodbye. They sat on the porch, and in the dark, he grasped her hand and whispered, "Meet me at the schoolhouse." Once her parents and Junior were asleep, she slipped out of the house and followed the path through the woods, across the center of the island.

Eddie was waiting for her behind the schoolhouse, on a blanket he had spread over the wet grass. He kissed her with a fevered urgency and tugged at the buttons on her blouse. Rachel could think only that she had longed for this revelation, to know what it felt like to have a man's hands on her breasts and to be admitted to the mystery of sex. There was something more, though, which she knew even that night, as they awkwardly undressed. Their speechless grief could not be expressed, but they could run their fingers through each other's hair and press their bodies together, and for a few moments, maybe it would be enough. Their touching was tentative and clumsy at first. She was frightened to move her hand below his waist, uncertain if this was what he expected or wanted, but when he guided her there, she felt the strange, electric delight of knowing she could give him pleasure. He rolled on top of her, gently working his way inside, and she held him tightly, feeling the muscles in his back beneath her hands like lengths of rope. Afterwards they lay side by side in the cool air, hands linked, deeply and sweetly exhausted.

The next morning Rachel boarded the ferry and waved to Eddie and the rest of the islanders as the boat pulled away. They both understood that what had happened the night before was not the beginning of anything. It was the end of the years she and Eddie and Phil had spent racing each other across the rocks at low tide. It was the end of there being three of them.

By the time Rachel returned to the island, she had met Kevin, who was unlike Eddie and the other island boys in every way. Any thoughts she might have harbored about Eddie had vanished. The night behind the schoolhouse was an aberration neither of them could explain. It was best left that way. Junior went off to Los Angeles, and Nate took Eddie into his business fixing cars and anything else the islanders or summer people needed repaired. Eddie was always around the house when Rachel came for a visit. They all understood. He had taken Phil's place, the only thing he could have done, the only thing they could have let him do. Ernie Brovelli, Eddie's grandfather, died shortly after Rachel and Kevin were married, and Eddie's parents moved to Florida. After that, Eddie celebrated the holidays at his brother's and at the Shattucks', splitting Thanksgiving and Christmas between the two houses, as if he were a member of both families.

Rachel had never told anyone about the night she spent with Eddie, except for a priest at a church in Pawtucket, which she had not attended before or since. She made her confession and stayed for the Mass, and, satisfied that she was absolved, did not speak of it again, even to Kevin, who believed what she told him, that she was a virgin on their wedding night. In a way, this was the truth. What she and Eddie had done bore a technical resemblance to sex, but it was really something else, the two of them clinging to any shred of life they could find.

The deserted beach stretched before her in an eerie blanket of white. Rachel lay on the damp sand, searching for a sky beyond the fog, until she heard someone approaching and raised her head to find Nick coming from the direction of the marsh. He swung a bucket from one hand and wore blue jeans caked with mud around the ankles. Rachel sat up.

"You've been busy this morning," she observed.

Nick set the bucket in the sand and squatted beside her, balancing his arms on his knees. "I wanted to catch the low tide."

Rachel peered at the clams piled in the bucket. "You got a lot."

"The summer people all go to the flats off the lighthouse. They don't bother coming over here. You've got to climb over all those rocks. You can always find a lot here. You know what time it is?"

Rachel glanced at her wrist, then remembered she was not wearing her watch. "It must be eight-thirty, something like that."

Nick squinted at the sky. "You can almost see the sun."

"Almost."

"So what do you do when you're not sitting on a foggy beach?"

"I teach at the elementary school in Barton."

"No, I mean what do you like to do?"

Rachel met his look. It was not the sort of question, frank and verging on the personal, that islanders asked each other. "I love to read. I guess that's why I became a teacher. My brothers used to complain they couldn't get me to come out and play because I was always reading."

Nick clasped his hands together loosely and nodded. "I like to read, too. Science fiction. And take apart radios and fix them. I've fixed about five so far this summer." He offered this information in a tone of guarded pride, as if he knew that fixing radios did not amount to much in the wider world, though he would take credit for being good at it. "Do you miss Snow?"

This was another question for which she was not prepared. "In a way. I miss the beach, the water."

"But not the middle of winter and being bored out of your mind?"

Rachel smiled. "No."

Out on the road a car horn sounded. Nick got to his feet, grasping the bucket by the handle. "That must be my father. So long."

Rachel watched as he crossed the beach, the clams rattling in the bucket, his feet sinking into the sand. She must have been like that when she was his age, young but not young, full of curiosity, longing to know the world beyond Snow.

Chapter Seven

"Where have you been?" Nate asked. He sat at the table, the leg in the cast resting on the floor, straight in front of him.

"I went for a walk."

"Pretty thick fog."

"It'll burn off, everyone says. Have you eaten?"

"Does it look like I've eaten?"

Rachel took the cast iron pan from the dish drainer, placed it on the stove, and retrieved butter and eggs from the refrigerator. Cracking four eggs into a bowl, she whipped them into a smooth, yellow liquid with a fork.

"How are you feeling?" she said.

Nate grunted. "I'm starving is all."

She let the butter melt in the pan and added the eggs, stirring them with the fork as they cooked. "Who's the president?"

"What president?"

"The president of the United States."

"Johnson, the big old fool. You think I don't know who the president is?"

"The doctor said to keep asking you things to see if your memory's all right."

"My memory's fine, thank you."

"How about headaches? Do you have a headache?"

"I always have a headache first thing in the morning."

"That's not what I'm talking about. The doctor said we should bring you back over if you keep being dizzy or have headaches. That could mean you've got brain damage."

"My brain's already damaged. Falling on my head probably made things better, not worse."

Rachel gave him an annoyed glance, dished the cooked eggs onto two plates, and carried them to the table.

"Jesus, those look good," Nate said.

She noticed the notebook as she sat down, a marbled notebook, the kind she had used in school and her students still used for practicing their letters. It sat in the center of the table, between them. Rachel reached for her fork and watched as Nate shoveled the eggs into his mouth, leaning awkwardly over the table, unable to bend the leg in the cast.

"What's this?" she asked.

"Something of your mother's."

Rachel opened the notebook to find the first page covered in her mother's handwriting. The fluid, looped script leapt off the page, so vivid that Phoebe seemed to have stepped suddenly into the room. The still images of photographs could no longer bring her mother back, but in the familiar handwriting, Rachel saw the quick turn of her mother's head and the flash of a smile. The date at the top of the page read *August 5, 1930*. She flipped through the notebook. Entry after entry passed before her eyes, each one dated, from 1930 and into 1931. She had not known that her mother kept a diary. The dates covered the year of her mother's marriage and her first months on the island, before Rachel was born. She looked up. Her father was still eating, eyes on his plate.

"Where did you find this?" she asked.

"In the closet, in your room."

"You never saw it before?"

He shook his head.

"And you read it?"

He shrugged. "Some of it. Pretty boring if you ask me. Mostly it's just the weather."

Rachel felt certain that he was lying. There was more than the weather in the pages of the diary. "How could you?"

"How could I what?"

"How could you read this? It wasn't meant for you."

"I suppose it was meant for you."

"No. It wasn't meant for anybody to read."

"Then how come she left it lying around?"

"She didn't leave it lying around. She hid it."

"Not that good."

Rachel closed the cover of the notebook. "We should put it somewhere it will be safe and save it –"

"For what? The grandchildren?" Nate pushed his plate toward her.

They stared at each other for a long moment, until the sound of a horn blaring outside broke the silence, and Eddie pulled up in the truck. He came through the door in his work boots and jeans splattered with paint. "Ready?" he said to Nate.

"Sure. Just get those cigarettes for me." Nate pointed to the bedroom.

"It's gonna be hot," Eddie said as he crossed to the bedroom and took the pack of cigarettes from the table by the bed.

Through the window, Rachel saw that the sun was breaking through the fog.

"Nate's going to keep us company while we finish working on the porch, be a sort of foreman," Eddie said to Rachel. He reached for the crutches on the floor and handed them to Nate.

"He shouldn't be out in the sun," Rachel called after them. "And if he has a headache, bring him home."

"Don't worry," Eddie responded. "He can sit in the shade."

Rachel watched through the window as Eddie helped her father into the truck. When they were gone, she ate her cold eggs slowly and studied the notebook. He had left it there. He had left it there because he wanted her to read what was inside. Rachel reminded herself that though her father was an uneducated man of apparently basic impulses and aims, nothing was simple with him. He was far more calculating, and in many ways smarter, than anyone she had met in college or during the years she lived in Providence, with the exception of Kevin. She knew from experience that it paid to be suspicious with her father, to approach each situation slowly, trying to see it from all angles, but she could not see her way around this one. Would her mother want her to read the diary? That was the real question, one that could not be answered.

Stacking the dirty plates, she took them to the sink, where she washed them as she listened to the foghorn. Its low drone intensified the silence. She returned to the table and ran her hand over the notebook. Finally she opened it. The first lines read: *You can see the water everywhere on the island. Wherever you are, the water is there, a constant view. I find it quieting, comforting. I am Mrs. Nate Shattuck now. Phoebe Shattuck—I keep saying it over to myself, trying to get used to the sound. Yes, I am a new person with a new name.*

She could hear her mother's voice. It was unnerving. Rachel closed the notebook. Going out to the porch, where the air was hot and sticky, she went down the steps and walked up the hill, away from the dock. The path was visible at the end of the dirt road, a thin line through the trees. She stepped into the shade of the woods and followed the path toward the center of the island. When the path forked, she went to the south, in the direction of the cemetery. The stone wall came into sight as she rounded a bend. She wound through the old headstones—Pierces and

Allins and Weedens—and passed the grave of John Sparr, with the inscription stating he was "Born of this island" and lived 1736–1772. There was a neat half-circle of missing stone at the top, like a slice made by a cookie cutter. Legend had it that a cannonball fired by a British ship in the bay had grazed the top of the stone and kept going. Rachel felt a kinship with those long-ago islanders, who had to evacuate when the British attacked and returned to find their houses burned and their gardens destroyed.

Her mother's stone was a simple square, set flat in the ground. A vase perched in the grass was filled with dead roses. The stone read: *Phoebe Hartwell Shattuck, 1910–1964*. Rachel reached down and traced the letters of her mother's name. She removed the dead roses by their stems, careful to avoid the thorns, and tossed them over the wall into the woods. A clump of day lilies grew at the corner of the cemetery lot. She went to them and broke off two orange flowers, snapping the thick stalks between her fingers. Her mother had always loved the day lilies. Rachel set them in the vase, arranging the flowers so they were turned outward, like two faces greeting her.

She watched as an ant made its slow, steady way across the gravestone. Sinking to the ground, sitting so that her feet were tucked beneath her, she listened as hard as she could, her whole body straining against the silence. She thought of the dead the way she thought of God. They lived far above the world, in a realm beyond the sky, and from this great distance, they saw and heard everything. Was it so far-fetched to think that her mother could give her a sign, granting her permission to read the diary or forbidding it? Rachel sat perfectly still for a long time, but other than the sound of the foghorn, far off and muffled, she heard nothing. The wind did not even stir the branches of the trees overhead.

Getting to her feet, Rachel looked down on the stone a moment longer before whispering goodbye and making her way out of the cemetery.

Following the path back the way she had come, she listened to a wood-pecker drilling into a tree trunk. When the path turned downhill, toward the water, she left the woods and emerged on the lawn beside Our Lady of Snow.

The casement windows in the square white building, set so primly on the patch of lawn, were open. Rachel thought she caught a whiff of incense as she went past. As a divorced woman, she could still attend Mass and receive communion, as long as she did not remarry, but she had not been to Mass since she left Kevin, though she had lied to her mother, assuring her that she went weekly and made her confession. The last time she had seen her mother was at Easter a year earlier, when Phoebe came and spent the night, and they went to Saint Joseph's on Sunday morning. Afterwards they had a noon-time dinner at Rachel's apartment. The pot roast was sliced, and there were boiled potatoes and carrots and salad, a feast by island standards. When the plates were served, and they were seated across from each other, Phoebe pursed her lips and said, "I spoke with Father Frater after Mass. He said he hasn't seen you in months. Have you lost your faith?"

"No," Rachel responded cautiously, "I haven't lost my faith. I just don't seem to have it in church these days. But I still pray."

Phoebe looked baffled. "Where? Where do you pray?"

"Here. In the apartment. Or out on the street, when I'm walking to school."

Phoebe made a clucking sound. "That's fine. It's fine to pray any-where, anytime, but it's not the same as receiving the sacraments. You know this."

Rachel did know what the Catholic church taught about such things; she was just not sure she believed those teachings, or that she could believe the teachings of any church now. What she believed seemed to exist apart from the church, in the privacy of her own mind and heart. Phoebe returned to Snow on the evening ferry, gazing at Rachel with silent disappointment as the boat pulled away.

They had spoken once on the phone after that, a conversation that was full of pauses. Phoebe could not begin to understand. If only, Rachel told herself, she had continued to attend Mass and given her mother that bit of comfort. If only their last visit had been like so many others, the two of them happily gossiping about the priests at Saint Joseph's and going over the island news. When someone died suddenly there were always *what ifs*, one more futile than the next. Rachel knew she could spend the rest of her life reviewing that final visit with her mother, coming up with a different ending, but it would change nothing.

Glancing back at the white façade of the church, with the simple cross over the door, Rachel remembered how she had loved Mass when she was a child, the strange incantation of the Latin words, the candles shining on the altar. The Sunday Mass seemed like a magic ritual the small band of island Catholics had invented on their own, a secret the rest of the world did not share. This sense was reinforced by the time she spent at the church with her mother during the week, when Phoebe did her work of dusting the pews and preparing the altar for the next Sunday. The church belonged to the two of them then. It was a true sanctuary, a place apart from the house where Nate and the boys ruled.

Rachel felt the heat on the back of her neck, and the dampness of the sticky air on her arms. She turned onto Bay Avenue, walking toward the dock. A collection of beach chairs sat on the rocky shore down below, waiting for their owners. Out in the channel, the bell buoys swayed like bobbing corks. Ahead of her she saw a man, walking in the direction of the dock and the store. She realized as soon as she spotted the dark outline of his sloped shoulders that it must be George Tibbits. Since he had returned to Snow some years earlier and taken up residence year-round in the twin houses, he made the walk around the island every morning at precisely the same time, arriving at the store at ten o'clock, before the morning ferry pulled in. He sat on the porch, or indoors by the stove in cold weather, until the ferry had come and gone, and then he made the walk back. Rachel's mother had told her that you could set your watch by George Tibbits. He circled the island in every sort of weather, making his slow, methodical way as though the fact of rain or snow was a mere footnote.

George wore a pair of brown suit pants reminiscent of the forties, a pressed white shirt, and a formal fedora. He turned his head at the sound of her footsteps and said good morning, tipping his hat.

"Looks like it's warming up," Rachel said, slowing her steps to walk beside him. She guessed he was not more than sixty-five, but he moved with the gait of an old man.

"We could use the rain, but I don't think we'll get it," George observed. "I have to be out there watering my garden every day with this drought. I save the water after doing the dishes, you know."

"So how's your garden doing?"

"Tolerable. It's too hot for the broccoli and cabbage and potatoes, but I should have plenty of tomatoes and zucchini, if I can keep the beetles off."

George did not appear surprised that she knew him and his garden. He took it for granted that everyone on the island knew who he was and did not concern himself with keeping all of them straight. Rachel remembered how she had been scared of him as a child, when he would come to the island for a day or two in the spring and walk the road like a ghost. People said that the experience of coming home from World War I and finding the dead bodies of the aunts who had raised him, one in each of the twin houses, turned him strange. Bertie had died of a heart attack, and Sarah, the addled sister, told no one, keeping the body laid out in the living room. When a telegram arrived, mistakenly informing the women that George had been killed in the war, Sarah took her own life. Rachel used to imagine Sarah's final hours in grisly detail, relishing the romantic tragedy of the story. Now it only seemed pointless and sad, and George nothing more than a reticent man who liked his routines.

They walked on, side by side, until they reached the store. George stepped back, letting Rachel take the path first.

The dimes she had collected the night before rattled in Rachel's pocket. She leaned against the porch railing while George went past her, climbing the steps and taking a seat on the bench. He held his hat in his hands and stared expectantly across the bay.

Joe Brovelli came riding up in his car. He pulled up beside the porch and swung out of the front seat in a way that seemed designed to make Rachel and George aware of his size. Resting one arm on the porch railing, he searched the horizon. "Where's the ferry?" he asked.

"Haven't seen it yet," Rachel answered.

Alice came out onto the porch, a white apron wrapped around her waist. "The ferry's stuck over in Barton. The engine won't start again."

Joe shook his head. "That Guido. What's wrong with him?"

"I don't know what's wrong with him and I don't care. I just want him to get that ferry running." Alice pushed a stray lock of hair behind her ear and went back inside.

"Guido got water in the gas tank a while ago, in that nor'easter we had," Joe said. "I told him the last time he was having trouble he'd have to drain the whole thing if he wants to solve the problem, but he doesn't listen to anybody but himself. Just keeps putting more gas in, hoping the water will go away."

Within moments, a small crowd had gathered by the porch of the store, mostly summer people. Joe announced to each new arrival that the ferry would not be coming that morning, and they didn't know about the afternoon or the evening run. "This is the third time this summer. Alice has got food over there spoiling, waiting to be delivered, and the mail and newspapers, and I don't know what else." Joe kicked at the gravel with his thick-soled black shoes.

Rachel stood on the porch, listening to the summer people trade remarks about just what they had planned to do that day and why they needed to reach the mainland not tomorrow, not this afternoon, but right now. A collective sense hung in the air that somehow they could will the ferry to arrive, or at least speed the repair, by gazing anxiously at the silhouette of the mainland across the water. In the summer and on weekends the rest of the year, Captain Guido was supposed to make three trips a day to the island. Some days in the summer all three runs were crowded, with people lining the deck.

George Tibbits remained on the bench, rotating his hat in his hands, as though unaware of what was being said around him.

Alice stepped through the door again. "The ferry's not coming," she told George, speaking quietly.

He checked his watch, obviously confused.

"Guido's having engine trouble. The ferry might make it this afternoon, but it's not coming this morning."

George was not certain how to proceed now that his routine had been disrupted. Replacing the hat on his head, he stood up slowly. "I'll be getting back to my garden then," he said, making the announcement to the empty dock as much as to Alice.

"I can send someone over to let you know if the ferry's coming this afternoon," Alice said.

George responded in a solemn voice, "Thank you, Alice."

Holding on to the railing, he went down the porch steps. Rachel and Alice followed his progress up the path. When he reached the road, he turned resolutely toward the far end of the island, as though he had settled back into the familiar pattern of his days, the absence of the ferry forgotten.

"I don't know why I worry about him," Alice said. "He's really more sane than anyone else on the island."

She gave Rachel a rueful smile and tugged open the screen. Rachel stood back, making way for the summer people who followed Alice inside. If they could not get to the mainland, they would have to settle for what Alice had to offer.

Rachel climbed the hill and crossed Bay Avenue, going on up to her father's house. The screen door slammed hollowly behind her as she went inside. It took a moment for her eyes to adjust to the darkness of the house after the glaring sunlight. She reached for the notebook on the table and carried it to the couch, where she sat, holding it in her hands. The worn cover had the softness of an old person's skin.

Chapter Eight

August 5, 1930

You can see the water everywhere on the island. Wherever you are, the water is there, a constant view. I find it quieting, comforting. I am Mrs. Nate Shattuck now. Phoebe Shattuck—I keep saying it over to myself, trying to get used to the sound. Yes, I am a new person with a new name. I feel as if I am watching her, this strange woman moving through a strange life, and yet it is my life. The freedom of the island is wonderful, and the freedom of being with Nate. I can say or do anything. It's as if someone opened all the windows and let in the light. There is nothing but sun here—sun and wind and water. My eyes hurt from the brightness and beauty of it.

Nate met me on the bus yesterday morning, as we had planned. Mother and Father believed what I told them, that I was going to Boston overnight for the audition at the music conservatory. I could not eat breakfast and had one attack of fear after another. What if he did not come? But there he was, standing at the bus stop. He gave me a huge smile and tipped his hat. Mrs. Sykes was waiting for the bus, and Morris Barnes. Nate and I did not speak to each other or sit together. I had to explain to Mrs. Sykes that I was going for my audition, and I felt like a terrible fraud. Once we reached Providence, Nate and I were able to meet across the street from the bus depot and disappear into the crowds. We got our license at City Hall and had the ceremony immediately. Two secretaries were our witnesses. Even so, there was a wonderful, solemn feeling to it, and when I said those words (I do), I had to brush back tears. Nate said he wished he could have taken me out for a fine meal, and we could have spent the night at the Biltmore, but we don't have the money for such things. We had a hot dog from a vendor on the street and sat on a bench holding hands, and I thought it was the best wedding reception possible. We hitched a ride back to Barton with a truck driver, who thankfully did not ask many questions. We waited in Gilley's until the ferry was due to leave, running out at the last minute. There was no one there who knew me. So we escaped detection, and now I am here, sitting on the porch, waiting for Nate to come back from the store. He says he better go explain to the islanders that he's married, before I show up and everyone wants to know who I am.

August 6, 1930
Nate has gone off quahogging. I understand. This is the busiest time of the year, and he can't afford to miss any days. Bill Daggett has taken him in on his boat, and they left first thing in the morning, just after sunrise. Yes, I confess that getting up so early is not easy for me, but I must learn to like it. No one sleeps past six on the island, except the summer people. There is too much to do. I cooked Nate eggs for breakfast, which did not turn out half bad, and he gave me a huge kiss and picked me up off the ground and said we would have more of our honeymoon tonight. He makes me blush and laugh like a twelve year old. I spent the morning cleaning the house—sweeping the floor and washing the windows and scrubbing down the table and the sink. The place is small but homey, and I see already how much I can do with it. I'll make some curtains and paint the floors. Each day I'll think of something new to surprise Nate.

August 8, 1930

I mailed the letter to Mother and Father from Providence, so they would get it the next day. I knew they would have the letter before they expected me home. I didn't want them to worry. Today the answer came, from Father. He says that I have hurt them more than I can imagine and that they no longer consider me their daughter. I guess I should have known this would be their response, but I felt so deflated, so hopeless. And there was nothing, not a note or a signature from Mother. I sat on the sofa, staring out the window. Nate put his arm around me and just sat beside me. I knew they would be angry, of course, but I imagined they could forgive me for marrying Nate, at least in time. But the tone of Father's letter was so severe, and the fact that it came from him, with nothing from Mother, scares me. I wrote to the women on the literacy committee, too, and Mrs. Maroni at the children's home. I hope they understand. As much as I know this is right, I feel terrible about simply leaving them all with no warning. I so wanted to tell the men at the factory the last time I met with them to go over their reading, and everyone at the children's home when I helped serve the noon meal on Monday, but of course I could not say a word. Yes, I felt like a criminal, packing my bag and listening to Mother wish me good luck with the audition. I must remind myself I am not a criminal, that my life is my own. Nate and I have done nothing wrong.

August 13, 1930

How strange it is to have everything different. Sometimes I feel like Nate and I are in a play, acting at being man and wife. Other times it feels like the most natural thing in the world. We are more shy here on the island, alone in our own little house. We have to get to know each other all over again—or get to know each other in another, new way. I will tell the truth—the nights are wonderful, when we curl together beneath the covers and lose ourselves in the dark. At first we were awkward and hesitant, but with a little practice we have become quite good at what Mother would call "relations." We don't bump heads and fumble to get out of our clothes anymore. We fall into each other, we melt into each other, we forget about the rest of what passes for ordinary life—food and work and the tooting of the ferry's horn as it goes in and out every day. What an overwhelming and wonderful thing. I am fortunate to have a man who appreciates me and makes me feel he wants to know me, every inch of me, down to the soles of my feet. I think of Mother and Father, of everyone back home. The letter they sent weighs on me, but I wouldn't trade this happiness for anything.

August 19, 1930
Mrs. Cunningham, the lighthouse keeper's wife, stopped by and invited me to come over for coffee some afternoon and brought a cake she had made. She had polio and uses crutches, but she got right out of the car and came up to the porch, with Mr. Cunningham behind her bringing the cake. An impressive woman. She makes you forget about her infirmities the way she talks in such a strong voice and seems to take no notice of them herself. I was terribly embarrassed because I was not dressed, though it was nearly nine o'clock. I went back to sleep after Nate left and had just gotten up and had to answer the door in my bathrobe. Mrs. Cunningham took no notice of this, either, though I tried to explain. But I appreciated the invitation. I have met people mostly down at the store—Walter Johnson, who runs the place, and Mrs. Daggett, who lives next door to us, and Mr. Brovelli, the game warden. They have all shaken my hand without saying much, which surprised me. I thought with so few people living on the island, they would be interested in someone new. Nate says it's because the summer people are still here. Everyone's too busy to take much time with me. Once the summer people are gone it will be different, he says. Then the island will be "normal"

again. I've been riding my bicycle in the afternoons, down to the sandy beach. I lie in the sun until I am so hot I can't stand it and then go running into the water. I'm getting a lovely tan. No one in Barton would recognize me going around in an old pair of Nate's mother's pants and a big shirt, my skin brown, my hair free.

August 25, 1930

I went picking blueberries in the woods yesterday. Nate told me where to find them. We had steamed clams for supper and bread, and blueberries and cream for dessert. The most simple things seem wonderful here. Yes, I must pump the water from a handle by the sink and take the path to the outhouse when I need to use the toilet. I must carry Nate's wet work clothes in a basket that seems to weigh fifty pounds and hang them on the line. We have to heat pans of water on the stove to take a bath in the tin tub that sits in the center of the kitchen floor. Everything takes longer here, without the conveniences I took for granted living in Barton. But that only makes me appreciate what we have that much more. We are focused on the real things here, what really matters—the goodness of a simple meal eaten on the porch as the sun sets, the wonderful days full of light and air, the cool nights when the sky is covered with stars. Isn't it strange that I hardly knew this is what I wanted, hardly knew this other life existed, but now I have it, everything feels so right? There's another hand at work in our lives.

August 29, 1930

I sat on the porch in the sun yesterday, shelling the beans Mrs. Brovelli gave Nate. I thought of all the times I searched for the outline of the island across the bay when I was a girl. The island was the place I went to in my mind when I wanted to get away. I remember going to the window at night and imagining I could see the island out there in the dark.

There was a magic about it—the little rise of land in the water, the white ferry making the trip out and back. I guess it's true with everything, but the real place is different from what I imagined. I hadn't thought of it being so quiet here, so empty. There's nothing but sky and water. But I love the wide open feeling of this place. I love letting my hair go loose and wearing old clothes and not caring what I look like. I love living by the sun's rhythms instead of the clock's. Nate and I fall into bed at nine or nine-thirty and lie there listening to the sound of the waves breaking on the rocks. I don't know how I lived without this sound all my life. Or how I lived sleeping alone. It is wonderful to wake in the middle of the night and find him there beside me. I'm still surprised. I have to remember all over again that we're married, that this is our bed, that I live on Snow Island.

September 3, 1930
The summer people have gone. They crowded the deck of the ferry two days in a row, and that was it. The windows of their houses are boarded over, and the island has become suddenly, completely quiet. No more cars driving back and forth on the road below the house. No more groups of children gathered on the porch of the store and mothers in their beach chairs perched by the water. The quahoggers row out to their boats in the morning and go down to Gooseneck Cove, but otherwise there is far less boat traffic in the bay. I find myself searching the water and seizing on any distant shape. The stillness is a sort of revelation. I can think here in a way I can't back home. There's room for my mind to wander.

September 9, 1930
Nate came running up to the house yesterday afternoon and said I wouldn't believe what came on the ferry. A huge crate, addressed to me. I went down the hill with him, trying to think what it could be, but as soon as

I saw the crate, I knew—the Steinway spinet. My heart sank as I watched the men get it on a dolly and roll it down the dock. I knew what Mother and Father were saying to me with this gift, if you can call it that. They are telling me that I am gone from their house completely. The men got the piano into the back of Walter Johnson's Model T truck. I followed the truck up the hill, feeling thoroughly useless and thinking that everyone was staring at me, the woman who had caused so much trouble and for what—a piano. Needless to say, the islanders don't see much use for a piano on Snow. It was quite a job to get it into the house. They removed the door and carried the piano through sideways. But once it was inside and they set it up in the corner of the main room, I was overwhelmed with joy at the thought I could play again. I've been waking in the night from dreams that I was playing the piano, my fingers moving back and forth. Nate stood over me and said to play something for him. I felt suddenly exposed, uncomfortable. I told him I would have to practice first, to get used to it again. My fingers are rusty, like the fingers of some old person with arthritis. He laughed and said, "It's just a piano." True, but the piano is such a personal thing for me. You don't just bring your fingers down on the keys. There is more to it than that, but I have never been able to explain this to anyone. Finally I played a bit of the Mozart Sonata in F Major. Nate kissed me and said it was pretty, then carried me into the bedroom. We are still on our honeymoon, he says. We drew the curtains and spent the rest of the afternoon in bed. Scandalous! Wonderful!

September 11, 1930
I wrote a letter to Mother and Father yesterday morning, thanking them for sending the piano. I have heard nothing from them since Father's letter, though I write at least once a week. I have kept my letters cheerful. I tell them how I am getting on and say that I miss them. My hope is that

they will relent in time. I will try to go back for a visit, maybe this month or next. Sue Hupert will probably let me stay with her, and once I am there, can they refuse to see me? But first there is the matter of paying for the piano. Nate came home last night and came stomping through the door and flung his jacket on the sofa. When I asked him what was the matter, he said my parents didn't pay to have the piano sent over on the ferry. They simply put it on the ferry and said we would pay on delivery. Now Captain Tony wants five dollars from us. "That's five dollars we don't have," Nate said. "For a stupid piano we don't want. I'd send it right back to them, but then we'd have to pay for that, too." He called Father a cheapskate. He's right, but I was hurt to hear him say it anyway. Just when I was feeling so happy to have the piano, when I was thinking perhaps it was a goodwill gesture, though there was no note that came with it. Nate went out after supper without telling me where he was going and didn't get back until after ten. I sat waiting for him, too miserable to play the piano or do much of anything else. He went straight to bed when he came back. I told myself to be patient and understanding, but I lay there listening to his snoring for a long time, wishing I had somehow managed to bring more money with me.

September 18, 1930

Indian summer. It was close to eighty yesterday, and it looks like it will be the same today. The days have developed a pattern. I wake early, when I hear Nate get out of bed. I go into the kitchen while he is out back and start on breakfast. He needs to eat a big meal. Bill Daggett comes to pick him up, and they head off. I can see the boat from the kitchen window going down to the cove. The morning hours are a luxury. I clean and work on my projects—the new curtains. I go down to the store at noon and get anything I need. Walter Johnson at the store doesn't talk much. I'm scared to open my mouth for fear I will say the wrong thing, but I am trying to be friendly to him and all the others. Sometimes I wonder if I am trying too hard. In the afternoon I play the piano and ride the bicycle down to the sandy beach.

It's a shame Nate didn't plant a garden last spring. There aren't many vegetables down at the store. With this heat, we would still have tomatoes. Next year we'll plant a garden. Things I miss: fresh lettuce and cucumbers. The radio. Shelves full of books. The men at the pin factory and our reading sessions. Things I don't miss: Father's forbidding stare at meals. The stupid, endless parties. Mother constantly reprimanding me because my hair was a mess.

October 1, 1930
Nate came home yesterday the way he does, tired and quiet. I followed him into the bedroom when he went to change his clothes, anxious to tell him about going over to Mrs. Cunningham's. Maybe I should have waited, but I was so happy. She wanted to know about my music and the composers I liked best. I did not have to explain—she knew all the composers, even some of the piano compositions by name. I felt that we had found each other here on Snow, compatriots. She must be close to sixty, but the difference in our ages doesn't seem important. I was going on, telling Nate all this, when I realized he wasn't listening. He was sitting on the bed, tugging off his wet socks. I put my arm around him and asked what was wrong. He moved away and said nothing was wrong. I knew he wasn't telling the truth. I asked again. He yelled then, said he just wanted to change his clothes without being chattered at. I was terribly hurt. I could not even look at him. I left the room and went to play the piano. While I was playing, I heard him go out of the house. He did not come back until after dark, and we ate supper in silence, like two people who didn't know each other. Before bed, he said he was sorry. He put his arms around me and we kissed, and I couldn't think how this had happened.

We were both surprised and ashamed. We fell asleep with our arms around each other. I think we both felt that we never wanted this to happen again.

October 6, 1930

The silence is overwhelming. I have never known such quiet. There are whole days when no cars go past on the road below. Then there's Walter Johnson, with his grunted "good morning." My mind gets strange and loopy. I think of God. I wonder if He's watching me. God is more real here than on the mainland. At home I dismissed the idea of God. I was smarter than that, I told myself. Here God is around every corner. The days are cooler now. No more swimming. I have been playing the Debussy Arabesque over and over. It is not an especially difficult piece, but it is so delicate that the timing must be just right. That, of course, has always been my downfall. I rush through the music, anxious simply to master the notes, without thinking of the thing as a whole, how it moves. Each time I play a piece like the Debussy, it's different. I hear moments in it, nuances I haven't heard before. It's incredible that human beings can create works of such beauty. What would it be like to compose music? I can't imagine creating something so perfect.

October 10, 1930

I have realized that I must find something to do with myself besides cleaning and cooking and playing the piano. I don't know what exactly I thought before coming here, but somehow I expected there would be many ways I could contribute. I have to admit that I imagined the poor islanders and how I would help improve their lives. I was a pioneer heading off for new territory. But all I've done is move a few miles across the bay. Still, I might have gone to Outer Mongolia, there's so little connection between this world on the island and the one back there. How stupid we human beings are. We invent such grand schemes for ourselves. We picture our lives like stories in books, and then we get there, and how our lives really are has nothing to do with the great things we imagined for ourselves. So here I am a pioneer on Snow Island. But no one wants to be a pioneer with me. They are quahoggers, store keepers, mothers and wives, fathers and husbands. They don't seem to want to get to know me, let alone take any help I might have to give. I know I must be persistent. It takes a while to break in. I will see if I can volunteer to help sort the books at the Improvement Center. There's a small lending library, and the books are piled all over the floor.

October 15, 1930
He calls me Lady. I admit I feel like a fool every time he comes up behind me and kisses the back of my neck and says, "Lady." I'm ready to drop whatever I am doing. I could not have imagined the happiness of this time until it was here. We don't know our own capacity for happiness. It's a miracle of sorts. I guess this is what you call love. I'm a terrible cook. We laugh about this. It's how he started calling me Lady. My pie crusts are a disaster—like cardboard. I have been trying so hard. Mrs. Cunningham gave me her recipe for chowder and some of her pie recipes. The first time I made the chowder, it was too watery, the second time too thick. This last time was better. At first there was silence when I served supper. Neither of us knew if we should acknowledge how bad it was. Then one night Nate said, "I guess they didn't teach you how to cook over there, Lady." He smiled in that way of his, devilish but sweet, to show me he didn't mean to criticize. Now he says, "Lady, did you try the cookbook?" and we laugh. He listens to me play the piano at night, and he truly seems to appreciate the music. The other night he asked if that was Mozart I had played. Of course, it wasn't Mozart. It was Chopin, but I felt terribly glad that he was at least trying to recognize the music, to learn.

October 20, 1930

This afternoon I went down to the Improvement Center, where they have the lending library. Mrs. Brovelli was there with her daughter-in-law, Donna. They were speaking Italian when I came in and stopped talking abruptly, as though I had caught them doing something wrong. I felt terribly awkward and couldn't think why I had come. They were busy putting the books in order. Clearly I was intruding. "You want a book?" Mrs. Brovelli asked. Yes, I said, not knowing what else to say. She pointed to a shelf of mysteries, and I took one. Mrs. Brovelli said that the summer people made a big mess of everything. They take books and don't even bring them back. I tried to make myself offer to help them, to ask if there was anything I could do, but it was obvious that they didn't need my help. So I said thank you and left with a mystery I don't want to read. When I glanced back, I saw them both watching me. I tell myself I'm being foolish, but it seems that the islanders are always staring at me. Am I that different, that strange? I imagined that the small world of the island would be a place where people had a great deal to do with each other, but just the opposite seems to be true, or perhaps I do not yet understand how friendships work here.

October 23, 1930

I have been hoping for a letter from home, week after week, but nothing has come, not even an answer from Brandon. I told Nate last night that I wanted to go over to Barton for a couple of days and visit them all. He said he couldn't see any point to it, when they won't even write. If I could just see them and speak to them, I feel certain I could make them understand and forgive me. I told Nate this. He said, "I'm still trying to pay Captain Tony for the piano." I thought that we had paid off the five dollars weeks ago. "No," Nate said. "I still owe him two bucks. When your family sends the money for you to take the ferry, then you can go." He said this as though there was no question of discussing it and picked up the newspaper. I felt paralyzed, unable to respond. Later I cursed myself. I should have asked him why he hasn't paid Tony back and told him I had to have the money for the fare, but I didn't. I went and washed the dishes, and we didn't speak to each other for the rest of the night.

November 3, 1930

Mrs. Cunningham came over this afternoon for tea. She is the one person on the island I feel I can call my friend. Her husband drove her over and came back later to get her. I spent the entire morning scrubbing the floors and dusting, feeling despair that I could not make the place look better. Her house is so bright and clean, even though it is right on the beach and Mr. Cunningham must track sand going back and forth to the lighthouse. I don't know how she does it on those crutches. She insisted I play for her. I felt suddenly shy, aware of how inadequate my playing is. I decided on the Debussy. She applauded afterwards and said it was wonderful. I couldn't tell if she meant it or she was just humoring me. She has promised to give me a lesson in making pie crusts.

November 12, 1930

Today I went down to the store as usual. Mr. Johnson gave me a strange look when I came in. When I set my purchases on the counter, he told me we would have to pay something on our bill soon. But Nate gave you money last week, I said. I spoke quickly, without thinking. Mr. Johnson shook his head. He opened the ledger book and showed me the numbers under Nate's name. Nearly thirty dollars. I stared at the penciled figure, speechless. I was too surprised to pretend I knew. How could this have happened? Each week I have asked him about the bill at the store, and every time he has told me it's paid. But worse, as I stood there I thought, how can we possibly come up with that money, unless Nate has it hidden somewhere? Mr. Johnson let me take the groceries. I told him I would have some payment for him soon. All afternoon, I thought of how I would speak to Nate. I practiced the words in my head, but when he came home, he swept in and kissed me. I couldn't bring myself to say any-thing. He was happy to see me. He said the bean soup I had made was delicious and the bread better than his mother's. I knew he was lying, but I was flushed with happiness myself and foolish pride. I couldn't break the spell. How fragile happiness is when it depends on another, when it is not just your own.

November 13, 1930
I searched the house. I found a couple of dollars underneath his shirts in the drawer, but nothing else. I took the two dollars down to the store and gave it to Mr. Johnson. I did not buy any groceries today, and I won't buy any tomorrow. Somehow we will have to get by on less. I wish now I had paid more attention to what went on in the kitchen at home. Those light suppers we had on Sunday nights. But there was always bread and cake and fruit, and of course every sort of meat. Here all I have to work with are eggs and flour and quahogs, beans and rice and potatoes. It's odd—I imagined loving having my own kitchen and what pride I would take in becoming a good cook, a good housekeeper. Now the very things I imag-ined seem to turn on me and mock me.

November 14, 1930
He discovered the missing two dollars as soon as he came home. I will not repeat here what he said and did. He was very angry. I could not even explain. Then later when he came back from wherever it is he goes, I told him what Mr. Johnson said about the bill not being paid. He did not respond. He did not tell me where the money has gone. I do not think we will even be able to afford a turkey for Thanksgiving. There was

something terrible in his eyes. I wanted to crawl under the bed like an animal and stay there, but I didn't. I held my ground. I stared back at him. We ate dinner in silence and went to bed without speaking to each other. I hate this more than anything—the silence between us. I feel like I am choking for air, like I can't breathe. In the morning, all I wanted was his touch. I didn't even care about the money or what he had done with it anymore. But he gave me that same cold look as he got out of bed, as though he wished I would disappear or die. I rolled over and pretended to go back to sleep and let him fix his own breakfast.

November 18, 1930

The days are clear and cold, and the wind never stops. It comes under the door and around the windows. The house is full of chill air. I worry that we won't be able to pay for another order of coal when the barge comes. Still there is something wonderful about these mornings. The frost sparkles on the lawn, and the water of the bay is such a thin, cold blue in the sun. Watching the sun come up over the water is a spectacle, day after day. I never fail to be amazed by it.

November 21, 1930

Nate and I are friends again. He still has not explained about the money, but he gives me a dollar or two now to take down to the store. After those terrible days, when he wouldn't speak to me or touch me, everything shifts. He came home one night last week and kissed me and held me by the waist, and I felt the firmness of his fingers through the waistband of my skirt and cared about nothing else. Am I a fool? I guess I am, but I love him, rough and strange as he is. We went tumbling into the bedroom and didn't get up to eat supper until nine o'clock. This is the greatest sweetness. I can't think once we have it again why we ever let it go, why it can't be this way between us every day. It can be like this every day. I know it can. I simply have to try harder not to make him angry, to be ready for whatever happens when he walks through the door at night, to make the time together good.

November 25, 1930
Mrs. Cunningham has invited us for Thanksgiving, and she has insisted we bring only a pie. I have said nothing to her, but somehow I feel she knows about the bill at the store, the scant groceries I am able to buy. I wonder if Bill Johnson talks. It's a terrible thought—that everyone on the island knows our trouble, but they all pretend to know nothing, to believe what they see, the happiness of the young couple. We are happy, we are the young couple they see. It's just that other things are true, too.

November 28, 1930
The dinner at the Cunninghams' was lovely—a table full of people, good food. We had a lively discussion about Prohibition and whether the movement to repeal it will succeed. All agreed that this would be a good thing, as the banning of liquor has brought no end of trouble. Mr. Cunningham said he was proud to serve his homemade hard cider, and Ernie Brovelli could come arrest us all if he wanted to. There were ten of us around the table—the Cunninghams' son, Ethan, home from college, and their daughter who lives in Connecticut and her husband and children, plus me and Nate. It was so good to be part of a family. Sometimes I think that the little problems between me and Nate come from there being only the two of us here in the house. It feels too empty. This is a terrible thing to confess, but there are days when Nate comes home that I can't think what to say to him, beyond asking how the quahogging went. And he doesn't like that. Last week he snapped, "It was wet and cold and we barely got a bushel of clams. How do you think it went?" I remember how Nate and I talked when we met. That first time, at the

town council meeting, when he presented a petition from the islanders to have the island road graded, and I presented the request for money for the children's home. I felt like we were co-conspirators, facing that row of dour old men. As I walked back to my seat, Nate smiled at me and winked. "Good job," he said to me after the meeting was over, and we were all filing out. "Now let's see if they do anything for us." He said he would see me at the next meeting, and I felt that we had made an unspoken pact. He did not disapprove of me, like Father, who said I had no business speaking in public and mixing in politics. As if getting money for the children's home was politics. I saw from the first that Nate admired me. What a feeling that was after living for years like an intruder in my own house, constantly reprimanded and told to behave, told to be someone else, less impulsive, less flighty, less idealistic, less *me*. And then the next time I ran into Nate down by the docks, when I was on my way back from the pin factory and he was over on the mainland selling his quahogs, and he asked me if I wanted to go into Gilley's for a drink. Of course he expected me to say no, but I went right across the street with him and sat there drinking a beer. He told me about growing up on the island, hunting deer, going to the one-room schoolhouse. It sounded magical, like another world. He told me how he had cared for his mother when she was sick and dying last year. After that, when he came over in Bill Daggett's boat and we met in the late afternoons in the park, we talked about so many things—my work teaching the men at the pin factory to read, and his plans for getting his own boat, and how neither of us cared what other people thought. What mattered in life was this, right here, what we felt, not anything else. I can't remember the particulars of all those conversations, but it seemed that we already knew each other. The words we said were simply confirmation of what we understood instinctively about each other. There was an ease to those first conversations, a sense of discovery on both sides. Our talk had its own life. Now there are times when we seem to be complete strangers searching for something to say. How do you live with someone every day and keep that sense of newness, of discovery? I am full of questions I can't answer.

December 1, 1930
The wash takes me the better part of a day—soaking Nate's work clothes, scrubbing them with a brush, hanging them on the line. The pile does not seem to grow smaller, no matter how many times I fill the tub with clean water and set back to work. Everything smells of fish. The clothes, his hands, the house. I try not to be disgusted, but sometimes I can't hide it. I want to run out the back door when he comes in. "What is it?" he says. "Nothing," I answer. He can't smell it on himself, of course. A couple of times I have suggested that he wash his hands before we eat. He asks me if I think I'm his mother. At night I dream of seaweed and fish and murky water. I wake feeling that I'm choking. Then I realize it's the smell. It never quite leaves him. I feel ashamed. I don't want to recoil from him. There are so many things I never thought of. It's as if there is one world, the one I used to think existed, before I came here, and there's the other world, the one I know now. That first world seems a complete fabrication, something I dreamed. Of course I am a fool and I have always been a fool. I did not have the slightest idea what I was choosing. Choosing? Did I really choose this? It feels now like something which was not a choice. I had to go, and Nate was the way to leave. And I loved him. I remind myself of this, but I begin to doubt the idea of love itself, I begin to think it is just one more story we tell ourselves, one more fabrication.

December 4, 1930
I read what I have written here, and I seem to be reading the words of a stranger, someone I have never met. I did not imagine myself having the kinds of thoughts I have now. Of course I love Nate. To suggest anything

KATHERINE TOWLER

else is ridiculous. He is so fine in so many ways—his tough strength and then his sudden gentleness, the way he laughs at me, the way we laugh together. There is a terrific honesty about him. He never pretends to be something he is not, he does not care what others think. I admire this about him. I admired it when I first met him and I still do. But how do you keep up that feeling of love every day? I did not think about this before, but I believed, without giving it any particular attention, that I would go on feeling just the way I did when we first met forever, that every day when he came in the door my heart would jump and his eyes would captivate me, hold me a near prisoner. All right, I will tell the truth—it's not like this. But writing this down is wrong and stupid. For it is still like this sometimes, when he says he's not hungry for dinner and we go into the bedroom like two people who will die if they don't get there as quickly as possible. When he unbuttons my blouse and I feel a lightness and heaviness come over me at the same time. When we lie in the dark, arms wrapped around each other. But there are the other times, too, when he comes home in a silent funk and barely looks at me. I am so sad then and hungry for any attention, any affection. I feel like a child begging to be noticed, then I hate him for making me feel this way. And I wonder how this can have happened, how we can have gone from loving each other so much to acting as though we didn't matter to each other, or worse, as though we were adversaries forced to inhabit the same house. We become like a couple of caged animals pacing off our territory.

December 9, 1930

I spent the morning with Mrs. Cunningham, watching her make pies. She explained the key to pie crust—only roll it out once. I roll mine out three or four times, trying to get the dough to stick together and the shape right. This is why it gets tough, she says. She has her kitchen set up so she can sit at the table and measure her ingredients and do everything else. Mr. Cunningham has made a cart for her, with wheels, so she can get the plates from the table to the oven. Still it is something to watch her scoot across the floor in her chair or hobble around on her crutches. I kept offering to help, but she waved me away. She's used to managing, she said. I feel ashamed when I think of my petty complaints and then think of what she endures. And she is so cheerful. She does not feel sorry for herself. That's a lesson. I am constantly feeling sorry for myself and for what? Silly little things. Mr. Cunningham came in from trimming the wicks in the lighthouse, and they persuaded me to eat the noon meal with them. They are so kind to each other. He calls her dear and is always watching to see if she needs help. Then he does things for her without being asked. I can't explain how it feels to be with a couple like that. You sense how comfortable they are with each other, and that makes you comfortable, makes you even feel included. Mrs. Cunningham gave me a jar of blueberries she put up to take home. I am going to save it until Christmas and surprise Nate with a pie—and a pie crust that is light as air.

December 15, 1930

This diary has become my companion, my friend, the one I talk to. I have never kept a diary before, but I brought this notebook with me, thinking I should keep a record of my new life. I didn't imagine this notebook would become almost like a person to me, someone in whom I can confide what I don't to anyone else. How strange it is not to talk more. Sometimes I feel like I am losing my voice, like the next time I open my mouth, nothing will come out. I asked Nate last night what we would do for a Christmas tree. I found it too hard to believe he had not even thought about it. He roused himself after a moment and said he would try to find one in the woods. I have searched the house without finding any ornaments, besides a little china Santa. His mother must have done something to decorate. We don't have money for anything. I have been spending the afternoons stringing popcorn and making paper stars. This will have to do. I can't think now about Christmases of the past—the house blazing with candles, the food, the weeks my family and I spent wrapping presents and making fruitcake and putting together baskets for the neighbors. Everything is pared down here. It's like living a skeleton life.

December 22, 1930
The tree Nate cut down takes up half the room. I don't know where he found such a thing. Down at Gooseneck Cove, he said. There aren't many pines on the island. I tried not to let it show, but I felt instantly disappointed when he dragged the thing into the house. It was so gangly and way too big. It is out of scale with everything else in the room. And with no ornaments to speak of, it looks so odd and bare, like a tree simply stuck in the house. Every time I look at it, I see the living room back home. I can't help it. How is it that those trees were always so perfect? Shaped so nicely, they took up one corner of the room, covered with gold balls and the little white candles in their holders. I remember living whole years of my childhood for the sight of those lit candles in the dark room on Christmas Eve. What magic. It was like something conjured, something dreamed.

I have a few things for Nate—some tobacco and a pipe I brought with me. I've sewn some handkerchiefs for him. Mrs. Cunningham showed me how to cut down the cloth from old linens and turn the edges. I don't know why I didn't think of a way to bring more with me when I came. I didn't think of things like Christmas and birthdays. I didn't imagine there would be so little to work with here.

December 24, 1930
Nate laughed when he came in last night and saw the tree. Kind of a mess, isn't it? he said. I laughed, too. He went to the shed and came back

with a little saw. He trimmed some off the bottom of the trunk, so the tree is shorter, and pruned the branches. The shape is much better now. It looks almost respectable. I put the strings of popcorn on it and the paper stars, and it felt like Christmas. Nate said I know how to brighten up a place. I played some carols on the piano and then we sat on the sofa, wrapped in that old afghan his mother crocheted. The smell of pine that fills the house is lovely.

December 26, 1930

Nate took the day off for Christmas, but this morning he headed out as usual. The weather has been good—cold, still days. The men have to take advantage of every day they can go out in the winter. Nate gave me a bracelet for Christmas—a little silver chain with a silver heart. He wouldn't tell me where he got it. I thought of the money. He's never told me what happened to the money that was supposed to go for our bills at the store. But the bracelet could not have been too expensive. It's just silver plate, and the chain is awfully thin. I kept it on all day and wore it to bed. I think that pleased him. He seemed to like the gifts I had for him. I felt badly there weren't more. I spent half the morning in the kitchen with the pie. I wouldn't let him watch. But when I sliced it open, the blueberries came running out in a watery mass. Nate knew immediately—I hadn't used thickening. I almost cried, but he said it tasted fine, and the blueberries were a great surprise. The rest of the meal was cod filets and boiled potatoes and soda bread—better than our usual fare, but hardly Christmas dinner. In the evening, there was a party at the Improvement Center. Miss Weeden made her mulled cider and cookies and gave presents to all the children. Mr. Brovelli dressed up as Santa Claus and read "The Night Before Christmas" in his Italian accent. Most amusing and festive.

Chapter Nine

Rachel raised her eyes from the page when she heard the ferry's horn give out a single blast that floated over the water. A crowd had once again gathered, and the ferry was chugging toward the dock. Scanning the figures down below, she found Eddie standing beside his brother, and George Tibbits on the porch of the store. Eddie's truck was parked in the lot, the passenger door hanging open. He and her father had not returned for lunch, and she had read off and on through the afternoon, moving out to the porch, setting the notebook down and picking it up, uncertain whether she wanted to read more. Each time she closed the cover, she vowed she would not open it again. Instead, she took up her quilting, joining the fabric squares in long rows, but as she sat in the shade of the porch sewing, the words her mother had written kept returning, repeating themselves in her mind, and she found herself opening the cover again.

The person in the diary was a stranger she had known all her life. She recognized this woman, but could not place her. Perhaps, Rachel thought, it is impossible for us to know our parents fully, as people of complex and ambivalent impulses. We are not capable of seeing them the way we do others. We must cling to the belief that they are simple, one-dimensional creatures whose motives can be reduced to the most basic elements—love or hate, affection or rejection. She had created a myth about her mother. She was a mistreated woman who suffered in silence for the sake of her children, enduring a bad marriage and life on the island. It had never occurred to Rachel that her parents might have loved each other once, that there could have been a certain romance to the early years of their marriage. She had known, of course, that her parents must have had sex, but her mother's references to this fact were surprising to encounter, like discovering they had committed some unspeakable act. Equally startling was the understanding that a series of random occurrences, one hinging on the next, had brought her parents together—city council meetings, encounters by the docks. What if any one of these had gone in a different direction? What if her mother had somehow been prevented from marrying Nate and moving to the island? Rachel recognized that her own existence, the existence of any human being, hung by a thread of chance.

She had heard the story before, how her parents eloped to Providence and then came to the island. Her father used to recite the details when she was younger, saying with a laugh, "I stole your mother out of the cradle." Even as a child, she did not take this exaggeration seriously, yet her parents' history was clear to her, a part of the collective story of her family, as far back as she could remember. Her mother's parents, the grandparents she never knew, had died shortly after Phoebe and Nate were married. When she was older, Rachel gradually came to understand that her mother's parents had disapproved of the marriage, but this fact remained a simple outline of the truth, like a silent movie. Phoebe seldom spoke about her parents or her life growing up in Barton. It was as if those earlier years belonged to a person she had ceased to be when she came to the island. Now the answers to questions Rachel reproached herself for never asking, things she had not stopped to wonder about, became clear.

Down below, Brock carried boxes of supplies off the ferry while

Guido unloaded the newspapers and the mail bag. Once this business was taken care of, the people who had waited anxiously all day to see if Guido would get the boat fixed boarded, and moments later, the ferry pulled away, sounding its horn. Eddie climbed into the truck and started up the hill. Rachel retreated into the house, setting the notebook in the exact spot where Nate had left it on the table. He would not know that she had read the diary, not if she could help it. Settling into a corner of the couch, she took up her sewing. When her father thumped through the door with Eddie behind him, she was bent over her needle and thread.

Nate crossed the room and dropped to the couch beside her, letting the crutches fall at his feet. "You're still here," he said in an accusing tone.

"You thought I was leaving?"

"I told you to go ahead with your vacation in Maine."

"I'm not going." Rachel finished a stitch and tucked the needle through the fabric. "I'm spending my vacation on Snow."

"Couldn't leave your old man in this state, huh?" Nate said.

"No," she answered, getting to her feet.

Eddie stood by the table, peering from under the brim of his baseball cap, a six-pack of Coke cradled in his arms. "I was going to make Nate supper."

"I can make supper." Rachel set the piecework in the canvas bag and went to the sink.

"What are we having? More of that frigging soup?" Nate asked.

"You've graduated to beef stew." Rachel took the can of stew from the cupboard over the sink and waved it with a mock flourish.

Eddie set down the six-pack, flipped the tops off three bottles with an opener he produced from his pocket, and handed a bottle to Rachel. "You didn't get heat stroke out there today, did you, Nate?"

"No. I wish to God everybody would stop asking me how I am."

Rachel opened the can and dumped the contents into a pot on the stove. "So Guido got the ferry going?"

"Yeah. Alice looked about ready to kill him. That guy is really hopeless. He's no mechanic." Spreading the newspaper on the table, Eddie flipped the pages.

"How far back are the Red Sox?" Nate asked.

Eddie turned to the sports section. "Thirty-one games out of first place. Kansas City is thirty-one and a half."

"Christ. Why do we bother to follow those poor slobs?"

"They've got to get better one of these years."

"Sure, and do what they did in the '46 Series? Break our hearts again?"

When the stew was heated through, Rachel ladled it into bowls and carried them to the table. Nate hobbled across the room on the crutches. Neither of them acknowledged the presence of the notebook. After her father fell into a chair, Rachel reached for the notebook and carried it to the end table by the couch. She watched Nate for some reaction as she returned and took her seat across from him, but he simply picked up his fork.

"Could you pass the butter?" Eddie asked. He had taken off his baseball cap and draped it over one blue jean–covered knee. Like all the other island men, Eddie would never be caught wearing shorts, even if the temperature rose past ninety.

Rachel handed him the butter plate. The words she and Eddie had exchanged that morning seemed to hang over the room, but she understood that they were both going to pretend the conversation had not occurred, that they were going to eat quietly, bringing food carefully to their mouths, as though any sudden noise or movement might start their earlier talk going again.

"Think you'll finish the Farnwells' place by tomorrow?" Nate asked Eddie.

"No. I've got a couple more days there at least, if the weather holds."

Nate wanted to know where Eddie would be working next. He had another roof job, he said, over at Snow Park, the Cheavings'. He was thinking maybe Will Daggett would help him with that one, in the afternoons, when he was done with quahogging. After that he had to paint the lighthouse for the Coast Guard. They wanted it done once a year, and they paid mainland wages. He wasn't going to let anyone muscle him out of that job.

When they had finished eating, Eddie passed around second bottles of soda, and Nate got out the cribbage board and cards. Rachel reached into the pile of cards her father fanned across the table, cutting for the deal. The three of them played one round of cribbage and then another while the sun set and, beyond the windows, the view of the water faded into darkness.

"I'm beat," Nate said when Eddie pegged out, winning the second game. He said good night and clomped across the floor on the crutches, pushing the bathroom door closed with his shoulder. Rachel followed his uneasy progress, wondering if he would take the diary, but he passed the coffee table without giving the notebook a glance.

She picked up the cards and shuffled them, avoiding Eddie's gaze. The flushing of the toilet sounded, followed by water running in the sink. Finally Nate emerged from the bathroom, heaving himself forward and closing the bedroom door behind him.

Eddie shifted in his chair, stretching his legs out. Holding the Coke in both hands, fingers laced together, he perched the bottle against the waistband of his jeans. "So what happened—did Kevin cheat on you?"

"God, Eddie, what kind of a question is that?" After a pause, she added, "It just didn't work out."

"I'm sorry. You were the one who got away—went to the city, got an education. Everyone admired that."

"Really? I thought it was more like resentment."

Eddie smiled. "Sometimes it's hard to tell the two apart. Maybe you're a little too sensitive."

"Maybe I am."

"Well, nobody was happy to hear you were getting divorced." Eddie took a sip of soda and set the bottle on the table. "You been seeing anyone over in Barton?"

"No. I'm not particularly interested, if you want to know."

"I've been seeing the schoolteacher."

Rachel was so startled by this announcement, she couldn't think what to say. Eddie saw the look on her face and laughed. "Is that so surprising?"

"No, it's just that nobody's mentioned it."

"You mean Alice and the rumor mongers didn't let you know?"

"They've fallen down on the job apparently. How long have you been seeing her?"

"We started dating back around Christmas, if you can call it that. There aren't a whole lot of places to take a girl out around here. She's staying with her folks in Cranston for the summer. I'm going over to visit this weekend."

"Sounds serious."

Eddie reached for the soda bottle again. "Yeah, I guess it is. Laura's only twenty-two. Sometimes I wonder if she's really happy with an old guy like me, but we have a nice time."

Rachel thought of her own marriage. She was the same age, twenty-two, when she married Kevin, who was over thirty. If she had been older would she have recognized the signs of trouble earlier? She wasn't sure her blindness had anything to do with age.

"I'm kind of used to living by myself," Eddie said. "I worry that I'm too comfortable like this."

"It's easier living alone."

"But is it better?"

"Depends what you like."

"Is it what you like?"

"Yes." Rachel left her response at that. There wasn't, really, more she could say. After a pause, she asked, "Do you still go to Our Lady of Snow?"

"Of course. I'm a Brovelli."

"I stopped going to Mass."

"What are you doing, flirting with hell?"

"I guess. Do you really believe all that—the Virgin birth, the resurrection, heaven?"

"Sure, as much as I believe anything. Whether you believe it or not is beside the point. You just go to church and say the prayers and do what you're supposed to, and on a good day you come out feeling better."

"And on a bad day?"

"You feel just the same as when you went in, but at least you didn't sit around feeling sorry for yourself at home for an hour."

"You have an answer for everything, Eddie."

He reached across the table, taking the cards from Rachel's hand, and smiled. "Want to play another game?"

She saw that the conversation was over. He would not reveal more. Rachel said sure, she would play another game, and watched as he spread the cards across the table, wondering what this Laura was like. She remembered her from their one brief encounter at a school board meeting in Barton as a mousy blonde, someone who would not attract any particular notice walking down the street.

Eddie turned up the two of hearts. Rachel reached into the pile and chose the nine of diamonds.

"How come you always win the deal?" Rachel asked as Eddie scooped up the deck, shuffled, and dealt.

"Luck," he said with a shrug.

They played the hand without speaking, other than counting out their cards as they laid them down. Rachel thought of all the games of one sort or another she had played with her brothers and the Brovelli boys. She took on the boys with a dogged determination and became the most competitive of them all, but tonight she could not manage to beat Eddie. He pegged out when she was still ten points behind.

"Do you ever lose?" Rachel said, throwing down her uncounted cards.

"I get a lot of practice at cribbage." He smiled sheepishly as he got to his feet. "Time for me to hit the hay."

"All right, but this match isn't over."

"You're down three games to zip."

"I know. I'll catch up. You'll see. I'm just rusty."

"You're still a little spitfire, Rachel." Eddie turned and went to the door, waving his hat before placing it on his head.

The truck started up outside and drove off, the beams of the headlights swinging across the window. Rachel watched the taillights grow smaller as the truck reached the bottom of the hill. Instead of turning, Eddie continued on down to the store. Rachel went to the front window, where she had an unobstructed view of the dock. Eddie parked beside the gas pump and stepped inside the phone booth, which lit up as he pulled the door closed. He stood there with the dome light like a halo over his head, the receiver held to his ear. He could be calling his parents down in Florida, but Rachel knew it was a petite blonde wearing red lipstick on the other end of the line. She could tell by the way he ducked his head, as though trying to keep the conversation private. Rachel remained in the shadow of the curtain, watching. Finally, irritated with herself for caring whether he stayed on the phone all night or not, she returned to the table and took up the cards, dealing a hand of solitaire.

The light from the lamp by the table was dim. She remembered the electric lights on the island as always being like this, not quite as strong as those on the mainland, glowing with a jaundiced light that made her peer at the numbers on the cards. Why hadn't someone told her Eddie was seeing Laura Hopkins? Her father, at least, might have mentioned it. Here she was making all kinds of assumptions about Eddie, even feeling vaguely sorry for him. She realized now that she had consigned Eddie to being single for the rest of his life. Of course this was unjust, but somehow she had assumed that he would always be there when she returned to the island, still gruff and untamed, leaning over a car engine with her father, a taller version of the boy she had once known.

Playing solitaire with a mechanical stupidity, Rachel dealt out the cards and glanced at the window, expecting to see Eddie's headlights move off down Bay Avenue. She lost the game she was playing and dealt out another. The old cards were greasy. The black gunk of car parts followed her father everywhere. She turned the cards up, one after another, moving them back and forth in a sort of trance, building up her piles. When she had at last won a game, she scooped up the cards and went to the window. The phone booth was dark, and Eddie's truck was gone.

Rachel stood gazing at the expanse of water past the dock, thinking of how she had fallen so thoroughly in love with Kevin, when there was nothing likely about the two of them being together. The day when it first dawned on her that something might be happening between them, she was pushing a cart through a narrow aisle in the library at college, shelving books. Kevin came toward her, as he often did, pressing his back against the shelves, but this time he stopped and whispered, leaning close to her ear, "I trust, my dear, that you will not forget to wear a slip tomorrow." He darted past before she could respond, glancing back to catch her convulsed with laughter at his imitation of Mrs. Herman, who had reprimanded one of the other girls with these exact words earlier that morning. In addition to committing the crime of not wearing a slip, the girl had worn a filmy dress that clung to her body, leaving no doubt about the extent of under-wear beneath. Rachel just had time to wink at Kevin before he ducked around the end of the aisle, and she found Mrs. Herman staring reprov-ingly at her from behind the reference desk.

Kevin Ellis was the circulation librarian and supervisor of the student workers. Their half-hour lunch break came at the same time, and they ate together in the staff room, sitting across from each other at a small metal table. Each day she waited to see what he would produce from the plastic containers he brought from home and left in the staff refrigerator. "I made veal scaloppini last night," he would say, unsealing the container with a flourish. Another day it would be eggplant parmesan. He was working his way through an Italian cookbook, one recipe at a time. "Want a taste?" he would ask. "The eggplant isn't too mushy. I hate that. You have to bread it just right—not too much—and fry it in just a little oil." As the months passed from winter into spring, Rachel came to feel there was something illicit in even the quick hellos she and Kevin exchanged when she arrived for work, though they had done nothing more than eat lunch together and imitate the way Mrs. Herman stared over her glasses, down her pinched nose, her thick lips quivering in outrage.

That summer Rachel stayed on campus, finishing the requirements for her education degree. Her lunches with Kevin lasted longer, with the campus so quiet, the library less busy. One day he asked her to dinner at his house. "Wait 'til you taste what I make right out of the oven," he said. He lived on a residential street up the hill from the college, in a small house with a lawn and border of roses out front. Inside, the living room was sparsely furnished with a couch and easy chair, but one entire wall was covered with shelves full of records. "I love classical, opera, Elvis, everything," he explained, gesturing toward the turntable and speakers in a cabinet on another wall. As they ate roast chicken and potatoes and sautéed mushrooms, she told him about her mother, recalling the piano pieces she had played through the years of Rachel's childhood. Kevin said it was tragic, really, that her mother did not have a career in music, when she was so clearly talented. Rachel felt, for the first time, that she had met someone who might understand her in the way she had always longed to be understood.

They were friends at first, though she secretly wanted more. He was eleven years older than she was, which made the idea of anything beyond friendship out of the question. As they continued to meet in the evenings, walking downtown to get ice cream and to sit by the train tracks, watching the trains come and go for Boston or New York, the sense that they knew each other in a way people didn't commonly know each other grew. Rachel thought of it later as something that had happened without help from either of them, an inevitable growing closer they had not sought or even encouraged. When he asked one night if he could kiss her, and then leaned down and brushed his lips over hers, she was not surprised. She realized that this is what they had been heading toward all along, whether they had admitted it to themselves or not. The improbability of it, with the difference in their ages, only made her more determined to prove that their love was real.

She took an apartment, which she shared with two other girls from school, and went to work as a student teacher. By the winter, she and Kevin were engaged, and the following June they were married on the island, at Our Lady of Snow. They returned to Providence and moved her few cartons of belongings into his house. She felt terrifically grown up, having a house and a husband and a job. This sense of herself, as someone who had arrived at the place where she was meant to be, carried her through eight years of marriage, until she was forced to understand who her husband was, and then to accept the even harder truth, that it couldn't go on.

Through the window, the low hum of a radio carried from a summer place down the road, the lazy sound of jazz floating on the air. When the radio went silent, she roused herself, checking one last time to make sure the phone booth was empty before leaving the window. She crossed the living room, taking the diary from the coffee table as she passed. The cover seemed to be teasing her, daring her to open it. In the bedroom, she undressed and slipped the nightgown over her head. The sheets were cool against her bare legs. She sat for a few minutes, propped against the pillow, holding the notebook in her hands. Rachel had wanted to tell her mother the truth about her marriage and divorce, but they had no vocabulary for speaking of such things. Her mother had died believing that Rachel and Kevin were unable to have children and that it was this sadness which drove them apart. If Rachel had somehow found the way to tell her mother the truth, would Phoebe have encouraged her to divorce Kevin and make another life? Rachel feared that no, her mother's response would have been the same. Marriage is a sacred vow, Phoebe told her, a sacrament. The sacrament mattered most of all.

Chapter Ten

January 6, 1931

Nate has been funny for days, like he had something to say but didn't want to say it. Last night he came in beaming. After we finished supper, he said he wanted to show me something. I looked around the house, wondering what it could be. Not here, he said. Come with me. He took me by the hand and led me out of the house and down the hill. We went down Bay Avenue, toward the lighthouse. I could barely see in the dark, but I followed him across the beach and onto one of the docks. He still had hold of my hand. He took me all the way to the end of the dock, pointed across the water, and said, There she is. I didn't understand at first. There who is? I asked. Our boat, he said. I could just make out the thing moored out in the channel in the dark—a quahog skiff. The Phoebe Louise, he said. Phoebe for me, Louise for his mother. Is this what you did with the money? I asked. I saw immediately it was the wrong thing to say. He let go of my hand and went quickly back up the dock. I called after him, but he didn't wait. When I caught up to him, he wouldn't speak. I said it was a wonderful boat, and I knew it would make a difference for him to have a boat of his own. I babbled like a fool, trying to make up for what I had said. He remained stone-faced, all the way back to the house. When we were inside, he said, Why do you have to ruin everything? I didn't mean to ruin anything, of course. I simply wanted an answer to my question. It seems to me we should decide these things together, make a plan. If he wanted to save money for a boat, he could have told me. We could have done this together, without going into so much debt at the store. It might have taken longer, but wouldn't it have been better that way? I didn't say these things to him. He would not have listened. I went to play the piano, and he left the house. I was in bed when he returned, and this morning he left without speaking to me. But I watched through the window and saw him heading out in the new boat by himself. I am certain he cannot have made more than a down payment on it. I know he can bring in more money with his own boat instead of going out with Bill Daggett, but will it be enough to pay for the thing, especially in the winter? It drives me mad not to know these things.

January 7, 1931

Nate was silent when he came home last night. I asked him how he liked the new boat. Fine, he said. That was all. I only asked if that was where the money went. It was an entirely logical question. It was not an accusation, a judgment, but that's how he took it. That's how he takes everything I say to him. What is the use? Anything I say is wrong. I look at him, and I've looked at him the wrong way. I make the most simple observation, like a comment on the weather, and he contradicts me. You don't know how to read the sky, he says. They didn't teach that in your fancy schools.

Sometimes it feels like we are creating a monster, this third presence the two of us become together, a thing that is ugly and twisted. I don't want to participate. I want to walk away.

January 16, 1931

The weather has been bad and the water rough for days. Nate has not been out quahogging. The wind here is ferocious, not like anything I remember on the mainland. You can hardly stand up in it. The storm itself has passed, but the bay is still too rough for the men to go quahogging. Inland it was probably snow, but here we had only rain. Driving rain that pelted the windows. I could hardly sleep. Nate goes out during the day, over to Silas Mitchell's, the one who owns the dance hall. He comes back at suppertime. I worry about so many things. How will we come up with the money for payment on our bill at the store when he's missed almost a week of work? I can't talk to him about these things. Since the night with the boat, I have not spoken of money, and neither has he.

February 3, 1931

Mr. Johnson mentioned the bill again when I went down to the store this morning. I saw he didn't want to speak to me, that it pained him to do it. He waited until Mrs. Daggett left, so no one would overhear. I find myself grateful for any small kindness these days. I have thought about it all afternoon. I must speak to Nate. I even went over to the Union Church. I knelt in the front row and asked God to tell me how to speak to Nate. I have never prayed like that before, on my knees. In the Congregational church at home, we did not kneel. We scooted forward on the edge of our seats and dipped our heads. More dignified, I guess. I never actually prayed then. I practiced pieces on the piano in my mind, going over the fingering. It never occurred to me to use the time in church for anything else. Now I am drawn to prayer. I can't say why, except that living such a quiet life makes me consider the possibility of God in a way I didn't back home. It is different to kneel. You feel humbled then. In the Congregational church, we didn't want to admit God had any power over us. It was so cold in the island church I could see my breath. I said to God, this is all I can bring you—cold air, doubt, fear. When I came home, I felt no more certain of anything, but perhaps a little comforted.

February 12, 1931

I had made up my mind by the time Nate came home. I could see he was tired. But he's always tired. There will never be a good time, I told myself. We need to come up with a plan for paying our bill at the store. I said the words first in my mind, then took a deep breath and said them out loud. "A plan?" he said. "You want a plan? How's this for a plan? We can starve. We can stop eating. The price they're paying for quahogs dropped twenty-five cents last week, and they say it will drop again. I can't even cover the cost of the fuel."

I was stunned. I should have known, of course. If I had gone to the sewing bee at Mrs. Cunningham's, I would have heard about it, but I couldn't bring myself to go. I felt so down that morning. I couldn't think how I would be able to talk with Mrs. Brovelli and Donna and Mrs. Daggett. If I spent time down at the store, I would have heard, but it's the same thing there. I feel terribly awkward just hanging around the store, the way some of the women do in the afternoons. And when I come into the store, they seem to be careful what they say, as though they need to protect me from their conversation. They all stare at me like I'm an exhibit in a museum.

Nate said there were the payments on the boat to make, and if he couldn't keep up, he would lose the boat, and then where would we be? Bill Daggett isn't bringing in enough now to take Nate out with him, so if we lose the boat, he will have no work. He gave me a triumphant look, like he was pleased somehow to deliver this news, to show me how stupid and insensitive I had been. Everyone knew about the drop in the price of quahogs, everyone but me, his look said. If I truly cared or truly understood, I would have known, too. I would not have asked, at this worst possible time, how we were going to pay the bill at the store. I did feel stupid and insensitive. If only I had known. I said I was sorry. He grunted and left the house. He came back after midnight and went right to sleep and snored all night long.

February 17, 1931

Nate seems to have forgiven me. He came home last night in an easier mood, for the first time in days. He said somehow we would manage. If we can make it to the summer, he can work on fixing the summer people's cars and other things, and go out quahogging. It will mean long days, but he thinks he can do both and with the extra income, we should be able to make the payments on the boat and pay off the bill at the store. He brought it up when we sat down to eat. I was determined to say nothing, to stay away from topics that only cause grief. He told me not to worry. He got up from his chair and came around the table and hugged me. Look at that face, he said. You're going to get lines if you keep going around looking like this. He kissed me and I smiled, realizing how long it had been since we smiled at each other, or God forbid, laughed. The days are getting longer, the light lasting until suppertime. That's a relief, too.

March 2, 1931

I believe I am pregnant. I have not had my period. I feel tired, no matter how much sleep I get, but maybe that's nothing new. I think I have known for weeks now. I just didn't want to admit it to myself. In the back of my mind was the tiny thought that I might leave. I could not imagine how this would happen, but the fact of it was there, like a secret door I could open if I wanted. This door was there from my first days on the island. If I am honest, I have to admit this. I did not know where I would go or how I could do it, but the idea of leaving was there from the moment I saw this little shack of a house. If it got that bad, I told myself, I didn't have to stay. Now it's different. It's not just me. How I long to want this baby. I have been going to the church to pray in the afternoon. I pray that I will want this baby.

March 11, 1931

Nate came home last night and asked why I go to the church. People are talking, he said. He made it sound like the worst possible thing—people talking. I go to pray, I said. Pray? About what? he said. Of course I had no answer. Whatever it is that people pray for, I muttered. He glared at me. You didn't used to be the praying type, he said. Now I am, I answered. This silenced him. I had planned to tell him about the baby, but after that I said nothing. It seems strange I am the only one who knows. Just me and this child inside. I like the idea of that. In the past, when I thought of having a child, I imagined it as a very public affair. I thought of how I would tell everyone, proudly, and imagined some vague group of women who would help me with the things I needed to know and heap praise on me. But now that it's happened, there's no one to tell.

March 16, 1931

I stay in bed in the morning. I am too sick to get up. Nate says nothing. He fixes his own breakfast and goes out. Everyone on the island is strapped now, with the price of quahogs so low. Walter Johnson has no choice about giving credit. If he didn't, we would all starve. But our bill must be the oldest and the largest. Still, he does not mention it when I go down to the store these days. I wait until the afternoon, when the sickness subsides. There's almost nothing I can eat, anyway—a little bread and the soup I make from potatoes and broth. I try to drink milk when we have it, but I find myself gagging on it. Why didn't anyone ever tell me these things? My mother or Aunt Beth—they never told me about the nausea, about how hard it would be to eat. My body is like a child itself, with a mind of its own. I can't make it do anything—get out of bed, eat a normal meal, make the walk out back to the outhouse. I have been using the chamber pot because just the idea of the outhouse makes me sick. God save me. I pray all the time.

March 30, 1931

There's a slight bulge to my stomach. I hold my hand there, but I feel nothing. It does not seem possible there is a baby inside, a person who will look like me or Nate or both of us. It's more than a miracle. It's so unbelievable as to seem absurd, like some preposterous myth we made up. Is this really the way people come into the world? Through a woman's belly and out between her legs? The result of months of nausea and fear? I want to feel happy for this child, but I am terribly afraid of everything. Of telling Nate, and of whether the child will come out deformed because I have had nothing to eat, and of the birth itself. I can't even think of that. I seem to spend all my time these days pushing things away—food, my thoughts, the future. Not to mention Nate. I am afraid it will be bad for the baby if I give in to his advances. I plead being sick, which is the truth, and I stay up sewing until after he is asleep. But the other night I woke to find him on top of me in the middle of the night. I saw it was best to let him go ahead. I know what to do to make it be over quickly. I prayed that the child was safe. Does this make any sense? One minute I'm praying to lose the child, and the next I'm praying she will be born healthy. How do I know it's a girl? I'm scared to admit it, but I feel she's a girl.

April 8, 1931

I went down to the store today. Walter Johnson gave me strange looks. I thought it was about the money again, but then Mr. Brovelli came in, and he kept glancing at me, too, as if there were something wrong with me. It wasn't until Nate came home that I learned the news. My family's house burned down. Nate had the paper from Barton. There was even a picture. Almost nothing was left—the chimney and a couple of walls. The rest was piles of rubble. It happened at night. The firemen said it started in the kitchen. They all got out except Father. He was making sure Brandon was out of the bedroom upstairs, and he became trapped. They are calling him a hero. The smell of smoke has been in my nostrils ever since Nate told me. I feel sick and black inside.

April 9, 1931
I must go to Mother. I told Nate this morning, and he sneered. They don't care about you, he said. Why should you care about them? That's not the point. I can't stand by and do nothing. I can't pretend the past does not exist. I believed that once—that you could make the past not exist. I don't believe it anymore.

April 10, 1931
I dreamed of Father last night. There was a knocking at the door, and when I went to answer it, he was standing there, covered in soot. He was ghastly—a black ghost. I shrank back, and he said, It's all right. Then we were walking together, down the street in Barton. He was telling me how he would rebuild the house. He went on for a long time describing his plans. It would be bigger than the old house, he said. There would be a whole room for music. I woke thinking of that—a whole room for music—what a wonderful thing. I felt that I had been with him, and that, for the first time, there was peace between us.

April 13, 1931
I took the ferry over for the funeral. On the way across, I felt the baby move. It was like the fluttering of wings inside me. I had to stop myself from getting down on my knees on the deck of the ferry and thanking God. I had convinced myself she was dead, that I would spend nine months with nothing inside. Now it is real. Now I believe in this child. I am calling her Rachel, after Grandmother Lawrence.

I went straight to the church. I saw Mother standing outside as I approached. She turned away without speaking. So that is how it will be, I thought. What a proud, cold woman. It is senseless. I sat in the back of the church, but I could see her throughout the service. Her head did not move. It remained fixed on the minister. Even now, I realized, she will make a good appearance. She will not disgrace us with a show of too much emotion, she will not be inappropriate. Never. Brandon sat beside her. I cried silent tears, and when they carried the casket out, I felt a wave of shame. Who was I to judge my father? To turn away from him as I did? I wished there had been another way. Brandon spoke to me as he passed my pew. I'm glad you came, he said. Mother went on down the aisle without even acknowledging I was there. There was a wildness in Brandon's eyes. I saw he wanted to say, to ask so many things, but we were like distant acquaintances fenced off on either side of a great gulf. Still, at the same time, I felt how profoundly and completely we knew each other. I knew his terrible control and what it cost him. He knew my impulsiveness. You're all right? he asked. Yes, I said. He grasped my hand and hugged me. I was undone then and cried openly. He gave me his handkerchief, then hurried away. I left by the side door of the church, not wanting to speak to anyone I knew. I sat on a bench by the dock until the afternoon ferry left.

April 16, 1931

I don't think I knew before how profoundly my old life was over. Now I do. I cannot force Mother to respond to me. For years, I believed it was Father who controlled our lives, who constantly made us be something we were not. I realize now that perhaps it was Mother all along. She hid behind him and blamed him. Now it seems clear that she was the one who cared most. I was too stupid to see it. I have been writing my weekly letters to her because I felt it was the best way to reach Father. Her stone face at the funeral told me otherwise. I didn't reach either of them and now I never will.

April 29, 1931

The child moves inside every day now. She sleeps when I sleep and wakes when I wake. How amazing it is to have this silent, lively companion. I feel for her a love more fierce than anything I have ever known, and I have not even seen this baby yet. I don't go to church in the afternoons these days. Nate doesn't want me to seem strange. I pray here in the house, on my knees by the kitchen table. I pray my thanks. I think it is the first time I have felt truly thankful since coming to Snow, thankful with all my heart. What I felt before was just selfishness. If God can do this, make a child inside me, He can do anything. Who am I to question His will, to question where He has brought me? The lilacs are in bloom. The smell is glorious.

May 4, 1931

I told Nate last night. I thought of it all day, how I would present him with the news. He was tired when he came in, as always. He does not like to talk when he first gets home. I have learned to be quiet, to let him take off his boots and raingear and sit back in his chair before I say much. I try to be careful, even then, not to talk too much. He hates chatter, as he calls it. Sometimes I forget, and the words spill out of me. There are so many little things to tell him—Mrs. Cunningham coming to listen to me play the piano, the first summer people arriving to open their houses, the pair of deer I saw in the woods. I know none of these things matter, really, yet they do matter to me. They're the things that make up my day. Is it too much to expect they might matter to him, too, just a bit? But last night I had it planned out. I would not say anything until the food was on the table. I was about to tell him when he said, "Can't you come up with anything to fix besides potatoes?" I was instantly deflated, turned back from my purpose. Then he told me about the boat. He needs some part for the motor. It will take half a day to go over to the mainland and back, and then he'll have to get it on credit. If they'll give him credit. Everyone's stingy these days, he said. Everyone's watching their own back.

I thought of waiting to tell him. But it would be no better the next night or the next. So after we finished the soup, I simply said it. I'm going to have a baby. He asked, You're sure? I nodded. He let out a great whoop and came and picked me up off my feet and twirled me around. Everything was suddenly changed. We had something to hope for together. Even more, there was something undeniable we had done together, made together. I felt the terrible rightness of this and I was so glad I cried. What are you crying for? he said. You're a silly goose. He told me not to worry, that we would go to the mainland when it was time for the baby to come. For the first time, I longed for my mother. I ran out back, pretending I had to use the outhouse. I sank my face into the lilacs and cried, too confused with happiness and fear and loneliness to stop.

May 7, 1931
The last page of my notebook. I have tried to write as small as possible and to leave no blank spaces. I don't have another notebook, and there's almost no paper in the house. It goes without saying that there is no money for such things. Maybe when I go to the mainland to have the baby, I can find a way to get another notebook and the other things I miss so much, like my Lux face soap. When I came to Snow, I thought I was a person who didn't care about having nice soap and new clothes and pretty shoes and hats, but I'm finding that I didn't know myself as well as I thought. Nate is so excited about the baby. He waits on me when he comes home at night and insists I leave the worst of the cleaning for him to do. He is so full of anticipation about becoming a father, he makes me feel it, too. Why do I worry so? Women have been giving birth for thousands of years. I am just one of many.

Chapter Eleven

The sound jolted her out of sleep. Something had fallen, crashing to the floor with a reverberating thud. She opened her eyes, trying to locate the source of the noise. In the next room, she heard her father. "God damn it," he yelled.

Rachel jumped out of bed and ran to the other room in her nightgown. She found Nate lying on the floor, groaning, the crutches splayed on top of him. Kneeling beside him, she retrieved the crutches and set them to the side. Nate pushed himself to a sitting position. "This thing is like a frigging piece of concrete."

"If I hold onto your arms and pull, do you think you can get up?" Rachel said.

"Maybe."

Rachel went behind her father and held him under the armpits, extending her arms in front of his body. Steeling herself, she heaved him up from the floor, feeling his weight push against her as she struggled to her feet. The leg in the cast was balanced straight in front of him, capable of toppling them both. After a long, wobbling moment, Nate got his good leg underneath him and stood up. She guided him toward the bed. He shook his head. "I'm sick to death of this stupid room. Take me to the couch."

Hopping forward, he grabbed the bedpost and waved one hand toward the crutches. Rachel picked them up and gave them to him. Nate positioned the crutches under his arms and swung himself out to the couch, just reaching it before falling sideways, landing on the worn cushions and letting the crutches drop to the floor. Rachel stood over him. "What month is it?"

"August."

"Who's the president of the United States?"

"It's still that idiot Johnson, and we're still fighting the commies in Vietnam. There is nothing wrong with my memory. I'm just dizzy. I stood up too fast or something."

"You look pale."

"I ain't been in the sun in more than a week."

"No, it's not that. You've got no color in your face."

Closing his eyes, Nate sank back on the cushion. His upper lip glistened with sweat.

"Were you dizzy yesterday?"

"Sometimes." He answered without opening his eyes.

"What's that mean?"

"I don't know. Off and on."

"Were you dizzy when you went to bed last night?"

"A little. It goes away when I lie down."

"I'm going to call the doctor, and if he says we should come over, we're taking the ferry back to the hospital."

Nate let out a groan. Rachel returned to her bedroom and hurriedly pulled on shorts and a blouse. "Don't get off the couch," she said as she made her way to the door.

A child's bicycle lay on its side in the grass by Alice's house. Rachel took note of this fact and went on down the hill, covering the distance in long strides. When she reached the phone booth, she felt for the coins in her pocket, deposited a dime, and asked the operator for the hospital. It was almost eight o'clock. The doctor might be in already, doing morning rounds, or he might have completed them and left for his office. She would track him down. The switchboard operator at the hospital transferred her upstairs to the nurse's desk. Yes, the nurse said, the doctor was still doing his rounds. She would take down the number and have him call back. Rachel hung up the phone, stepped from the booth, and glanced up at the porch to find Joe leaning on the railing. "Everything okay?" he asked.

"My father fell down when he got out of bed. He's still dizzy. I'm waiting for the doctor to call back."

"Did you get him up after he fell?"

Rachel nodded.

"I bet that wasn't easy. That happens again, you come get me."

Joe went back into the store, leaving Rachel leaning against the side of the phone booth. Out on the water, Will went by in his quahog skiff, headed toward Gooseneck Cove. He raised his hand and waved. She waved back. The air was still and hot, once again. Rachel imagined that it was the sort of summer day she had loved when she was a child. She would have her chores to do—helping with the dishes and sweeping under the kitchen table—but once those were done, she would be free until the midday meal. She and Phil and Eddie would run down to the water, leaving Junior, the baby, at home. They would hunt for mussels clinging to the rocks and smash them open to find the rubbery orange flesh inside, then pull long pieces of thick string from their pockets and tie the open mussel shells to the ends. The bait ready, they would perch on a rock and trail the lines in the shallow water, waiting for crabs. They had to sit completely still, careful to keep their reflections from darkening the rocky bottom and scaring the crabs away. Rachel remembered the thrill of seeing a tiny claw appear from beneath a rock, followed by the rest of the crab's body, emerging bit by bit. The crabs would scuttle back and forth, circling the bait, darting behind a rock and back out. Finally they would seize the mussel in their claws and attempt to drag it off to darkness and safety. It was important not to pull the line up too soon, before the crab had secure hold. She was scared to touch them, but she had learned how to grasp a crab from behind, by the shell of its body, so it could not nip her with its claws. She and Phil and Eddie would drop their catch into a bucket and run over to the store to see if there were any fishermen looking for bait. The men paid them five cents a crab, which seemed like an enormous sum. When they could not sell the crabs, they would put them back in the water, enjoying the sense that they were gods giving the animals another chance at life. The crabs scuttled back under the rocks with what looked like nervous glee, as if understanding that they had been saved.

The ringing of the phone brought Rachel back to the present. The doctor identified himself and asked how he could help her. Rachel told him about Nate's fall that morning and the bouts of dizziness. It didn't sound serious, the doctor said. Sometimes it could take as long as a week for the dizziness to go away. Nate should stay in bed and rest.

Rachel thanked the doctor, hung up, and made her way up the steps to the store. Inside she found Alice behind the counter and her mother, Evelyn, seated in the armchair by the stove, knitting. Joe leaned against the shelf where the milk and sugar was laid out, a cup of coffee in his hand.

"I think I need some of that," Rachel said, gesturing toward the coffee. "The doctor says my father just has to rest. You know how easy that is, to get him to stay still for a day."

Evelyn pursed her lips and smiled. "He's not the most agreeable patient, huh?"

Rachel shook her head and took the cup of coffee Alice handed her.

The door swung open and two women wearing shorts with matching blouses entered. They called hello to Alice and went around gathering up groceries. Alice poured a second cup of coffee for Nate, and Rachel paid her and carried them over to the shelf, where she added milk and sugar to both.

"We didn't have a thing in the house for breakfast," one of the women said as she set her purchases on the counter. "Those men eat everything in sight. You think you've at least got cereal and milk, and you turn around and the refrigerator's empty."

The other woman added, "Vacation. I love that. Who's on vacation here? We're cooking for an army. Next year I'm putting my foot down. We're going somewhere they've got restaurants."

Alice responded with a forced smile as she began to ring up the groceries. Behind her, Evelyn clicked her knitting needles together and said, "I've been saying that for years. What this island needs is a good restaurant. You're absolutely right."

"I don't know how you can stand it," the second woman responded. "My husband's family used to come here when he was a kid. I had no idea when we rented the Barrett place. The kids are used to miniature golf and going out for hotdogs, you know, that kind of thing."

"A lot of people are surprised when they get here," Evelyn said. "They think because we're just a half-hour ferry ride from Barton, we must have restaurants and stores. Well, you're looking at it."

Rachel exchanged an amused look with Joe. Evelyn was the only islander who would openly criticize the island in front of a summer person.

"If you need any help up there, let me know," Joe said to Rachel. "I mean it—if he falls again or anything, you come and get me."

"I will. Thanks, Joe."

Rachel said goodbye to Alice and Evelyn and carried the coffee outside. Up at the house, she found her father on the couch where she had left him. He opened his eyes and said, "Johnson. Johnson is the president."

Rachel sat in the chair beside the couch. "I got you some coffee at the store."

He reached for the cup and greedily drank.

"I talked to the doctor. He said you need to rest, which means stay in bed. All day."

"So you're serving me breakfast in bed?"

"Yes. Well, breakfast on the couch anyway. How's your head?"

"Fine."

"You're not dizzy now?"

"No, nurse Rachel."

She ignored the sarcastic tone in his voice and went to the refrigerator, removing the eggs and milk. She made four pieces of French toast, floating bread in the batter she whipped up and then dropping the slices into the frying pan. Nate took the plate she handed him and propped it on his lap. "You stayed up late last night, huh?" he asked.

"Not really."

"I know you like to read before bed."

Rachel had set her mother's diary back on the table by the couch the night before. It was still there, where she had left it. She was not going to let him know she had read the diary. "We played another game of cribbage and then I went to sleep."

"Eddie won, huh? He always wins. It's enough to make you stop playing with him."

"Why didn't you tell me he was seeing Miss Hopkins?"

Nate shrugged. "It didn't come up."

"It's kind of significant information. Eddie doesn't exactly do a lot of dating."

"No, and I don't want you mucking around in this. She's a nice girl. Very nice. So don't go sticking your finger in the pie."

Rachel glared at him, so incensed she could not think how to respond.

"You know Eddie. He's so damn stubborn. If he thinks anybody around here wants him to get married, he won't do it, so don't go making any comments about her, good or bad. The less any of us say, the better. "

"What about Eddie? Does he want to get married?"

"Eddie keeps his cards close to his chest. Speak of the devil." Nate pointed toward the window.

The truck pulled up in front of the house, and Eddie bounded up the porch steps.

"I'm a frigging prisoner," Nate called as Eddie stepped inside. "Nurse Rachel here ain't letting me out of bed."

Rachel explained the doctor's orders.

"So no foreman today, huh?" Eddie said. "Who's going to dole out the cigarettes?"

"Guess you're gonna have to manage without me."

"All right. You two behave yourselves." Eddie went to the door and said he would see them later.

When Eddie's truck had pulled away, spewing exhaust, Rachel took the plates to the sink and filled it with water. By the time she was done washing the dishes, Nate was asleep, his head resting on the couch cushion, his mouth hanging open. Rachel remained standing at the sink, gazing at the bright surface of the water in the distance, thinking of the pages she had read the night before. What stayed with her most was the revelation that her mother had prayed that she would lose the baby she was carrying. Rachel had always assumed that of course her mother wanted her, as she had wanted all her children, no matter what else her marriage entailed. Rachel and her brothers were the one purely good piece of her mother's life, she had believed, but the story, it appeared, was not that simple.

Down below, one car passed and then another on the dirt road. It was not yet ferry time. The presence of traffic could mean only one thing— the dump was open. She finished her coffee and turned to the pile of trash bags out on the porch. Lugging bag after bag to the car, she filled the back seat of the Ford coupe. Inside the house, she took the key from the hook where it hung by the door. The car started uneasily when she pulled out the choke, pressed the starter, and gave it gas. She took her foot off the gas as soon as it caught and pushed in the choke, hoping the engine wouldn't flood. After a moment it ran steadily.

As she neared the dump, Rachel joined a procession of cars slowly winding along Bay Avenue. She followed them through the opened gate in the fence and pulled up next to a mountain of trash. Brock McGarrell stood in front of the pile in his green coveralls, directing traffic. He wore canvas gloves and went from car to car, helping unload bags of garbage and broken lawn chairs and old mattresses. Anything that could still be of use was set to one side, but the rest was thrown together in one foul-smelling heap. Overhead, a flock of gulls screeched loudly.

Brock came over as Rachel got out of the car.

"Welcome back, Rachel," he said. "I was sorry to hear about your father. That was a nasty accident. This is quite a collection." He gave her a furtive smile as he helped unload the paper bags full of beer bottles and soup cans.

Rachel ignored the remark, remembering why no one on the island liked Brock. He had not learned the first rule of island life, that you do not comment on other islanders' business, even when it is staring you in the face.

"Everybody was real relieved to hear Nate wasn't hurt too bad," Brock said. He stood in front of her, pulling on the ends of his gloves. A tee-shirt frayed at the neck showed beneath the coveralls. "It's a good thing you can come help out. I know that place needs some attention."

"Alice told me you've been taking the boxes I send up to the house.

Thanks."

"Happy to do it."

"Hey, Brock, do you want this?" a man called from another car as he waved a rusted toaster in the air.

Brock said goodbye to Rachel and skirted around the edge of the trash heap, taking the toaster from the man and placing it with an odd assortment of broken furniture and battered appliances by the front gate. This was the "picking pile," from which the islanders and summer people were encouraged to help themselves.

Rachel heaved the last bags onto the trash mound and climbed into the car. Brock had moved on, assisting a woman in a pink skirt. Rachel waved and pulled out. Brock McGarrell was known for being a talker. Whenever he came up among the islanders, someone would say confidentially, "He's from Iowa." This fact, it was understood, explained quite a bit. People from Iowa were a little too friendly.

She remembered the day in the fall of 1945 when Brock stepped from the ferry, asking for the girl who worked at the store. Astonished to discover Alice had a secret boyfriend in the service, the islanders talked about nothing else for weeks. Brock had been stationed at the Navy base on Snow during the war, before shipping out to the South Pacific. They were married at Christmas time at the Union Church. When Brock discovered Alice would not leave her mother, he agreed to live on the island. He was a stubborn but unambitious man, who drove the store's delivery truck and managed the dump.

Rachel searched the faces behind the windshields of the cars coming toward her, but there was no one she knew heading for the dump. She waved to each car she passed anyway, and the drivers waved back. As she came up to the dock, she passed George Tibbits, which meant that it must be almost ferry time. George raised his hat as she went by, nodding toward the car with that distant expression on his face.

The coupe let out a belch of black smoke when she shut off the engine. This, Nate had explained, was nothing to worry about. The car was a 1950, and it ran damn good, as far as he was concerned. Rachel slipped the keys in her pocket and went inside. Nate was still asleep.

Retrieving her sewing bag, she went out to the porch. It was cooler there than in the house. She sat in the old lawn chair and arranged the quilt squares in her lap, choosing colors for a new row. Andy liked the brightest shades—reds and yellows and oranges. She tried to make the quilts she sewed for him bright as a summer day on Snow. Kevin used to laugh as she assembled her scraps of fabric, saying that she had an eye for the most garish patterns. "Where do you find this stuff?" he would ask.

Kevin had gone with her to visit Andy twice. After the second time, he said the state school was just "too depressing." He sent gifts for Andy, stuffed animals and chocolates, but he couldn't face going back. She became accustomed to making the trip across town once a month by herself. It was on one of these Saturdays that she returned home and walked into the house to find Kevin and a man she did not know on the couch, naked. The curtains were closed, and a record was playing so loudly they did not hear her come in. The man lay on top of Kevin, his head resting on Kevin's chest, unaware of her presence until Kevin pushed him away. He might have been asleep. She puzzled over this—were they sleeping?—as she stood there, unable to avert her eyes while they sorted through a pile of clothes on the floor, their backs to her, and scrambled to get dressed. The hypnotic sound of Gregorian chant filled the room. She recognized the record, a favorite of Kevin's. The music was as difficult to take in as the sight of their rounded buttocks and undershorts around their ankles. The man with blond hair finally tugged on pants and socks and a pair of loafers, grabbed his jacket from the back of the easy chair, and hurried out the front door without saying a word, as if intent on simply vanishing, on convincing Rachel that he had never been there and did not exist. Crossing the carpeted floor, Kevin went to the record player and lifted the needle, plunging the room into silence. He slipped the record back into its cover and began to cry. "I'm sorry," he said over and over.

They had been married eight years then, eight years in which she had avoided the truth. At first she and Kevin had seemed no different from any other couple, in her inexperienced view. Though he was reserved in ways that surprised her, undressing in the bathroom and arriving ready for bed in a pair of neat pajamas, he would initiate sex often enough. After the first few months of their marriage, these times became less frequent. Rachel waited patiently for him to show interest, but he would say he was tired and apologize, giving her a quick hug. She would press her body to his, trying to coax him into desiring her, and he would run his fingers over her face, kissing her closed eyelids, before falling asleep. When she gathered all her courage and asked him what was wrong, he said that it was just taking time, that he would become comfortable with her eventually and be able to "perform."

Rachel blamed herself. She was not beautiful enough, not attractive enough. She had not made Kevin love her fully, the way a husband should love a wife. She was not as cultured and knowledgeable as he was, and she suspected that sometimes he was bored with her. After coming home from work, she would listen to his records and read the books on the shelves, and rehearse interesting conversations they could have that night. She would light candles and pour wine, waiting for him to walk through the door. She would dress in a new, tight-fitting blouse and spend an afternoon washing and setting her hair. Eventually she became resigned to the fact that sex was not a part of their marriage. She told herself this was not so unusual. They remained the closest of friends, cooking together, taking long walks around the city at night. She told herself this was enough.

For months after she returned home to find Kevin with the man who remained nameless, he was contrite. He promised it would not happen again. She woke more than once to find him lying beside her in bed, crying. When she put her arms around him and whispered that it was okay, he shook his head. "It's a sickness," he said. "I shouldn't have given in to it. You're so good to me. God, you're so good."

He went to a psychiatrist, who said he could cure Kevin of his desire for men, but it would take time. Rachel learned not to ask about the weekly sessions. Kevin only became irritated, waving his hand dismissively and responding that once in the doctor's office was enough. He didn't want to go over the sessions again. She noticed things she had not noticed before, how *queer* and *faggot* were the worst taunts the children at school could hurl at each other on the playground. There was one boy they teased more than the others. He was small and thin, with large eyes, and easily given to crying. Did the children know something about him he did not know about himself? Was this what it had been like for Kevin? She found herself studying men on the street, in stores, and wondering about them. Perhaps it was a sort of rite of passage, an indulgence. Perhaps there were more men drawn to this than she imagined. She believed Kevin when he said that it would not happen again, that it was a temporary lapse, a sudden impulse, though she was painfully aware of how he struggled over what he saw as a sin. The categorizing of sins had never interested or bothered her; in fact, she was not at all sure she believed in sin, which made her an impossibly flawed Catholic. Still, it hurt her to see him hurt, and at the same time, she felt wounded and violated in a way she could not begin to voice, even in her own mind. She vacillated between extremes, angry over what he had done to her, done to their marriage, and equally angry at a world that would see her husband as someone beneath acknowledgement or contempt. But she did not want to be ruled by anger or blame or hurt. She wanted simply to return to companionable friendliness, to feeling Kevin was the one who knew her better than anyone else in the world. She tried harder to be attractive and happy and smart, convinced she could make him forget anyone else. It was as if they had embarked on a secret mission which gave their marriage a sudden urgency and vitality.

One night the following summer, Kevin stayed after work for a meeting of the Rotary Club. The air in the house was close, and Rachel decided to walk into town, thinking there might be a breeze by the river. On one of the back streets, she saw him half a block ahead, walking with a man she did not recognize. Slipping into a doorway, she watched until they disappeared down a short flight of stairs, into the basement of a brick building. Rachel remained hidden in the doorway. Other men descended the steps and went inside, most of them arriving alone. When she finally stepped back onto the sidewalk and went down the street, she saw that the door was not marked in any way, but the sound of music came from inside. She hurried past.

For the rest of the summer, Kevin was frequently out in the evenings at Rotary Club meetings. Rachel did not bother to follow him or to walk down the street by the river again. This much was clear—he was living another life. What hurt the most was that he did not tell the truth about where he went, that he kept himself hidden from her. Not that she wanted to know the details of where he was or what he did. She did not want to know, though she tortured herself with wondering and imagining.

There were times when he did not leave at night, when he played records and cooked, and they curled together in bed, and it felt like the days when they first knew each other. Rachel lulled herself into believing the crisis was past. Her duty was to support him, to help him be the husband he now seemed bent on proving he could be. There was no point in searching for secrets, in accusing or judging. Then suddenly he would take up one of the Rotary Club projects again and be gone several nights a week, and they were back to the old pattern of being evasive and remote with each other. Rachel became furtive, complicit with him in keeping his secrets, though she hated herself for it.

In the winter, she discovered he had stopped seeing the psychiatrist. When she pressed him about it, he answered tersely that there was no point to it. She woke at three one morning a few weeks later to find the space beside her empty. Wandering through the house, she stared at the shapes of chairs in the dark as if they were wild animals waiting to spring. She did not know how she could leave. It would mean becoming a different person. Rachel lived with the idea for months, turning it over dully in her mind, willing it to go away and leave her alone, but it did not go away, not when Kevin would again stay out all night, returning an entire day later to act as if nothing out of the ordinary had occurred. It was one of these times, when he did not come home all night or the next morning, that she filled a suitcase with clothes and the framed photos of her family she kept on the dresser, and went to stay with one of the teachers at school. She could not find another way to tell him. When the women circled around her at school, full of concern, she suggested, without being explicit, that he had hit her. They patted her hand, giving her grave and knowing looks, and did not mention it again. Later she felt ashamed of this lie—Kevin never would have hit her—but there were no words for the truth.

Rachel pulled the needle through two squares of fabric, careful to make the seam straight, the stitches even in size. She had hoped that he would fight to keep her, though she recognized this was senseless, but he did not contest the divorce. In the end, he made it easy.

Chapter Twelve

The days passed in a hot, lazy blur. Nate slept on the couch or sat in the shade on the porch reading the paper. Rachel prepared meals and swept the floor and took her walks to the beach. They fell into an odd, uneasy rhythm, inhabiting the same house yet keeping a wary distance with each other. This is what it meant, Rachel told herself, to be *home*, a simple word that carried far more weight than it seemed able to bear.

On Sunday morning, she stood out on the porch, watching the cars on the road down below. Eddie went past in his truck, followed by Joe and his family, all of them piled into the police cruiser. Others she did not recognize, summer people from Snow Park, drove by, headed toward Our Lady of Snow. Rachel waited until there were no more cars before starting off on foot. She would arrive after Mass had begun and leave before it had ended.

She could hear voices as she climbed the hill to the church. They were saying the *kyrie*. She had safely missed confession and the first prayers. Reaching into her skirt pocket, Rachel pulled out the lace mantilla she had found in the dresser in her bedroom and secured it to her hair with bobby pins. A couple of people turned, noting her late arrival, as she slipped into the last pew. The Brovellis were seated in the front pews. Rachel made the sign of the cross over her chest. It was, she recognized, a habit, an involuntary gesture that had perhaps lost all meaning, though she found it comforting.

The priest, a thin man with a pinched face and gray hair, read the collect in a rapid staccato, his eyelids fluttering nervously. Rachel could not get used to hearing the prayers in English. She agreed with, even applauded, the changes the Catholic church was making, yet in practice she found the new Mass strangely disorienting. Mass was no longer a secret, Latin ritual that belonged to the priests. The congregants kneeling in the pews participated more fully, but the prayers they voiced in the everyday language of people walking down the street were stripped of their mystery and power.

Rachel stayed for the readings, the sermon, and the offertory. When the priest began the prayer of consecration leading up to communion, she moved to the end of the pew, genuflected, and went to the door. Outside, she blinked in the sunlight and walked up the hill, taking the path through the woods home. She felt foolish attending church in this half-hearted manner, but she could not bring herself to make a confession, which would require admitting she had not been to Mass in more than a year, and without making her confession, she could not receive communion. Still, she had to go to church. She had always attended Mass on Snow, except when she was sick, or during the winter when the island was iced in, and the priest could not come from the mainland. Even then, Eddie's grandfather or father would lead the prayers, with readings from Scripture, a stilted affair that counted as a substitute for Mass.

It was dark and cool in the woods. Rachel breathed in the smell of dirt and pine needles. When she came to the fork, she went to the right, following the contour of the hill as the path headed back toward the road. She emerged onto the dirt road, her steps raising a small cloud of dust. It would have to rain sometime. The summer could not simply go on and on, eternally bright and hot and dry.

She spotted her father on the porch as she approached the house. "You went to church?" he asked.

Rachel put her hand to the mantilla. She had forgotten to remove it. She tugged at the bobby pins and slipped the mantilla in her pocket. "Yes, I went to church. Why?"

Nate shrugged. "Your mother said you weren't doing that anymore."

"She told you that?"

"Yeah, after she came back from visiting you one of those times."

The last time, Rachel thought, it was the last time she visited me, but she did not say this. Instead she said, "I felt like going to Mass. Is that a crime?"

"Did I ever say anything about you going to church, you or anybody else in this family?"

Her father had said plenty about her mother going to Mass, but Rachel saw no point in pursuing that old argument. She sank to the top step and said tonelessly, "I wish it would rain."

Nate squinted at the sky. "Ain't looking like it any time soon."

Rachel followed the progress of a lone sailboat tacking across the channel out on the bay. The boat looked like an apparition in the heat, shimmering on the glassy surface of the water. "How's your head?"

"Great." Nate tapped his forehead, smiling in that impish way of his.

"Are you dizzy?"

"Not really."

"What's that mean? Answer the question yes or no."

"I was dizzy when I got out of bed, but that's normal."

"No, it's not," she answered resignedly. "Want something to eat?"

"Nah, I had some Corn Flakes already."

Rachel went inside, leaving her father on the porch. Out of habit she had not eaten before Mass, even though she was not receiving communion, and now she was ravenously hungry. She poured herself a bowl of cereal and sat at the kitchen table, reading the front page of yesterday's paper. "Marines Defend Burning of Village," a headline declared. The article began: "A U.S. military spokesman outlined today for the first time some of the combat rules set down for American Marines fighting in South Vietnam. 'Marines do not burn houses or villages unless those houses or villages are fortified.' Reports from Danang had described American Marines sweeping through the village of Comne and setting fire to huts despite the pleas of villagers. The spokesman stressed the evidence the Marines had first considered that the village was communist controlled."

Rachel folded the front page, trying to ignore the other headlines about the riots in Los Angeles. One photo showed an entire city block on fire, another looters carrying television sets through broken store windows. She knew what her father would say—you make sure Negroes can vote and see what they do? About the war, he had only one comment: "Damn commies." She had to admire the simplicity of his views. There was no middle ground. But the fight to protect the right of blacks to vote was a fight for democracy, wasn't it? You couldn't believe in democracy selectively. The fight in Vietnam was a fight for democracy, too. They had to stop the spread of communism. She believed this. She only wished it could be accomplished without war, without burning villages, without killing.

Pushing the paper and its headlines away, she finished the cereal and left the bowl in the sink. Outside, her father remained in the battered lawn chair, the only piece of furniture on the porch, paging through an old issue of *Popular Mechanics*. Rachel went to her bedroom, where she changed into her bathing suit and dropped a towel and an Agatha Christie mystery into a straw bag of her mother's. She pulled a sleeveless cotton dress over the bathing suit and slipped her feet into her sandals. As she headed out of the house, she took a floppy hat from a peg by the door, the one her mother had worn when she gardened. Nate was leaning back in the chair, his eyes closed. They fluttered open when she let the screen close behind her. "Going sunbathing?" he asked.

She nodded.

"Don't get burned," he called.

Rachel glanced back. "I won't."

Her mother had been the one who badgered her endlessly about staying in the sun too long. Her father had never cautioned her about it before.

Retracing her earlier walk, Rachel followed Bay Avenue toward the south end of the island, passing Our Lady and going on to the beach by the lighthouse. The crescent of sand was covered with beachgoers—women seated beneath umbrellas and children dashing back and forth to the water, men standing in a cluster by the shore with their arms folded awkwardly over their bare chests. Rachel skirted around the knots of people and made her way to the point at the far end of the beach, where there was just enough sand between the water and the beach grass to place her towel. She pulled the dress over her head, took a pair of sunglasses and her book from the straw bag, and stretched out. The words floated in front of her in the bright light as she read, sentences meandering up and down the page. The sun was piercingly hot, but there was a breeze off the water that ran over her skin, hinting at coolness without quite achieving it. She read a page and then another. She was only on the second chapter of the book she had found in the bedroom, but already it appeared obvious that the sister was the murderer, though Rachel guessed she must be wrong about this. The book couldn't be that simple.

When she was so hot she could stand it no longer, Rachel removed the sunglasses, dropped the book in the straw bag, and ran to the water. The cool depths enveloped her, and for a moment, as she plunged beneath the surface, pulling her body through the water, she felt everything fall away. Opening her eyes, she searched the sandy bottom. There was another world here, on the floor of the ocean, a world that belonged to tangled trails of seaweed and barnacles clinging to rocks and the hidden homes of crabs and fish and clams. As a child, she had imagined being transformed into a sea creature and going to live in this strange world. Now she wanted to make this fantasy a reality simply for the sake of staying cool, but as she came to the surface, her face meeting the air, she felt the heat of the sun on her skin again.

Emerging from the water, Rachel dried herself with the towel and pulled on her dress. She slipped her feet into the sandals, and, gathering up her things, made her way over the sand to the path. The dusty road shimmered in the heat. She walked past the inn with its empty rocking chairs and passed the summer cottages where clotheslines were festooned with bathing suits and towels in an assortment of blues and reds and yellows.

She was almost to the dock when Eddie pulled alongside her in his truck. He came to a stop and leaned out the open window. "I thought I saw you at church."

Rachel nodded.

"Why didn't you stay?"

"I told you, I haven't been to Mass in a while."

"I always thought of you as a good Catholic girl."

"I'm not a good Catholic girl since I got divorced."

"You can still attend Mass."

"I know. I used to fantasize about becoming a nun, when I was thirteen or fourteen. Sometimes I think I would have been a lot better off if I'd gone straight from the schoolhouse to a convent."

Eddie smiled. "I never imagined you as nun material."

"How was Cranston?"

Eddie had gone to visit Laura on Friday and had returned that morning on the ferry, in time for church. "Not so hot. We broke up."

Rachel studied his face, trying to gauge how to respond. He balanced one hand loosely on the steering wheel, his eyes on some distant point down the road. "I'm sorry to hear that," she said finally.

"Yeah, well, that's how it goes." Eddie reached into his breast pocket, took out a cigarette, and held it between his fingers without lighting it. "She thought I was coming over there with a ring and when I didn't produce one, she was kind of upset. She actually started crying. God, I don't know what to do when women cry. I really don't. I just clam up and stare at them like an idiot. Then, of course, that just makes her cry more. It wouldn't have worked, anyway. I don't know what I was thinking. She's not Catholic. And she told me right away when I got there Friday night that she didn't want to live on the island, like she'd been rehearsing it or something. She said she couldn't raise children here. It wouldn't be fair to them. What the hell does that mean?"

"You can work out the Catholic stuff and where you want to live."

Eddie shook his head. "Nah, I'm not giving up my house that I built with my own hands." Tucking the cigarette behind his ear, he started up the truck. "I've gotta work this afternoon or I'll never get that porch done. You and Nate got any plans later?"

"Not exactly."

"Maybe I'll come by." Eddie took off down the road, trailing dust.

Rachel turned off Bay Avenue and spotted her father in front of the house, beside a car with the hood raised. A man she didn't know stood beside him. The man extended his hand as she approached and introduced himself as Harvey Baum. "I hope you don't mind my putting your father to work here," he said.

Nate leaned against the edge of the car, propped on the crutches, a dirty rag in one hand and a socket wrench in the other. "Spark plugs are fouled," he said. "I cleaned them off, so it should start up okay now, but you should probably put some new ones in. I can send over to the mainland for them. If that doesn't take care of it, we can try something else. It could be the valves are going, but I think it's just that the choke was sticking."

Rachel went up the steps and into the house, where she made her way to the bathroom and shut the door behind her. Peeling off first the dress and then her wet bathing suit, she stepped into the tub and turned on the shower. The water ran over her skin, washing away the dried salt. She rubbed the soap over her arms, thinking of Eddie. Was he right that there was no future for him and Laura, or was he only making excuses, avoiding the discomfort of having to deal with a woman who just might, on occasion, cry? There were worse things than a crying woman, though she imagined it would be hard to convince Eddie of this. She was not one to persuade others of the benefits of marriage, she realized; yet it was disturbing to watch Eddie dismiss the idea so quickly and easily, as if he had merely been discussing the possibility of meeting Laura somewhere for dinner and now had changed his mind. Rachel let the water run down her back, flicking her wet hair over her shoulder. She felt fresh and cool as long as she remained under the shower's spray. As soon as she shut off the water, the heat would crawl over her body again. She stood there a moment longer, then reached for the faucets. Through the open window, she could hear her father on the other side of the house, still talking to Harvey Baum. She patted her skin with a towel and dried her hair. Wrapping the towel around her body, she opened the door and crossed to her bedroom. Outside, Harvey was saying, "I wish I had a mechanic like you back home."

"Summer people are always saying that to me," Nate answered. "Guess it's hard to find somebody reliable."

"That, and somebody who doesn't rob you blind."

Rachel dressed in shorts and a blouse and ran the comb through her hair. The men exchanged more words, and then the car started up. Nate shouted some instructions over the coughing engine. The car drove away, and Nate came into the house.

"You're supposed to be resting, not repairing cars," Rachel said.

Nate eased into a chair, dropping the crutches. "I ain't exactly straining myself."

"I saw Eddie out on the road. He and Laura broke up."

"Oh hell, I thought this one was gonna work out."

"What do you mean, this one?"

"He dated the schoolteacher we had before Miss Hopkins, too."

"What happened with her?"

"I don't know. She didn't have a sense of humor. Eddie said he couldn't marry somebody who didn't have a sense of humor."

Rachel went to the cupboard and took down a can of tuna fish. Eddie could no doubt come up with endless reasons for not getting married. Clamping the can opener to the lid, she found herself wishing that someone would come along who silenced his excuses.

Chapter Thirteen

"Are you gonna read this thing?" Nate pointed at the notebook on the coffee table. The diary had remained there for days.

Rachel had just emerged from the bathroom and was barely awake. She pushed her hair back from her forehead and rubbed one eye, turning toward the table. "No," she lied.

"Then put it back in the closet, would you?"

She gave him an annoyed glance and went to the refrigerator, removing a pitcher of Tang. She poured a glass and stood at the window, gazing out at the crisp view of the shoreline and the mainland across the water. A thunderstorm had moved through the night before, and the air was wonderfully cool. Her feet actually felt cold on the bare floor. This, she thought, was the island she remembered, a place of sudden clarity and expansive light where, on a day like today, you felt you could see to the edge of the world when you looked out at the water.

Rachel carried the cereal and two bowls to the table, and went back for the milk. Nate hobbled over from the couch, swinging the cast in front of him. "I ain't been dizzy since yesterday morning," he said. "If I can just get this blasted thing off my leg, I'll be the same as ever."

"You've got five more weeks until the cast comes off."

"Jesus. You know my leg goes to sleep inside there. It's enough to make you stark raving mad. And it itches. It itches like crazy all the time."

Rachel poured cereal and then milk into her bowl without responding to this litany of complaint. They were almost finished eating when Eddie drove up and came bounding through the door. "What do you say, Nate? Are you up for working?"

Nate pushed his chair back, and, gripping the edge of the table, got to his feet. "Just hand me those crutches."

Eddie retrieved the crutches from the floor.

"We were waiting for you to come over for cribbage last night," Rachel said.

"Sorry. Joe roped me into a project over at his house. He's building bunk beds for Theresa and Rose. You sure you're up for this?" Eddie asked Nate. "You're feeling better?"

"I'm feeling fine, except for this lead weight I got on my leg."

"All right then, let's finish that porch before Mrs. Farnwell has a fit."

The men bantered back and forth while Eddie helped Nate up into the truck. They sounded like boys setting off for a day of uncharted adventures. Eddie seemed close to euphoric, which struck Rachel as strange. Was this how he truly felt or simply a cover for his disappointment over Laura? Rachel thought she knew him well enough to believe that his happiness was genuine. Perhaps he was one of those people who was most comfortable being alone. Perhaps she was one of those people, too.

"You can throw those stupid crutches in the bay," Nate said, his voice carrying through the screen.

"Then how are you going to walk, chief?" Eddie shot back.

A moment later the truck started up, and their voices were lost. Rachel thought of the time when she had lived like a dead person with Kevin, moving through the days as though drugged. His other life was like a huge piece of furniture they kept walking around, without ever acknowledging its presence in the room. There was no question that being alone was better than what she endured then, though she could not help wishing that others, like Eddie, would find that one person who was meant for them. It might not be right for her, but she needed and wanted it to be right for everyone else.

Rachel went to the coffee table and retrieved the notebook, carrying it to the bedroom. Her mother's clothes were gone from the closet, a discovery which had surprised her. There was nothing of her mother's in the other room, either. Nate must have made arrangements to give Phoebe's belongings away, though she could not quite imagine how this had happened. Perhaps he had taken everything to the dump and thrown it all out. Rachel's own clothes hung in the closet now, beside a collection of empty hangers that rattled against each other. A cardboard box full of blankets and towels sat on the floor.

Pulling aside the blankets, Rachel leaned over, ready to nestle the notebook at the bottom of the box. It was then that she saw the stack of notebooks, five in all, hidden beneath the old blankets. She stopped, staring at them with a sense of awe. The notebooks had not been there earlier in the week. She had looked in the box, thinking there might be others, and found nothing.

Rachel edged the bedroom door closed with her foot, anxious to make sure Nate would not see her if he returned. Opening the cover of the first notebook, she found an entry dated September 20, 1931, shortly after her own birth. She turned the cover of each notebook, discovering entries dated 1938, 1940, 1942, and 1945. He had left the diaries here deliberately, knowing she would find them. Rachel could not understand the strange nature of this game. She only knew that this time she would be a match for her father. She would not give him the satisfaction of revealing that she had found them, and certainly not the satisfaction of letting him know she had read them.

She placed the original notebook on top of the blankets, in plain view, and hurried out of the house to the store. She waved to Joe, who was standing next to his police car talking to a man she didn't know, and went up the porch steps. Alice was not behind the counter. Instead she found Nick paging through a magazine, and the black and white cat curled in the armchair by the stove. Nick folded the magazine and shoved it under the counter, though not before she had caught the title *Scientific American*.

"Nice day, huh?" he said.

"Beautiful. I'm glad the heat broke."

"Me, too. Some people around here were getting a little cranky." He smiled, raising his eyebrows as though sharing a private joke.

"Yeah, well, even though it's cooler, I'm going to get cranky if I don't have some coffee."

Nick poured coffee from the pot. "Miss Hopkins quit," he said as he handed her the cup.

"What do you mean?"

"She quit the job at the schoolhouse. She called this morning."

Rachel tried to take in what he had told her. "Just like that? She just quit?"

"Just like that. I don't think she ever liked it here. You know—island life."

"But there's only a couple of weeks until the start of school."

"Yup. If we don't find a teacher, I'm not going to graduate."

She handed him a dollar and waited while Nick made change. "You'll graduate all right. If you have to go to the mainland, you'll still finish school."

"I don't know about that. The Brovellis don't want anyone to go over to the mainland. They say that'll be the end of the schoolhouse."

Rachel carried her cup over to the shelf. She turned back to face him as she stirred the coffee with a wooden stick. "The schoolhouse isn't going to close."

He smiled again, giving her the same vaguely conspiratorial look. "If you say so."

Rachel made her way to the porch, where she met Joe coming up the steps.

"You hear about Miss Hopkins?" he asked.

"Nick just told me."

"I was down here first thing, when the store opened. I pulled up in my car, and the phone was ringing. I said hello and just like that she says she's quitting. I asked who she thought we were going to get now, at the eleventh hour, and all she said was 'Sorry' and hung up. That takes nerve. You'd think she'd at least care about the kids. She signed a contract. Do they do that over on the mainland, just up and leave right before school starts?"

"Sometimes." Rachel tried to imagine the situation from Laura Hopkins' point of view. Maybe she couldn't face coming back, knowing she would have to avoid Eddie. Maybe she couldn't face another winter on Snow.

"Hell, we were hoping things would work out with her and Eddie. We were all as nice to her as we could possibly be, even when it got a little crazy over at the schoolhouse. Everybody gave her the benefit of the doubt, and this is what we get in return. You know anybody over on the mainland? Anybody who could take the job? We've got to find someone before the school board gets wind of this and tries to shut us down."

"I can't think of anyone, but I can make some phone calls."

"Could you? That would be great."

Rachel went on up to the house, spotting Alice coming down the hill as she crossed Bay Avenue. Ellen, her older daughter, skipped along beside her in a pair of red sneakers. "Morning," Alice called.

Rachel returned the greeting. Ellen danced in a circle around the women.

"Did Nick tell you about Miss Hopkins?" Alice said.

"Yeah. I'm really sorry."

"I just hope she told Eddie before she told us. I don't know what we're going to do now. I suppose that's no concern of hers."

Ellen stuck out her lower lip in a pout. "Miss Hopkins was mean. All she did was yell. We want a nice teacher. Did you used to go to the schoolhouse?"

"Yes," Rachel answered. "Miss Weeden was my teacher."

"Miss Weeden's almost a hundred."

Rachel and Alice exchanged a smile. No one knew Miss Weeden's exact age, which she refused to divulge, but it was generally believed that on her last birthday, she had turned ninety or maybe ninety-one.

"Was Miss Weeden nice?" Ellen hopped from one foot to the other.

"Yes, she was. Sometimes if we were bad we had to sit in the corner, but she didn't yell."

"Were you ever bad?"

"No. I was never bad."

"Me, too. I'm never bad, but the boys are. Miss Hopkins hit Scott's hand with a ruler."

"When did that happen?" Alice asked in a tone of alarm.

Ellen kicked a stone across the road. "I don't know. Last year."

"Why didn't you tell me?"

"I don't know. I forgot."

Alice shook her head. "There were a few problems last year," she said to Rachel. "These kids could use a decent teacher."

"I'll see if I can get any leads for you."

"Come on, Mom," Ellen said as she took Alice's hand and pulled her down the hill.

Rachel said goodbye and continued on to the house. To quit like this, so soon before the start of the school year, was completely outrageous. Maybe, Rachel reflected, this was precisely why Laura Hopkins had done it.

She went to the bedroom and closed the door behind her, standing at the window, staring out at the brown grass. She could be just as smart and calculating as her father. This is what he had taught her in the years when he came home drunk. She had learned how to fool him into drinking a cup of coffee, how to coax him from the living room to the bedroom, talking to him the way you would talk to a deranged animal, her voice gradually calming him into compliance. She had learned to think fast, anticipating his sudden outbursts of temper, the quick shifts in mood that would frighten her brothers. She had learned how to be smart without revealing she was too smart, for fear of setting him off. More than anything, he hated the idea that people knew things he didn't. Rachel had perfected the dance they did to an art, never letting him see that she questioned his dominance or his judgment. He was the father, and she was the daughter, and so it would always be. Pulling the curtains closed, she left the window and went to the closet, where she reached into the box.

Chapter Fourteen

September 20, 1931

Rachel Lawrence Shattuck, born September 7, 1931 at 6:48 a.m., six pounds, ten ounces.

October 2, 1931

How frightening it is to hold your own child in your arms, and how wonderful. She is breathtakingly beautiful. I can't take my eyes off her. When she sleeps, I sit by the cradle and stare at her. I could do this for hours. Nate picks her up when she cries at night and brings her to me. If she doesn't want to be fed and still cries, he walks the living room with her, back and forth between the table and the stove. She is so small against his chest. I think she feels safe then. She almost always stops crying when he holds her. This is the happiness we have waited for.

October 13, 1931

I have never loved anyone the way I love this tiny squawking baby. The feeling is overwhelming, something so much bigger than myself it is scary. I am filled with a fierce sense of love that pervades even what little sleep I am able to get. Of course I could not have understood what it would mean until I held her in my arms, but she is mine, entirely, absolutely. She belongs to me as no one has ever belonged to me before. I feel guilty when Nate catches me gazing at her. I look up and find his eyes on me, and I wish I could say that I love him as I love her. Did I ever feel this way about Nate? Or my parents or my brother? I don't want to admit it, but if I search my heart I have to say that I never loved any of them the way I love Rachel. Perhaps Nate cannot tell how I feel. I try not to let him know that she fills everything now, that I wonder if there will ever be a place for him again, alongside Rachel. Is this what nature does to us women, making us choose our children first? There are times when it seems cruel. I go around flushed with happiness and then paralyzed with guilt, praying that Nate does not realize what I feel for him is paltry compared to what I feel for her.

October 22, 1931
I am more tired than I can say. The baby woke four times last night. She howls as though she is in the worst sort of pain. You think her lungs will burst. I want to scream myself. Nothing and no one can comfort her. I begin to think she is possessed, that I am possessed, too. I long only to understand what it is she cannot tell me, the fear or discomfort that makes her cry until she is gasping for air. I crave silence. If I could have one wish, it would be to sit in silence for an entire day, with no one needing or wanting me.

November 5, 1931
Nate is off quahogging every day, and I spend my time with Rachel. It's a strange routine, if you could call it that. No sooner have I finished feeding her, when she needs to be changed, and then she throws up all over herself and me, and we both need to be cleaned up, and then it's time for a short nap, and then she feeds again, and then she needs to be changed, and on and on. Every woman has probably said this, every woman who's

a mother, but I feel like a cow, a hideous dispenser of food. My stomach sags with all the weight I have gained, and my breasts are so big I go around in Nate's shirts. I am an absolute sight. I can't imagine Nate will ever want to touch me again. Worse, I can't imagine wanting to be touched again, seeing my body as something worthy of being touched.

November 30, 1931
Rachel noticed her hands yesterday and spent hours examining them, as though they were some fantastic discovery. I wish Nate had been here to see it. He misses so much, being gone all day. I vowed that I would record each milestone here, but there is no time. Weeks pass, and I write nothing. I will try to do better.

December 27, 1931
Rachel's first Christmas. We set the cradle by the tree, and she stared at the stars I made from tin foil. It is a miracle to see the world through her eyes. Everything is magical to a baby. The smallest thing—a key, the firelight when the stove is opened, the crinkling of paper—is something to be marveled at. I pray she never loses this. Her eyes are so bright and attentive. I see intelligence in them, and an endless capacity for love. We went to the Cunninghams' for dinner on Christmas day, and Mrs. Cunningham gave us a beautiful little sweater she knitted for Rachel. People have been so kind. Mr. Johnson gave us a free bag of groceries, and Mrs. Daggett brought a batch of Christmas cookies. Everyone loves Rachel. The women carry on over her and make me feel she is the most beautiful baby ever born, as of course she is.

January 6, 1932
I don't have a moment to myself anymore. Sometimes I literally think I am losing my mind, running from keeping the fire going to feeding the

baby to washing the endless mounds of diapers. I try to time the washing to coincide with her naps, but this doesn't always work. Yesterday I
had to dash to the clothesline with one diaper at a time, afraid to leave
her awake and alone in the house for too long. The diapers are stiff as
wood when I bring them in, and then I sit by the stove with Rachel in
my lap, trying to warm the diapers and soften them by folding and
refolding them, rubbing the frozen cloth in my hands. There is no time
to think, no time to argue with Nate, hardly time to sleep. I haven't
played the piano since Rachel was born, not once. I wish I could have
it removed from the house so I don't have to see it there, constantly
accusing me.

February 12, 1932
Nate rolled on top of me in the night and begged me. He said he couldn't
wait any longer. It's been months, he said. How can I explain? My body is
so foreign to me now. It belongs to someone else, the baby constantly crying for my breast. I let Nate do what he wanted, but had the strangest feeling that it was a betrayal of the baby. She has a right to my body now, she
comes first. Afterwards Nate fell asleep, satisfied, and I lay there listening to
Rachel's tiny breaths from the cradle, wondering if I will ever feel normal
again.

March 8, 1932
I am producing far less milk. I feed the baby, but she still cries. I don't
think she's getting enough. She's able to eat some cereal now, so I know
she's not starving. Still, I worry. I know that I found the breastfeeding
exhausting, that I wished so many times to be done with it, but I didn't
wish for this. When Nate came home and I told him, he gave me a
pained look and left after changing his clothes. He came home later with
the smell of liquor on his breath and fell asleep immediately. He doesn't

get up with the baby anymore. That's my job, he says. He has to make a living and can't spend half the night up with the two of us.

April 4, 1932

I don't have the will to write here anymore, though this seems like one more sign of my lack of focus. The days should not be so hard, but they are. I love having Rachel with me all the time. I love her wonderful bright eyes. She says "dada" now and crawls across the floor. I am as proud of these achievements as I would be if she had invented the car engine or cured polio. But always I have the feeling that I just want to *be* with her, which is never possible. There's the endless list of chores that are never finished. Still, she is a cheerful baby. She laughs when I shake a dried gourd and make it rattle. She reaches for it and seems just about to tell me what is going on inside that lively little mind.

April 28, 1932

I write these words to make myself believe them. I am pregnant again. How can this be? We haven't even finished paying off the bill to the doctor for Rachel's delivery. I told myself I would be careful, that I would not give in to Nate. But he catches me off guard in the middle of the night. I am so tired, I don't know what I'm doing, night or day. I can't even remember if we've been together when I get up in the morning. It's like a haze-covered dream, a fantasy brought on by exhaustion. Did he lie on top of me, pushing his way in? I don't know. I don't want to know. I could pretend this is not true, that I've imagined the first signs, but I know them too well—the nausea, the lack of appetite, the crazy fear. I will go mad with another baby. I will shoot myself. I don't see how it will be physically possible to wash that many diapers. Please, God, send me strength.

May 14, 1932

The nausea grows worse every day. There's no mistaking what is happening to my body. I should be happy, but I feel like a drowning woman who has been thrown overboard trying to claw her way back into the boat. I will not tell Nate until I have been to the doctor and know for sure. My mind is so strange these days, I could convince myself of anything, even a pregnancy that isn't real.

June 5, 1932

Now that there are two ferries running each day, I was able to make the trip to the mainland to see the doctor. Nate said it wasn't necessary. The baby is fine, he said. She's growing just the way she should be. What's the sense of spending money on a doctor when we don't need to? We should save it for when it's really important. I told him I wouldn't let another month go by without taking her over. There are things only a doctor knows, things we can't see. Nate wouldn't speak to me the night before I went over. He went off to Silas Mitchell's and came back in the middle of the night. He took off early in the morning and did not return to help me get on the ferry. I feel so alone. There are not words for how alone and empty I feel sometimes. Of course I was right. I'm pregnant. The doctor beamed at me and said, "Congratulations, Mrs. Shattuck." I had to bite my lip to keep from bursting into tears in front of him. The baby should come in December, which means I will have to leave the island in November if the weather is bad and take Rachel with me. How will we find the money? I can't even think about it.

I met the Catholic priest on the way back from the mainland, on the ferry. He's young, just out of seminary, and his name is Father Slade. I was standing by the railing with Rachel in my arms, and he came up beside me and said she was a beautiful baby. I felt so grateful at that moment for a kind word. This is his first summer coming to the island to conduct

Mass at Our Lady of Snow. He has a very calm, quiet way about him. I don't know why I spoke to him as I did—perhaps it was the way he had of seeming to listen so intently—but I told him that Rachel had not been baptized, and I felt badly. He said he understood. It is difficult living on an island, when you can't get back and forth to the mainland easily. The church made exceptions in such cases. I realized then that he thought I was Catholic and hastened to explain I was not. He apologized and actually blushed. I don't know what came over me next, but I told him I was expecting another child. I tried not to cry, but I could not stop myself. I told him I was scared, that I didn't know how we could afford another baby. There was no one I knew on the deck, just some summer people, and I don't think they noticed. He patted my shoulder. "Children are always a blessing," he said. "God will help you care for your children." I saw that he was right. Children are a blessing. I should be grateful. When we got off the ferry, he said if there was anything he could do to help about getting Rachel baptized or anything else, to let him know.

June 6, 1932

It was just like the last time. I told Nate after supper that we were going to have another baby, and he jumped up from the table and danced me around the house, smiling and laughing. I had expected just the opposite—alarm, concern, worry—talk of money and how we would manage. But he was delighted and proud. I understand now that he sees the children as a reflection of himself. He feels he is doing what he was meant to do in the world. In moments I feel this way, too. But then there are the other days, when I question everything. I imagine I am not fit to be a mother, I feel such despair. I imagine they will put this new baby in my arms, and I will give the child back, run screaming out the door and go as far away as I can. Do other women long for this the way I do, simply to vanish, to walk out of my life and leave it all behind? These days of blackness are more frightening than anything else. It's all I can do to pick up Rachel when she cries and place the bottle to her lips.

June 18, 1932
I was out walking with Rachel, trying to find a breeze to cool us both, and I ran into Father Slade down by the lighthouse. He had come over on the afternoon ferry to say Mass tomorrow. He was wearing his collar with a short-sleeved shirt but no jacket. He seemed like a regular person, not a priest, in his shirt sleeves. He came up behind me on the road and said hello and asked how things were. I told him that I was well, and Rachel was well. "She seems like a happy baby," he said. For some reason, I take an idiotic pride in comments like this, as though having a happy baby were my doing, something I have accomplished with my expert mothering. We walked along without saying anything for a few minutes. Then he asked, "Do you have a faith you can turn to?" "Yes," I answered, barely able to do more than whisper. The question felt so personal and intimate. I explained that I had grown up attending the Congregational church in Barton, but that since coming to the island, I didn't go to the Union Church because my husband didn't want to. I told him that I prayed on my own. I felt terribly shy saying this, as though I had revealed a great secret about myself. He nodded and said, "Prayer is a comfort." We turned around when we reached the lighthouse and walked back. When we came to the church and the little cottage where he stays, we said goodbye. I walked home wondering how it is that some people can make you feel you have always known them, even when you have just met, and with other people, you can know them for years and still feel you have not gotten inside them.

July 1, 1932
Nate works long hours now, fitting as much into each day as he can.

After he is finished with quahogging, he works on the cars. He has three different cars he's trying to get running for summer people. He comes in at eight or eight-thirty, when he can't see what he's doing any longer, and we have a late supper. He hasn't been over to Silas Mitchell's once. It feels somehow as if we have turned a corner. Rachel is sleeping better and fusses less when she's awake. We have made a couple of payments on our bill at the store. I sense that Nate understands. He has a family now. He can't think of himself first all the time. He seems determined to show me he can make enough money this summer that the winter will not be as bleak as last year. The nausea has subsided, most days. I am trying to prepare myself to love this child, to be ready, though sometimes I can't imagine dividing the love I feel for Rachel, sharing it with another baby.

July 7, 1932
Another bad day. I walked Rachel down the road and, when no one was looking, ducked inside Our Lady of Snow. I had never been inside the church before. It is plain, with wood pews like the Union Church, but there is a statue of Mary at the front, and little candles in blue glass holders. I sat before the statue and prayed. I prayed that I would love my children, Rachel and the one to come. I prayed that I would find a way to get through the summer, to do what I have to do each day, without so much sadness. I prayed that this new baby would be a boy, for Nate's sake. I prayed to understand what it is that God wants of me, to understand why my life has been made the way it has. Praying before the statue is different. I felt I was speaking to Mary, that she could understand, a mother herself, a mother who was asked to give up her only son.

July 13, 1932
I go to the church every day now, except on Sundays, of course. I go in the morning, when Nate is out in the boat. It is the only thing that gives

me relief from my fear and dread. I lie in bed at night, listening for Rachel, and count the months until the new baby will come with a sense of terrible foreboding. I tell myself to stop, I am cursing my unborn child. I should not invite this darkness. But I can't stop. I imagine every horror. I imagine sneaking onto the ferry somehow after the baby is born and leaving Nate to care for both of them. Then I cry silently for myself, appalled that I am a harsh, unloving woman who can consider abandoning her own children. I think of Rachel and how beautiful she is, how desperately I love her, and I am so ashamed I want to hurt myself. I used to believe I was a very balanced person. Now there seems to be nothing balanced about me. I feel so weak and helpless and stupid. I should be better than this. I should be able to control my wayward feelings, but I cannot.

July 17, 1932

Father Slade found me in the church this morning. It was terribly awkward. I jumped up when he opened the door and apologized and tried to slip past him to leave. He smiled in that way he does, slowly and patiently. "You're welcome to come here," he said. "There's no reason to apologize." "But I'm not Catholic," I blurted out. "The church should be for anyone who needs it," he said. I think it was his use of that word— need—that caught me. Up to then I had told myself that the church was just a quiet place, a place where I could think in peace. I liked sitting before the statue of Mary. I felt she had become a friend who truly listens to me. But when he spoke, I saw that I did need the church, in more ways than I knew. I asked him what I would have to do to become a Catholic. He looked surprised. I thought of my mother pointing to the Italians and Portuguese filing down Front Street for the Saturday evening service at Saint Joseph's and calling them cheap. But I long ago gave up on winning her approval. She would be horrified. Everyone in my past life would be horrified. I don't care. The church is the only thing that calms me now, that makes me feel I can go on. Father Slade asked me if I thought Nate would convert, too. This stopped me. I told him I did not think so. Would Nate agree to have the children raised in the church? I said I thought this was possible. Father Slade said I should discuss all this with Nate, and if we are in agreement, he would be happy to meet with me when he comes on the weekends, to go over the Catechism. After I have completed the instruction, if I still want to join the church, I can. I went home feeling lighter and stronger, and happier than I have in days. To think that it might not have happened if Father Slade hadn't come on the early ferry and caught me there praying. But of course there are no accidents in this life. If I have come to believe in God, I must believe this, that our lives are shaped by God, and what is meant to happen does, even when it seems the farthest thing from what we want or expect.

July 25, 1932

The Brovellis and the others, mostly summer people, stared at me when I entered the church yesterday. Father Slade said I should come to the Mass, though I can't take communion of course. I felt that everyone was watching me. I didn't know when to kneel and when to stand, when to cross myself, or any of the prayers. I kept thinking I shouldn't be there. It's their church, not mine. But then I would look at the statue of Mary and feel her steady encouragement. The Latin is so strange and beautiful. It didn't matter that I couldn't understand the words. I understood their message, the strength of what lay behind them. Father Slade speaks in a clear voice. He is reassuring and inspiring at the same time. I am amazed by how sure he seems of himself for someone his age, and how comfortable he is with his role as a priest. Nate took care of Rachel for the hour while I was gone. He has agreed that if I am determined to join the church, he will not object to raising the children Catholic.

August 3, 1932

How is it that everything can seem so bleak one day, and the next I am so grateful to be alive? Thunderstorms went through last night, and the terrible heat of the past week lifted. I was able to work in the garden this morning, with Rachel sleeping in a basket on the porch. We will have a real crop this year—tomatoes, carrots, potatoes, cabbage. I am already imagining the meals I will make with our own food. I find myself even looking forward to winter, to those nights when the stove is going and I have a good meal to put on the table. Perhaps what matters is as simple as this, the satisfaction of canned tomatoes opened in January and the warmth of a fire. Rachel cries less now. That makes a difference. Nate is busy with all the work he does for the summer people. It's better when we are both busy, when the nights are just as full as the days. And I have my meetings with Father Slade. I am trying to spend whatever time I can find preparing, reading the books he has left me, memorizing the Catechism. I have a rosary now and have learned how to pray with the beads. Nate laughed when he first saw it. "I never thought I'd have one of those in my house," he said. But he was not angry. I say the rosary after he leaves in the morning. I love the feel of the beads between my fingers. They make the prayers tangible. Rachel reaches for the beads and smiles, and I feel she will grow up with faith. This is what is most important.

August 12, 1932

I am canning. The days are so hot and long. Mrs. Cunningham came to help me the first day and showed me how to get the jars to seal properly. It does seem like madness to boil huge pots of water on the hottest after-noons of the year. Between the garden and the laundry and seeing that Rachel and Nate are fed, it's a small eternity from the time I get up to when I fall into bed. No problem sleeping now. I almost fell asleep stand-ing at the stove yesterday. But I am so proud of the jars lining the shelves in the kitchen. I am not sure I have ever felt so proud of anything I've done, except giving birth and performing my high school piano recital.

August 22, 1932
My belly is big enough now that everything is tight. I wear the house dresses I wore when I was pregnant with Rachel, big, tent-like things. My hair is dry, and the curl is gone. I look like some sort of bloated scarecrow. Why must women be the ones to bear children? It hardly seems fair. We get saddled with everything—pregnancy and childbirth, cleaning, cooking, washing out the clothes—and then we have to be pleasant and attractive for our husbands. We have to keep up appearances, as they say. What have we done that God asks so much of us, that He punishes us in this way? I try to smile and say something nice when Nate comes in from work. But there are nights when I don't even have the energy to speak, when I want to scream, "Look what you have done to me!" The only thing that makes me feel sane is prayer, though sometimes when I say the words over and over they become so mechanical, like a frenzied wish, that I wonder if I even believe them anymore.

August 29, 1932
I met with Father Slade again on Saturday night, at the cottage that serves as the rectory. We sit at the table by the kitchen sink. He always begins with a prayer. We go over church history, and then we review the sacraments and different parts of the Catechism. There's a wonderful order and beauty to it all. I don't know what I absorbed from all those Sundays at the Congregational church, but it doesn't seem to amount to much now. Catholicism is so much richer. What I knew of church and the Bible in the past feels like a pale comparison to this. I understand now also that the Catholic church is the true church, with the priests and bishops descended directly from the Apostles of Jesus. Of course such

things were never spoken of or explained when I was a child. I thought every church was the same as another, except that the Catholics were mostly poor and had bad taste, according to Mother. Now I see that the church of the poor is the church of Jesus, without question. He did not come to serve people like my family, living in the best of circumstances in Barton. He came to serve the abandoned, the poor, the sick, the destitute. I cannot exactly count myself among these, but maybe I am closer to them now than I used to be. Closer in my heart, at least. And I imagine even Jesus would acknowledge that Nate and I are poor.

September 1, 1932
It won't be long before I go to the mainland. I am praying for a boy. Now that my pregnancy is getting advanced, I am not having classes with Father Slade. We will put off continuing until the spring, after the baby has been born, and I can take the time again. I should be accepted into the church next summer. I am too much of a sight to be out in public much.

September 5, 1932
The summer people are gone, and the island is empty, swept clean. I go down to the store in the mornings, carrying Rachel on the mound of my belly. A sort of pensive silence hangs over everything. I watch for Nate's boat, Bill Daggett's boat, Owen Pierce's boat. Sometimes they come round the east side of the island. They work their way along slowly, in no hurry now that the summer has ended. Nate has no work in his fix-it shop. We will have to rely on quahogging alone. I just hope it will be enough to see us through the winter.

September 6, 1932
I guess this is not a fit topic to write about, but changing and washing

diapers has to be the most disgusting thing in the world. At first I was so dewy-eyed with love for my beautiful baby that I hardly noticed. I thought even her soiled diapers were precious. Now I can't bear it. I have to stop myself from gagging when I wash them out. I ask myself every day how I will manage with another baby. Nate is so cheerful suddenly, so eager for the new one to arrive. He doesn't seem to have the slightest idea what it will mean for me. I begin to wonder if he is deaf and blind. Of course I am glad that he wants another child, and thankful I can give him one. But he is just so oblivious sometimes. "What's wrong?" he asked me the other night. "I'm dead tired," I said. "Didn't Rachel take her nap?" he asked, as if that might be the entire explanation. I honestly think he imagines that I spend the afternoons when she is asleep lounging around reading magazines. If you ask me, going out and hauling quahogs for a few hours is nothing compared to washing out three tubs of diapers and clothes, feeding the baby, doing the dishes, baking a loaf of bread, making chowder for supper, scrubbing the floor, going down to the store for groceries, mending Nate's work pants and shirts, bringing the washing in off the line and folding it all, and feeding the baby again and giving her a bath. And that's just a fraction of what I do in a day.

September 7, 1932
Rachel is one year old today. Is it possible she has been with me a whole year? The time has flown. I want to slow time down, to make these days when it is just the two of us last. She is so big. She pulls herself up on the table edge and teeters there with the most triumphant expression on her face. She has taken a few steps by herself already. I think she will be ready to walk soon. I am amazed by how much she understands. When I say clock, she points to the clock over the sink, and when I say deer, she points out the window. I feel that she understands everything I say to her. It's just a question of time until she can form answers, talk back in whole

sentences instead of isolated words. I wanted to make a cake for her birthday. I spent half the morning on it while she crawled around the floor and played with the wooden blocks Nate made for her. I sampled a piece at lunch. The cake is awfully dry. It crumbles in the mouth, though it doesn't taste bad. What is the secret to baking? I have not discovered it, whatever it is.

October 2, 1932
Nate came home from Silas Mitchell's last night, drunk. There have been other times I smelled the liquor on his breath and saw the unfocused look in his eyes. This was different. He came lurching through the door and stumbled to the bedroom. He fell across the bed and passed out. I had to remove his boots and take off his clothes. When I tried to move him on the bed, he raised his head and yelled at me, cursing. I left him there and spent the night on the sofa with Rachel beside me. He was like an animal. I felt that I did not know him, that I had never known him. God help us.

October 11, 1932
I have made arrangements to stay in the rooming house in Barton, at Mrs. Worthington's, when the baby is born. I will take Rachel with me and Mrs. Worthington will care for her when it's time to go to the hospital. Nate will stay on the island. We cannot afford to have both of us in town and to lose the income if he's not working. He says if the quahogging isn't good in December, he'll try to come around the time the baby is due. I suspect the quahogging will still be good, unless we get storms early this year, in which case he might not be able to make it over anyway. He has been quiet and apologetic since the night he came home drunk. I stayed away from him in the morning, still frightened. He said he was sorry and put his arms around me and asked me if I could forgive

him. I guess the answer is always yes, I can forgive him. He is not a bad man. Whole weeks pass when we are happy together, when he kisses me every night when he comes in from work, and we sit at the table and talk. He tells me about his day out in the boat, I tell him about Rachel's latest discoveries. We are companions then, friends. I don't know what causes him to become someone else, to turn dark and brooding, to go off like that and drink. I only know that when it happens I want to shake him until the old Nate, the one I know, returns. He has not been over to Silas Mitchell's once since the night he came home so drunk. We have not discussed it, but I understand that he is trying to tell me it won't happen again, that he is sorry and wants to make it up to me. My prayers have been answered.

November 8, 1932
The baby inside me never seems to sleep. He kicks all day and night. He must be a boy. Rachel was not like this. I feel like a battle is raging in my belly. I wonder if this baby will be born early. It certainly seems to want to get out. I lie in bed in agony no matter how I position myself. It seems useless even to try to sleep. Next week I go to Mrs. Worthington's. I am looking forward to it as though it were some glorious vacation.

November 17, 1932
I nearly cried when the taxi deposited me at Mrs. Worthington's door yesterday. She helped me into the house and made me a cup of tea. I sat in her wonderful parlor in a sort of trance, unable to believe that some-one else was going to look after me now, cook my meals and even help me with Rachel. She doesn't need to help with Rachel, but she does sim-ply out of kindness. I have a small room, in the back of the house off the kitchen. It is bright and cheery. Rachel sleeps beside me in an old crib that Mrs. Worthington keeps for visits from her grandchildren. She has

left a bell on the table by the bed and told me to ring it if I need anything in the night. I feel that this baby could be born any minute. When I see the bell beside the bed, I'm not so scared. There's an odd collection of us around the table for supper, with all the boarders who don't live here but come for meals. I remember some of them, others are new to town or people I simply never would have crossed paths with. The new people don't even remember my family, which seems so strange. It's as if we vanished from this town. The place where our house stood is still an empty lot. Mother lives somewhere in Connecticut, I hear. I don't even have her address. Brandon wrote once, months ago, telling me that he was moving to New York, and the bank was for sale. It is just as well, I guess. I could not go back to that house, even if it did still exist.

November 25, 1932
We had a wonderful Thanksgiving dinner around Mrs. Worthington's table. It was me and Rachel and Mrs. Worthington and all the single men with nowhere else to go. Even though I could not eat much, I enjoyed just looking at the food spread from one end of the table to the other. She is a magician in the kitchen. She creates meals out of almost nothing, which is what we all have these days. So many of the men are out of work. They show up at the door during the day, begging for any bit of food she can spare. It's heartbreaking. Mrs. Worthington always has something for them—a roll or a slice of bread, an apple, a cup of coffee.

November 29, 1932
I spend my days sewing and knitting for the new baby, washing out Rachel's diapers, napping in the rocking chair. It seems to be the only place I can sleep now. I am beginning to think I'm carrying an elephant inside me. I am so big I can barely get out of the chair. I look thoroughly ridiculous. But even with the waiting and the discomfort, there's a

peace to these days. Rachel has been so good. She plays with her toys and amuses herself and does not cry. At first I was so relieved to be away from the island, to be free of the daily drudgery of keeping the house going and cooking for Nate. Now I find the time weighing on me and even look forward to going home. I miss Nate. This is the truth, though I wouldn't have expected it. Why is that sometimes we can hardly tolerate the people we love most, and then when we are apart from them, we feel how important they are to us, how incomplete we are without them? Human beings are so restless and inconstant. I long to stop wishing for things to be different all the time and to accept what I have.

December 6, 1932
I cannot go to church in my condition, but Father Slade came to see me on Sunday. He prayed with me and blessed Rachel. I could tell Mrs. Worthington was surprised, but she said nothing. Father Slade said he would come to visit me in the hospital, and we could have Rachel and the baby baptized in the spring at Our Lady. What a comfort he is to me.

Phillip Hartwell Shattuck, born December 8, 1932, 8 pounds, 4 ounces.

Chapter Fifteen

The last entry, recording her brother's birth, was written in the margin, at the bottom of the notebook's last page. How much her mother had felt, Rachel thought as she closed the notebook and went to the window, gazing down at the dock. The ferry had come and gone, and the parking lot was empty. She had felt things Rachel could not have imagined, like her desire to run away, to leave not just Nate but all of them. She was full of conflicts Rachel had never guessed at. If only, Rachel told herself, she had paid attention, if only she had understood.

There was one thing she could do now—pack the diaries in her suitcase and take the ferry back to Barton. She could spirit the record of her mother's life to the mainland, just the way her mother had wanted to leave all those years ago, when the thought of another baby to care for was more than she could bear. Rachel considered this course of action as she watched the police car come into view, moving down Bay Avenue from the direction of the lighthouse. The block-like shape of Joe Brovelli's head was just visible behind the wheel. Following the car's progress as Joe turned in at the store, pulling the cruiser up beside the gas pump, the slow realization came over Rachel that, as much as she might want to protect the words her mother had written and take them away from her father's house, this was where they belonged. No, she would not be leaving, with the diaries or without them. She was going to stay.

She went out to the porch, cleared the steps in a single leap, and hurried down the hill. Joe was still standing beside the police car in his uniform, surveying the parking lot as though it might become a crime scene at any moment. She made her way down the path to his side. "I'd like to apply for the job," she said.

"At the schoolhouse?" he responded in a tone of disbelief.

"Yes."

"We didn't think you'd be interested or we would have asked you. Sure, you can apply for the job. You can have the job. I'm offering it to you right now."

Rachel extended her hand, and he shook it. "Does it still come with Owen Pierce's house and a car?"

Joe nodded. "Yup, the house and the car. And $4,500 for the year. Plus a budget for books and supplies, and we supply the wood for the stove."

"At the schoolhouse or at Owen's?"

"Both."

"Quite a deal."

Joe smiled. "You mean it?"

"I mean it."

"Okay then, I'll bring the contract by later."

Ducking his head, Joe strode across the parking lot and went up the steps to the store. The stiff, restrained movement of his body seemed to signal what Rachel had agreed to. She was an islander once again.

PART II
The Schoolteacher

Chapter Sixteen

Closing the door of her house, Rachel stepped into the sun. She had forgotten how still the island could become in October. Across the expanse of the bay, the mainland was etched on the horizon in the sharp light. This morning the tide was low, and the mud flats stretched beyond the rocks, a mucky wasteland strewn with seaweed. As she gazed over the rock-strewn landscape, the dream came back to her. She was with Kevin, in a large house with many rooms. They walked up a flight of stairs and went down a long hallway. He held her hand, leading her down the hallway, protective and reassuring. He took her into one of the rooms and pulled her toward him, his arms around her, his lips on hers. There was something sad in the kiss, as if they both knew it would be their last. In the confused logic of the dream, she thought, "We can't do this anymore," and then she thought, "Why not?" and pulled him closer, not letting go.

Rachel stood for a moment by the car, holding the key between her fingers. She did not want to dream about Kevin. She not even want to think about him, yet he kept coming back, refusing to stay put, safely in the past. Since she had moved back to the island, she found herself remembering him at odd times. She attributed it to being in a different place, a place that was peopled with ghosts—the ghost of her own younger self and the others she couldn't forget, her mother and Phil and

Andy. Now Kevin had joined them, as if he had died or been locked away, too. She had to remind herself that he was very much alive and walking the streets of Providence, though she might prefer to think of him as no longer in this world.

Rachel climbed into the Ford and stepped on the starter, then cautiously gave it gas. Easing the car onto the road, she drove by the lighthouse, where ladders lay on the ground, waiting for the arrival of Eddie and her father. The men were a team again, painting the lighthouse, now that the cast was off her father's leg. Nate still limped a bit, but he had more or less recovered.

When she reached the dock, Rachel turned down the hill and parked next to the gas pump. The children were gathering in the parking lot. She waved to Ellen and Lizzie and went into the store. The fire going in the woodstove made the place so warm the door had been left ajar. Rachel said good morning to Alice and waited while she poured a cup of coffee and slid it across the counter.

Outside, a tremulous, high-pitched voice carried across the porch. "Ellen, pull down your skirt. It's indecent." Evelyn Daggett came through the door a moment later. "I don't know what's wrong with those children," she said, as though she and Alice and Rachel were resuming a conversation already in progress. "They don't listen to a word I say. Honestly."

Evelyn pushed Arthur the cat from the easy chair by the stove and took his place. "I don't know how you can stand spending all day with that horde. It would give me a terrific headache. Don't get me wrong, I like children, but sometimes they're a gang of monkeys. That's what my mother used to call us. She was right. Honestly, we were savages."

Alice continued straightening the shelves behind the counter and ignored her mother, who went on about how lax today's parents had become. In her time, children didn't talk back. They'd get tanned for it, and they knew it.

"You know we used to have teas for the girls at the schoolhouse," Evelyn said. "It was Miss Weeden's idea. She felt just because they lived on an island was no reason the girls couldn't learn how to act in society. They even wore white gloves."

Alice tossed an empty cardboard box over the counter. "I never wore white gloves."

"Maybe that was before your time at the schoolhouse," Evelyn answered vaguely.

"Did the kids have breakfast?" Alice asked.

Evelyn paused, as though she had to think about it. "Yes. I made oatmeal. And Nick had about five cups of coffee. He shouldn't drink so much coffee. We weren't allowed to have coffee until we were twenty-one, honestly. Or cigarettes, either. Some things were for grown-ups."

"You try to get him to stop drinking coffee."

"Oh really, Alice, are you saying he can't live without it?"

"I'm saying that he does what he wants, at least as far as coffee is concerned."

Evelyn sniffed. "Maybe that's the problem."

Alice caught Rachel's eye and frowned. It was true that Nick, who brought a thermos with him to the schoolhouse, drank too much coffee, and that he was proud of his independence, but Rachel did not think these were particularly grave faults.

"Well, it looks like taxes are going up again," Evelyn observed. "Did you see the paper from day before yesterday? They have to pay for that new high school over there on the mainland somehow. Why not wring it out of us over here? They figure we won't bother to take the ferry over to protest. Do you know what the taxes were on our house when you were growing up? Twenty-five dollars a year. Now look what we're paying. You'd think we lived in Newport."

Evelyn addressed her words to Alice, who was counting the packs of cigarettes on the shelves. "If we're going to be a part of Barton, I guess we have to contribute," Rachel said when Alice did not respond.

"Oh, what do they do for us? Nothing. They want to live high on the hog over there, fine. Just don't make us pay for it. I haven't noticed a new schoolhouse on Snow."

Rachel realized that Evelyn was expressing a view shared by most of the islanders. Perhaps her own perspective was different after living in Barton. She knew that they truly needed a new high school, that it was not an indulgence or a luxury.

"And don't get me started on that fancy police station they built last year," Evelyn went on. "That's a glass palace if I ever saw one."

Rachel nodded, seeing no point in disagreeing. "I guess it's time for school," she said, before Evelyn could get started again.

"Don't take any guff from those kids," Evelyn called.

"I won't." Rachel waved at Alice and stepped onto the porch.

She loaded the children into the car, Ellen and Lizzie in the front beside her, and their cousins, Scott and Bob Daggett, in the back. As they drove past the marsh beyond the lighthouse and the old inn, the tall fronds of grass turned from gold to silver in the early light. The rows of windows on the second floor of the inn looked like sightless eyes, staring back blankly. The boarded-up summer homes across the road only completed the sense that Snow had been abandoned, left with nothing but the shells of deserted houses for the winter. They reached the schoolhouse just as Joe Brovelli pulled up, coming from the opposite direction. The doors of the police car opened, and the four Brovelli children spilled out.

Nick had come on his own, too grown up to ride with his sisters and cousins in the Ford. The old Army jeep he drove was already there, parked on the edge of the grass. When Rachel ushered the children inside, she found him seated at his desk, reading a science fiction paperback, his long legs stretched into the aisle. He closed his book as they entered and came to the vestibule, where the students left their coats.

"Do you think it's cold outside or something?" Nick asked his sister, Lizzie, playfully.

"Yes." Lizzie held up her hands. "I wore mittens."

"I noticed." Nick tugged off the mittens and helped Lizzie out of her jacket.

"Nick! I can't reach!" she squealed, holding up her jacket imploringly.

He took her jacket, hung it from a peg on the wall, and brushed his hand over her hair. Lizzie slipped from beneath his touch and ran into the schoolroom.

"I don't know why everybody's so short around here," Nick said to Rachel.

"Maybe it's just that you're so tall."

When he stood in front of her, Rachel had to look up to meet his eyes, a fact she found vaguely unnerving, accustomed as she was to teaching younger students. Glancing around the schoolroom as she went through the day, she would catch a glimpse of him off in the corner, bent over an assignment at his desk, and wonder what that man was doing in her classroom.

The children darted through the doorway, shouting out greetings. Rachel and Nick followed them into the schoolroom. The children scattered to their places. Rachel placed one hand over her heart and began the Pledge of Allegiance, pausing to let the assortment of voices join in. For the first few weeks, she had passed the days at the schoolhouse in a state of exhausted excitement. She was never more than five minutes ahead of the children in figuring out what came next. Nick's eyes followed her around the schoolroom, as if watching a race, curious to see if she would keep up. It was entirely different to teach in a classroom where her students covered such a range of ages, from Paul Brovelli, who was six, to Nick at eighteen. None of the nine children from three different families who made up her charges were in the same grade. After Paul, there was Lizzie, who was eight, and Rose Brovelli, who was nine; then Bob Daggett, aged ten; Ellen McGarrell, eleven; Theresa Brovelli, twelve; Scott Daggett, thirteen; Lou Brovelli, fourteen; and Nick, off by himself in senior year. This teaching tested her constantly, in a way her work in Providence and Barton had not. There were times it nearly made her dizzy, and yet at the end of the day, she felt triumphant, as though she had pulled off a small miracle.

The sound of chairs scraping over the wood floor filled the room as the children settled behind their desks. "Miss Shattuck," Paul called out. "I have to go to the bathroom."

The others burst into laughter. "Already?" Ellen said.

Rachel gave Ellen a reproving look, trying to stifle her own smile. "You may be excused, Paul."

The boy scrambled to his feet and hurried to the hallway leading to the kitchen. Rachel wrote the date and the day of the week on the board in yellow chalk. When she turned to face the class, Rose was waving her hand wildly in the air.

"Yes, Rose," she said.

"Today is my day to be teacher's helper."

Rachel nodded, motioning Rose to the front of the room. She gave the girl a stack of papers and told her to pass out the spelling quizzes, which she had drawn up individually and marked with each student's name. Rose went flouncing from desk to desk, until she came to Bob Daggett. "Miss Shattuck, he has a squirt gun! He just stuck it in his pocket." She pointed accusingly at Bob.

Rachel thanked Rose and suggested she continue passing out the quizzes. Paul reappeared, his shirt untucked and the fly of his jeans unzipped. Making his way slowly across the room, he kicked the soles of his sneakers against the floor, the image of aimlessness. Once he was slouched in his seat, Paul's brother leaned over and whispered to him to zip his fly. This was cause for more snickers of laughter. Rachel told them all to settle down and begin work on the quiz, then strode to Bob's desk and said in a low tone, "I'd like that squirt gun, please."

He glared at her, but removed the blue plastic gun from his pocket and placed it in her hand.

"Dangerous thing, a squirt gun," Nick said when Rachel went to check on him.

"In the schoolroom, yes, it is."

"Want to search my desk?"

"Have you got a squirt gun in there?"

Nick made a show of rummaging in the desk, pulling out crumpled pieces of paper, pencils, and a roll of Lifesavers. "I thought I had one in here. I don't know where it went."

Rachel smiled. Reaching into the pile of papers, she extracted a pencil drawing he had done of a deer. "That's nice."

"Oh, that's just a buck I saw down at the old Navy base. It's not much good."

"It's very lifelike."

Nick shrugged. "He's at least five years old. You can tell by the antlers and their necks. The older ones have thicker necks. My father and I tracked this buck last year but never got a shot at him."

"Are you going to try this year?"

"I don't know. I think he's earned the right to live, but my father will probably want to go after him."

Rachel set the drawing back on the desk. "How far have you gotten with *The Grapes of Wrath*?"

He flipped through the worn paperback. "I'm up to chapter twelve. He's a wordy guy, Steinbeck."

Rachel nodded and told him to read to the next chapter, then went to see how the others were doing with their quizzes. The rest of the morning passed quickly, as she went from group to group, supervising lessons in history and reading and writing. Rose followed her like an anxious puppy, constantly asking what she should do next, until she sang out, "Miss Shattuck, it's time for lunch."

Nick pulled on the jacket slung over the back of his chair and reached for the bag that contained his lunch, off to eat in the jeep. He just missed bumping into Gina Brovelli as she came through the doorway with a cardboard box in her arms. The smell of tomato sauce filled the schoolroom, as it did most days when Gina arrived with a hot meal for each of the Brovelli children. "Everyone behaving today?" she asked.

"Oh, sure," Rachel answered brightly. "Take your seats, boys and girls. No eating until everyone is at the table."

Rachel herded the children into the kitchen and took cartons of milk from a wheezing refrigerator, which had been hauled from the dump. Gina set the plates she had brought in front of Lou and Theresa and Rose and Paul, removing tin foil to reveal fat slices of lasagna and garlic bread. The other children had long ago accepted their cold lunches and took the wax paper from peanut butter and jelly sandwiches without giving the fragrant lasagna a glance. The situation was in fact just the opposite of what Rachel had initially imagined. It turned out that the Brovelli kids hated their hot lunches and the embarrassment of having their mother noisily invade the schoolhouse each day. What they wanted most in the world was a paper bag containing a slim peanut butter and jelly sandwich, an apple, and cookies.

Rachel took her place at the head of the table and unwrapped her own sandwich. Gina, a self-appointed lunchroom monitor, hovered around the table, swooping down to retrieve dropped napkins. The children concentrated on their lunches, ignoring her. They ate quickly and jumped from their seats when they were dismissed, dashing outside and scattering across the lawn, leaving the table covered with debris.

"Lou doesn't give you any trouble, does he?" Gina asked as she helped Rachel clean up. "He's being a bit of a teenager at home."

"No. He's good with the other kids." Lou had his sullen moments, but Rachel did not feel they were worth mentioning.

"He likes you better than Miss Hopkins."

Rachel nodded.

"She didn't know how to handle a boy like Lou." Gina gathered the dirty plates and set them in the box. "I knew that woman was trouble the day I set eyes on her. It's a good thing we're rid of her. Thank God Eddie saw the light." Gina went to the door, calling over her shoulder, "I know you're not going to make the mistakes she made."

Rachel wiped down the table with a sponge and wondered exactly what mistakes Laura had made, or Gina thought she had made. She reviewed the afternoon's lesson plans at her desk, keeping an eye on the game of tag in progress outside. Even Lou had joined in, though some-times he refused to participate because he was too old for that "baby stuff," as he called it. Nick remained in the jeep with his book. The entire half hour of recess passed without the need for her to rush out and inter-vene in a fight or bandage a skinned knee.

The afternoon began with Ellen reading to the younger girls and Lou quizzing the boys in history while Rachel went over algebra with Nick. She pulled a chair up next to his and opened the textbook to the chapter on polynomials. Nick took a piece of notebook paper from his desk and set to work. Rachel watched him with a certain wonder. She decided from their first day together that she had no choice but to learn the second year of algebra with him. It was utterly foreign to her, and he quickly out-stripped her, moving through the problems with mechanical precision. His mind worked in ways she found hard to fathom. The equations clearly meant something to him that they did not to her. He did not need to translate the language of mathematics; he understood it instinctively.

Rachel was still puzzling over the first problem, trying to work it out, while he had finished number five. He glanced up and laughed when he saw the expression on her face. "It's not torture."

"Not for you."

"Here, I'll show you." He wrote out the equation. "See?"

"Yeah, but I'm not sure I could have done it myself."

"Keep trying. You'll get it. Miss Hopkins just handed me the book and walked away last year. I had to figure it out by myself."

"But you're not the teacher."

"It's not your fault they don't do algebra in third grade."

Rachel nodded, grateful for his acknowledgment that she could not be expected to become a high school teacher overnight.

Ellen finished the story, and the Daggett boys began tearing around the desks. Rachel went quickly to the head of the room, clapping her hands to restore order. Gathering the younger children together, she started a science lesson about weather while the older students worked on their English compositions and Nick sat by himself, lost in algebra. When the hands on the clock over the blackboard pointed to three, Rose shouted, "School's over, Miss Shattuck."

Rachel checked the clock, surprised to discover she was right. She dismissed the children and, as they raced each other to the vestibule, called out reminders of homework assignments. Nick helped Lizzie get dressed, said goodbye to Rachel, and went out to his jeep. She watched through the window as he pulled off the grass and onto the dirt road, giving a quick wave. The Brovellis climbed into their father's car and took off behind Nick.

The McGarrells and the Daggetts settled in their places in the Ford, and Rachel headed toward Bay Avenue, listening to the girls chatter about Halloween. Ellen was going to be a witch. When Rachel looked in the rear view mirror, she saw Scott gazing out the window. "What are you going to be, Scott?" she asked.

He shook his head in disgust. "Nothing. I'm too old for Halloween."

Rachel should have known this, she realized. She had not meant to embarrass him. She pulled up next to the store, and the children scrambled out of the car, calling goodbye. Lisa Daggett, Will's wife, was waiting on the porch.

Driving up the hill from the dock, Rachel welcomed the sudden silence, surrounding her like a gust of wind. After a day at the schoolhouse, she wanted nothing but to be still, knowing that she could finish a thought without being interrupted. She waved at her father and Eddie as she passed the lighthouse. Eddie stood on a scaffold he had erected to paint the tower. Nate was on the ground, swabbing a brush over the base. They raised their paintbrushes in greeting as Rachel passed.

Chapter Seventeen

The house still smelled vaguely of Owen Pierce's pipe smoke, though numerous summer residents and teachers had come and gone since his death. Rachel let herself inside and set her canvas bag full of school folders on the table. In the bedroom, she changed into her corduroy pants and an old pullover sweater. It would be cold that night. She could feel it already.

She ran a comb through her hair, adjusted the rumpled collar of her blouse, and crossed the main room. Stepping back outside, into the clear air, she went up the road, away from the lighthouse, toward Miss Weeden's.

The elderly woman was sitting on the porch, bundled in a wool coat that covered her knees. Miss Weeden liked to spend a few minutes outside each day, even in the coldest weather. It kept her healthy, she said.

"How'd it go today?" Miss Weeden called as Rachel approached.

"Pretty good. No major catastrophes."

Miss Weeden got to her feet slowly, pushing herself out of the wicker chair. Rachel held the door and followed her into the house. The teapot sat on the table, steam rising from the spout. She helped Miss Weeden out of her coat and hung it on the rack by the door. When they were seated at the table, Miss Weeden reached for the teapot and filled the cups, giving Rachel a pointed look, as though trying to gauge her mood.

"It never gets any easier," the old woman said as she passed a small pitcher of milk. "Even after all those years, I couldn't sleep before the first day of school."

"But you must have gotten used to all the different ages and figured out –"

Miss Weeden clucked her tongue, cutting Rachel off. "I don't know that any of us ever figure out anything. We get more experienced, maybe. But I wouldn't say I ever got it figured out."

"You kept us busy all day long. You made it seem like you had a plan."

Miss Weeden brought the cup to her lips and smiled. "Yes, I had a plan, but I can't tell you how many times I threw away my plans and started over on the spot. That's the thing about children. They aren't predictable. And teaching them isn't predictable. But up until the last day of the year, you can always try to do better, try to get to that one child who isn't listening. I think that's what kept me at the schoolhouse so long. I should have retired sooner, but there was no one to take my place, so I just kept on showing up. I hope you're planning to stay."

Rachel gazed at the summer places across the road through the window. It seemed that the squat cottages with their boarded-over doors and windows should reveal the contents of her future. She had taken the job with the intention of only staying that year, but she was liking the children and the chaos of the one-room schoolhouse far more than she had expected. "I promised to stay for this year. I'll have to see after that."

"I used to think you could be a teacher. You were so thoughtful and patient as a child."

Rachel took a sip of tea, amused to hear herself described this way. Had she been thoughtful or just withdrawn? Patient or simply cautious? "I guess every teacher hopes at least one of her students will become a teacher, too."

"Of course, but it's hard to get the smart ones to consider college.

And I don't know that I want them to leave. We need them here on the island."

Need them here for what? Rachel wondered. She drank her tea and listened to Miss Weeden talk about the early years at the schoolhouse, back at the turn of the century, when the island was more populated. She had twenty-six, twenty-seven pupils some years. As adults, many of them had left. The island seemed empty to her these days.

Miss Weeden's hand shook as she raised the cup to her lips, and there was a tremor in her voice, but other than these signs, she did not show her age. She wore a floral print dress that buttoned up the front, the collar fitting closely around her wrinkled neck, and old-fashioned black shoes with laces and rounded toes.

Down the road, the silence was broken by the sound of a vehicle approaching. The truck from the store pulled up outside, and Brock McGarrell swung out of the cab with a box of groceries in his arms. Rachel went to the door.

"Afternoon, ladies," he called out jovially. "Am I in time for tea?"

Miss Weeden started up nervously. She was about to make her way to the kitchen when Brock waved her back. "Only kidding, Miss Weeden. I can't stay. Alice has got a whole list of things for me to do back at the store. We're making improvements." He winked, as though indicating they both knew that there was no real improving the store, but Alice had to be humored in her projects.

Brock carried the box into the kitchen and set it on the counter. "We had everything on your list but the beets, Miss Weeden. We should get a shipment tomorrow. I put in two packages of those throat drops."

Miss Weeden eased back into her chair and thanked him.

"Least we can do for our oldest customer." Brock stood in the doorway, arms folded over his chest. "You ladies watch yourselves with that tea, now. Don't overdo it."

Rachel smiled in spite of herself at his stupid joke.

"You got anything that needs attending to in the garden, Miss Weeden? Might be a frost tonight, with the full moon."

Miss Weeden shook her head. "I brought in the last of the tomatoes the other day."

"All right, then. You let us know if you need anything." With a tip of his hat, Brock stepped outside.

"I don't know why he has to keep reminding me I'm their oldest customer," Miss Weeden said when the truck had driven away. "It's hardly flattering to be told you're a near relic."

Rachel drank the last of the tea and reached for a chocolate chip cookie. Miss Weeden made a batch each week and kept them in a tin on the kitchen counter decorated with a picture of three kittens sitting in a picnic basket.

"Do you want help putting the groceries away?" Rachel asked.

"No. You've got work to do." Miss Weeden squeezed her hand. "I know you're doing a good job."

"Thanks." Rachel felt suddenly emotional. She cared about the children and doing the best she could, though she had been uncertain at first that she should stay.

Rachel went to the door. The sun was low in the sky, just visible over the tops of the trees. It did feel like there might be a frost. Back at her house, she took sheets of newspaper from a box next to the potbellied wood stove, wadded them into balls, and placed them inside with a few pieces of kindling. She struck a match and watched to make sure the paper caught. The old stove was temperamental, prone to emitting sudden billows of smoke. She had learned to build a small fire to start with, generating enough heat so the flue would draw, before adding any logs.

Delivering the wood to her and to the schoolhouse was another of Brock's jobs. A few weeks earlier, he arranged to have a cord of wood brought over on the ferry, in a farmer's truck. He stacked it against the side of Rachel's house in alternating rows, creating a neat pile that gave her a sense of security. Nate had argued with her at first, saying he saw no sense in her freezing in that little shack by the water when she could live in her own home with him, but she held firm. If she was going to stay on the island and take the job at the schoolhouse, she was going to have her own place.

She fed more newspaper and kindling into the stove, closing the door so the smoke would not escape. After a few minutes, the stove began to send out heat, and through a chink where the door did not quite close, she could see the orange light of flames. She added two logs, stacking them at angles, one on top of the other, and went to the table. Removing the spelling tests from the folder, she glanced out the window at the water. The tide was going out again, exposing the rocks. She knew what people believed—she had stayed because of her father. The truth lay elsewhere. She did not owe her father anything, and the fate of the school-house and the island children did not rest on her shoulders. No, it was not a sense of duty that made her stay and take the job, nor was it some misguided notion of righting past wrongs, of making up for being a neglectful daughter. She had stayed for her mother, not her father.

Going through the stack of papers, she attached gold stars to the tests with perfect scores and red stars for eighty percent or above. She took the small stars from the cardboard box she had brought from the mainland and balanced them on her fingertip, then licked the backs and fixed them to the papers. The diary Nate had given her remained exactly as she had left it, on top of the blanket in the box in the closet, untouched by either of them. The other diaries were still hidden in the bottom of the box. In the last weeks of August, she had been back in Barton, preparing to move, and then all through September, her father was home most of the time, his leg still in the cast. There had been no opportunities for her to be alone in the house, to reach to the bottom of the box and pull up another notebook. Now that Nate was working again, she would find a time.

She finished grading the papers and heated up some macaroni and cheese left over from the night before, and opened a can of peaches. She ate at the table, facing the view of the water beyond the porch. Within moments, light drained from the sky, and the bay became an inky pool of black stretching to the erased horizon. When she was done eating, she slid the dishes into the sink and pulled on her wool jacket. Stepping out the door, she followed the worn path across the brown grass to the road. The air had a sharp, raw feel that hinted at the coming winter. She took her gloves from the jacket pockets as she passed the lighthouse, watching the beam sweep over the shuttered summer places and the tops of the trees. The pay phone outside the store was already ringing when she reached the dock. She stepped inside the booth and picked up the receiver.

"Hi," Babs said in response to Rachel's greeting. "I've been sitting here with the phone ringing for two whole minutes." Babs called every Thursday at seven.

"Sorry. My watch must be slow."

"I had lunch with the new science teacher." Babs paused to let the effect of this news sink in. "He is very…serious. Not that that's bad. I just don't think he's ever going to ask me for a date. God, I'm afraid I talk too much. Do I talk too much? He's sort of quiet, and I knew I was just bab-bling like an idiot, and then I thought, God, he's going to hate me."

"Maybe he's taking his time."

"He might have time, but I don't. Honestly, I'm turning into an old bag."

"You're not that old."

"Oh, come on, Rachel. If I don't have children soon, I'll be the age of a grandmother by the time it happens."

Rachel kept her eyes on the empty road above the store. The street-light cast a white circle on the pavement that gave the surrounding dark-ness an impenetrable depth.

"You know that Laura Hopkins is a bit of a ditz," Babs said.

In a strange bit of symmetry, Laura had taken Rachel's job at Barton Elementary. "Really? How so?"

"She does this weird thing where she bites her lip and giggles all the time. No matter what you say to her, she giggles. I guess she's an okay teacher. When I walk by her room, the kids are all sitting at their desks anyway. She's just kind of breathy, you know what I mean? It drives me crazy in the lunchroom. So how's your father?"

"He still limps a little, but he's doing all right. He's working again. Everyone says it's amazing."

"And what about you? Are you going spend the rest of your life over there?"

"No."

"I hope not. I know they need a schoolteacher, but it's a waste. You'll never meet a man if you stay there."

"How's Sheila?" Rachel asked.

"She's not exactly her cheery self. She's got this little map of Vietnam on her desk. Whenever she gets a letter from her son, she sticks a pin in the map, if she can figure out where he is. I don't know, it just makes me kind of sad."

"They're saying the war shouldn't go on much longer."

"Yeah, that's what everybody tells her. When are you coming over? Metzger's has got the cutest things for winter—wool plaids from England and these adorable sweaters. Don't tell me you don't need clothes any-more."

Rachel smiled. "No, I need clothes. I wear a skirt or a dress every day to school."

"That's a relief. You shouldn't let yourself go, Rachel. Really. Just because you're living like a hermit over there. Come over and have your hair done. Get on that ferry."

Rachel agreed that she would come some weekend, said goodbye, and hung up the phone. Retracing her steps, she climbed the hill to the road, passing the darkened store. Now that the summer people were gone, Alice closed by six.

She was almost at the top of the hill when she heard the uneasy chugging of an engine and saw headlights coming toward her. At first she thought it was Joe, making his night rounds, but as the vehicle approached, she realized it was Nick. He said hello through the open window, without adding the "Miss Shattuck" he used at the schoolhouse.

Rachel pushed her gloved hands into her jacket pockets. "Where are you going?"

"Just driving around, looking for deer. Want a ride?"

She said sure and climbed up into the jeep. "It gets cold down in that phone booth," she added, as if she needed to give an explanation for accepting his offer.

He glanced at her without making a response and went on toward the lighthouse, passing the turn to his house and her father's. As they came up to the inn, he said, "You know I read that American history book last year."

"What do you mean?"

"Miss Hopkins had me read it."

"Why didn't you tell me?" Rachel felt both incensed and mystified.

Nick shrugged. "I thought maybe I was supposed to review it or something."

"On the mainland they have American history senior year. I just assumed that's what we would do. That's a huge waste of time, reading that textbook again."

Nick pulled the jeep over at her house. Across the seat, his face was a veiled mask, except for a flash of amusement in his eyes. She opened the door and said, "Nick, if there's something you want to study that we're not, or something that's not going well, you have to tell me. I won't know otherwise."

"I'll tell you, Miss Shattuck." A hint of a smile moved over his lips. "I will, really."

Rachel swung out of the jeep and said goodnight. He waved at her, one hand flat above the steering wheel, before he turned around and headed back toward the dock. It was then she spotted Eddie's truck parked in the gravel at the side of the house.

"Feel free to break into my house any time," Rachel said as she stepped inside.

"The door was unlocked."

She took off her jacket and hung it from the coat tree. Eddie had left his denim jacket and baseball cap hanging from another peg. He sat at the table, a bottle of beer in his hand. "You and Nick out joy riding?" he asked.

"No, we were not out joy riding. He gave me a ride from the dock. I was talking to Babs on the phone." Rachel went to the stove, filled the kettle with water, and put it on to boil. "He spends a lot of time driving around in that jeep."

"Guess it's better than being cooped up in the house with your sisters and parents and grandmother."

"It can't be easy being the only kid his age on the island."

"He's always been a bit of a loner. He doesn't hang around with the summer kids much. He'd rather be off in the woods."

"Is that so strange?"

"I didn't say it was strange. I just said it's what he likes to do."

The kettle began whistling as the water came to a boil. Rachel took a mug and a tea bag from the cupboard.

"I've got another beer if you want it." Eddie pointed to an unopened bottle on the table.

"Not on a school night." She dropped the tea bag in the cup and added hot water.

Eddie smiled. "I keep forgetting you're Miss Shattuck."

"Technically I'm Miss Ellis, but I can't stand being called that. If I'm not married anymore, I'm not going to keep that name."

"No, it never really suited you."

"The name or the husband?"

"The name. Rachel Ellis. It didn't sound quite right."

"You should have pointed that out before I got married."

"I don't think you gave me the opportunity."

Rachel carried the mug to the table and slid into the chair across from Eddie. "No, I guess I didn't."

Eddie brought the beer to his lips and reached for the deck of cards on the table, fanning them in front of her. They both selected a card and turned it over. "Look at that," she said. "For once I win the deal."

"Lot of good it will do you."

She gathered up the cards and began shuffling. "I believe I'm only two games behind."

Eddie smiled in that distant, knowing way of his. "A lead is a lead."

She felt the smooth surface of the cards as she dealt the hand and wondered if anyone could have talked her out of marrying Kevin.

Rachel won the first game and lost the second. The third game was close all the way to the end, when Eddie won by only three peg points. "That's too bad," he said as he scooped up the cards. "You almost cut the lead to one game."

She reached for a crumpled napkin on the table and tossed it at him.

Eddie pushed his chair back and got to his feet. "There's always next time."

"If I agree to play with you again."

"I think you will." He went to the coat rack and retrieved his jacket and hat, slipping the unopened beer in his jacket pocket.

"Thanks a lot, Eddie."

"Any time. See you around."

Rachel sat at the table after he was gone, listening to the truck start up outside. When the sound of the engine had faded away, she went to the bedroom and stood at the window, staring out into the dark. This is what her life had come down to, she thought ruefully, playing cribbage with Eddie Brovelli and making the trip around the island every morning and afternoon, as predictably as the tides going in and out. She supposed it could be worse.

She opened the closet door and surveyed her clothes. She would wear the red wool skirt in the morning, with a white blouse and her red cardigan sweater. Taking her nightgown from a hook on the door, she undressed and climbed beneath the covers. A battered hardback of *Ethan Frome* she had found at the Improvement Center sat on the table by the bed. She opened the book carefully, propping it on her knees, and turned the brittle pages slowly, thinking of the dried wings of dead moths and flowers pressed between the covers of a dictionary, the colors of the petals faded to a dull white. She imagined all the people who had followed the sad story of Ethan and Mattie in this copy of *Ethan Frome* while sitting on the beach or lying across a sofa on a rainy afternoon. She had read the book before, when she was in college, but the story struck her as utterly fresh and surprising, as if she were reading it for the first time. That was the mark of a good book.

The room grew colder as she turned the pages, lost in a snowy New England winter. Rachel set the book on the bedside table and went to add more wood to the fire. Turning out the lights, she crossed the floor in her slippers and lay with her head turned toward the window, waiting for the beam from the lighthouse to swing round. The light flashed every sixty seconds, clearing the roof of the house and sweeping across the water, cutting through the dark. It made her think of another Ethan, Ethan Cunningham, who had been the lighthouse keeper when she was a child.

The old keepers had trimmed the wicks and polished the lens, and woken at set intervals to make sure the light was still going. Now the lighthouse was automated, with no need for a keeper. Ethan Cunningham had taken over the job in his late twenties, when his father died suddenly. Ethan was tall and far too handsome to be a lighthouse keeper or an islander. He wore khaki pants with a crease down the legs and crisply pressed white shirts open at the collar, an outfit that made him look like he was about to step onto a city streetcar. Once, when Rachel was eight, Miss Weeden took all the school children for a tour of the lighthouse. Ethan led them up the spiral staircase in silence. When he began speaking, his deep voice resonated in the tower. She remembered the sure tone of his voice, and his hands, gesturing in the air as he described the workings of the light. The ends of his fingers were covered in dabs of brown and black and red paint. When he was not looking after the lighthouse or his mother, he was up in his room painting landscapes on square canvases. This gave him even more of a foreign air.

Ethan went off to serve in World War II, leaving his mother and sister to tend the light. There was not much for them to do, since the lighthouse was blacked out for the duration of the war. When the war ended, the Coast Guard took the final steps to automate the lighthouse fully. Ethan moved to New York with the girl he had married, and Mrs. Cunningham went to live with her daughter in Connecticut. No one had tended the lighthouse since, other than the Coast Guard delegation. The men showed up every few months to clean the windows and polish the lens, and recharge the battery that powered the light. They had none of the romance of the old keepers or Ethan, who was so unsuited for the job but had captured Rachel's young imagination.

It seemed to Rachel now, as she closed her eyes and drifted toward sleep, that Ethan Cunningham was a dashing figure she had invented, a piece of some distant childhood dream. It did not seem possible that he had actually existed and that he might be walking the streets of New York tonight, his shoulders slouched forward, his dark hair framing that narrow face.

Chapter Eighteen

It took four tries to get the car to start in the cold the next morning. She pressed the starter and then the gas pedal gently, careful not to flood the engine. This was one of the lessons her father had taught her when she learned to drive at the age of fourteen. All the vehicles they had ever owned were difficult to handle. She had become adept at a variety of tricks and could remember, if she forced herself to go through the litany of cars and trucks, the special quirks of each one.

Rachel arrived at the store before the children. She was about to climb the porch steps when the sound of raised voices inside, carrying through the open crack in the door, stopped her.

"Where are we going to get money for that?" a man said.

"There's scholarships, there's jobs," Alice answered.

"I just don't see the point. All that money for what? He ain't gonna be happy."

"He's smart, Brock."

"He's not that kind of smart. He doesn't really care about school. He just wants to fool around with his radios and go hunting."

Rachel considered quietly retracing her steps and waiting in the car, but she could not make herself move. Alice and Brock must have been so engrossed in their conversation that they had not heard her pull up outside. After a pause, Alice continued. "If he's not enrolled in college, he could be drafted. He's already sent in his registration."

"Is that what you want? You want him to go to college so he can't get drafted?"

"That's not what I said, Brock. It's just that he's good in math and science, and he's always reading…" Alice trailed off, a certain hopelessness in her voice.

"I'm proud I served my country. I'd be proud if my son did, too."

"Of course you should be proud, but maybe Nick has a choice."

"That's a crummy choice if you ask me. Your country calls on you and you go twiddle your thumbs with a bunch of college kids. You think Nick's too good for the Army?"

"No, I don't think he's too good for the Army," Alice said in a tone of disgust.

There was a long silence, before Brock said, "I better go see if the kids are ready."

The door flew open, and Brock came striding down the steps. Rachel tried to make it appear that she had just arrived. "Good morning," she said.

"Morning," Brock answered brusquely.

He brushed past her and climbed the path to the road.

Rachel wished she could let Alice know she had heard the conversation and agreed with her, but once inside she took the cup of coffee Alice handed her like any other morning, without saying anything.

Alice's face was flat, empty of expression. There was no sign of the argument that had just transpired. She looked tired more than anything else. Rachel noticed for the first time the creased wrinkles around Alice's eyes and mouth and remembered the girl she had admired at the schoolhouse. Alice had been smart, too, and even back then, before the war, people said she was so capable, she could go on to do anything. *Capable—*

what a New England compliment. Yet what the islanders said was true. Alice was capable, and she could have done anything she set her mind to, but she stayed on Snow with her mother and ran the store. You couldn't blame her for wanting her son to have a chance at more than that.

"Doesn't it seem early for the first frost?" Rachel said as she poured sugar into her cup.

"Sometimes it's October, sometimes it's November. Miss Weeden says it'll be a bad winter because the caterpillars' stripes were skinny, but I don't know if that really means anything. Owen Pierce could tell you. He was the best weather forecaster on Snow."

"I keep expecting to find him sitting on the porch."

"So do I, and it's been ten years."

Voices sounded outside, and the door swung open. Lizzie and Ellen went running toward the counter, followed by their grandmother. "Everyone's here, Miss Shattuck," Ellen announced.

Rachel downed the rest of the coffee, dropped the cup in the wastebasket, and said goodbye to Alice and Mrs. Daggett. The girls skipped behind her out the door and headed for the car. When the children were settled, Rachel started up the car. After a series of chugging coughs, the engine turned over. She released the emergency brake and climbed the hill. The girls went on about the frost. They could see their breath that morning. This was an event.

Rachel should have considered the possibility that Nick could be drafted, though she had not thought about it. The editorials in the newspaper said the war would be over in another year at most. The Vietcong were poorly trained and equipped and out-numbered. It was just a matter of time. Rachel had assumed Nick was safe, and that when he graduated from the schoolhouse, the war would at least be winding down, but what if Alice was right?

In the schoolroom, they found Nick by the stove, with his hands spread above the iron top to absorb the heat. The children gathered around the stove with him, stamping their feet. "Thanks for starting the fire," Rachel said.

Nick shoved his hands in his pants pockets. "It was cold in here."

Rachel went to his desk and retrieved the American history book. "Good riddance?"

"Good riddance."

She set the book on the bottom shelf of the bookcase by her desk, pulled out a worn copy of a textbook on European history, and handed it to him. He accepted the book with a half-smile which made her feel that now they were truly friends.

The younger children did not stumble over their reading that morning, and the math problems did not feel so difficult to explain. Maybe, Rachel thought, she and the students were both making progress. Nick informed her that there had once been bears in Europe, but they had all been killed off. When she asked if he had learned that in his new history book, he laughed and said, "No, it's just something I know."

At lunch time, Gina Brovelli arrived with plates of sliced ham and Waldorf salad. Paul pointed at the pieces of chopped celery covered in mayonnaise. "Yuck. I hate celery."

"That's good for you, and you'll eat it, Paul Brovelli," Gina snapped. She rolled her eyes at Rachel.

The others downed their lunches quickly, but Paul was left at the table, pushing the bits of salad around with his fork. "Two more bites," his mother said, "or no recess."

Paul stared mournfully at his plate while Rachel and Gina cleared the table.

"You want recess?" Gina said.

He nodded.

"Then eat."

Paul let out a prolonged sigh, reached for his fork, and took one bite followed by another. He barely waited for his mother's permission before leaping from his chair and running to the door.

Gina reached for his plate and stacked it on top of the others. "I heard Alice wants Nick to go to college."

Rachel gathered up the empty milk cartons and dropped them in the wastebasket, wondering how Gina had come upon this piece of information.

"You think he could get in?" Gina asked.

"If he wants to, sure. He's a good student. He could go to the state university."

"Joe says Brock's not too crazy about the idea. You know how that goes. The husband thinks one thing, and the wife thinks another. Joe and I don't have that problem. Ever since we met, we agree on everything. People say they can't believe it, but it's true. We're just suited to each other, I guess." Gina gathered up the box. "Well, I better get back. Joe's waiting for his noon meal."

Rachel watched Gina cross the lawn, call goodbye to her children, and drive off toward Snow Park. Maybe Brock had told Joe about his argument with Alice. She couldn't think how else word of it would have gotten around. Gina's obvious enjoyment of the dispute made her uneasy.

When the hands of the large clock above the blackboard read three o'clock, she loaded the Daggetts and the McGarrells into the Ford. The sun had warmed the air, so that no one needed gloves. They passed the maple and birch trees in their fall foliage, sudden bursts of orange and yellow. Rachel pulled up beside the gas pump, and the children jumped out of the car. Ellen ran inside the store, but Lizzie remained behind, looking up at the sky.

"I can't see my breath anymore," she said. "My father says when you can see your breath, it's the angels touching it. They're all asleep now.

They just come out early in the morning or at night."

"Really? I'll have to watch for them."

"Oh, you can't see them, Miss Shattuck. But sometimes you can feel them. They touch you with their wings."

"What does that feel like, when they touch you?"

"Very soft. Softer than Arthur. Some people are scared of the angels, but I'm not."

Lizzie reached up and took Rachel's hand. Together they climbed the porch steps. Ellen was already seated behind the counter eating a donut.

"Donuts!" Lizzie shrieked.

Running to the counter, she ignored her mother's outstretched arms, waiting to give her a hug, and dragged a stool next to the chair where her sister was perched. Scrambling onto the stool, she took a donut from the open box.

"It's nice to see you, too," Alice said.

Lizzie smiled, her mouth too full to speak.

"She was just telling me about the angels," Rachel explained to Alice. "When you can see your breath, the angels are touching it."

Alice grimaced and said, "That's some story her father told her. Our house is full of angels and fairies and little people. I ignore them myself, but I'm always getting yelled at for stepping on them."

Rachel went to the cooler and peered inside. "You got a delivery."

"Yes—hamburger, chicken, pork chops. For once, they sent everything I asked for."

Taking a package of hamburger from the cooler, Rachel carried it to the counter, adding buns as she passed the bread rack. She returned to the shelves for a can of peas. Alice packed the groceries in a bag and made change. She would see them all later, Rachel said, and made her way to the car. When she reached her house, she changed out of her skirt and blouse into her corduroy pants and a sweatshirt. After a quick run of the comb through her hair, she set off walking back down Bay Avenue with the bag of groceries in her arms.

Absorbed in painting, Eddie and her father did not notice her until she reached the base of the lighthouse. "Looks good," she called up to Eddie on the ladder. Nate was working on the lower portions from the ground. Both men wore old work clothes dotted with flecks of white and baseball caps liberally splattered with paint.

"I got some hamburger for dinner," Rachel told her father. "How much longer do you think you'll be?"

"Eddie, how much more of this you wanna do before we knock off?" Nate asked.

"Another hour, I guess, as long as the light lasts. That okay?"

"You're welcome to come for dinner, Eddie." Rachel squinted up at him.

"I already told Gina I'd go over to their place."

"Okay. See you."

When she glanced back, they were both facing the section of wall they were painting, concentrating on their work. Rachel pulled her jacket close and went on down the road. The tide was high, the waves washing over the rocks. The full moon that night made the tide higher than usual. Rachel thought of the '38 hurricane, when the water had engulfed the road, the waves crashing with a stunning force and violence over the roofs of the houses along the shore. Many of the summer places had been lost, and the store was gutted. Rachel was just five years old then. She did not remember seeing the churning water overtake the island, though she had heard the story many times. What she remembered was fear, and the terrible howling of the wind as she and her brothers and her mother and father crouched in the tin bathtub, holding on to each other. Her father kept saying they would be all right. She believed him. It was only later, when she was older, that she understood how close they had come to being swept away.

Rachel let herself into the house and placed the wrapped hamburger meat in the refrigerator. Glancing at her watch, she peeled off her jacket and left it on the couch.

Chapter Nineteen

May 4, 1938

A new notebook at last. I've missed those stolen moments in the after-noon when I sat down to record my thoughts. I never sit down these days. I've learned to live without so many things—sleep, quiet, being able to hear my own thoughts, even having thoughts. I love my children, but I have to admit there are days when I want to scream, when I want my old self and my old life back. If I met that other Phoebe Shattuck on the road, I might not recognize her. How young I was. How young we both were, Nate and I. We were full of ideas. I don't have time for ideas now. I don't have time for anything but washing and cooking and caring for the children. But I will try to make time to write again and play the piano.

May 13, 1938

Today I opened the Cheavings' house and cleaned it from top to bottom. It was sunny and warm, and the children played on the lawn while I worked inside. Rachel is old enough to be a real help now. She thinks up games to play with Phil and Junior, and then when they get tired, she sits with them and goes through the book of nursery rhymes. She's such a lit-tle mother. I worry we've made her take on too much responsibility, but she doesn't seem to mind. She loves being "in charge" and telling the boys what to do. Tomorrow I will work on the Allertons' house if the weather is good. They have sent the money for the cleaning in advance, thank God.

May 19, 1938

I am making time to play the piano, at night after the children are in bed and Nate has gone off to Silas Mitchell's. Every time I come back to the piano, I don't know how I have lived without it. The music feeds me, even when I am so out of practice I play badly. I am thinking of Father Slade, of course. He will be staying at the rectory again soon, and now that the Cheavings have given their piano to Our Lady, he said that perhaps I could play something for him when I come to fix supper. It is hard to imagine Mrs. Cheaving would simply give such an instrument away, but she said it was taking up too much room, and nobody ever played it. She would have given it to the Union Church, of course, but there's no room there, either. So it's my gain. I am working on the Mozart Sonata. What divine music. It is breathtaking. I must go deeply into the music, deeply into myself, if I am even to begin to do justice to it. Nothing makes me feel more alive than when I am playing a piece that asks this. Tonight when I had finished, I went in to check on the children. They were sleeping so peacefully. I felt an overwhelming love for their little faces and their little hands. Yes, they exhaust me, but I love them terribly.

June 6, 1938

Nate has lost the boat. I guess I have been waiting for this to happen ever since he bought the thing, but it is far worse than I imagined. He went over to the mainland with Silas Mitchell. They played poker at Gilley's. He told me some long involved story about an accident, the boat smashed to pieces. I knew it wasn't the truth. I took the children and walked to Silas Mitchell's. I told him I would ask Ernie Brovelli to start an investigation if he didn't tell me. He cleared his throat, said I should ask Nate, and tried to go back in the house. I said I wasn't leaving until he told me what had happened. Phil and Junior started to cry. He motioned me inside the door, where the children couldn't hear. Nate wagered the boat and lost. Any of the locals wouldn't have taken it, but this man was from Providence. He came first thing in the morning and towed the boat away with a motorboat. Silas said he was sorry. It was his fault, he suggested they go over to the mainland. How many times I've cursed the invention of the outboard motor. Once Silas rigged up his boat with that motor, there was no stopping them from going across the bay any time of the day or night. I walked home carrying Junior, with Rachel and Phil trailing behind. Anger was gone this time, ebbed out of me. I told Nate I knew, and he put his face in his hands. He said he was worthless to me or anyone else in this world. I felt so desperately sad to see him like that. The boat doesn't matter, I said. We'll find a way. Though I don't know how we will find a way.

June 9, 1938

Nate has spent the last two days going around the island telling everyone that his fix-it shop is open for the season. Some of the summer people are here already, and he has two cars to repair this week. Somehow we will survive. I went down to the store and knew instantly that everyone had heard about Nate losing the boat. They wouldn't look at me. I find myself thinking about that stupid boat constantly. It seems that everything that has gone wrong with our lives had its start with Nate buying the boat. From the beginning, the first night he showed it to me, it caused us nothing but grief. Maybe it's for the best that it is gone. Maybe we can make another kind of life now that Nate is not going out quahogging. I think of Bill Daggett and the day of the accident, when they found his boat drifting off the west side. Every woman on the island lives with this fear, that she'll become like Evelyn Daggett, left alone with two children and no means of support. Evelyn manages now that she runs the store, but just barely, like the rest of us. Sometimes she looks so tired, sitting there behind the cash register. I wish I could do something for her, but I have to face the truth that I can't do more than get my own family through each day.

June 13, 1938
Cold again and rain, but I didn't care. Father Slade came to stay over Saturday night and say the Mass on Sunday. I was at the rectory, putting the sheets on the bed, when I saw him out the window. He came walking down Bay Avenue with his umbrella. Someone should have given him a ride. Now that it is warmer, he is staying at the rectory again, instead of with the Brovellis. It was as though no time had passed since last year. He sat at the kitchen table, and I served him supper. I had saved a jar of my tomatoes, the last. I made a sauce with the tomatoes and baked it with macaroni and cheese. He didn't say anything, but I could tell he liked the meal. He barely spoke while he ate, yet it was as if we were talking to each other all the while. How can I explain this? We speak to each other in the silence. It's strange to remember how I used to chatter at him, the first summer. Now I understand there is not always a need to talk. I have never felt this way with someone before. I seem to know what he is thinking. After supper I played the Mozart for him on the piano in the church. I wanted it to be flawless, for once. I wanted to play with my soul in my fingers. Of course I wanted this so badly that I got off to a terrible start. I was nervous, and the phrasing was off. But then I settled in and played as well as I ever have. At least that's how it felt. My hands had a certain freedom. When I was finished, he sat for a long time in silence. I felt frantic for his response, but I didn't want to look at him, to appear too eager. He got up from the first pew and came to the piano. He smiled. "Your playing is very strong," he said. "You've

been practicing. It was wonderful. As good as the soloist I heard in Providence."

I shook my head.

"Really. You have that grace and precision in your playing. It's remarkable."

I repeated his words in my mind over and over as I walked home. They were like food, something I have been hungry for.

June 14, 1938

The rain ended in the night, and by morning it was clear, though still cool. I made my confession with the others before Mass. I do not look at his face on the other side of the screen, even glance at his profile. Still, I can't shake the sense that I'm talking to him, that we might be speaking over the kitchen table. There's something so secret and intimate about the confessional, though we almost always say exactly the same thing. Father Slade preached a wonderful sermon about forgiveness. The con-gregation dragged on the hymns, though I tried to keep the tempo up, and Donna Brovelli sang off key, as usual. I don't know why I bother to rehearse with her.

June 17, 1938

Rachel went with me to clean the church today while Nate watched the boys at home. I tried to get her to be quiet, but finally gave up and let her run through the pews. She has such a hard time being still. I was sweep-ing the floor when she came running up to me and said, "The Blessed Virgin smiled at me." She says the most remarkable things. I can't help being pleased to think that she has a real faith. She listens to the sermons at Mass, and she seems to understand more than I would think a six year old could. I imagine how proud Mother would be if she saw Rachel. She would recognize instantly how smart Rachel is. But I don't even know where Mother lives now. I think this is more inconceivable than anything else in my life. Between my work at the church and cleaning the summer people's houses, and Nate's work on the cars, we almost have as much coming in as before he lost the boat. I am trying to think of anything else I can do this summer to make money. Maybe some of the summer people will want piano lessons for their children.

June 27, 1938
I think sometimes of that day when I met Father Slade on the ferry, and how close I came to not finding God. I could have gone to the mainland some other day. It just happened that I chose that particular Saturday and returned on the late boat. When you think back on moments like this, you realize that our lives could so easily go in one direction or another. It's our arrogance as human beings that makes us think we can control the direction our lives take. Of course, my conversation with Father Slade that day was meant to happen. If we hadn't met then, God would have found another way. Still, it was that crossing on the ferry, talking to Father Slade, which brought me to Mass. Now I would call what I felt in Father Slade that day holiness. Then I didn't have a word for it, though I recognized his depth of faith instinctively. I wonder how someone his age, not long in the priesthood, can achieve such wisdom. He makes anything seem possible and everything bearable.

July 2, 1938
I put up a sign at the store about the piano lessons, and a couple of summer people have responded. Nate is working every day. The summer people want all kinds of things fixed—toasters, stoves, lamps. He's even caning chairs. Ever since the loss of the boat, he's been a different person. He doesn't go over to Silas Mitchell's anymore, and he's quiet and considerate around the house, watching the children, asking if I need help with

supper. It seems like a fair trade. The boat is gone, but I have my husband back, the Nate I remember who used to sit on the sofa with his arms around me and whisper in my ear. I know such longings seem like a complete indulgence now. I have no business with such thoughts, but the truth is I have not forgotten how we were with each other in those first months when I came to the island and everything between us was new.

July 11, 1938
I worked on the Chopin Scherzo in E all week to play for Father Slade, but I saw as soon as he arrived there was something wrong. He was anxious, preoccupied. After he ate the supper I prepared, I waited for him to ask what I was going to play that night. This didn't happen. He said he had something to tell me. I stood at the sink with a dish towel in my hand, feeling foolish. He said that Saint Joseph's couldn't afford to pay me anymore for playing the music and cleaning the church and being housekeeper for the rectory. The diocese has so little. The churches can't raise money the way they used to, with everyone out of work. Mission parishes like the one on Snow will have to make do with volunteers.

"I know it's unfair," he said. "I know you count on what you make here. I can't ask you to do the same work without being paid."

"Of course I'll keep on," I said. The answer came immediately, instinctively. I knew it was the right thing to do.

He argued with me, briefly, but I did not waver. I reminded him that this is the Lord's work. Besides, I said, who will you get to cook for you? Donna Brovelli? He laughed then. I had to get home, so I did not play the Chopin. I said I would play for him next week.

July 12, 1938
I told Nate how I would no longer be paid for my work at the church. I imagined he would be disappointed, worried, but it was worse than that.

"You can't be the housekeeper for free," he said.

He was angry. I could not understand why. I explained it would be my contribution to the church. I would do the cleaning at night, after I was done with my other work. It wouldn't interfere. And why shouldn't I play the music if I'm going to be in church anyway? There's no one else who can do it.

"At night?" he said, snorting the way he does. "You're going to the church alone at night? Not if I have anything to say about it."

An old quarrel. Why should he have anything to say about it? My time at the church is mine. It has nothing to do with him. But he does have something to say about this and everything else, way too much to say.

"People will talk," he said.

This is always his accusation. People will talk. Yes, they will. On Snow Island they will talk about anything. So what?

I asked him what he meant.

He said, "You can't be going over there making the bed and cooking his meals for free. A married woman. It doesn't look right."

I was so baffled I couldn't come up with a response. Would a single woman be more appropriate? "He's a priest," I said.

"I don't care if he's the Pope. It doesn't look right."

Look right. What does look right? Nothing to Nate. He sees deception in everything, even in something as wonderful as my friendship with Father Slade.

July 13, 1938

Jealousy. It's a terrible thing. Nate is jealous of the time I spend with Father Slade, brief as it is. He has been jealous ever since I joined the church—jealous of my faith and the time I spend praying, jealous of my playing the hymns, jealous of my having this other life. Is it a crime to care for someone who is generous to me, encouraging, someone who wants to know what I think, who shares my faith and helps it become stronger? No. I have done nothing wrong. I have made a friend, that is all. Even this threatens Nate. He does not want me to have friends, except for the boring women with their quilting bees and chicken suppers. I can do anything I like with them. That's normal. My friendship with Father Slade is not normal. People will talk. People have talked. I don't care. How could I expect anyone on Snow to understand the conversations I have with Father Slade, the time when he listens to me play the piano? The fact that they can't understand only confirms what we share, only makes me more determined to keep this friendship in my life. A terrible thought, but sometimes it seems that Nate would deny me any happiness, no matter what it is. My being happy is a threat. But I am happy when I am playing the piano for Father Slade, when I'm cooking his supper, when I listen to him preach at Mass. I will not give up this happiness.

July 14, 1938

I have told Nate that I will continue working at the church. I waited until after Rachel and the boys were in bed. Then I told him. I wanted him to understand there was no question of discussion.

"You're not my wife if you do this," he said.

We stood staring at each other in the middle of the room, then he went slamming out the door. He came home late, when I was already in bed. He climbed in beside me and fell asleep without saying anything. I lay there awake half the night, praying. In the morning, he ate breakfast and went out to the shop without speaking. He talked to Rachel and the boys, of course. He was all love and light with them. He does this on purpose, to torture me. Tonight it was the same. He did not speak to me during supper and now he has taken off again. The children do not seem to notice that we are not speaking to each other.

I have prayed to God. I cannot believe Nate actually means what he said. He wants me to obey him. He has always wanted this. He can't tolerate the idea that I am a person, too, with my own thoughts and feelings independent of him. It doesn't matter what we're arguing about. It's the fact that I won't do what he says. I have backed down again and again. I have let him have his way. I have been quiet and good. I can't do it this time. What is right? Am I only doing this for myself, or is there something bigger here? Father Slade needs me, the church needs me. Nate does not believe in having a calling, in God's will. I do. It is God's will that I play the hymns on Sunday and clean the church, not mine. I cannot turn against God's will, but there is no way I can make Nate understand this.

July 15, 1938

The silence between us continues, broken only by single sentences. "Will you eat now?" "Mrs. Cheaving is bringing her car over at eleven." The stupidity of it. Each look, each short exchange, is full of other meanings. I do not want to participate in this. We are like children, but we can't stop ourselves. I pray for forgiveness.

July 16, 1938

I went to the rectory as usual tonight. Nate was outside working on the Cheavings' car. He looked up when I left. I hurried down the hill and did not glance back. I knew that he knew where I was going. I left Rachel and the boys at the Brovellis'.

"So you're here," Father Slade said when he found me setting the table.

I thought I might cry. He understood that I did this only out of charity, generosity, what is right. Not out of some other selfish motive. Not out of a desire to hurt Nate. I don't know how he does it, but Nate turns everything into a battle in which it looks like I have set out deliberately to hurt him. But this is not true.

Father Slade was pleased with the meal I fixed—fish fillets and potatoes, cobbler for dessert. Nate even accuses me of serving better meals to Father Slade. I want to tell him it makes a difference when someone appreciates the food you set on the table, when someone says thank you. I knew I could not stay long, that there would not be time to play the Chopin. A sort of sadness crept over us. It was as if Father Slade understood that things were different now.

"My husband is displeased," I blurted out as I cleared the dishes. I don't know why I said it. I couldn't stop myself.

Father Slade looked troubled. "If this is causing problems, I don't want you to do the work."

I shook my head. Again, close to tears. I asked if we could pray together. With my head bowed, hearing the steady tone of his voice, I felt that everything was clear again. I will keep on, I told him, and then left quickly, before he could argue with me.

July 18, 1938

I left for church, still without Nate speaking to me. Father Slade asked me to stay after Mass. He said, loud enough so others could hear, that he wanted to talk about the hymns for next week. We had already chosen the hymns for next week. I knew this as well as he did. Rachel went skipping around the church. He waited until everyone was gone. Then he said, "I don't want this to be a problem for you at home. I can make other arrangements."

"Nate is just using this to pick a fight," I said.

"That doesn't matter. Your first obligation is to him."

Obligation—what an ugly word. No, my first obligation is to God. Though with God, it may be a duty, but it's a happy one, freely given.

Rachel came up to me and tugged on my dress. It was easy to leave without saying more. Home to continued silence from Nate.

July 20, 1938

I feel a sort of panic when I think of losing Saturday nights at the rectory. It's foolish, of course. I did not know how much it meant to me until I saw the possibility of this time being taken away. Even just meeting him at the church and going over the hymns, if I could just have that much, I would not feel so sad. More than sad. Crazy, dejected, lifeless. I tell myself I must pull together. I wake in the morning and say the rosary. I call on God. I haven't played the piano all week. It seems useless if there's no one to play for.

July 21, 1938

Reason, hope, purpose—all taken away. I feel the way I did when I was pregnant with Phil, those moments of thinking I had lost all hold on reality. I honestly believe if I lived somewhere else, on solid ground that wasn't surrounded by endless water, I would not come unhinged so quickly and so easily.

Nate will not give in. Last night he stomped around and shouted. Rachel woke and started crying. He said it was bad enough to have a wife who was a loony Catholic, who spent half the day mumbling under her breath and talking to saints. But he wouldn't have me going over to the rectory by myself, washing out Father's undershorts when I'm not getting paid for it. I was so disgusted I nearly left for good that moment. I have never washed out any of Father Slade's clothes.

"Don't you see how it looks?" he shouted.

I told him, "You're the one who makes it into something wrong."

He picked up the little pitcher Mrs. Cunningham gave me and threw it at the wall. He said, "You go over there, and I'm moving into that shack by the lighthouse."

He lives on anger. It makes me sick. But I see that he means it this time. I have written Father Slade a letter to say I cannot do the work anymore.

July 24, 1938

I went to Mass this morning. Nate cannot stop me from doing this. And I played the hymns. Father Slade asked me if I was sure. I said yes, I can at least donate my time to play the music. I arrived early, so we could go over the hymns. Father Slade said he was sorry to receive my letter. He said it was his fault, to put me in that position. I said no, it was just Nate's way. When I asked Father Slade what he had done for supper, he said he fixed himself some soup. I felt the shabbiness of it. He comes all this way to say Mass. He should have something more than tinned soup.

After Mass, Mrs. Brovelli said she heard I was not working at the rectory anymore. I explained that Saint Joseph's couldn't afford it. She said she would organize the women to bring in meals. I felt better then.

July 29, 1938

It's as if I have given up something fundamental, let Nate cut off an arm or a leg. I wake feeling dead inside, knowing I have let him do this. What choice did I have? None. I think of Rachel and the boys. I have done everything for them. I know that someday I will see the results in the lives they live. I tried to play the Chopin Scherzo this afternoon, but I couldn't.

August 6, 1938

I watched Father Slade walk up the hill from the dock and down Bay Avenue. He could not see me in the shade of our porch. I felt a mad sort of longing just to speak with him for a moment. I will have to console myself with confession tomorrow. It makes all the difference to know that he will be there on the other side of the screen and that I will receive absolution from him. I know this is a form of heresy—absolution is absolution, no matter which priest gives it. But the truth is it feels different when I make my confession to him. I feel heard in a way I don't with other priests. I guess this is only natural, given how we know each other. I believe this is a gift—his knowledge of me and mine of him. I can't see it any other way.

August 11, 1938

I have been practicing the Chopin. The women are holding a sewing bee Saturday night. I will say that's where I'm going and then surprise Father Slade. I know what it would mean to him to hear it.

August 15, 1938

I did go to the sewing bee, but I left once it was dark. I told them I was-n't feeling well. I met no one on the walk to the rectory, fortunately. As soon as I saw the light in the window, I realized the madness of what I was doing, but I was not about to turn around and go home. I knocked on the door.

Father Slade was wearing his collar and shirtsleeves, his jacket off. He looked alarmed when he saw me. He asked if anything was wrong.

No, I said, I had just come to play the piano. "Is it all right?" I asked.

"Of course. You can play the piano anytime," he said.

We stood there for a long moment. Then I said, "I'll just go up to the church then."

I imagined he would offer to come with me, but he didn't. I felt ashamed. I told myself I shouldn't have come. I heard Nate saying it doesn't look right. Of course nothing really true or important looks right to other people.

I climbed the hill and felt the rough gravel under my feet. I could hear the bell buoy out on the water. Otherwise it was quiet. I felt more stupid than I can say. The last thing I wanted was to play the piano, but it would have looked even more absurd if I went away without doing so. I struggled through the opening of the Chopin Scherzo. My fingers felt clumsy and lifeless. How is it that one day I can race over the keys and the next it's like fingering mud? I was overwhelmed by a sense of my own vanity and stupidity. Why did I think it made a difference to him to hear me play? Why did I have to prove myself to him? Then I heard the door open. I glanced up just long enough to see him take a seat in one of the back pews. I had not turned on the lights, just the lamp on the piano, so he was in darkness. But I felt him there. My hands instantly became more responsive. A miracle of sorts. I felt myself moving over the keys. I felt the music moving in response.

When I finished playing, he slipped out. I understood. We could not meet and talk in secret, but I could play, and he could listen. A terrible discovery, that I play my best when he is present, but a good discovery, too.

The next morning, he shook my hand after Mass and said, "The music was beautiful." I knew he did not mean the hymns, but what I had played the night before. I walked home feeling lighter.

September 7, 1938
Rachel's birthday. I cannot believe she is so old. I had to bite back tears when she went off to the schoolhouse for the first day of school. I look at her and see the baby I nursed, the baby I rocked in the night. How strange that children have no memory of this time. I am her mother, yes, but she takes this for granted. I have always been there, and I will always be there. It's nothing special. Sometimes it's absolutely maddening. I want to shake her and say, "Do you know I changed hundreds of your diapers, cleaned up after you when you vomited?" In her eyes this is just my job. She doesn't feel she owes me anything. And she doesn't. I know this. Still, I keep looking for some tiny bit of acknowledgment, a thank you. I made a white cake with butter cream frosting. Nate made her a wooden car she can pull around on a string. She stuck out her lip and said she wanted a doll from the mainland. I would have sent her to her room if it

hadn't been her birthday. Later, she apologized to Nate and played with the car, as if trying to prove she really liked it. I felt there was some hope that she will turn into a grateful child, one who understands what she has been given.

September 9, 1938

The summer people have gone, and I am busy cleaning the houses one last time, putting linens in moth balls and covering furniture. I dread the coming of winter. I know I should be better than this, that I should rise above these feelings. I can't. When I first came to Snow, I didn't mind the cold weather. It was a challenge. Trying to keep the house warm was a part of the adventure. It made me feel alive. Now living on an island simply seems like work, pointless work. I should not write these words down. I should pray instead. I am a terribly weak person. I commit the sin of coveting everything but what I have. Why can't I be content?

September 13, 1938

Nate is around the house more, now that the summer people are gone, and he doesn't have much work. Something has changed since our last fight. I feel numb. There's a part of me that won't go out to him anymore. I think of when we were first married and how stunned I was by the force of our fights. And then the making up. We were so sorry. We sat in front of the stove and held hands. Now we move past these times of not speaking to each other, we return to something like normal life, but we don't make up. There seems to be an agreement—we don't need to speak of these things anymore. What's the difference? We just go on. I can't feel good about this, but I can't see any other way, either.

September 19, 1938

It's as if the summer never happened. The island is so still. We go back to being a small community of odd people, family but not family. Evelyn Daggett says she doesn't know if she'll have the money to keep the store stocked through the winter. I wonder if she's just mismanaging the place. I can't blame her for making threats. She's trying to tell us she can't put us all on credit for months. Of course not. But everyone else is in the same shape she is—no money and nowhere to get it. I have a bundle of bills in a jar, hidden in the kitchen cupboard. One hundred and eighteen dollars. It's all I could manage to save from what we made this summer. We'll have to make it last.

Chapter Twenty

Checking her watch, Rachel slipped the notebook back into the box in the closet. She went to the main room and took the broom from the corner where it was propped by the sink. When her father came stomping up the porch steps, she was busy sweeping the floor.

Nate threw his hat on the table, fell into the chair, and removed his work boots, tossing them across the room. They landed by the couch. Rachel leaned the broom against the back of the easy chair and picked up the shoes. She carried them into the bedroom with the odd sense that there were two people in the house with her now—the man in the other room and the person her mother wrote about in the diary. They were the same person, and yet they were not the same.

Rachel went to the refrigerator and took out the hamburger, setting the wrapped package on the counter. When she removed the brown paper, the meat lay there gleaming, a marbled pink. Nate unfurled the newspaper he had brought home and leaned back in the chair. She shaped the meat into patties and placed them in the frying pan. Reading this section of her mother's diary, she had found herself wishing for something she could not quite acknowledge. If only, she kept thinking, Father Slade were not a priest, and if only her mother were not married…but this was absurd, like wishing that her parents had never met, which was the same as asking not to have been born.

"It's about time Alice got a delivery from the butcher," Nate said when she set the cooked food in front of him. "They always fill the island orders last. Who cares about those nuts over on Snow? They can eat quahogs every day, right?"

Rachel had grown tired of these sweeping pronouncements about people on the mainland, as if they represented some alien race bent on making life difficult for everyone on Snow, but she knew there was no point in disagreeing.

"Eddie and Gina and Joe invited us for dinner on Sunday," Nate said. "They got Alice to order a pot roast."

"I was thinking of going over to the mainland."

Nate shoveled the peas into his mouth. "What for?"

"I'm going to visit Andy." Rachel had formulated the plan at that moment, but she knew that she should follow through with it.

"If you go tomorrow, you'll be back by Sunday."

"I was going to stay overnight with Babs and take the afternoon ferry."

Nate grasped the hamburger bun in two hands. "You know it ain't been easy for Eddie since he and that girl broke up."

"I know that. I've been perfectly nice to Eddie."

"He thinks of you like family."

"I think of him like family, too."

Nate shrugged, as if to say it didn't really matter to him, and went on eating, chewing his hamburger noisily. When his plate was empty, he pushed it away and wiped his fingers on a paper napkin.

Rachel finished her burger and stood to clear the plates. Nate glanced up at her. "Does he still like cookies?"

"Does who still like cookies?"

"Andy. He always liked those chocolate chip cookies." Nate reached into his pocket and produced two dollar bills, which he set on the table. "Buy some for me and take them to him, huh?"

Rachel slipped the bills into her pocket and carried the plates to the sink. Nate resumed reading the paper. She filled the sink with warm water and added soap. Dunking the dishes in the soapy water, she imagined Andy seated by the couch, banging his wooden blocks on the floor. He would clutch the blocks in his chubby hands, refusing to go to bed, until he fell asleep sitting up, and they had to pry the squares of wood from him. Long after Andy went away, the blocks still smelled like him, a mingled scent of baby powder and clean, damp skin. She used to take them from the toy box and hold them against her cheek.

The dishes were set in the drainer, and the table was cleared. Rachel went to the sofa, pulling on her jacket. "I guess I'll be going," she said.

Nate lowered the newspaper. "See you."

The cold air bathed her face as she stepped outside. At Alice's house, the yellow squares of window broke the dark. Through the thin curtains, she could make out Brock stretched on the couch. He appeared to be asleep. Evelyn sat in the armchair, knitting, with the floor lamp beside her. The rest of the family was not in view. Rachel hurried past the house and on down the hill, crossing the road to the phone booth. She fished in her jacket pocket and found enough change to make the call.

"Babs," she said. "It's me. Rachel."

"Oh, hi," Babs answered. "Wait a minute. Let me turn down the TV."

Rachel listened to a wave of canned laughter on the other end before the noise went suddenly still.

"What's up?" Babs said when she returned.

"I was thinking about what you said about how I should come over. I was thinking maybe I'd come this weekend and stay overnight, if that's okay."

"Sure. You can always have the couch."

"You don't have plans?"

"Plans?" Babs laughed. "What kind of plans do you think I would have? Nah, I was just going to go to the movies."

"What's playing?"

"That new Cary Grant movie, *Walk Don't Run*."

"I'm going to visit Andy in Providence. I'll take the bus back and get to your place middle of the afternoon. We'll still have time to go to Metzger's."

"I was drooling over the blouses in the window when I went by today. I've got to do something to get that science teacher to look at me. The thing is I want to look sexy but not *too* sexy, if you know what I mean. He's kind of conservative."

"I'll help you pick out something. I'll see you tomorrow."

The sound of the waves breaking carried from down below. Rachel placed the receiver in the cradle and listened to the coins drop into the box. She was looking forward to seeing Babs, she realized, looking forward to getting off the island and feeling a sidewalk beneath her feet. As she climbed the hill to the road, she watched the white crests of foam covering the rocks, trying to isolate one wave from another in the dark. They broke farther out now as the tide receded. The trancelike rhythm of their motion rolled over her, a rhythm that seemed to contain the shape of her life, going forward and then back, forward and back.

She was almost to the inn when she saw car lights coming from the direction of the lighthouse. She sensed it was Nick before she could make out the vehicle in the dark. He brought the jeep to a stop and rolled down the window. "Miss Shattuck, need a lift?"

Nick was her student, yes, but they were also friends. She told herself there was no reason she shouldn't accept his offer of a ride. She opened the door and climbed into the passenger seat.

"I was headed down to Gooseneck Cove," he said. "I've finished my homework, if you're worried about that."

"No, I'm not worried about that, Nick."

He drove on toward the dock without turning around, and she realized that, though she had not exactly agreed to it, she was going to Gooseneck Cove.

"I've only been out to the cove once since I've been back. Isn't that funny? You live on this little island, and you never even see half of it." The words seemed to come out of Rachel's mouth in idiotic jerks. She felt suddenly nervous and couldn't think what else to say.

"It's nice out there. Nobody's around."

Nick drove quickly, rounding the bend by the dump and taking the turn toward the sandy beach. When they passed Eddie's house, she caught a glimpse of a light in an upstairs window.

The jeep rattled over the gravel as the dark shapes of the trees bounced past. There was nothing beyond Eddie's house besides the ruins of the Venable mansion out by the cove.

"I found some deer out here in the woods, sleeping in the afternoon," Nick said. "Three of them, a doe and two fawns. I hid behind a tree and watched them. They looked like huge cats curled on the ground."

"I used to go looking for deer in the woods. I spent a whole summer once trying to find some asleep like that, but I never did."

He slowed the car as they reached the turn by the mansion and pulled over. The water of the cove shimmered through the trees, a wavering presence. He stepped out of the car. "I'll show you where the deer were."

Rachel followed him down a path which led away from the road, out to the point. Across an overgrown field, the stone walls of the mansion rose up in the dark. Mrs. Venable still owned the castle-like structure which had been built in the early fifties, but she never came to Snow. Only half of the mansion was completed before Mr. Venable died in a train accident in Europe. Mrs. Venable did not have the work finished. Empty shells of walls still stood, surrounded by a crumbling foundation. The portion of the house that had been completed was never lived in or furnished. Windows had been broken, and the grass grew thick and tall, giving the place an eerie, abandoned feel. The island children said it was haunted.

The crunch of Nick's footsteps sounded on the path. Walking behind him, Rachel kept her eyes on his shoulders, on the wide, dark space they made in front of her, moving into the lighter darkness beyond. Halfway to the point, he took a side path. He stopped in a clearing in the skinny pines and pointed at a spot of ground. "They were right there."

The pine needles were soft underfoot. Rachel breathed in the cold air and studied the ground where the deer had slept. There was no sign of them now. "How did you happen to come this way?"

"I was going over to the flats, to look for clams. I came back the next day, but they weren't here."

"Maybe you'll see them again."

"Maybe, but I never did before, and I'm in the woods a lot."

He said these last words as if he were proud of the time he spent in the woods, and Rachel felt, as she had before, that he lived a secret life she knew little about.

Nick sat on a large boulder at the side of the path. "You're not bad for a teacher, you know."

Rachel smiled in spite of herself. "You're not bad for a student."

"I've only got until June. Then I'm a free man."

"Is the schoolhouse a prison?"

"No. I just get bored sometimes, that's all. But it's been a little less boring this year."

Rachel realized that she was supposed to take this as a compliment. "What about after you graduate?"

He shot her a quick glance in the dim light. "My parents can't afford college."

"You could probably get a scholarship at the state university."

"I don't know. My father says we don't have the money. Besides, I want to start a repair business, for radios and other things. I already know how to do that."

"I still think you should consider college."

"Why?"

"Because you're smart."

He raised his eyes to hers. "I didn't know you thought I was smart."

There was something about the way he said the word *smart*, making it sound suddenly intimate, that gave her pause. She went on, covering any uneasiness she might feel. "You're a good student. You should do something with it."

"What's wrong with having my own repair business?"

"Nothing. It's just that if you go to college, you might discover there are other things you want to do."

"Like what? Be a lawyer?" He reached for a twig on the ground and broke it in two. "There's only one thing I'm really good at—taking radios apart and fixing them. And I'm good at finding animals in the woods, but you can't exactly make a job out of that. You do what you're good at, right? Like you. You're a teacher because you're good at it."

This observation brought Rachel up short. She had not gone into teaching because she thought she would be good at it. In fact, she still doubted whether this was the case. She had gone into teaching because it was a job that was available for young women. She did not have dreams, like her mother, of being a pianist or of pursuing some other lofty, creative calling. She was not *gifted*, as her mother had been; she was simply determined and maybe a bit stubborn.

"I didn't really know if I would be good at teaching," she said. "It's the sort of thing you don't know if you're good at it until you do it, and even then it's hard to say. I always liked children. I guess that's why I went into it."

Nick gazed up at her in the gray light. She thought she saw disappointment in his look. "When I'm taking apart a radio, I don't know what time it is or anything else. I can sit there for two or three hours, and it feels like five minutes. It's the same way in the woods. I can wait forever to see a fox. I love that, when you forget about everything else. "

Rachel felt a twinge of envy. "That's a wonderful thing, to have something you love like that."

He continued to give her a look tinged with pity, the pity of a young person for someone who, over thirty, is already old. Then he stood up. "Aren't you getting cold? I am."

Rachel nodded and followed him back down the path. The dried fronds of marsh grass rustled as they went past, making a faint whispering sound. She did not want to be more like Nick with his awed wonder for the natural world. No, it was worse than that. She longed to trade places with him, seeing the world through his eyes, to absorb his certainty about what mattered and what didn't. He knew himself, despite his age and inexperience; he understood what would make him happy and did not hunger for something else, something more.

When they reached the car, he opened the passenger door and waited for her to climb in. "You are good at teaching, Miss Shattuck."

"Thanks." She grasped the door handle and pulled it closed.

He came around to the other side and slid behind the wheel. "It's not just me. The other kids like you, too."

Rachel felt an uneasy gratitude for his comment. It should not matter what the children thought of her, but of course she cared.

Nick started up the car, and they went rattling over the rough road. On the way back, he drove even faster, going quickly past Eddie's house and making the turn onto Bay Avenue. When he reached her house, he shut off the engine and said, "You really think I should go to college?"

"I think you should do what you want to do."

"That's the thing, isn't it, figuring out what you want to do. I'll think about it."

"Good."

She opened the door and climbed out, calling goodnight. He waited until she was in the house to take off. Through the window, she watched the car cross the road and turn back toward the dock. She pulled the shades with the unsettling sense that Nick was older than his eighteen years and knew this, and understood that she knew it, too.

Chapter Twenty-one

The passenger cabin smelled of cigarettes and coffee. Rachel sat on the bench, her jacket draped over her lap, listening to the banging of the radiator. The small space was oppressively warm, but the alternative was to stand out on the deck in a numbing wind. Through the clouded surface of the window, she could see Guido pacing back and forth across the deck. She was the only passenger that morning.

When the horn sounded and the ferry slowed down, inching toward land, Rachel pulled on her jacket, retrieved her overnight bag, and went out to the deck. Now that they were out of the channel, the wind was not as strong. She stood at the railing, watching the streets by the dock come into focus as they drew closer. The long brick building of the old pin factory took up half a block along the waterfront. It was abandoned now, the windows broken and a sheet of plywood nailed over the main door, with the words "No Trespassing" scrawled in black paint. Under a gray sky, the pin factory appeared smaller than she remembered, a squat, unimpressive structure asking to be torn down. The man who ran the ferry office, selling tickets and handing out schedules, stood on the dock. Guido tossed a line to him as Keith, up in the wheelhouse, stilled the engine. When the boat was secure, Keith and Guido lowered the gangplank in place. Tipping his hat, Guido gestured toward the gangplank like a maitre'd in a fancy restaurant and said, "Miss Shattuck."

Rachel carried her bag up to the street. The bus to Providence would not come for another half an hour. She made her way past the tangle of docks and quahog skiffs and entered Frank's, where she found May wiping down the front table with a rag. May dropped the rag and called out, "Rachel Shattuck, as I live and breathe."

Rachel set down her bag and gave May a hug.

May stepped back, looking her up and down. "What are you eating over there? You've lost weight."

Rachel shook her head. "No, I haven't. This skirt just makes me look skinny. See?" She spread her hands over her thighs, smoothing the wool skirt, as if to show how wide she really was.

"Hmmm. Well, I'm getting you a donut and a cup of coffee. On the house."

Rachel tried to protest that she had already eaten breakfast, but May bustled behind the bar and returned with a cup of coffee and a sugar donut on a plate. "I got that donut fresh from the bakery this morning," she said. "I want to see you eat every last bite."

Taking a seat at the table, Rachel broke the donut in two. "Where's Frank?"

"He had to go over to Woonsocket for a funeral. Some cousin of his I never met. You know how many cousins Frank has? About a hundred. And that's just first cousins. Forget about second and third. I guess he and this guy used to play together when they were kids, but they hadn't seen each other since then. Cancer. He was sixty-two, just retired. I'm telling you, I don't plan on ever retiring. Everyone I know who's retired, they die within a year. I'd rather drop dead right here at the bar."

"I think you've got a while before you have to think about anything like that."

"You're sweet, Rachel, but I turned fifty-eight last month. I ain't no spring chicken. I don't know what else we could do, though. Frank's been in this place seven days a week, twelve hours a day for twenty years. Before that there was Gilley. He had the place until he was more than seventy-five. So I guess we can do the same, God willing and knock on wood." May rapped the surface of the table with her knuckles. "Besides, none of our kids are interested in the business. You know, they've all got their jobs and families and everything. Barton ain't exactly a draw. So how are you liking it over there?"

"I like the kids and teaching at the schoolhouse. It's totally different from teaching on the mainland. You never have any idea what one day or the next is going to be like. And it's good to be back on the island in a way. It's just…"

"There aren't any men to meet?"

Rachel laughed. "No, there aren't any men to meet."

"You're doing a good thing, helping them out this year, but you don't have to stay next year. Think of yourself, Rachel."

"Seems to me I don't think about much else."

"You know what I mean. Do what's right for you. Your father can take care of himself now, can't he?"

"Oh, yes. He eats nothing but cans of pork and beans if nobody cooks for him, but he's fine. Better than fine. He'll outlive all of us." Rachel took a bite of the donut and followed it with a gulp of coffee. "I've got to catch the bus to Providence."

"The bus won't be here for fifteen minutes." May tapped the edge of the plate with her finger. "Eat the rest of the donut."

Rachel dutifully made her way through the remainder of the donut, washing it down with coffee, while May watched attentively. When Rachel was done, she dusted her fingers with a napkin and thanked May, adding, "Tell Frank I say hello."

"He'll be sorry he missed you. He's always saying, 'I wonder how

Rachel is. Seems kind of funny not to have her in here on the pay phone.'"

"Now I'm on the pay phone over on the island. I guess I'll never have my own phone."

May placed her hand on Rachel's shoulder. "Yes, you will."

Rachel smiled. "If you say so, May."

Picking up her overnight bag, she made her way to the door and hurried around the corner to Front Street. A teenaged boy and an older woman with a kerchief tied around her head sat side by side on the bench at the bus stop. Rachel leaned against the wall of the bus shelter. The leaves had fallen from the linden trees, leaving an arch of bare branches overhead. The damp air smelled like winter.

When the bus pulled up, billowing exhaust, Rachel let the others board first. She made her way to the rear, where she took a seat by the window. They left the town of Barton behind quickly, heading north, past a few miles of fields and farms before reaching Havendale. How alike these small towns were. In the center of each, you found the straight line of a main street with its drug store and movie theater and post office and dime store, bordered by the undulating shoreline of the bay on one side and neighborhoods of triple-decker houses and squat capes on the other. Towns like these defined the meaning of ordinary, with their understated dreams. She wondered what it would be like to live in a different landscape, like the West, where mountains and sky ruled. Were the people there more tough and ambitious, another breed? Did they refuse to settle for less?

She thought of her mother's diary as she stared out the window. How strange to discover that there had been a secret to her mother's life, even there on the island, where it seemed that secrets could not exist. Rachel watched the streets go past and tried to convince herself that her mother had not been in love with Father Slade, though what her mother had written felt like the words of someone who was in love, whether she had acknowledged it or not. What did it mean to be "in love"? She couldn't say anymore. Her mother and Father Slade were friends, that was all. Certainly they were never lovers. Such an idea was too strange, though the character of their friendship was deeper than most, or was this a fantasy on her part, what she wanted to see in the diary, projecting the longing her mother had felt onto a young, Catholic priest who was soft-spoken and gentle, the antithesis of Nate? Rachel studied the bare branches of the trees, blurred as the bus moved down the road, and tried to remember what Father Slade looked like all those years ago, when he was young. She did not recall him as being particularly handsome, and now she could envision only a fat, bald man in a white robe, conducting the funeral Mass. It was hard to believe that this figure had inspired her mother to practice the piano with such intensity.

When the bus reached Providence, Rachel joined the throng of exiting passengers and crossed the street, where the bus that would take her to the state school was waiting. She paid her fare and tucked her overnight bag beneath her seat. This bus was warmer than the first. She unbuttoned her jacket and turned to watch the city streets go past. She had walked these streets in every season, making her way from home to work or downtown to shop. Providence was big enough to be a city, and yet it felt like one of the small towns along the bay on a grander scale, with more people and more stores and more traffic but the same narrow streets, the same contained views. Rachel scanned the faces of the people milling along the downtown sidewalks, half-hoping to find Kevin among them. She did not want to speak to him; she simply wanted to look at him, to search for a sign that he missed her.

Reaching for the cord above her head, Rachel rang the bell for the next stop. She exited through the back door and waited at the corner for the light to change. Traffic swirled past, and the wind blew dried leaves about in the gutter. She luxuriated in the sense of being surrounded by life, which was so absent on the island. You could meet anyone standing on a street corner in Providence; you could board a bus or a train and go anywhere in the world.

Rachel crossed the street and entered a corner grocery store. A plump woman wearing an apron stood behind the cash register, gesturing and speaking in a foreign language. Italian, Rachel realized after listening. The person she was addressing stood on a step stool in one of the darkened aisles at the back of the store, a young woman in a short skirt and high heels, with teased black hair piled on her head. Rachel nodded at the older woman and took a bag of chocolate chip cookies from a shelf. When she set them on the counter, the woman gave her a gap-toothed smile and said, "What's with this weather already, huh? Too cold."

Rachel slid one of the bills her father had given her across the counter and nodded. "It looks like snow today."

"Ah, snow, don't tell me snow!" The woman made change and placed the cookies in a paper bag. "I don't like that snow."

Rachel thanked her and left, clutching the paper bag in one hand and her overnight bag in the other. She turned off the avenue, down a side street. At the end of the street, she came to the gates of the state school. She walked up the sidewalk that bordered the driveway and went through the front door. The familiar smell of the place met her, cooked vegetables and overdone meat from the cafeteria laced with the scent of ammonia and floor polish. There was a new person at the front desk, a thin girl who appeared no older than sixteen. Rachel signed her name in the guest book, then turned down the hall which led to Andy's room.

Through the open door she saw Andy, seated in the chair, staring out the window. Next to the bed by the door, a man sat in the room's other chair with a belt strapped around his waist to hold him in. This was a new roommate. Rachel wondered what had happened to Jeff, the last one.

"Andy," she said. "It's Rachel."

He turned his head as she approached. Leaning down, she kissed him on the cheek. He arched his neck and made a gurgling sound. He was dressed in baggy blue jeans and a red sweatshirt, with thick cotton socks and slippers on his feet. The quilt she had made the year before was wrapped around his shoulders. He pointed at the paper bag as she set it on the bed, making another rough sound from deep in his throat.

"That's dessert," Rachel said. "You can have them after lunch."

She took a tissue from the box on the bedside table and wiped his nose, before removing her jacket and taking a seat on the edge of the bed. "I'm living on the island now, Andy, on Snow. I can't come to visit you as often. I have to take the ferry over to come and see you."

Andy craned his neck and went back to looking out the window. After a moment, he began crooning, letting out a low continuous sound as he rocked back and forth. Rachel glanced at the roommate to see if he took any notice of the noises Andy made, but he was leaning back in the chair with his eyes closed, a small man with blond hair and gnome-like features.

An aide entered the room in a white dress and thick-soled shoes. "Andy's singing again, is he?" she said, going to the chair and placing a hand on his head to smooth his hair. "He loves to sing. You're our little songbird, aren't you, Andy? Middle of the night we come in and find him lying there in bed, singing away." The woman laughed. "Okay, it's time to eat, Andy. No more singing for now." She spoke in a raised voice, as though the volume might make her words more comprehensible.

"What happened to Jeff?" Rachel asked.

"He passed away last month. This is Luke, Andy's new roommate."

Luke made a groaning sound when the woman said his name and banged his curled hand on the arm of the chair. The aide went out to the hallway, returning with a tray which she set on a rolling cart.

"They don't eat in the dining room?" Rachel asked.

"Not anymore. We take them down for supper, but not for lunch. They all eat lunch in their rooms. We don't have the staff to get everybody down there more than once a day. You know how it is. Budgets, budgets, budgets." Taking a cloth napkin from the tray, the woman tied it around Andy's neck. "You want to help him eat?"

"Sure."

Luke banged his fist on the chair arm again. "Just a minute, Luke, I'm getting your lunch in just a minute." The aide took his hand, stilling it. "You have to be patient, sweetheart."

Luke made another groaning noise as the woman returned to the hallway.

Rachel pulled the cart close to the bed and reached for the fork. "Turkey tetrazini. Can you say turkey?"

Andy rolled his head back, staring at the ceiling. Rachel took a forkful of the soupy noodles and sauce and called to him, "Andy, don't you want to eat?"

He turned back, his lips parted. Sometimes it seemed that he understood every word she said, and other times nothing.

"Here comes the train," Rachel said. "Choo, choo. Ready? The train's going in the tunnel." She slipped the fork between his lips. He clamped down with his teeth. "Okay, now let the train out. Open up."

After a moment, he released the fork and began chewing. They repeated the ritual until he had finished the turkey and noodles, some cooked spinach, and a bowl of applesauce. *Train* had been one of the words Rachel was teaching him before he left the island. She used to read him a picture book about trains. She liked to think that somewhere in the inner reaches of his mind, he remembered the word, though he could not show her that he did.

Rachel was wiping the food from his face when the aide returned and said, "Andy, you cleaned your plate. Look at that. He always eats good. He's so sweet. Everybody loves Andy. He's never any trouble, are you, Andy? All right, let's take that nasty old tray away."

The aide whisked the tray away and added it to a rack out in the hall, returning with a meal for Luke, which she set on the rolling cart. Seated on the other bed, she tied a napkin around Luke's neck and proceeded to feed him with a spoon.

Rachel took a cookie from the bag and held it toward Andy. "Cookie? Do you want a cookie?"

"Andy loves cookies, doesn't he?" the aide said. "We go easy on the desserts because we don't want them to gain too much weight, but it's nice for them to have treats once in a while. You know, break up the routine a little."

Andy threw his head back and began crooning again.

Rachel said, "These are from your father. Daddy. Daddy sent these to you."

Andy did not respond until she placed one of the cookies in his hand. Then he brought it to his mouth and bit down on it. Crumbs cascaded from his lips and down the front of the sweatshirt. Rachel let him eat two more before rolling up the end of the package, setting it in the drawer of the bedside table, and brushing up the crumbs. Andy went back to crooning with his neck arched, as though trying to make his music reach the ceiling or some point beyond. Rachel took her sewing kit and some quilt squares from her overnight bag.

"Did you make that quilt for him?" the aide asked. "He never lets go of it."

"I'm making a new one for Christmas."

"That's pretty, all the different colors. He really responds to colors. He hates his gray sweatshirt. What a racket he makes when you get that one out, but as soon as he sees the red sweatshirt, everything's fine."

The aide finished feeding Luke and gathered up the tray. As she left, she called over her shoulder, "You boys be good now. You've got a visitor."

Rachel listened to the squeak of the wheels as the woman rolled the lunch cart down the hall. The people who worked at the state school were unfailingly cheerful. Rachel felt ashamed as she watched them breeze in and out of the rooms and talk to the patients as if they were engaged in ordinary conversations. She could hardly bear to stay for an hour, and here they were day after day, without complaining. Their calm acceptance seemed to contain a silent reproach: she should be caring for her brother, not leaving him in the hands of underpaid strangers, but the shape of Andy's life had been set long ago, when her father brought him here. She was not even sure it would be good for Andy to take him away now.

When another half hour had passed, she told herself she could go. She put away her sewing and, wrapping her arms around Andy, gave him an awkward hug and kissed his forehead.

"Rachel has to go now," she said.

Glancing back, she saw that he was staring out the window again. She walked quickly down the hall, keeping her eyes averted from the open doors she passed. Outside the wind had picked up. Rachel's hair swirled around her face. She boarded the bus. When it reached down-town, she carried her bag across the avenue to Betty's, the lunch counter next to the depot. Booths lined one wall and a counter with stools the other. The wall behind the counter was plastered with hand-lettered signs advertising the specials: two eggs, bacon and toast; tuna plate; a hot dog and baked beans. Rachel sat at the counter and ordered an egg salad sandwich and a coke. She and Kevin had eaten here once, on a Saturday when they came downtown to the department stores. Kevin actually enjoyed shopping, unlike the husbands of the other teachers at school. Rachel remembered the envious looks the women gave her when she described her shopping trips with Kevin.

When she and Kevin first met, they seemed to share thoughts without needing to voice them. She used to think of that scene in *Jane Eyre*, when Mr. Rochester tells Jane he feels that there is a string tied under his ribs, which is attached to a corresponding string tied to the same spot in her body. She and Kevin were linked in a fundamental way, just like Jane and Mr. Rochester. How intoxicating it was to be known so completely. Kevin was a friend and a brother, a lover and a parent, all rolled into one. Even at the end, when she knew she had to leave, this sense stayed with her. There was a part of her that Kevin would always know better than anyone else.

Rachel paid her bill at the cash register and went outside to the bus stop. She pushed her hair back from her face and, setting her overnight bag on the ground, wrapped her jacket tightly over her chest. She should have worn pants. Covered only in a pair of thin stockings, her legs were freezing.

When the bus arrived, she labored up the steps and deposited her fare in the coin box. On the outskirts of Barton, she rang for her stop and walked the block to Babs' house. Babs opened the door as soon as she knocked and ushered her inside, saying, "Rachel, thank God you're here. I've been wandering around this place trying to clean all afternoon. I don't know what to do with myself."

Rachel set down her bag. "What's wrong?"

"I had a date this morning."

"A date?"

"Yes. With that science teacher, Howard Needham. He called last night and asked if I wanted to go out for breakfast. I was such a nervous wreck, I dropped a whole forkful of egg in my lap. I wasn't sure if he noticed, so I just sat there, waiting for him to look away, and then he leaned over and said, 'Is that a spot on your dress?' It was absolutely mortifying. He'll never ask me out again."

Rachel laughed. "That's not so terrible. If he likes you, he won't care."

"You don't understand. He's so, I don't know, proper. When he realized it wasn't a spot, he said, 'Oh dear,' and then neither of us said anything for about five minutes. The whole thing was so awkward."

"How was it when you said goodbye?"

"He said, 'Thank you for having breakfast with me.' That was it. Like I was his maiden aunt or something."

"First dates are always awkward."

"Yes, but I just feel so big and fat and –"

"Babs, don't talk like that. You are *not* big and fat. And everybody drops food in their laps."

"He just doesn't seem like somebody who's going to go for a klutz like me."

"You're jumping to conclusions."

"I guess, but listen, we can't go to Anthony's tonight. That's where we went this morning. I can't go in there again. We'll have to eat at the diner. Let's go shopping. I've got to get out of this place."

Babs pulled on her wool coat and slung a purse over her shoulder. "It's just that I thought about this for so long, and then when it finally happens, it's nothing like what I imagined," she said as they left the house. "I can't stand that."

They walked up Front Street into town. The dime store window was festooned with cardboard cut-out orange pumpkins and black cats and white ghosts. They went on to Metzger's. Inside the department store, Babs marched by the cosmetics and jewelry counter to the women's clothing section.

"See?" she said, turning to Rachel. "Look at these skirts. Imported wool."

Rachel fingered a green and black plaid skirt with narrow pleats down the front. "Don't you think this is a little short?"

"That's how they're wearing them." Babs riffled through the racks, eyeing the blouses quickly as she rattled the hangers. Finally she extracted one, blue-and-white striped with a bow at the collar, and held it up to her chest. "What do you think?"

"It's fine."

"No, it's not. It's too schoolmarmish. I was just testing you. Really, Rachel."

Babs went back to flipping through the blouses. Within a few minutes, she had a pile of wool jumpers and skirts and blouses over her arm.

"Aren't you going to try on anything?" Babs asked.

"I don't need anything right now."

Babs shrugged and carried her haul to the dressing room at the back of the sales floor. Mrs. Webb, who had run the women's department at Metzger's for years, followed them. "Would you like to try those on?" she asked.

She ushered Babs into the dressing room and pulled the curtain closed behind her. Rachel went to a table displaying crew neck sweaters and studied the colors. She could use a new sweater, but she couldn't decide between the rust brown and navy. When Babs emerged from the dressing room, she was wearing a gray skirt and a tight-fitting red blouse. She looked like a cross between a cheerleader and a member of the altar guild. "This skirt's too long, isn't it?" she asked.

Rachel said no, she thought it was perfect.

Babs fingered the cloth. Mrs. Webb appeared from behind a rack of winter coats and said, "That's a lovely flannel. The cut's so flattering on you."

Babs returned to the dressing room with a flounce of the skirt. Mrs. Webb and Rachel avoided making eye contact as Mrs. Webb went back to marking prices on the coats.

Babs came from behind the curtain in one outfit after another. Rachel nodded her assent to the ones Babs liked and agreed that others were too tight, too long, or just plain "funny looking." In the end, Babs chose a jumper, a skirt, and two blouses. Rachel took one of the navy blue sweaters from the table.

"You're getting one of those sweaters?" Babs said, her disapproval barely disguised.

"Yes. Why?"

"You could use something more feminine."

"I don't want something more feminine. I want a warm sweater I can wear with pants."

Babs raised her eyebrows. "I'm just trying to help you out, Rachel."

Without saying more, Babs carried her purchases to the sales desk. Rachel followed her with the offending sweater in her hand. Mr. Metzger greeted them behind the cash register. "Ladies, it's always good to see you. Did you find everything you wanted?"

"Yes. The new wools are very nice," Babs said.

"I hand-picked them myself." Mr. Metzger peered at them through his bifocals as though they were the lowly store owners and he was the important customer. "Would you like this on your account?" he asked Babs.

She nodded yes, and he totaled the items on a receipt pad, then wrapped each piece of clothing in tissue paper and set them in a card-board box. With a flourish, he opened an oversized shopping bag and set the box inside. When it came to Rachel's turn, she paid cash and was given her sweater in a plain paper bag without a handle, though he did take the time to wrap it in tissue. Mr. Metzger thanked them with a bow of his head and walked them to the door, which he held ajar.

"There are so few places left where you can get service like that," Babs said as they made their way down the street to the diner.

Chapter Twenty-two

She could hear the radio before she entered the house, blaring a football game. She knew the moment she stepped inside that he was drunk. The house was cold, the fire gone out. The room stank of beer, and empty bottles lay on the floor by the couch and covered the table. Nate was sprawled on the couch with the radio propped beside him, the volume so high that the announcer seemed to be next to him, shouting wildly. Rachel went to the radio and lowered the sound. Nate turned his head, as if just realizing that she was present.

"Rachel, sweetheart. You came home. Me and Eddie are listening to the game."

"Where's Eddie?"

Nate glanced around, confused. "I don' know. How's Andy? You go see Andy?"

Rachel stood over the couch, staring down at him in disgust. "Andy's fine."

"You give him the cookies?"

"Yes."

Nate sank back on the couch.

Glancing at the bottles, Rachel determined that they were all empty. On the kitchen counter, she found an empty pint of whisky. She filled the kettle with water and set it on the stove to boil.

"Didn't you have dinner at the Brovellis?" she asked.

Nate swung his unfocused eyes across the room.

"You were having Sunday dinner with Gina and Joe," she said.

Her words still did not appear to register. After a moment, he shook his head from side to side, as though trying to clear his fogged mind. "Dinner. Yeah, we had dinner. Damned good cook, that Gina."

Rachel had gotten something to eat with Babs and taken the ferry back. Enough time had passed since Nate's noon meal at the Brovellis for him and Eddie to do some damage. When the water had boiled, she poured it into a mug and added a heaping teaspoon of instant coffee from the jar on the kitchen counter.

"Here," she said, holding out the cup.

He pushed it away. "I don't want that crap."

The coffee sloshed over the cup and onto Rachel's hand. She went to the sink and held her hand under the cold water until the skin turned pink, and she couldn't tell if it was burned or not. She was still standing at the sink when she heard the excited voices of children outside and footsteps on the porch. Halloween. She had forgotten. Hurrying across the room, she reached into her purse for the candy she had purchased in Barton. She ripped open the bag of candy corn and went to the door just as the children shouted, "Trick or treat."

Alice stood behind the girls, her hands on their shoulders. Lizzie, dressed as a ghost, lifted the sheet from her head to reveal her face. "Hi, Miss Shattuck."

"Lizzie," Rachel said in mock surprise. "I didn't know it was you."

Ellen, in a clown costume, tugged on her sister's sleeve. "Don't, Lizzie. Put the sheet back. You're supposed to make them guess."

Lizzie dropped the sheet back in place and giggled.

Rachel took a handful of candy corn. Before she could drop it into the girls' bags, she heard Nate behind her, lurching toward the door. He staggered into her and asked, "What's all the noise?"

"It's the McGarrells. They're trick or treating."

"Trick or treating?"

"It's Halloween!" Ellen squealed.

Nate knocked the clown hat from Ellen's head. "Don't!" she said, stooping to retrieve it.

Alice gave Rachel a grim look and pulled the girls close to her.

"Look, Lizzie, candy corn," Ellen said, thrusting her bag forward.

Rachel dropped the candy into the waiting bags while Nate breathed his sour breath on her neck.

"Who told you to come over here?" Nate asked, eyeing Ellen.

The girls turned to Rachel, confused and frightened. "He forgot it was Halloween," Rachel said.

Nate leaned toward the children, and Rachel stepped in front of him, trying to push him back. "Thanks for coming by," she said.

Alice herded the girls across the porch, glancing back and mouthing the words, "Do you need help?"

Rachel shook her head. Ellen and Lizzie called out their thanks and went rustling down the steps, clutching the bags of candy. Rachel pushed her father inside and shut the door. "Come on," she said tiredly. "Let's go drink that coffee."

Nate sank onto the couch and mumbled, "I ain't drinking that crap."

Rachel gathered up the beer bottles scattered on the floor, piling them into a paper bag she found beneath the sink. When she turned around, she discovered her father was lying down with his eyes closed. After a moment, he let out a grunted snore. Going to the bedroom, she took the ragged blanket from his bed and carried it back to the living room, draping it over him.

She thought of the notebooks and went quickly to the other room, pushing the door closed halfway, and rummaged beneath the blanket for the diary she had not yet finished reading. Opening the cover, she consulted the date—1938. This was the one. She slipped it beneath her sweater and made her way through the living room.

Outside, she started up the car and eased down the hill. Lights glowed in the windows at Alice's house. She searched the road as she made the turn onto Bay Avenue, but she did not see the trick or treaters. They had probably gone down to Miss Weeden's. Rachel had promised that she would be at her own house when the children came, but she was going to break this promise. She passed the dump and took the fork out toward Gooseneck Cove. When she came to Eddie's, she pulled into the driveway behind his truck. The lights were on downstairs. She banged on the door, listening to the heavy tread of his boots inside. The door swung open, and he stood there staring at her uncertainly, a cigarette between his lips. Behind him the radio played a Temptations song.

"Hi, Rachel." He took the cigarette from his mouth. His breath smelled of alcohol. "How's Barton?"

"Barton is the same as the last time I was there, but I came home and found my father drunk."

Eddie leaned forward, unsteady for a moment. "Wanna come in?"

Rachel stepped inside, letting him close the door behind her. The room was littered with all sorts of debris. Dirty dishes were scattered on the table, and empty milk bottles lay on the counter by the stove, with a pile of discarded eggshells beside them. A generator sat on the floor, on a stack of newspapers, surrounded by tools and piles of nuts and bolts. Two copies of *Playboy* lay next to it. Eddie went to the table and stubbed out his cigarette in an ashtray overflowing with butts.

Rachel remained inside the door with her coat on. "What are you doing, getting my father drunk?"

Squinting at her, Eddie grasped the back of a chair for support. "I didn't get him drunk. He got himself drunk."

"You brought him the beer. And the whisky."

"We were listening to the game and we decided to have a tailgate party in the house, make it a special occasion. You know, Rachel, you want everybody to be perfect, and the thing is, everybody ain't perfect."

"This is not about being perfect, Eddie."

"Yeah, well, seems like it to me. We were listening to the game. I had an extra six-pack out in the truck, and I went out and got it, that's all."

"Next time before you bring an extra six-pack over or a bottle of whisky, maybe you'll think about it."

"Maybe I will."

She held his look for a long moment, feeling a sense of complete futility. It was pointless to have this conversation now.

He stared back at her. "Was that you in Nick's jeep, going down to Gooseneck Cove the other night?"

Startled, she buried her hands in her coat pockets.

"You're making that a regular thing, riding around with Nick, huh?"

"Don't be ridiculous, Eddie."

The chair on which he was leaning rocked forward. Eddie lost his balance for a moment before righting the chair. "Nick's a handsome kid. He could turn anyone's head."

"Well, he hasn't turned mine." Rachel went to the door.

"Hey, don't go." He came over and placed his hand on her arm. "I can clean up this mess."

She shook her head. Eddie squeezed her arm, then let go. As she stepped outside, she saw him leaning toward her, as if thinking of following her, a slightly perturbed, puzzled expression on his face. Rachel went to the car. He was still standing there, framed in the doorway, when she started up the engine and drove away.

She did not pass anyone on the road as she traveled back to Bay

Avenue, drove by the darkened store and the dock, and went on to her house. The children were home by now, eating their Halloween treasure. Rachel parked the car in the gravel next to her house and carried the groceries she had purchased on the mainland inside, anxiously repeating the conversation with Eddie in her mind. Why had she gotten into Nick's jeep? What a stupid thing to do. She would not do it again.

She removed her jacket, hung it by the door, and went about making a fire. When she could see the flames through the chink in the stove's door, she closed the damper halfway and went to the sink, filling the tea kettle with water and setting it on the stove. What she had told Eddie was the truth. Nick had not turned her head. Still, she had to admit that he made the days at the schoolhouse something to look forward to. He made her laugh. Her made her forget herself. Eddie was jealous, she supposed. She took a certain satisfaction, along with alarm, at this thought.

The water came to a boil, and she poured the hot water into a cup, then dunked the tea bag. Carrying the cup to the table, she switched on the radio. The crooning of a man's voice filled the room—Bob Dylan singing "Like a Rolling Stone." Yes, we were all alone like the person he sang about, she thought, we were all unknown. It wasn't the words of the song, but the way his voice carried them, with that peculiar blend of exhilaration and longing, that conveyed the feeling of what it meant to be invisible, a stone rolling along with no idea where you were going. For a moment, the song captured the romance of being freed of possessions and money, but it was saying something else, too, that rich or poor, we are all encumbered by our own loneliness. She thought of Eddie, alone in his place by Gooseneck Cove, and her father, sleeping it off on the couch, and herself, here in her own silence.

Chapter Twenty-three

September 23, 1938

Our world has been completely transformed. I would not have believed that an act of nature could do this until I saw it with my own eyes. It was on Wednesday. The sky turned dark after lunch and the wind came up. Nate came in from the shop and said it looked like a bad storm coming. We expected heavy rain, some wind, nothing more. The children came back from the schoolhouse just before the hurricane hit. Within minutes, it seemed, the sky was black and the wind so high and the rain so thick you could see almost nothing. We had glimpses of the water down below, huge waves washing over the ferry dock, and then we could see just a swirl of leaves and tree limbs and rain beyond the window. The sound of the wind was incredible, a horrible roaring. Nate pushed furniture up against the door and the windows. I honestly wondered if the house would hold. We all got in the tin tub and sat there pressed together in the middle of the room. If the house was swept away, we thought, we might be saved in the tub. We are lucky to live up the hill, away from the water. This is what saved us. The children cried, and Nate and I sang every silly song we could think of to quiet them. I tried to pray, but I was so frightened I could hardly concentrate. I just kept saying, "Please, God, please, God" over and over in my mind. Finally the wind went still, and

I scrambled out of the tub, but Nate said it was only the eye of the storm passing over. A few minutes later we were plunged back into it. Then at last the worst was over. It still rained heavily all night, but the wind subsided. The children were too frightened to sleep in their room. We all piled together in our bed and somehow the children went to sleep. I lay there looking at their small heads on the pillow, thinking how precious they are, and praying that everyone on the island survived. In the morning we learned that no one had been lost on Snow—a miracle. But what a scene of devastation. The ferry dock is gone, and the store was almost completely destroyed. Many of the summer houses close to the shore by the lighthouse have simply been washed away, without a trace. The beach is strewn with pieces of furniture, broken planks of wood, bits of clothing and bedding. It's a completely unreal landscape. I haven't been to the other side of the island, but Nate says that, too, is unrecognizable, though most of the houses in Snow Park are intact because they were far enough up the hill not to be engulfed by the water. Today the sky is clear and the bay utterly still. It's impossible to believe that such a short time ago the bay was a seething monster. It will take months, maybe years, before we can recover.

September 26, 1938
The men have rigged up a temporary place for the ferry to dock, and today we had our first contact with the outside world. Captain Tony reports that hundreds of people died along the coast from Connecticut to Providence, and many roads on the mainland are still closed due to downed trees and power lines. He brought us the newspapers—the photos are incredible. Everyone is faulting the weather bureau. There was no warning. Ten women on a church picnic were killed in Misquamicut. It's hard to imagine. They have run out of coffins, and the funerals are scheduled one after another for days to come. Here on the island we are mostly worried about

the lack of food, but we have been so fortunate. We have lost roofs and houses but no lives.

September 29, 1938
Evelyn Daggett has threatened to leave the island. She says she does not know how she can rebuild the store. Mr. Brovelli and Mr. Cunningham went over to her house and seem to have persuaded her to stay. The men will rebuild the store for her as soon as we can get lumber from the mainland. Everyone is sharing what food they have. It's all we can do until things are back to something like normal on the mainland, and Captain Tony can begin deliveries again. The children are still too frightened to sleep in their room. I can barely sleep myself. I keep thinking I hear the wind howling around the house. What a horrible sound. I hope I never hear the wind blow with such force again.

October 3, 1938
The summer people have been coming over, one or two each day, to see what is left of their property. Some have the money for repairs and rebuilding. Others say they don't know what they will do. The Cheavings have already hired Nate to make repairs to their roof. I hate to say it of something so terrible, but the hurricane may be what saves us, for this winter at least. All the summer people have been stopping by, asking if Nate is available. How strangely twisted everything is. If Nate had not lost the boat last summer, he would have lost it in the storm. Now he is in better shape than the other quahoggers because he spent the summer advertising his services for repair work around the island. Of course there will be more than enough work to go around, and Nate will need the other men. But I can't help thinking that the loss of the boat was somehow meant to be.

October 5, 1938

I received a letter from Brandon today, informing me that Mother and Aunt Beth were lost in the hurricane, at Aunt Beth's house on the Connecticut shore. He had no way to notify me sooner, with the mails such a mess and phones out everywhere. They have already been buried, in the Hartwell family plot. Of course it made a difference to know that my mother was in the world somewhere, even if I never saw her again. I guess I never would have seen her again. She made it clear. I no longer existed. I have tried to think of her as being dead all these years. But she wasn't dead. She remained with me in some strange way. I feel bereft now, and I cannot stop thinking of her. How we fought in those last years before I left home. I blamed her for being so judgmental and scolding, but I know I played my part. I feel so ashamed when I think of those fights now. They seem so stupid. I should have gone to Connecticut to visit her, I should have forced her to acknowledge me, but the truth is that I was scared. She probably would have refused to see me. The sadness contains so many layers, I can't get to the bottom of it.

October 7, 1938

I went to Our Lady and said prayers for Mother. Not that she would have appreciated the Catholic prayers, but it was a comfort to me. While I kneeled there, it seemed that God understood why I had to leave my family and why Mother had to react as she did. Afterwards I was over-come. I sat in the woods and cried, not wanting Nate or the children to see me like that. I cannot say what I feel. Despair, I guess, that things could not be different, that they ended the way they did. Maybe my memories of her will always be like this, one emotion fighting another.

Nate and all the other men are busy from first light to sunset. There is so much to be done before winter comes. They have already begun work on the store. I look out the window and see the place where the dock once stood, and I am overwhelmed. My children are safe. The hurricane has put everything in perspective. I am so grateful to be alive. Nothing else seems to matter now. I think of Mother and Aunt Beth and how easily we could have met the same fate, and I want to fall on my knees and say thank you to God for saving us. I will not take anything for granted from now on. I will remember this lesson and be thankful.

October 9, 1938
Father Slade came on the morning ferry and said Mass at noon today. There were not many of us, with the summer Catholics gone. I made my confession and felt unburdened of so much. Father Slade said he was so sorry to hear about my mother and my aunt. He led us in prayers for all the dead from the hurricane. He has the most soothing voice. Mrs. Brovelli had him over for supper, and he stayed the night with them, as there is no heat in the rectory cottage. So I had only a few moments to speak with him after Mass, but that was enough. When I am with him, even briefly, I feel that I know myself again. My place in the world is clear to me for a moment.

October 10, 1938
I went down to the ferry to say goodbye to Father Slade this morning. As we were shaking hands, he said, "Here is that article I mentioned," and gave me an envelope. I did not know what he was talking about—he never mentioned an article—and returned to the house with a strange sense of foreboding. There was no article in the envelope, just a letter. I understood as soon as I unfolded the page that he did not want Mrs. Brovelli or the others to wonder what he had written. He has asked to be transferred to Chicago, and the bishop has agreed. Since his father's death, his mother is alone. He wants to be near her. We will all get an official letter from Saint Joseph's in a few weeks, but he wanted to tell me

himself. He wrote that my friendship and music have meant so much to him. He didn't want me to learn this news in an impersonal letter. He said he would always remember my service to him and the church on Snow, and he would keep me in his prayers. The time with Father Slade is the one thing that has seen me through these last winters. I should be grateful to have had his friendship at all. But such thoughts are not much consolation.

November 15, 1938
I have written nothing here for weeks. There is nothing to say. Nate is still busy hammering shingles on roofs, and the children have recovered from their fear of the hurricane. The store is almost finished. We all dream of having coffee again. The days have been still and unseasonably warm. I spend most of my time doing laundry and cooking. Phil is old enough now to play with Junior and keep him amused while I work around the house. Nate and I both fall into bed at night, exhausted. I have not played the piano once. Sometimes I think I will never play it again, though I realize this is spiteful and foolish. No doubt music will come back to me, the way it has so many times before.

November 21, 1938
Darkness. There's the actual darkness—the sun sets so early and the days are so short—and then there's the other darkness that follows me around all day. I wake from the reverie of doing the wash or cooking to find the boys on the floor, looking up at me expectantly. They depend on me for everything. Sometimes it is so overwhelming, I want to run out of the house screaming. Fix your own lunch, come up with your own games, I want to yell. It's been cold and rainy all week. I'm stuck here in the house with the boys all day. I know this is the reason for my gloom, but that doesn't make me feel any better.

November 28, 1938
Father Slade's last Mass was yesterday. I had hoped to have a moment alone with him, but there was no chance of this, with Mrs. Brovelli and Donna flocking around him and carrying on. He pressed my hand as I left the church and slipped a piece of paper into it. He wrote a brief note, saying that he would keep me in his prayers and that if I wanted to remain in touch, he would be happy to hear from me. He included his address in Chicago. He is going to teach at a Catholic high school and work in a parish right in the city. I know he will do such good work. They need him there more than we do here, though I will miss him terribly. I did not go down to the ferry when he left. It seemed pointless, and the children were all fussing so badly, I could never have gotten them dressed and out of the house.

December 12, 1938
A cold, freezing rain today. It hits the window panes and just the sound of it makes me shiver. Nate is off working with the other men despite the weather. They are trying to get one last roof repaired. Evelyn has the store open again. It seems almost cheery—food on the shelves and a fire going in the stove. If I didn't feel so strange and awkward with the women, I would go down and spend an hour at the store just for the company. Instead I played the piano this morning while the boys built towers out of their blocks. I thought at first that my hands would not respond, but after a few moments the old movement returned, and I lost myself in the music, flying over the keys. What happiness music is. There's nothing else so pure and simple and beautiful. I have not had a letter from Father Slade, though I wrote to him within days of his leaving. Even this didn't seem to matter as I played the music. I felt that somehow he was listening.

December 16, 1938

Nate has not had a drink for months now. When he is busy and has work, when he feels needed, he does not drink. Everything changes. A sort of hope comes over the house. But how many times have I felt this hope only to have it taken away? This time I am praying it will be different. The work will last through the winter and into the summer, with many of the summer people who lost their houses talking about rebuilding. Nate is the one they come to first. He has the tools and knows more about carpentry than Silas Mitchell or John Brovelli. I am certain that having work will make a difference and keep him from falling back into bad habits. There are times I have felt so angry and disgusted, wondering at this person I married and how he has become someone else, but then I must remind myself how hard it is for Nate to struggle with making money and supporting us, how it wounds him not to be able to give us whatever we need. I think this is what drives him to drink—feeling powerless. He does not mean to hurt us. He just can't overcome his own frustration, and then Silas is always there to lead him down the wrong path. But this winter I feel will be different. I am trying to be understanding and supportive, not to do anything to drive him away, out of the house.

December 20, 1938

I received an answer from Father Slade today—a true Christmas present. Evelyn Daggett gave me an odd look when she handed me the letter down at the store, but did not comment on the return address. Usually she announces who the letter is from before she gives it to you. She is a terrible snoop and gossip. I try to think charitable thoughts about her, but the way she goes on, prying into everyone's business, is enough to make you sick. He wrote two whole pages describing the parish in Chicago, his students, the other priests. He misses being near the water, he says. Lake Michigan is not the same. He misses seeing the lighthouse on the horizon and the outline of the island. He asked if I was working on a new piano piece and how are the children and Nate. I can see his face when I read the letter. It's as if he is here, in the room. How quickly we lose a sense of people when we are separated from them, but then suddenly they return, and we are struck all over again by the force of who they are. He says that he continues to pray for me. This means more than anything, to know that he says my name in his mind each day. I pray for him, too.

February 2, 1939

The days are dark and gray and cold. I find myself staring at the water out the window. What am I looking for? I don't know. It snowed last week and the children were so excited. I had forgotten how magical snow is to children, that overwhelming sense of wonder. I know I felt the same sort of ecstasy over the smallest things when I was younger, but it seems inconceivable now. Life does wear us down. I don't like to admit this, but it's true. The one bright spot was a letter from Brandon last week, with a hundred dollars enclosed. He says that he will put some of the money from mother's estate into an account for me and the children. I did not expect this.

April 7, 1939

The days are the same, one after another. What can I say, to myself or the pages of this diary? The truth is that I live for a letter from Father Slade, but I have not heard from him since that letter in December. I know he is busy. He is teaching and coaching basketball, and he has his duties at the church. But I can't help wondering if he has forgotten me. I fear I have imagined I am more important to him than I am, that he wrote that letter out of charity. The nights when I played the piano, our conversations at the rectory—I begin to think it was all a fantasy I created in my own mind. He felt sorry for me, stuck here on the island with Nate and

the children. Now he has moved on to another life, and the pale house-
wife who cooked for him doesn't matter anymore. I am such a vain creature. I ask God to forgive me, but I can't stop these thoughts, can't get
over feeling hurt, even though I know it's ridiculous.

April 18, 1939
A letter at last. I have been going down to the store every time the ferry
comes, just to see if there is a mail delivery. Today I was rewarded. I let
the children run down to the beach and sat on a rock, out of view of the
store. As soon as I opened the envelope, I knew how foolish I had been
to think his silence meant anything. The children are in the living room,
playing. I am here in the bedroom, reading the letter again. More vanity. But how much it means to me. I did not know how much I needed
this letter until it was here.

    Dear Phoebe,

        Forgive me for not answering you sooner. I have had your let-
ter on my bedside table for weeks, where it has been giving me
reproving looks. You don't know what a comfort it is to hear from
you and to remember the island. Here I am pulled in many direc-
tions at once and have hardly a moment to myself from the start
of the day to the end. I think of the nights when you played the
piano, and then when the music ended, how we sat and listened
to the sound of the waves breaking. I cannot find quiet, or beauty, like that in Chicago. I guess you could accuse me of romanti-
cizing the island. I know that you work hard and that your life is
not easy, especially since the hurricane. But remember to pause
for a moment when you go about your work and look out at the
bay for me.

        I am enjoying the teaching, though it is a challenge. It's

harder than I thought to get the boys' attention and keep it for fifty minutes, which can seem like an eternity, believe me. Then there are the days when it doesn't seem like an effort at all, and the time flies by. They make up for the others. I have been so busy getting settled and preparing for classes and saying Mass that I haven't had much time to get out in the city. I'm hoping I will be able to get to some concerts eventually. I haven't even been to the museum, but I'm taking a group of students there next week.

You must be having spring weather by now. Have you done any planting yet? How is Nate doing with all the repair work? I hope this finds you and Nate and the children well.

In Christ's love,
Daniel

May 5, 1939

Nate came in last night and kissed me. I couldn't remember the last time he had done that, walked through the door at the end of the day and put his arms around me. For a moment I felt that old senseless longing, that eagerness. "Look at you," he said softly, so the children couldn't hear. "Not a smile in sight. Come on, Lady." He held my face in his hands, and I did smile then. He can still do this, he can still make me laugh in spite of myself, he can still make my knees go weak. But I protect myself against that desire. I do not want another baby. Nate doesn't understand. I give in to his advances as little as possible, at times of the month when I think it's safe. He says it seems that my period lasts for weeks. That is just one of my excuses, but perhaps I do use it too much. I wish all these things were not so complicated. It seems that you should be able to pin down what you feel, to get hold of it and understand it. I feel a million things at once, all canceling each other out.

Chapter Twenty-four

She pulled her new sweater over her head and checked her reflection in the mirror. She did not care if it was not "feminine" enough. The sweater looked just fine, cute even, over a striped top and her blue skirt. She ate her breakfast standing at the kitchen counter and hurried out to the car, buttoning her jacket on the way.

Alice called out good morning when Rachel stepped inside the store.

"Morning," Rachel said. "Sorry about last night. I hope my father didn't scare the girls."

"Not really. They were just disappointed they didn't get to trick or treat at your house."

"I know. I'm bringing candy for recess today. Eddie said my father didn't drink anymore."

Alice went to the hot plate and poured some coffee for Rachel. "I haven't seen him like that in a long time."

As Rachel went to add milk and sugar, she felt Alice watching her. Was it an island conspiracy, she wondered, to defend her father no matter what? Before she could say anything more, the door burst open, and Brock entered with Lizzie and Ellen. The girls skipped across the floor and reached into the glass jar by the cash register, each taking a red licorice whip.

"Did I say you could have those?" Alice said, glaring at them.

Lizzie shook her head, her eyes wide with apprehension. She held the limp piece of candy over the jar.

"Don't put it back!" Alice barked.

Lizzie remained frozen, uncertain whether to bring the licorice whip to her mouth or hide it in her pocket.

"You said we could have one yesterday, for Halloween, and then we forgot and went home," Ellen said.

Alice eyed the girls reprovingly. "All right, you can have them, but ask next time. Don't just grab."

Falling into the easy chair by the stove, squashed together side by side, Lizzie and Ellen bit off pieces of the licorice and concentrated on chewing. "They told me you said they could have them," Brock explained sheepishly. "I said it was okay."

Alice gave him an annoyed glance but made no further comment, merely asking, "Where's mother?"

"Up at the house. She's got one of her headaches."

"Great. She was going to make dinner."

Brock shifted his weight nervously from one foot to the other. "I can help with that."

From the dismissive look Alice gave him, Rachel concluded that Brock was not much use in the kitchen. Outside, children's voices sounded, and footsteps reverberated on the porch. Rachel finished her coffee and turned to Lizzie and Ellen. "Time for school."

Brock leaned down and gave each of the girls a kiss on the cheek. "You girls behave, now."

"We will," Ellen responded, waving to her mother as she steered her sister toward the door. When Rachel glanced back, she saw Alice and Brock, still facing each other over the counter.

The boys dashed across the parking lot, playing a game of tag. Rachel clapped her hands. "Come on. Time to go."

Scott Daggett darted in and out of the parked cars, chasing his brother, who shrieked in anticipation of being caught. Finally Scott grabbed Bob and yelled, "You're it."

Rachel clapped her hands again. Slowly the boys filed to the Ford, retrieving book bags and lunch boxes they had left in the dirt. Rachel climbed into the driver's seat.

"We didn't get to go trick or treating at your house, Miss Shattuck," Ellen said.

Rachel pulled out the choke and started up the car. "I know. I'm sorry."

"You said we could come trick or treating at your house."

"Yes, I did, and I'm sorry, Ellen. If you want to wear your costume to school tomorrow, you can."

"Can we all wear our costumes?" Lizzie asked.

"Yes, you can all wear your costumes."

The girls let out excited squeals.

"Miss Weeden gave out popcorn balls with caramel coating," Ellen announced.

"That's what she gives every year," Scott said.

"Yeah, but they're homemade."

"I like candy bars better," Bob said.

The children went on, comparing notes on the candy they had collected. Rachel parked the car on the grass in front of the schoolhouse, and they spilled out. "Everyone inside," she called as they darted across the lawn. "This isn't recess."

Reluctantly, they filed through the schoolhouse door. Nick was seated at his desk, reading the newspaper, and the Brovellis were milling around. Rachel helped the younger children out of their jackets while the boys gathered around Nick's desk.

"I'll trade you my *Popular Mechanics*," Scott was saying to Nick as Rachel entered the schoolroom.

"What for?"

"That transistor radio, the one you got for parts."

Nick shook his head. "I still need it for parts."

"Okay then, will you help me fix my dad's old radio?" Scott asked.

"Sure."

Rachel went to the blackboard, and the children took their places at their desks. After giving the older children a quiz in history, she gathered the younger ones into reading groups, and then went to Nick's desk. He looked up from the newspaper and asked, "You went shopping on the mainland, huh?"

"How'd you know that?"

"You're wearing a new sweater."

She nodded.

"It looks nice."

His words hung in the space between them, a dare of sorts. She realized, with a start of recognition, that he was flirting with her.

"Aren't you supposed to be reading *Julius Caesar*?" she said quickly, trying to cover her confusion.

Nick folded the newspaper, rattling the pages. "I'm starting to think I'm going to spend the rest of my life reading *Julius Caesar*."

"How about just focusing on the next scene?"

He held her look as he reached inside the desk and produced the collection of Shakespeare plays. Rachel turned away, moving across the room to the younger students, trying to convince herself that she did not feel his gaze on her back. He had bantered with her before, even teased her, but this was different—the pointed way he looked at her and the suggestion in his voice.

For the rest of the day, she avoided sitting down with Nick. When it came time for math, she handed him the worksheet and went off to read with the younger children. He gave her another of those looks, vaguely taunting, taking note of the fact that she was not participating in the algebra lesson. Had she encouraged him? She was afraid that she had, afraid she had welcomed, even sought out, his attention. Now she did not know what to do. She could not simply erase the friendship between them, but she could not let it go on, either.

When the time for dismissal came, Nick was going over a science lesson with Lou. As soon as the hands on the clock reached three, he pulled on his jacket and went out to the jeep. Rachel told the rest of the students they were dismissed and helped Lizzie into her coat. Outside, the children talked noisily as they climbed into the car. Rachel drove to the other side of the island, hearing the steady stream of their voices without listening to what they said. When they passed the lighthouse, she recorded the fact that her father and Eddie were there, painting. At the store, Lizzie and Ellen jumped out of the back seat and ran up the porch steps. Rachel followed them.

Inside, the girls skipped across the floor and ducked behind the counter. Alice hugged them both and asked, "How was school?"

"Fine," Ellen answered. "I got to read out loud."

"Me, too," Lizzie said.

Alice glanced up and saw Rachel. "Girls, why don't you go up to the house? Daddy's waiting for you. He'll help you with your homework."

Lizzie and Ellen went clattering toward the door. "But don't make too much noise. Your grandmother has a headache," Alice called.

In the silence after the girls were gone, Alice stood there leaning on the counter, her face drawn. She absently petted the cat, asleep by the cash register. "How's Nick doing?"

For a moment, Rachel thought that somehow Alice knew about the compliments Nick had paid her, the way he looked at her. She was overcome by an awareness of her own furtive guilt. She never should have gotten in Nick's jeep and gone off to Gooseneck Cove with him. She reminded herself that this was all she had done, nothing more, and yet it felt tantamount now to something forbidden.

"As far as I can tell, he spends all his time out looking for deer. I just wanted to make sure he was doing his homework," Alice added.

"He's keeping up fine."

"I'm trying to talk Brock into letting him apply to college. Brock says we can't afford it."

"I think he could get a scholarship. I mentioned it to Nick."

"What did he say?"

"He wasn't sure. He said he just wanted to start a repair business and why should he go to college for that?"

Alice sighed. "I don't care what any of my kids do as long as they're happy, but Nick's different..."

Rachel nodded. "I'll encourage him to think about it."

"Thanks, Rachel." Alice looked relieved for a moment.

Outside, Rachel climbed into the car, wondering how she would find a way to talk to Nick again about college when she did not want to talk to him about anything. Driving up the hill, she went straight across Bay Avenue to her father's house. She pulled over beyond the porch steps, shut off the engine, and reached into the glove compartment. The notebook was still there, where she had left it that morning. She slipped it beneath her jacket and made her way quickly inside the house. The air had a flat, stale smell to it, though the odor of beer was gone. Rachel went to the bedroom and placed the notebook beneath the blankets. As she returned to the main room, she heard the truck rumbling up the hill. She had hoped to avoid seeing her father and Eddie, but now it could not be helped. She reached for the broom and began sweeping the floor.

The door opened, and Eddie entered, still in his painting clothes. He eyed her uneasily. "Hi," he said.

"Hi."

"Your father stopped at the store. He'll be up in a minute."

Rachel propped the broom in the corner. "That's okay. I wasn't planning on staying."

Eddie took off his hat and dropped it on the kitchen table. "Hey, I'm sorry about yesterday. I wasn't too coherent when you came by."

"No, you weren't. Neither was my father."

"Yeah, we got carried away, listening to the football game. You know, Sunday afternoon and everything."

Rachel felt a certain vindication in his discomfort. "Sunday afternoon. That always was a favorite time for drinking around here."

"All right, Rachel, I get the message. No more extra six-packs."

"I'm going to hold you to that."

Eddie nodded. When Rachel realized that he was not going to say anything more, she took her jacket from the couch and pulled it on. "I'll see you later," she said as she stepped out the door.

She passed her father at the bottom of the hill, as she was about to make the turn onto Bay Avenue. He raised his hand in an awkward wave. Turning the corner, she drove on to her house.

PART III

Departure

Chapter Twenty-five

Rachel slipped out of the house, into the dark. The April wind was warm, blowing off the water, bringing with it the scent of mud and salt, a harbinger of spring. She buried her hands in her pockets and took the path by the lighthouse down to the shore. The days were growing longer at last, and the first hints of green had begun to appear in tight buds on the branches of trees and tentative shoots of grass. She made her way carefully over the rocks, moving away from the lighthouse on down the beach, listening to the hush of the waves coming in and going out. She had missed that sound when the island was iced in. Winter brought a profound silence to Snow, broken only by the groaning of the wind.

The store was dark, the dock beyond illuminated by a single streetlight. Rachel stepped into the phone booth and pulled the door closed. After a couple of minutes, the phone rang. The receiver was cold in her hand when she picked it up.

"Rachel?" Babs said.

"Yes. Who did you expect to answer the phone?"

"I don't know. It's a pay phone. Anybody could answer it. Are you sitting down? I have something to tell you."

Before Rachel could explain that there was nowhere to sit down in the phone booth, Babs blurted out, "I'm engaged!"

"You're engaged?" Rachel heard herself stupidly echoing Babs' words and tried to think how this had happened since they had spoken a week earlier.

"Yes, I'm honest to God engaged with a big rock on my finger. A gorgeous diamond. Wait 'til you see it. You'll faint it's so beautiful. I wake myself up at night and stare at it. You can practically read by the thing in the dark."

"Howard gave you a ring?" Rachel asked, still trying to take in the news.

"No, Principal Reid gave me a ring. Yes, of course it's Howard. He asked me out to dinner on Sunday night, and he walked me back to my house and came in. Then he took this little box from his pocket. I played coy, but I knew what it was the minute I saw it. I had to bite my tongue to keep from shrieking and running up and down Front Street telling the whole world. God, Rachel, you haven't even met him. You've got to get over here and meet him, especially since you're going to be one of my bridesmaids. I'm thinking baby blue for the bridesmaids' dresses—knee length, with pretty little spaghetti straps and big skirts. How's that sound?"

"Great."

"We're planning on June, the 18th. You can make it, right?"

"Sure, I can make it."

"Good. My sister has to be the maid of honor. I hope you understand. But you'll be next in line, right beside her. We're doing it at Saint Michael's, and then we'll have the reception at the VFW. I've already got Anthony's signed up to do the food. And I'm thinking that the colors for the decorations will be baby blue, like the dresses, and buttercup yellow. Doesn't that sound perfect?"

Rachel nodded, forgetting that Babs could not see her. It made no difference, as Babs went right on talking, telling her about Howard's family and how she had gone to meet his parents in Boston. "Thank God he doesn't care where we get married, and neither do his parents. The Episcopal church is just fine with them. You know that makes my mother happy. She always says the Episcopalians have class. Oh, did I mention we're buying a house? That cute little place just over the bridge on the way into town. It's got three bedrooms so you can come and stay with us. No more staying at the Priscilla Alden. That place has really turned into a dump, by the way. Mrs. Santos is getting positively senile."

Babs paused long enough for Rachel to break in. "I'm so happy, Babs."

"I know. I'm the luckiest damn girl in the world. He's smart and nice looking, and he knows how to pick out a diamond. Listen, I've got to go. Howard's coming over to look at china patterns. I got a whole bunch of brochures from Metzger's. That's where we're registering. So look, can you come over this weekend for a dress fitting? We've got to get the dress orders in if we want them here by the first of June."

Rachel said she could come over on Saturday. They agreed to meet at Metzger's.

"Mrs. Howard Needham," Babs said proudly. "How do you like the sound of that?"

"It sounds great."

"Yeah. Jeez, I still can't believe it. If I didn't have this hunky diamond on my hand, I wouldn't. Okay, behave yourself over there. I'll see you Saturday."

Rachel said goodbye and slid the receiver back into the cradle. Circling the store, she went on down the beach.

It was not a surprise that Babs was getting married at last. She and Howard had been dating all winter. After the third date she started to talk about him in a different tone, and then as the months passed, almost every conversation began with, "Howard says…" and "Howard thinks…" Rachel had accepted the fact that he was an authority on just about any topic. She was genuinely happy for Babs. This is what Babs had wanted for so long. Whether Howard was the right man or not hardly mattered. Babs would make it work. She made everything in her life work.

Rachel was passing the back of the inn when she heard a car in the distance and spotted headlights on the road above, carving a path through the murky darkness. Pausing in the shadow of the inn, she waited to let the vehicle pass, assuming it was Nick. He drove by her house almost every night. She kept the shades pulled over the front windows and when she walked down to the phone booth, took the beach instead of the road, avoiding him. She had been careful since the fall, at the schoolhouse and when she met him elsewhere on the island. She thought she had succeeded in establishing a certain distance, making sure there was no more bantering, no more flirting, that they stayed focused on the business at hand—English essays or science reports. Nick had declared, after Christmas, that he was not interested in applying to college. This disappointed her, of course, and so did the end of the easy exchanges between them, the raised eyebrows and small jokes, but if they were to get through the year at the schoolhouse, there was no other way.

Tonight a truck, not a jeep, came into view up on the road. She climbed the path and found Eddie waiting for her with the engine idling.

"You're going to kill yourself walking on those rocks in the dark," he said through the open window.

"I know them by heart."

"Yeah, but you can't see that slippery seaweed."

"Are you on your way somewhere?"

"Your house." Eddie flicked a spent cigarette end out the window. "See you there."

Rachel followed the truck the short distance to her door. She and

KATHERINE TOWLER

Eddie had reached a truce. He still drank his regular beers, but he had been true to his word not to supply Nate with more than one or two at a time.

"Babs is getting married," she told him as they entered the house. "I'm going to be a bridesmaid. In a baby blue dress."

Eddie slid into a chair at the table, draping his jacket over the back. "That's a good color for you."

"The first time she went out with Howard, she couldn't stand him. Now he's the best thing since sliced bread. He got her a diamond."

"That'll bring a girl around."

"That's what you think? Women can just be bought with jewelry and clothes?"

Eddie shook his head. "If it was that easy, I'd be married."

Rachel took the seat across from Eddie. "The wedding's in June. You want to go?"

"Are you asking me to be your date?"

"There's nothing worse than going to a wedding alone."

Eddie laughed. "That's a great invitation if I ever heard one."

"I'm serious, Eddie. I could use an escort."

"Fine. Do I have to wear a suit?"

"Yes, you have to wear a suit."

"Are you going to iron it for me?"

Rachel rolled her eyes. "All right, I'll iron it for you. That's a concession, you know. I didn't even iron for Kevin. He ironed his own shirts."

"Is that why you split up? Because you wouldn't do his ironing?"

"No. We split up because he liked men."

She had not expected to make this revelation, and the words suddenly hanging between them surprised her as much as they surprised him. She saw that he was trying to assess whether she was making a strange joke. Crossing his arms over his chest, he shifted in his seat. "That must

283

have been tough."

"You're the first person I've ever told."

Eddie was clearly uncertain what to say. She didn't blame him. She didn't know what to say herself. "I've never gotten that," he said finally. "There were men like that in the Army. I didn't go anywhere near them. Weirdos."

"Kevin wasn't a weirdo."

"Sorry." He shifted again in his seat. "I didn't mean he was a weirdo. But he didn't have any business getting married."

"He thought he would change. He went to see a psychiatrist, but it didn't help."

"So he was going around with men?"

Rachel wished she could avoid answering the question. She responded with a quiet, "Yes."

"What a bastard."

"It wasn't intentional."

"What do you mean, it wasn't intentional? Jesus, Rachel."

"I mean that he didn't set out to do that to me. It just happened."

"I don't buy that. He was cheating on you, wasn't he?"

She had never thought of it as cheating, or never thought of it only in those terms. "It wasn't like he was having an affair."

"He was just having sex with other people?"

"Eddie, please. You make it sound so...tawdry."

He did not speak. The expression on his face was his answer. Yes, of course, it was tawdry or whatever you wanted to call it, but Rachel did not like to reduce Kevin to such words.

"He didn't set out intentionally to fool me," she said slowly, trying to find a way to explain. "It's just how he is, it's just what happened."

"You're being pretty damn charitable."

"I left him, didn't I?"

Eddie nodded. She saw in his eyes a respect and admiration she wasn't sure she had seen before. Rachel got up and went to the kitchen counter. She returned with a bag of potato chips and the deck of cards. When she fanned the cards across the table, Eddie turned one over.

They played one hand of cribbage and then another, calling out the totals as they set their cards down. Eddie won the first game, and Rachel the second. When she pegged out ahead of him, she said, "We're even. I didn't think I'd live to see the day."

"You got lucky."

"You don't think there's any skill involved?"

"Maybe a little. You've improved."

"Don't kill yourself giving compliments." Rachel reached for the cards, shuffled them, and spread them out.

Eddie pushed his chair back from the table. "Let's save it for next time."

"Eddie Brovelli, you're afraid you're going to lose. You won't play another game because you know I'm going to win. Chicken."

Getting to his feet, he pulled on his jacket. "I'm just tired, that's all."

He placed his hand on her shoulder, giving her a small squeeze, and said good night. Rachel sat at the table after he was gone, listening to the truck start up outside. She had not realized how it would feel to say the words about Kevin out loud. Now the shame of her marriage was out in the light.

When the sound of the engine faded, she went to the bedroom and undressed. Kevin had struggled, at least at first. She had known his struggle as if it were her own, but there came a time when this fight no longer had to do with sin, or betrayal, or deceit, when she saw that if she loved him, she would have to leave. This is what she could not explain, that she had left him out of love more than anything else.

Sliding beneath the sheets, she wondered if anyone really knew what the word love meant. Love came in costume and assumed many shapes and guises. Nothing in life had prepared her to understand this. She had grown up believing that love was a fixed state arrived at between two people, who, once they had achieved this small miracle, would remain in its protective glow for the rest of their lives. Now she was old enough to know that people changed, and that what they felt for each other changed, and that love could contain equal measures of hate and resentment and anger, and still in some strange way be a form of love.

Chapter Twenty-six

Rachel squinted at the profile of the mainland as she drove past the light-house with the car full of children. They were giddy this morning with the promise of spring, the promise of shedding coats and gloves and, in a little more than a month, even shoes. Rachel remembered how it felt the first warm day when she would cast off her sneakers and walk through the grass, her toes curling in delight at the soft, clean feel of the ground. That first barefoot day marked the start of summer. Sometimes she had gone whole weeks without wearing shoes, though her mother was constantly reprimanding her for having feet covered with scabs. Rachel did not mind a few cuts and bruises, a small price to pay for the freedom of running barefoot across the rocks at low tide. She loved to turn and look back at the island, to see it from out on the water, imagining that it was some foreign land she had just discovered. How strange the inhabitants of this place must be, she would tell herself, and how quaint their little houses and boats. When she went out on the rocks with Eddie and Phil she was always bound to get hurt, because then it was a race. They dared each other to see who could reach Elephant Rock the fastest, starting from three different points. Struggling to keep up, she would slip and go crashing into the water, skinning a knee or stubbing a toe. She had learned to get back up, without pausing to inspect her injuries. The boys did not care, and they would not wait for her. She had learned to hurl her body from one rock to the next without fear.

It was warm enough that there was no need for a fire in the stove at the schoolhouse. They found Nick sitting not in his usual chair but on top of his desk, legs crossed, paging through a volume of the encyclopedia. Scott went running up to him and peered over the edge of the book. "What's that?"

"It's a bobcat. You ever seen a bobcat?"

Scott shook his head.

"Me neither. But someday I'm going to see a bobcat, up in Maine or New Hampshire."

"In a zoo?"

Nick laughed. "No, not in a zoo. If you know how to look for them, and you stay in the woods long enough, you might see one. But they're shy. You've got to wait for them."

"We had a raccoon with two babies at our house. They were cute."

"Bobcats aren't cute. They're wild and beautiful."

Scott examined the photo of the bobcat gravely. When Rachel called the class to attention, he darted to his desk. Later in the morning, Rachel approached Nick's desk to find him reading a slim pamphlet set inside the history textbook. He quickly closed the book, trying to conceal the pamphlet.

"What are you reading?" she asked.

"History."

Rachel pointed to the cover of the pamphlet, sticking up between the closed pages.

"Oh, that," he said sheepishly. "It's the instructions for my new radio kit. It came in the mail yesterday."

"Maybe you should save that until after school."

Nick gave her an annoyed and vaguely defiant look, but said nothing.

"You need to pass history if you want to graduate."

He extracted the pamphlet from the textbook and shoved it in the desk. "Am I not passing history?"

"No, you're passing at this point, but you need to do well on the next test."

He continued to stare at her, the expression on his face suggesting that the idea he might not do well on the next test was an insult beneath acknowledging. Rachel opened her copy of the textbook and began reviewing the chapter, keeping the tone of her voice neutral. There were days when he was like this now, moody and resentful of the authority she held over him. She tried to remain friendly but distant, firmly planted in her role as the teacher.

At lunchtime, Nick went out to his car as usual, and Gina Brovelli came bustling into the schoolroom, the cardboard box in her arms. Theresa peered over the edge of the box and followed her mother to the kitchen. "Ravioli," Theresa said gloomily, sticking out her tongue.

"Theresa Brovelli, shut your mouth and sit down," her mother responded.

Gina caught Rachel's eye as they distributed cartons of milk around the table and motioned her over to the corner of the room. "Did you hear?" she whispered. "Nick got his draft notice."

"When did this happen?"

"Yesterday. Alice is pretty upset."

"What are you whispering about?" Rose called from the table.

"Nothing, sweetheart," her mother answered. "Just something I had to tell Miss Shattuck. Eat your food."

Gina circled the table, encouraging the children to eat. "No recess unless you drink all your milk," she reminded the Daggett boys.

There was quiet as the children ate with concentrated speed, anxious to be done with lunch. Bob brought the milk carton to his lips and downed what was left in a single, prolonged gulp. Slamming the carton on the table, he announced, "I'm done."

The others drained their milk cartons and waved them in the air before scrambling out of their chairs and running to the vestibule. Gina gathered the plates her children had eaten from, setting them in the box. "I can see why Alice doesn't want Nick to go," she said. "I wouldn't want my Lou to go if I could help it. But if they're drafted, it's their duty to serve and our duty to support them, don't you think?"

"Yes," Rachel answered, though she wasn't sure she meant it.

Gina made her way out the door. Rachel waited until she had driven off to go outside. For a moment, she simply stood in the middle of the lawn, with the children running in circles around her. How blissfully unaware they were of everything, even her presence in their midst. Nothing mattered but their own world of childhood, their games and rivalries, their little tragedies and outsized boasts. She would give anything, she thought, to be that self-absorbed again.

Crossing the lawn, she went to the jeep. Nick went on reading the pamphlet with the instructions for assembling the radio. She cleared her throat. Startled, he looked up.

"Mind if I sit with you for a minute?" she said.

He shook his head and leaned across the seat to open the passenger door.

Rachel slid in beside him and pulled the door closed. "I heard you got your draft notice."

"Yeah, my classification notice. I'm 1-S. My father never even heard of that classification. It means I'm still in high school. It's good through graduation, then I'll get another notice. Don't worry, Miss Shattuck. I'm not going to drop out or anything."

Rachel watched the children racing back and forth across the lawn. "I'm going to sign you up to take the college entrance test."

"There's not much point to that now."

"You can get a deferment. If you go to the draft board and tell them you've been accepted for the fall, they'll consider a deferment."

"You don't want me to go to Vietnam?"

She turned to look at him. "No."

Nick moved his hand across the seat and rested it on her shoulder. She sat, frozen, ready to ignore his touch, until he slid his hand down her arm and over her thigh. The warmth carried through the wool of her skirt, sending a slow tingling up her leg. She reached for his hand, thinking for a moment that he might misinterpret the gesture, believing she wanted to hold his hand, and wondering if he would be right, if she did want to keep his hand in hers, before she pushed it away.

"Don't do that," she said softly.

"Why?"

"Because I don't want you to."

She opened the car door and stepped out onto the brown lawn, searching the faces of the children to see if they had observed anything. They were still running in circles, hair flying, bright faces red from the cold. When she clapped her hands, they swarmed around her, happily oblivious. If only she could join them in an endless game of tag.

She returned to the schoolroom, her mind a swirl of panicked thoughts. She had been so cautious all winter, avoiding his gaze as she went from desk to desk, keeping their conversations brief. Perhaps she had been fooling herself. She believed she had put a stop to comments that were too personal, looks that were too suggestive. She believed she had banished the idea of Nick, made him just another pupil who happened to be tall and good looking. She was too old to give a boy his age so much as a second glance. But had she given him a second glance?

The children filed in and took their seats. She went from desk to desk, organizing them in reading groups. Nick came in behind the others and took his place, but she did not look at him. She would pretend that he was not there.

"Miss Shattuck," Nick called as she distributed the readers to the younger children. "What do you want me to do?"

She looked at him for a brief moment. "Work on your English essay."

Pulling her chair up beside Lizzie, Rachel listened as the girl made her way slowly through the reader, moving a stubby finger beneath the lines of type. Her hesitant voice, stumbling over the words, was reassuring. If she sat beside this girl, if she let the music of her voice roll over her, perhaps Rachel could become a girl again herself, untouched by desire and confusion.

Rachel went from one reading group to the next, and when the reading lessons were done, passed out a spelling test for the younger children and worked with Lou and Rose on science. Nick sat at his desk, head bent over a stack of paper. Occasionally he moved the pen across a page. She kept her back to him and did not speak to him. At three o'clock he stood up, pulled on his jacket, and went out to his car. Rachel felt her limbs go slack with relief.

She drove with a mechanical detachment to the other side of the island. She could not say with certainty that she had completely discouraged Nick, that he had no reason to think she might respond. This was what haunted her, this and the thought of his draft notice. The war was not, as had been predicted, winding down. They were drafting more and more soldiers and sending them off. The newspaper published the casualty numbers every week now. Rachel wished she had put aside her misgivings and pushed Nick harder to apply to college.

The children chattered away in the back seat, but their words did not reach her. Maybe she could convince Brock that Nick should take the entrance exam, and Brock could convince Nick. She couldn't think of anything else.

"Is your father waiting for you at home?" she asked Ellen as they pulled up next to the store.

"No. He's fishing over at Snow Park."

Ellen and Lizzie jumped out of the car, slamming the doors behind them, and ran up the porch steps. Rachel swung the car in a circle and turned back up the hill, crossing Bay Avenue and going on to her father's house. Nick's jeep was not parked at the side of the road. He was probably out at Gooseneck Cove. She knew Brock's routine, when he went fishing in the afternoon. He would be back in another hour or so. She could wait.

Rachel parked at the side of the road and let herself into the unlocked house. The close air inside smelled of cigarettes and coffee. Her father and Eddie must have come home for lunch. They were working again, now that the weather had changed, repairing a dock at a summer place past Miss Weeden's house. Rachel went to the bedroom and stood a moment in front of the closet, looking down at the box, where the first of the diaries still sat on top of the folded blanket. Her father would not move it and neither would she. They had continued to play this strange, silent cat-and-mouse game with the notebooks all winter, neither of them giving any sign that they were aware of the existence of the original notebook perched atop the blanket, nor any sign that there might be others hidden beneath.

There had been few chances over the winter to be alone in the house or to take one of the notebooks over to her own place. Nate was around most of the time in the colder weather, spending days going back and forth from the house to the store, drinking coffee and trading whatever news could be found with Mrs. Daggett, the two of them seated by the stove and no doubt driving Alice crazy. He tinkered with a variety of cars, trying to get some of the old, abandoned ones down in the parking lot started again, but this was work that kept him close to home. Rachel could not be certain she would be alone for any length of time when she stopped by after school. She had managed to read one more volume of the diary in bits and pieces. Her mother wrote about the work after the hurricane and how Nate stayed busy all the next summer and fall. Father Slade continued to write. She found his letters between the pages of the notebook, the plain paper deeply creased, as if the letters had been folded and unfolded many times. Then came the winter of 1940, when work was again scarce, and Nate disappeared on two occasions, going to the mainland and staying for two and three days, coming home with no money and his eyes rimmed in red. That notebook ended in the spring of 1940 and the next notebook, which she had glanced at without yet reading, took up in 1942. The diaries were full of such gaps. Rachel could guess only that there were notebooks that had been destroyed, or that her mother had abruptly stopped writing and then started again.

Now there were only two slim diaries left, small notebooks, not the larger ones she had used before. Rachel had put off reading these. In one part of herself, she was afraid to discover what they might contain, and in another, she wanted to make the experience of reading the diaries last as long as possible, for once she reached the last page, there would be nothing left that her mother could tell her. She hesitated a moment longer and reached beneath the blanket.

Chapter Twenty-seven

January 8, 1942

How completely a single day—the attack on Pearl Harbor—has changed our lives. It's like the hurricane. Overnight our world has been entirely altered. It seems as I get older, I should adjust to the fact of change, but just the opposite is true. I find myself more surprised by turns of event now than when I was younger. I have an unnatural expectation that my life is finally going to stop changing, that I will reach a point where I know how things are going to be. This doesn't happen, of course. The lighthouse is blacked out, and we must put thick curtains over the windows at night. There are shortages of everything—gas, sugar, coffee, rubber. We are reminded of war in a million different ways every day. The Navy is building a base at the south end of the island. John Brovelli has enlisted. Nate says he will sign up next month. I am frightened of what this will mean for all of us, but I am proud.

January 20, 1942

Nate has decided to enlist in the Army. He does not have to enlist. They are not drafting fathers with children, but he says he can't stay here when so many others are serving their country. He will have a few months of training, maybe somewhere on the East Coast, and then who knows? He could be sent to Africa, England, the Pacific. I am praying for strength and courage, and for peace. The world seems to have gone mad, but we have no choice but to do everything we can to stop Hitler and the Japanese. Phil and Junior and Rachel understand that their father is doing the right thing. He's a hero, like countless other men who never expected to be heroes.

February 12, 1942
A strange, dark day. I don't know what I expected, but it was not what I imagined, watching Nate go off on the ferry. It all happened so quickly. He was busy packing and closing up the shop until late last night, and then this morning we barely had time for breakfast before we saw the ferry out on the water, heading for the island. I kept the children home from school to see him off. We all ran down the hill and got there just as the ferry tied up at the dock. There were only a few minutes for good-byes. Once the ferry pulled away, and I watched Nate standing there on the deck, waving to us, I realized he was really leaving. I don't think I quite believed it before that. Rachel cried, and the boys stood there stoically, waving back. Tonight Junior kept asking when Daddy would come home. What can I say? We have no choice but to tell the children that we don't know these days, that everything in the world is uncertain. The three of them were quiet at supper. We all felt the change without Nate there to tell jokes and prod Junior into eating something. They have never been separated from their father. Nate and I have never been separated, either, except for when I went to the mainland to give birth. Yes, of course, there have been times when I wished for this. If only I could leave, I thought, or if Nate would simply go and let us live our lives without him, in peace. But now it has come, this separation is not what I imagined. I am overwhelmed at the thought of being here alone with the children. I pray throughout the day, asking the Blessed Virgin

to watch over us. I know what I feel is no different from what thousands of women are feeling all over the country. We have become a country of women, left alone.

February 23, 1942

Thank God the children are in school. It's the only way I can get anything done. Everything seems to take longer these days—washing, cooking, cleaning up. I laugh when I remember how I imagined my life on the island when I married Nate. I saw myself like some missionary going off to Africa. I was going to bring culture and ideas to the natives. Now I have learned—life consists of doing the dishes over and over, of scrubbing the children's dungarees and hanging them on the line. This is what shapes our days—the same repeated routines. My life is no different from any other woman's. We all have to eat and bathe the children and get them dressed in halfway decent clothes. No letter from Nate yet. The mail is slower than ever getting through.

March 6, 1942

A brief note from Nate. He is at Fort Dix in New Jersey. He says they are in training ten hours a day and fall asleep the minute they hit the pillow at night. He wrote about the other men—a long list of names. His new friends. I can see he likes the other men, even likes the hard work. This is the first letter I have received from him since we met, and he wrote me from the island. It's strange, but writing to him and receiving his letter makes me feel we are those people again—young and knowing nothing, in love, ready to make a new life no matter what the cost. An odd feeling. Most of the time I see that old self, the young woman who came to the island, as a complete stranger. Then suddenly I know her again, can even imagine repeating the choices she made.

April 10, 1942

I have so little time for anything these days, but I must write the news that I am pregnant. Another child. I prayed that this would not happen, but now I am almost glad. It seems like a sign that life will go on, after this terrible war. So far the nausea isn't bad, and I am not too tired. I am hoping I can get through this pregnancy more easily. Maybe I can get Mrs. Cunningham to care for the children when my time comes, and I have to go to the mainland. I lie in bed at night imagining this new child and wishing I could tell Nate.

April 21, 1942

Another letter from Nate. He says he misses us, but he sounds positively happy. He had not received my letter yet, telling him I am pregnant. It's funny to have our letters keep overlapping in the mail. It doesn't quite feel like we are writing to each other. The Americans bombed Tokyo over the weekend—16 planes made the long trip and dropped their bombs without being hit. It's the first good news we've had and makes us all feel that maybe there is some hope.

May 10, 1942

I took the children over to Barton yesterday to the doctor. Captain Tony is running two ferries on Saturday again, so we were able to go over and back the same day. I was worried about Junior, with his earaches all winter, but the doctor says he will probably outgrow them. The doctor confirmed that I am pregnant—no surprise. The baby should come in October. I told Rachel on the way home on the ferry. She was so excited at the thought of having a baby sister. Of course, I would like another girl, though I know it is God's will, not mine.

May 14, 1942

Today Ethan Cunningham left. He is enlisting in the Signal Corps. Mrs. Cunningham's daughter has come to stay with her and to watch over the lighthouse. I feel for Mrs. Cunningham, having her son leave when she has barely gotten over the death of her husband. I still can't believe Mr. Cunningham is gone, though it's been more than a year. I keep expecting to see him on the path to the lighthouse when I go by. He always had a kind word for everyone, and he was so patient with Mrs. Cunningham. She is such a strong woman. She never let on what a shock it must have been, to find him dead on the floor of the kitchen with no warning, but I can see how much she misses him. I wonder if marriages like theirs are as rare as they seem.

June 2, 1942

Finally an answer from Nate. He was in transit, from Fort Dix to Fort Benning in Georgia. Soon he will get his orders and ship out. He writes he is happy to hear about the baby coming and hopes I can manage on my own. I guess I can manage, as I am day after day, but sometimes I don't know how. We are better equipped to deal with the shortages here on the island since we have always had to make do, but that's not much consolation when dinner consists of rice and the first lettuce from the garden. The boys have been going out clamming after school if the tide is low in the afternoon. I rely on them more and more. The truth is I would be happy not to eat another clam for the rest of my life, but when it's the only food you have, you eat them. Nate's paycheck should arrive soon. Then I can use more of the ration stamps and get some canned food at least.

June 15, 1942

A long letter from Father Slade today. This is the first I have heard from him since Christmas. It's strange to sit in bed and read his letter, without

worrying that Nate will see me. I am certain that Nate does not know
Father Slade and I write to each other. I have always gone down to the
store for the mail, and that dizzy Evelyn Daggett has not figured out who
writes me from Chicago as far as I can tell. He does not put his name on
the envelope, just the return address. Is this terribly wrong, to go on writing to Father Slade when Nate does not know? I have asked myself this
question a million times. I keep coming up with the same answer—how
can something that feels so right be wrong? If I love Father Slade—and
surely what I feel for him is love—it is only natural. He is like the other
half of myself. From the start, we knew each other in this way, as if we
were already linked by some deep understanding. We did not make this
understanding happen—it was already there. A friendship of this sort
happens once in a lifetime, if you're lucky. I cannot deny something so
essential and true. People have so few ways to talk about or imagine love.
There's the love between man and wife, parents and children, brothers
and sisters. Anything else falls outside what we define as love. So what
do you call what I feel for Father Slade and I feel certain, dare I say it, he
feels for me? This is not the love of a man and woman, and yet we are a
man and a woman, connected in some way we cannot explain. Still, I
cannot bring myself to call him "Daniel" or to address my letters to him
by his first name, though he has been signing his letters this way since
last year.

Dear Phoebe,

My thoughts are with you more than ever at this difficult
time. I am proud to know that Nate has enlisted, but of course I
wonder how you are doing by yourself. I will certainly keep Nate
in my prayers. Prayer seems to be a full-time job these days. I
have to admit that I can't bring myself to read the newspapers
every day. So much suffering and bloodshed—we can't begin to

understand it. Greed and hatred and power-hungry men started this war, like every other war. We human beings should learn to stop hating and killing each other, but we don't. Still, I pray that the world will come out of this a better place. Without such hope, I don't think I could go on. I do believe that good ultimately overcomes evil and that Christ did not die for us in vain. Perhaps one day people will look back at this dark time in history and see it as a turning point, truly the war to end all wars, as our parents said of the Great War. I hope you are managing with the food shortages and everything else we now take for granted as simply the way life is. I imagine on the island and all along the coast people are quite nervous. I have heard reports of German submarines right offshore. I trust you feel safe enough, and as always, I am praying for you. Forgive the brevity of this letter. There is so much more to say, but I wanted to get this off before another week passed without your hearing from me, especially as the mails are not particularly reliable, as I'm sure you know. Do give my best to your children and blessings on everyone on Snow.

> With warmest affection, in Christ's love,
> Daniel

June 20, 1942

The children are out of school. How different it is to be just us, without Nate here. A sort of lightness has come over the house. I am not watching for him all the time, waiting to see what his mood is today. It is a relief to be alone. I was terribly frightened that I would simply not be able to manage without Nate, but despite the fear that hangs over everyone these days, the children seem to be thriving. They go off clamming whenever the tides are right now that school is out, and Rachel is helping at the lookout tower. She is so proud to be supporting the war effort, as she calls it. Even Junior, young as he is, goes around collecting newspapers and tin cans and reminding us all to pull the blackout curtains. It is moving to see how seriously they take these things, but still it feels like we are having summer. We sit on the porch after supper and count the boats out in the bay. I play the piano while they fall asleep. Rachel says she can't go to sleep without music. When she says things like this, I know she is my daughter.

June 28, 1942
Father Frater came over to say Mass today. He rushes through Mass in a monotone and preaches the most boring sermons. Afterwards, when we all file out, he barely seems to remember us from one Sunday to the next. I wonder if he's going senile. I know that the quality of the priest should make no difference. It's the holy sacrifice of the Mass that matters. But the priest does make a difference. I keep thinking of Father Slade. I can see him there at the altar, elevating the host. There was a purity to how he conducted Mass. You felt the strength of his belief in every word. When I was younger, I could not have understood this, that there are differences in the depth of people's faith and how they express it. But why is this? It seems terribly unfair. Shouldn't God give every priest the gift of strong faith and strong preaching? Priests are human beings like the rest of us, I guess. Certainly Father Slade has reminded me of this more than once, when he has spoken of his own shortcomings, though I don't see them.

July 13, 1942
This week we learned that the Giberson twins are leaving. Pete is enlisting in the Navy, and Lydia is joining the Red Cross. Their parents will be left alone to run the inn, though they won't have much business this year

with none of the summer people coming over. The island is almost as deserted as it is in winter. In a way, I like it. For once, the island feels like ours in the summer. I take the children to the beach by the lighthouse, and there is no one there. They run around like wild animals, screaming and kicking sand to their heart's content. Those of us left here feel a sort of freedom. None of the usual rules apply in this time of war. But of course I'd take the summer people back in a minute if it meant the war was over. No sign of this happening, however.

July 17, 1942

I went down to the store at ferry time this afternoon. The children were with me, running ahead on the path. Another hot, clear day. The weather has been dazzling. We go swimming every day, and in the evening Rachel helps me in the garden. We will have a great crop of tomatoes this year. It is hard to believe, with the news from overseas, that we are having such a lovely summer. I feel almost guilty as I walk along the shore and watch the children splashing each other. I was thinking of Father Slade as I took the path to the store today. I will go entire days without thinking of him, and then suddenly he is there again. I am overwhelmed by a sense of him, as if he is standing beside me. Is it possible to communicate with someone across such distance, without words? The idea is frightening, but when I suddenly feel connected to him again, I can't help but wonder if he is thinking of me at that moment, perhaps even speaking to me in his mind the way I speak to him. When I entered the store, Alice was busy sorting through the mail. "There's a letter for you," she said. I assumed it must be from Nate, but when she put the envelope in my hand, I saw that it was from Chicago. I did not expect to hear from Father Slade again so soon. How did I know, as I went down to the store? Why did I think of him just then? Mysteries.

Dear Phoebe,

It has been over ninety degrees for a week here—the worst sort of heat wave. You can imagine what it is like to teach in these conditions. My students are not the best, either, boys who have failed English and must do extra work. When I think I cannot endure another minute in my stuffy classroom with all those boys staring back at me, I run the Chopin Scherzo in my mind. I found a recording of it, but I can still hear it as you played it that night at Our Lady of Snow. That was the last time I heard you play the piano. I guess that it is a long time ago now, but the music remains vivid to me. I trust you have heard from Nate by now and I pray that all is well. You must be strong, for his sake and for the children. I know you are busy with the children out from school, but write when you can. I can smell the salt air when I open your envelopes!

In Christ's love,

Daniel

July 18, 1942

It is after midnight, but I am still awake, sitting out on the porch. I can hear the children inside, stirring in their sleep. Fr. Slade does not know that I am pregnant. It did not seem right to tell him such news, before the baby is born. Am I crazy, or is it possible that in some way we are still listening to that piano music together? Tonight, sitting here in the warm air, with the moon making a track across the water, it seems not only possible but undeniable.

August 10, 1942

I feel the baby kicking more often now. She seems real to me at last. I am calling her "she" out of my foolish hope for a girl. When I play the piano at night, the baby settles down. How incredible it is to think that this little being inside me can hear the music. I play lullabies, the softest and quietest pieces I know. With Nate gone, this child feels like mine alone. Is this a terrible thought? I love the idea that I will get to know her by myself, that we will have so many quiet hours together while the children are at school. I will be able to devote myself to the baby without Nate to worry about and cook for. I guess these are terrible thoughts, but I can't stop them. The house feels suddenly so open, full of the summer air. I feel the same way, as though someone had washed me inside and out. Perhaps this is God's way of making me ready to be a mother again. All these years I resisted the idea of another child, and now it fills me with happiness. We don't know what we really want and need.

September 16, 1942
I am big as a house. It doesn't seem possible that this baby won't come for another month. Everything drives me to distraction—the children, the laundry, the smell of fish. I seem to be constantly reminding myself to stop snapping at the children, to stop feeling so sorry for myself, to stop cursing the war and Nate and this stupid island. I don't know how I am getting through the days. In two weeks I will go to the mainland and leave the children with Mrs. Cunningham and her daughter. I am looking forward to it like some prisoner being let out of jail. This is awful, I know. I should be worried about leaving the children, but all I want to do is escape them and this huge, bloated body of mine. I don't know why God has let me become a mother again. I am so clearly not fit for it.

October 3, 1942
I cried like an idiot when I said goodbye to the children and got on the ferry yesterday. Mrs. Cunningham kept reassuring me, but I felt an overwhelming despair, like I was leaving them forever. And how can I ask so

much of her? It is a terrible imposition, but the only other choice was Mrs. Brovelli, and she has her hands full with her own grandchildren and Donna in the house, with John gone. Mrs. Cunningham and her daughter, Martha, kept telling me not to worry, but of course I have done nothing else since I arrived. I spent all morning walking up and down Front Street. I figure if I keep walking as much as possible, maybe I will go into labor. I cannot wait another day for this baby to be born.

October 16, 1942

Andrew Hartwell Shattuck, born October 12, 1942, six pounds, two ounces.

November 12, 1942

I have not written here because I could not bear to put it down. A part of me has been living this past month in a dream, just hoping I will wake to find I have imagined it. Sometimes I wonder about my sanity. Entire days pass, and I feel nothing. I do not know if it is morning or afternoon. If the children didn't return from school, I would forget to make supper. And there he is, always, crying and squawking, his poor eyes staring at me. I did not see it when they put him in my arms at the hospital. I saw what I wanted to see—a normal baby. But when the doctor came to my room the next day, I knew something was wrong. He was so nervous. He kept glancing out the window and clearing his throat. So I said it for him. There's something wrong, isn't there? He nodded. He told me that Andy is a mongoloid. I saw it then—the flat nose and small features, as if the face had been squashed. His eyes are so vacant. They are not like the eyes of my other babies. I can hardly bring myself to look at him. It's cruel and heartless, but I recoil from him. He makes me too sad. It's all I can do to pick him up and change his diaper. I know that I love him, but I cannot feel this love. All I feel is fear and despair and a sickening shame. I have written to Nate that Andy was born, but I have not told him anything else. How can I, when Nate is off fighting God knows where? He doesn't need such news when he is so far from home.

December 3, 1942

I do not know when I have ever been so tired. I seem to spend all day trying to get the baby to feed. He cannot hang on to the nipple. His breathing is so labored. When he is finally able to suck for a minute, I'm afraid he's going to suffocate. He jerks away, gasping for breath. I try to clear his nose, but it doesn't seem to help. I go from one terror to another all day long. He cries a thin, feeble cry which is worse than if he screamed. I long to hear him bellow, to cry the way other babies cry. He does sleep at night, for much longer than the others did. This is a relief, but then I wake suddenly, my breasts spurting milk, and jump out of bed, terrified again.

December 7, 1942

Rachel came home from school today and asked me if Andy is retarded. I have said nothing to her or the boys because I did not know what to tell them or how. I had to tell her the truth, of course. Everyone on the island must know by now, though I hardly ever go out and don't take Andy with me if I can help it. I won't have people gawking at him or saying stupid things that are meant to be kind but only make me feel worse. I don't know what I have done to deserve a child like this. Or I do—I do know what I have done—and that makes it even harder. I have cursed the life God has given me when I should have been on my knees giving thanks. But I am haunted by other thoughts, too. Was it something I did while I was pregnant that made him turn out this way? Did I work too hard and not eat enough? Of course, I did work too hard, and we didn't have enough to eat, but how did these things affect the baby? I keep turning it over in my mind. I wake in the middle of the night and torture myself.

Was there something I could have done differently? The doctor said no, it was nothing I did or didn't do. These things just happen, he said. It's not your fault or anyone's fault. He might have been talking about the hurricane. There was something so cold about it, though I understood he was trying to reassure me. But his words had just the opposite effect. For I know that such things don't just happen. I can't shake the fear that this is God's way of speaking to me. Is He punishing me? Certainly Andy feels like a punishment, though I hate myself for writing this.

December 15, 1942
Mrs. Cunningham and her daughter came to visit today. She is so kind. She sat on the sofa and insisted I put Andy in her arms. She held him just like he was a normal baby. She said I must be strong, for the other children. We all have crosses to bear. Of course when I look at her walking with her crutches, I realize I am an idiot for feeling so sorry for myself, but this doesn't change the fact that I am exhausted and overwhelmed and constantly worried that my baby is starving. There are moments when I have wished that he would die. I should be killed myself for this, but what is the point of struggling so hard for a baby who will never be able to enjoy life, to experience the things the rest of us do? I know I should feel it's worth it—he's a living being, even if he is impaired—but sometimes I cannot find it in me.

December 18, 1942
If the ferry were not running so erratically with the bad weather, I would take the baby over to the doctor. Every day it's the same—an endless struggle to get him to eat. I have tried a bottle, but it's no better. This morning I sat on the couch and sobbed, the tears running all over my naked breasts. I have to stop myself from shaking him and screaming at him that he must learn to eat. Poor thing. It's not his fault. Thank God

the children were at school and did not see me sitting there. The doctor told me to write to him if I could not get over to the mainland. I sent a letter today, asking him what to do about feeding Andy. We don't have a scale, so I can't tell if he has gained any weight, but he looks so pitifully small and feels like nothing in my arms.

December 26, 1942
Mrs. Cunningham invited us to her house for Christmas. I could not think what the day would be like and was so relieved. I brought some blueberry preserves, and she made wonderful biscuits and chowder and served her pickles. She had saved her sugar to make gingerman cookies. The children were so excited. It actually felt like Christmas. I forgot about Andy for a little while. He lay in his basket and slept. He could have been any baby. As strange as everything in life is now, this day felt somehow like an ordinary Christmas, even though there was nothing ordinary about it.

January 5, 1943
I received an answer from the doctor yesterday. He said it is normal for mongoloids to weigh less, and Andy is probably getting enough milk even if he has difficulty feeding. He said it is important not to get anxious about feeding him, as the baby will sense this, and it will only make things worse. How am I supposed to do this? I am a wreck every time I hear him cry. I dread sitting down on the sofa with him. I have been trying to fool myself and the baby into believing this is not the case—we're just sitting there together and if he happens to feed a bit, that's fine, and if he doesn't, that's fine, too. But of course this is nonsense. The doctor says I should bring Andy over as soon as the ferry is running regularly again. Another hurdle—how to get all of us on the ferry, and then we will probably have to spend the night in Barton. Perhaps Mrs. Cunningham will watch the

children for me. I never imagined I would miss Nate as much as I do now. I dream about seeing him walk through the door.

January 19, 1943

This morning as I was trying to feed Andy, I fell asleep. I only slept for a few minutes, but when I woke up, he was sucking away, staring at me with his creased eyes. He actually looked happy. I was so relieved, I hardly dared to breathe. He slept more peacefully, most of the afternoon. I got down on my knees and thanked the Blessed Virgin. I know that she is here with me, every minute of every day, but so often I lose a sense of her presence. I forget to pray. I am just too tired, but I must do better. This morning was a lesson.

January 22, 1943

A letter from Father Slade. I wrote to him some weeks ago to tell him about Andy. His words mean so much, but I still feel like I'm crazy. I can't get hold of myself. I fantasize about getting on the ferry and never returning.

> Dear Phoebe,
>
> How sad I was to get your news. I can only imagine how difficult this time must be for you. I understand that this is a burden you did not expect, but I am sure that in time you will discover what this child has to give you and why he has come into your life. I think this is one of the hardest things for us humans to understand—why we are given things to bear that it doesn't seem possible we can bear. But I truly believe that God does not dole out anything in this life that we cannot handle, if we turn to Him for help. He does not forsake us, even in the darkest hours.
>
> I am sure it is not easy for you, having Nate gone and the other children to take care of by yourself. We are all asked to shoulder a

great deal these days, but you are being asked to shoulder even more. I include you in my prayers every morning. I will pray for your baby, too, now. May he be a blessing.

In Christ's love,
Daniel

March 6, 1943

I took the children to Barton to the doctor yesterday. He was not too concerned about Andy's weight. After he had examined all four children, he said he wanted to speak with me alone. I sent Rachel and the boys out to the waiting room. The doctor said that when the time comes, he will help me make arrangements to send Andy to the state school in Providence. He wanted me to know that there is somewhere we can send Andy, where he will get the care he needs. I didn't respond, because I hadn't thought that far in the future. The doctor seemed to sense what I was thinking. "You have other children," he said. "You can't spend everything on this child." I left the doctor's office feeling confused and relieved. It had not occurred to me that we would, or could, make such arrangements for Andy, and the idea was like a sudden bit of hope. We spent the night at Mrs. Worthington's, all of us bunked together in her small back room. She gave me such a pitying look when I unwrapped Andy and began to feed him that I wanted to scream. He's not a monster, but that's all people see. They look at his contorted face, at his slanted eyes and tongue hanging out, and they are revolted. It was the same way with the nurse at the doctor's office. I just want to hide him away where no one can look at him like that.

Rachel and the boys were very well behaved, especially at Mrs. Worthington's. It did them good to leave the island. They ran up and down Front Street with such abandon. I try to remember when something like a piece of stick candy or a comic book could make me so happy.

Yes, I bought the children these things, though I had no business doing so. But we should have money from Nate soon.

March 10, 1943

I am haunted by the idea of the state school. The doctor is right—I can't take care of Andy and keep up with everything else. I try to imagine what it will be like to have a toddler who can't be taught or made to understand the most simple things. And what about as he grows older? What will I do with him, all day here in the house? The thought of it fills me with so much despair I want to simply curl up in bed and stay there. It is fitting that I, who am such a poor mother and have never loved babies especially, have given birth to a child who will always be more or less a baby. I cannot bear the idea of being trapped here in the house with Andy. The doctor says it would be best to wait a few years, until he has grown a bit. Then the transition is easier. For his sake and for ours, I believe it is the best thing.

March 18, 1943

I still have not written to Nate. I cannot bring myself to do it. I know he has a right to know about Andy, but now does not seem to be the time. I fear what it will do to him, to receive such news so far from home. I've just had one letter from Nate since the middle of February. I cannot tell where he is or what is happening to him from what he writes. The censors don't allow anything to get through. National security—it's become an obsession, even here on Snow. Mr. Brovelli is always going around at night screaming at people to turn out their lights. He makes us feel that we don't take the war seriously and are completely unpatriotic. We're all making sacrifices. It shouldn't be a contest, but that's what he turns it into. All the time I am wondering where in the world Nate is and how he will react when he learns he has a mongoloid son.

April 21, 1943

It is warmer at last. I thought spring would never come. I can set Andy in a basket and bring him outside with me while I hang the clothes on the line or work in the garden. I do not feel so hemmed in. Every year I forget that the coming of spring and the longer days does make a difference. I become convinced that I will remain locked in the despair of winter forever. And then one morning everything looks different. Well, not exactly everything. We are still at war, and so many things are harder and harder to come by. Evelyn Daggett says she is sick of telling people she's out of everything they want at the store. How any of us survive is a miracle. Somehow I keep getting up in the morning and changing Andy's diapers and putting food on the table, though there are times when I feel like a sleepwalker moving through the day and wonder who this strange woman is inhabiting my body. Maybe this happens to everyone as you get older. You don't recognize yourself anymore. Or is it just me and my constant discontent? It seems I have always wanted to be someone other than who I am.

Chapter Twenty-eight

Rachel sat on the sofa with the notebook in her hand, staring blankly out the window. She was not surprised to learn that her mother had been conflicted in her feelings about Andy, though Rachel could not have imagined the depths of this conflict, but she was surprised to discover it was the doctor who suggested sending him to the state school. She had never heard mention of this.

Going to the bedroom, she set the notebook back in the box, under the blanket. She imagined she could see her mother standing at the sink, a dishcloth in her hand. After Andy was gone, she would find her mother like that often, gazing out the window as if she had forgotten what she was doing. There was no discussion of what had happened or why. When Rachel mentioned Andy in the weeks after he went away, her father would glare at her and say, "Let's not talk about it." Somehow, from the scraps of information she was able to assemble, she had formed the clear impression that her father insisted Andy go to the state school. No one explained that the doctor or the authorities in Barton might have played a role.

She was roused from her thoughts by the sound of a vehicle climbing the hill. The delivery truck from the store pulled up outside Alice's house. Brock stepped from the cab, went around to the back, and lifted a bucket and fishing rod from the flatbed. Rachel pulled on her jacket.

Brock whistled as he carried the bucket across the muddy expanse of lawn. When he reached the side of the house, he set the bucket on the ground and raised a square of wood fixed to the shingles with a hinge, creating a level surface on which he could work. By the time Rachel had come down the road and crossed the lawn, he had taken a fish from the bucket and was slitting it open with a knife.

"Miss Shattuck," he called when he spotted her. "Not a bad day after all, huh? I thought we were in for more rain the way the sky looked last night. You want one of these striped bass for supper? They've just started running over there on the west side, the little ones."

Rachel peered into the bucket. "Sure."

"I'll give you a couple for your father, too."

Brock cut the fish down one side and then the other, and scooped out the guts, exposing the white flesh. Rachel watched as he peeled the skin from the body of the fish. For a moment, she had no desire to raise the question about Nick and the test. She breathed in the pungent scent of the fish and watched him work. Inside the house, she could hear the muffled sound of voices. Nick had not returned. It was the girls she could hear on the other side of the wall, talking with their grandmother.

"You ever go fishing?" Brock asked.

"I used to go with my brother and Eddie, when I was a girl."

"There's nothing better on a day like today."

Rachel nodded. "I heard that Nick got his draft notice."

Brock wiped the blade of the knife on his blue jeans and reached for another fish in the bucket. "Yeah, it came in the mail."

"He could still take the entrance test for the university. He could still get a deferment."

He looked up, the fish grasped in his hand, pausing for a moment before inserting the knife. "Nick seems to have made up his mind. If he's drafted, he's going."

"I know. He told me that. I just thought maybe if you talked with him he'd consider taking the test. I'm going to the mainland on Saturday. I could go with him and make the arrangements. They can give him the test at the high school."

Brock sliced the fish without answering. He removed the skin and set the fillet to the side.

"He'll listen to you, Brock."

He reached into the bucket for another fish and slapped it down on the slimy board. "It might be good for him, being in the military. It might give him some direction."

"Sure, but he could get that in college, too."

"Look, I don't want to see him get sent off any more than you do or Alice. I'm just trying to help him figure what's right."

"Could you just see if he'll consider it?"

Brock set the fillet in the pile with the others. "Okay, I'll talk to him."

"Thanks," Rachel said, the relief so complete she could not find any other words.

She was about to turn away when Brock reminded her of the offer of the fish. He wrapped the fillets in a piece of newspaper he took from his tackle box and handed it to her.

"You've done a lot for Nick this year," he said. "Alice and I appreciate it."

She could feel the heat rise from her neck and over her face. She was aware only of what she had not done, trying to keep her distance. "Maybe, but he won't listen to me about this."

"He's like his father—stubborn." Brock nodded. "I know. I'll see what I can do."

Rachel turned and went up the hill, just as Eddie's truck turned off Bay Avenue. They met in front of the house.

"Look at that, Eddie," Nate said as he swung down from the cab.

"Our cook is here. What's for supper?"

"Brock gave me some fish," Rachel answered.

Nate made a clucking sound with his tongue. "It's that time of year already, huh?"

"I don't see either of you two out fishing." Rachel rolled her eyes and climbed the porch steps. The men followed her inside.

"I guess you heard Nick got his draft notice," Nate said. "Alice was looking pretty bad this afternoon." He sat down and kicked off his boots.

"I was over there asking Brock if he could convince Nick to take the entrance exam for the university this weekend. He said he'd talk to him."

Eddie set a six-pack of Narragansetts on the table and glanced at Rachel. "Maybe Nick wants to serve."

"Tell me you want to see him go to Vietnam."

"Jesus, Rachel, I don't want to see anybody go to Vietnam, but it's not up to me." Eddie removed his jacket and slung it over the back of a chair. "What're you becoming, one of those peace nuts, like that lunatic who burned himself at the Pentagon?"

"I'm not a peace nut. For God's sake, Eddie. It's just that Nick doesn't have to go. He can get into college."

Rachel shot Eddie an angry look. He gave her a knowing smile and asked, "Want a beer?"

He opened three bottles and handed them around. The cold liquid went down Rachel's throat, the taste a combination of bitter and sweet. She wanted it to wash away everything—the words in her mother's diary, the thought of Nick going off to Vietnam, her tenuous grasp on her own feelings.

Leaning back in the chair, Nate opened the newspaper. Rachel thought she caught a whiff of his smelly socks all the way across the room. She took a can of green beans from the cupboard and unwrapped the fish.

"Nick ain't the only one getting drafted," Nate said. "That rookie catcher for the Red Sox just got his notice. They're down to two catchers."

"You think it'll make any difference?" Eddie asked.

"They finally won a game down there in Florida."

"Yeah, but we're stuck with that idiot manager Martin again."

Rachel opened the can and emptied the contents into a pot on the stove, listening to them go on about the Sox and their chances this year, wondering what it would take for human beings to stop sending young men off to fight battles they understood dimly, if they understood them at all.

Chapter Twenty-nine

The day was clear and still, the sky dotted with puffy clouds. Rachel took the path to the dock. In the distance, the ferry inched toward the island. Joe Brovelli leaned against the hood of the police cruiser, and George Tibbits sat on the porch at the store. These were the only signs of life, other than a seagull perched on top of the streetlight.

Rachel exchanged greetings with George and entered the store. Alice raised her eyes from the newspaper spread across the counter. She gestured toward the headlines as Rachel approached. "I shouldn't read this stuff. It only gets me upset."

Rachel nodded.

"Brock's up at the house with Nick. He's trying to convince him to go over with you."

"Nick doesn't want to go?"

"I'm not sure. I'm trying to stay out of it. As of last night, Nick was saying that he'd make up his mind in the morning. I think he wants to get drafted. I think he wants to go to Vietnam. That's what scares me." Alice folded the newspaper and set it beneath the counter. "You want some coffee?"

Rachel said yes to the coffee and watched as Alice tiredly reached for the pot. She pushed the coffee across the counter, took the coins Rachel handed her, and dropped them in the cash drawer. Rachel was pouring milk into the cup when Nick stepped through the door. He glanced at her and circled the counter.

"The ferry's here," he told his mother. "I'll man the cash register."

"You don't have to do that," Alice responded.

"It's okay. You can go help Dad check in the deliveries."

Alice moved reluctantly toward the door. Rachel remained by the counter, stirring her coffee, uncertain whether to follow Alice or to stay. When Alice had left, she turned toward Nick.

"I'm not going to take the test," he said.

"I'm sorry to hear that."

"Yeah, you're so sorry, you won't even look at me."

There was anger in his voice and hurt. Rachel had convinced herself that his feelings for her were nothing more than a schoolboy crush. This might be the truth, but it did not make them less real. If they had known each other in another time and place, she might have been able to ignore the difference in their ages, to consider crossing that line, but there was no question of it here or now.

Outside the ferry's horn sounded one long blast.

"I *am* sorry that you're not going, Nick. I was hoping you would."

"It's not your life."

She shook her head. "No, it's not."

She went to the door, then turned back. She wanted to tell him that she cared about him a great deal, but even those words felt risky. Instead she returned his look, trying to say in this speechless form that she had not meant to hurt or reject him. Mumbling an inadequate goodbye, she stepped outside.

Brock carried a box down the gangplank while Alice consulted the list Captain Guido held in his hand. George remained on the bench, holding his hat by the brim.

"Looks like spring, doesn't it?" he said.

"Yes, at last. I'm going to the mainland. Do you need anything?"

George tipped his head back, glancing at the sky, as if the answer to her question might be found there. "I ordered all my vegetable seeds by mail, and Alice gets me whatever I need at the store. I can't think of anything."

Rachel smiled, in spite of herself, at the simplicity of his response. That was true happiness, she thought, to want as little as George Tibbits wanted.

When Brock had finished unloading the deliveries for the store, Captain Guido waved his arm, motioning to anyone planning to come aboard. Rachel said goodbye to George and crossed the parking lot. Brock and Alice regarded her gravely.

"Have a good trip," Alice said as Rachel headed toward the gangplank.

Brock raised his hand in a wave but said nothing. Rachel climbed the gangplank, paid Guido, and went to sit on the bench. Guido remained by the railing, gazing down at the crowd, then hauled up the gangplank with Keith. As the ferry pulled away from the dock, Rachel kept her eyes on the store, thinking that Nick might at least step out onto to the porch.

The ferry inched into the channel. George Tibbits watched it go, nodding in the general direction of the boat before turning and climbing the path to the road. The people gathered by the dock grew smaller, until they were mere shapes, and then disappeared entirely. Reaching into her canvas bag, Rachel took out quilt pieces and her needle. Nick could still change his mind and go ahead with the application, she told herself, or maybe he would fail his Army physical. She squeezed her eyes shut and mumbled two Hail Marys.

The sun spilled over the deck, saturating everything with its warmth.

She sewed with a steady concentration, feeling the sun on top of her head, until the ferry was close to land, and she went to the railing, looking out over the rooftops of Barton. Keith held one of the thick lines of rope curled on the deck. When Guido eased the ferry out of the channel and pulled it in beside the dock, Keith tossed the rope to the man who ran the ferry office. Guido cut off the engine as the man secured first one line and then another to the pilings. A moment later, Guido emerged from the wheelhouse to help Keith lower the gangplank.

"See you this afternoon," Rachel said to the men as she made her way down the gangplank.

She checked her watch as she went up Church Street toward town. Babs was standing outside Metzger's in a lime green coat. She waved her hand excitedly as Rachel approached.

"It's beautiful," Rachel said, examining the ring she held out. "Just beautiful."

Babs grinned. "I told you. He went all the way to Boston to get it. He said there was no place good enough in Providence. My mother says no girl in our family ever had a diamond this nice. And wait 'til you see the dresses. This dress is perfect for you, Rachel. You'll be a knockout."

Babs held the door for Rachel and then followed her into the department store. "Hello, Mr. Metzger," she called out loudly.

Mr. Metzger was with a customer in the men's section. He turned his head and nodded at Babs.

"He's been so helpful," Babs said. "Everybody has. I don't know what I would have done without these people. I don't know the first thing about ordering dresses and renting tuxedos and all that. There's been times when I thought I was going to have to take a leave from work to pull this off by June."

Babs went through the aisles to the women's section. "We've got an appointment," she whispered to Rachel as they approached Mrs. Webb, who was waiting by the dressing rooms.

Mrs. Webb asked them to sit in the chairs by the fitting area and retreated to the back room. She returned holding a dress aloft by its hanger. Wrapped in plastic, the dress ballooned out in front, appearing alarmingly large. With a flourish, Mrs. Webb removed the covering.

"Isn't it divine?" Babs said.

The dress was indeed baby blue, with a tight bodice accentuated by darts extending from under the arm to the breast, and thin little straps that looked unlikely to stay in place. It came in at the waist and fell in a full skirt that gave the dress a classic hourglass shape.

"You'll wear a crinoline underneath, so the skirt stands out," Babs explained. "And we've got to pick out some shoes. I haven't done that yet. My sister had her fitting last week. She looked wonderful, didn't she?"

"Yes. It's a lovely dress, one of our most popular for bridesmaids," Mrs. Webb said.

Mrs. Webb handed the dress to Rachel and ushered her inside the dressing room. Rachel removed her clothes and stepped into the dress, struggling to get it in place. What she noticed first was how stiff the fabric felt. The bodice stood away from her chest as if it were made of cardboard. She tugged at the zipper set into the side of the dress, hoping that this might improve matters, but when she looked in the mirror, she was overcome with dismay. The dress hung on her like a sack, and the spaghetti straps fell limply off her shoulders.

"How's it going in there?" Mrs. Webb called.

"Okay." Rachel remained in the dressing room a moment longer, staring at herself in the mirror. She was too old to be a bridesmaid. She would simply have to tell Babs this.

Opening the door, Rachel stepped onto the carpet in her stocking feet. She tried not to look at the two women, but she could not help catching their expressions of alarm. Mrs. Webb stepped forward quickly, tugging at the skirt and smoothing down the waist. "It's a little big for you, but I don't think we want to go down to a size six. Then the waist will be too tight. We can make some adjustments."

Stepping back, Mrs. Webb pursed her lips and looked Rachel up and down. She took a pin cushion from the table between the chairs and went to work, tugging at the dress from one direction and then the other, asking Rachel to turn back and forth. When she was finished, straight pins were set in lines along the darts and at the waist, and the straps were shortened with safety pins.

"I'll have to help you take this off with all the pins in it," Mrs. Webb said.

She held the door to the dressing room while Rachel squeezed inside, pulling the voluminous material of the skirt behind her. Rachel stood still, arms slack at her side, as Mrs. Webb carefully eased the dress down past her chest and her waist. She had worn her best underwear, but still she felt embarrassed to have Mrs. Webb see her practically naked, with her skinny knees looking like doorknobs.

Mrs. Webb held the dress gingerly by the shortened straps and maneuvered it out of the dressing room. If only, Rachel thought, a bridesmaid could wear a simple cotton skirt and blouse, with a flower in her hair. She got dressed in her old, ordinary clothes and stepped back onto the sales floor. Mrs. Webb had disappeared with the heavily pinned dress.

"I can't face the shoes right now," Babs said. "Let's go eat, okay?"

With a cheery goodbye to Mr. Metzger, Babs strode to the door. "How many people did you have at your wedding?" she asked as they turned up Front Street.

"Fifty or so. It was mostly just our families and the people on the island. It wasn't too fancy."

"We're having a hundred and fifty. I know that sounds insane, but

Howard has such a big family, and there's everyone from school. By the time you invite all the teachers and their husbands, you've got thirty people right there. Then my mother insisted we have to invite everyone on my father's side, which means twenty cousins I haven't seen since I was about five. I told her they never invited us to any of their weddings, so I don't see why I have to include them, but she said she wasn't going to have bad blood over my wedding, and it was everybody or nobody. What can I do? She's driving me crazy enough as it is. I'm not going fight over the damned invitation list. Oh, by the way, Howard's really sorry he's not going to get to meet you. He had to go up to Boston. Some uncle of his is visiting."

They reached Anthony's and went inside, taking a table by the window. Babs did not open the menu when the waitress placed one in front of her.

"Listen, I have to tell you I'm eating nothing but salads for the next three months," Babs said. "Honest to God, I cannot gain a single inch or a single pound if I want to get into that wedding dress. Oh, I forgot to show you the picture of my dress when we were at Metzger's. When we go back to look at the shoes, remind me. Mrs. Webb has got a picture in the wedding book."

The waitress returned with two glasses of water and took their order, a caesar salad for Babs and a grilled cheese sandwich for Rachel. When she delivered their plates, Babs pushed aside the container of salad dressing and reached for her fork. "No dressing, either. It's too fattening."

"You look great," Rachel said. "Really."

"Thanks. So what are you doing next year? Are you staying on that crazy island?"

"I don't know. I guess I'll have to make up my mind by the end of the month."

"You actually like it?"

"I like the one-room schoolhouse. It's completely different. And you don't have to go to staff meetings."

"I could live with that. It's been damned boring without you this year, you know. Laura Hopkins is a real ninny. She takes Principal Reid's side about everything." Babs speared a large piece of lettuce with her fork and brought it to her lips. "And Sheila's no fun anymore. Did I tell you her son was wounded?"

"No."

"He got hit with a grenade or something. He's going to be okay, but his leg is pretty busted up. He's at one of those military hospitals, down in Virginia. They think he's going to be able to walk, but he has to do a lot of physical therapy. He's had a couple of operations. Sheila was down there for a week."

"That's terrible. She was so worried."

"Yeah, well at least he's back and he's alive. That's what she keeps saying. But she's still worried sick."

Rachel tried not to think about Nick. "What are you going to do next year?"

"We've got to pay for that cute little house somehow, so I'm going to keep working, you know, until we have a family. God, Rachel, the last time I saw you I had no idea about any of this. And now look at me— buying a house and ordering bridesmaid dresses." Babs waved her fork in the air. "You never know. Everything can change like that." She snapped her fingers with her free hand.

When they had finished eating, they paid the bill and made their way out of the restaurant to the street.

"Okay, now we tackle shoes," Babs said, linking her arm through Rachel's. "They'll be blue, of course, to match the dress, and I thought satin would be nice. They're not wearing such pointy toes anymore. What do you think? Do you like that more rounded look?"

They walked back toward Metzger's, passing the movie theater and the Priscilla Alden. Rachel glanced through the glass door at the hotel, but the lobby was empty, with no sign of Mrs. Santos. "I don't know. I guess the rounded toe is all right."

"I think there's something clunky about that shape. They remind me of old lady shoes. Well, we'll see what Metzger's has got. You can bet Mrs. Webb will have an opinion. She has opinions about a lot of things when it comes to weddings."

Chapter Thirty

The street by the docks was empty of people or cars. Rachel sat on a bench, watching the shifting movement of the light on the water. Captain Guido had not yet arrived, and the ferry floated by the dock, the white shape of the boat an image of patient stillness. At the sound of footsteps, she turned her head to find Guido and Keith coming toward her. They waved and boarded the ferry, moving over the deck of the boat, checking the position of the lines and picking up stray bits of trash. After a few minutes, Guido climbed the stairs to the wheelhouse.

Head bent over her sewing, Rachel did not notice Guido come down from the wheelhouse or the muted conversation that passed between him and Keith. She did not see the two of them disappear into the cabin and go down below, to the engine compartment. She went on sewing, thinking of herself in that blue dress and satin spiked heels, a nosegay of roses clutched in her hand. For Babs' sake, she would become a replica of a china doll for one day. It was the least she could do.

Rachel checked her watch. Four twenty. It was then that she noticed Guido and Keith huddled together at the foot of the stairs to the wheelhouse. Keith was gesturing impatiently, and Guido looked angry. She had been listening unconsciously for the sound of the ferry's engine starting up, but the area around the dock was silent except for the screeching of gulls. She watched as the men went inside the cabin, slamming the door behind them.

Rachel held the canvas bag in her lap, her sewing put away. After another couple of minutes, Guido emerged from the cabin and came down the gangplank, tugging on the brim of his cap. "Looks like the battery is shot," he said. "I'm going to have to go up to Providence to get a new one."

"Today?" Rachel asked.

"Yeah, I'll call the guy and tell him to wait for me. He'll do that. But we won't be able to make the run 'til tomorrow. I'm sorry. We'll shoot for leaving at the regular time in the morning."

Guido pulled on the brim of his hat again, as if to signal that the conversation was over. Clearly it was no concern of his where she went for the night. Rachel got to her feet.

"Fine," Rachel said, turning away in disgust. "I'll see you in the morning."

"I'm sorry," Guido called weakly after her.

Rachel crossed the parking lot and went up Church Street. Babs would take her in for the night. Howard was not due back until the next day. Certainly Rachel had nothing pressing to do on the island, and it was a relief to put off seeing Nick, but she was annoyed nonetheless. This was not what she had planned.

As she turned onto Front Street, she heard the tolling of the bell in the steeple of Saint Joseph's. She wondered for a moment if the bell was being rung for a funeral, then remembered it was time for the five o'clock Mass. She did not know the priests at Saint Joseph's these days. She could slip into the church and sit in the back without being recognized or questioned. This was what she had always wanted, a church where she could be anonymous, alone with the words of the prayers. Going up the side street past her old apartment building, she saw the women in their spring coats and sensible heels climbing the stone steps of the church. Most of them were older, of her mother's generation. The men at their sides or trailing behind were older, too. They wore gray flannel pants and trench coats that flapped around their knees.

Rachel kept her eyes lowered as she went up the steps. Rummaging in her sewing bag, she found a square of white fabric, which she draped over the top of her head. This would have to do. Inside the church, she dipped her hand in the bowl of holy water by the door, made the sign of the cross, and took a seat in the next to last pew. An elderly woman played a quavering melody on the organ. Rachel dropped to her knees, wondering if God listened to those who prayed only out of expedience or necessity.

She had not attended church since last summer, at Our Lady. It was something of a scandal at first when the Catholics on the island realized that Rachel was no longer one of them. There were awkward moments when Gina Brovelli gave her pained looks, but then Gina seemed to forgive her. Having a decent teacher at the schoolhouse outweighed anything else. Even a lapsed Catholic was acceptable. Rachel sat back in the pew and waited for Mass to begin. She knew that by the definitions of the church, she was no longer a Catholic in good standing, though in her mind, it was not so easy to undo being Catholic. For better or worse, this is what her mother had chosen and how she had been raised, and in a fundamental part of herself, Rachel would always feel that she was a Catholic, whether she ever attended Mass again or not.

The organist started up the opening hymn. Rachel was fumbling with the hymnal in the rack and did not see Father Slade processing in behind the crucifer and altar boy. When she raised her head, she recognized him immediately, before he took his place at the altar, his back to the congregation. How strange it was to hear that voice again, the authoritative yet reassuring tone she remembered. Listening to his voice without looking at his face and the altered contours of his body, it was possible to believe he was still the young priest who had come to the island to serve his first parish, still the man her mother had written of in the diaries. Rachel was so distracted she could hardly follow the Mass, though she knelt at the appropriate times and stood again, holding the missal open in front of her. When the time for communion came, she remained in the pew, thinking of all the questions she would like to ask Father Slade if she could find the words.

During the final hymn, Rachel stared at Father Slade as he passed, processing to the rear of the church, but he glanced at her without making any sign of recognition. She knelt along with the rest of the congregation after the hymn had ended. She remained in this posture while people filed out of the church, chatting about the weather and asking after each other's families. They paused to greet Father Slade, one after another saying, "Good evening, Father." When the voices began dying out, Rachel stood. She waited until the last person had shaken Father Slade's hand and stepped from the pew.

He extended his hand automatically. He still did not know her. "Father Slade," she said. "I'm Rachel Shattuck."

"Rachel," he said, startled. "Yes, of course. I should have recognized you. How nice to see you. You're living in Barton now?"

"No, actually, I'm living on the island this year. They needed a teacher at the schoolhouse."

They went on talking, Father Slade explaining that he was just filling in for the regular priest at Saint Joseph's. Rachel listened to him and ran another conversation in her mind, one in which she told him about her mother's diaries, but what was there to tell, really? That she knew her mother had played the piano for him and that they had written to each other all those years? That his letters were still there, between the pages of the notebooks?

After an awkward pause, in which they both seemed to be considering whether they would let the encounter remain an exchange of banalities or whether they would move on to a conversation of actual substance, Father Slade regarded her gravely and said, "I meant to go over and visit the island when I came back to Havendale, but I never got around to it. I'm sorry about that now. Isn't that always the way? We put off the most important things."

"Did my mother know you were back?"

"I think she must have heard from Father McKenna. He was saying Mass on the island then. I was going to write your mother to let her know. We hadn't been in touch in a long time. But it was another one of those things I didn't get around to." He placed his hand on Rachel's arm. "I know the shock must have been very great. I hope you have been able to make your peace with it."

Rachel wasn't sure how to respond, so she said simply, "I was glad you were able to do the funeral."

Father Slade's face flushed, and he lowered his voice when he answered. "The coroner may have called it suicide, but your father didn't believe that she meant to take her own life, and neither did I. Your mother was a member of the church, a devout woman, and she deserved what any member of the church deserved." He glanced uneasily from side to side, checking to make sure that no one could overhear them. "It was the least I could do."

Her hands went cold. What he had just told her was not possible.

"I was grateful that your father called me, that he asked me to say the Mass."

She tried to think of something appropriate to say, something to cover her shock and confusion, but she could only nod mutely.

Father Slade removed his hand from her arm as footsteps sounded at the front of the church, and the crucifer and altar boy came down the aisle. "We didn't lock up, Father," the older of the boys said.

"That's fine. I'll take care of it."

The boys said good night and went on out of the church.

"I have to get back to Havendale or I'd ask you to have supper with me," Father Slade said. "Maybe another time."

He extended his hand, and she placed her hand in his. His skin was warm and slightly damp. "I always remember your mother in my prayers," he said.

"Thank you," Rachel responded in a near whisper. She hurried toward the door.

Outside, the sky had grown dark. She went on up the street, away from town. She could not face the familiar store windows and the Saturday evening shoppers. She walked as fast as she could, wanting to put distance between herself and the great stone structure of the church. One block passed and then another. She was among houses, in a cast-off neighborhood of Barton, where paint peeled on the clapboards and rickety front porches looked like they might collapse into the front yards. Now that she was far enough away, the tears came. She cried silently, in a numb fury, uncertain if her legs were moving beneath her, oblivious to the sidewalk that ran on before her. It had been a heart attack. Suicide. She could not begin to connect the word with her mother. The suggestion was inconceivable. Her mother could not have done such a thing. Rachel felt as if the air had been punched out of her. It could not be true.

She wandered the back streets of Barton, barely aware of the houses bordering the sidewalk or the cars that passed. Why had her father lied to her? She considered the possibility that Father Slade had somehow gotten the story mixed up, though it seemed unlikely he would be wrong about the coroner. Clearly he believed that she was aware of the circumstances, whatever they were. She felt sick with rage at her father and anyone else who had participated in this deception. Was it an accident, an accident that looked like suicide? If this was the case, why didn't her father tell her? There was nothing to conceal if it was an accident, no reason to keep the truth from her.

Rachel kept on walking, her mind a stunned place where anger and sadness fought with each other. She thought of the meals she had cooked for her father that year and all the times she had cleaned the house, repulsed by the awareness that she had felt responsible for him. She never should have come back to the island. She should have let him rot in that house by himself. So what if he was her father? She had no say about which family she was born into, she had no choice when it came to fathers. Her mother may have made the mistake of marrying him, but Rachel did not have to participate in that mistake and perpetuate it. To lie to your own daughter about her mother's death—could there be a greater deception? She wanted to strangle him, to seize him by his scrawny neck and shake the life from his body. For a long time, she had not thought of him as her father. Now he was beneath any notice at all.

Her vision blurred, Rachel fished in her pocket for a tissue. She blew her nose and glanced in confusion from one side of the street to the other. After a moment, she was able to orient herself and figure out the way back to town. She could not go find Babs now. It would be impossible to spend the night with her, having to pretend or, worse, telling her. In some distant part of herself, she registered the fact that she was cold and hungry, and that she could not stay outside all night. She walked back toward town. On Front Street, the lights seemed unnaturally bright. People were going into Anthony's for dinner, and the soda fountain was still open at the drugstore. The marquee over the movie theater glowed, announcing that *A Man and a Woman* was playing. Rachel went quickly past the theater and into the Priscilla Alden, where she found the lobby of the hotel empty. She crossed the worn carpet to the front desk and tapped the bell sitting there. After a moment, Mrs. Santos appeared from behind a curtain that hung over a doorway behind the desk.

"Rachel," she said in surprise. "Haven't seen you in a long time."

"The ferry's not running. Guido's gone to get a new battery up in Providence."

Mrs. Santos made a clucking sound with her tongue. "That's not the first time I got people coming in here who can't get to the island."

Rachel nodded. "I know. So I need a room for the night."

"I wish I could give you at no charge, but I can't do that." Mrs. Santos gestured vaguely toward the empty space of the lobby. "I got a business to run."

"I'm paying, Mrs. Santos. I don't expect you to give me the room."

"Well, okay then, but I'm sorry you got stuck like this." Mrs. Santos reached beneath the desk and produced a key. "I give you a room on the second floor, in the back. You got a nice view from there."

Rachel thanked her, scooped up the key, and headed for the staircase at the back of the lobby.

"I leave the front door unlocked until midnight. You just come and go," Mrs. Santos called after her.

As she climbed the stairs, Rachel thought of the last time she had stayed at the hotel, after one of their family visits to see Andy. Her father would not pay for more than one room, so Rachel and her brothers slept on blankets on the floor. She remembered the strangeness of those nights, listening to her father snore while she lay awake, staring at the gray ceiling. The hotel had not changed much since those days. Threadbare carpet covered the stairs and, when she reached the second floor, the corridor was shrouded in darkness until she flipped the light switch on the wall.

Rachel went to room twenty and turned the key in the lock. The door swung inward, revealing a simple room furnished with a double bed covered in a chenille spread, a dresser against one wall, and a chair against another. She closed the door behind her and, without turning on the light, went to the window. Beyond the old pin factory, the dark surface of the water was visible, stretching away from the docks. She placed one hand on the window and held it there, wishing that something—the cool surface of the glass, the view of the bay—could tell her what her mother had done and why.

In the morning, Rachel boarded the ferry and stood at the railing during the crossing, with the wind on her face. As she watched the island grow closer, she clung to the knowledge that there was one notebook of her mother's diaries left which she had not yet read.

Chapter Thirty-one

October 1, 1945

We are different people now. I guess this is no surprise. From the moment he returned, Nate has been cheerful and helpful around the house and busy all the time. He is putting in a bathroom. At last—indoor plumbing. He doesn't go out at night. He stays here and plays with the boys and asks Rachel about her schoolwork. We feel almost like a normal family— except for Andy. I was so afraid of how Nate would respond to Andy, but he treats him no differently from the other children. He holds Andy on his lap and talks to him and pulls the little wooden truck around on the floor, which makes Andy laugh. The other night, after Rachel and the boys were in bed, we sat out on the porch. I asked him what it was like over there. He said, "We were wet and cold and hungry a lot. We shot at the Germans and they shot back." I can't get him to say more than this. Maybe it's for the best. I don't want to dwell on the past three years any more than he does.

October 9, 1945

I waited to tell Nate about the state school. I can't go on like this. I am exhausted. When we were in bed last night, I told Nate that this is what is done for children like Andy and explained that the doctor would help make the arrangements. Nate shook his head. "He's our son," he said. "He's not going anywhere." I pointed out that Andy can't go to the schoolhouse. "We can teach him at home," Nate said. Teach. His use of that word made me furious. Who is going to teach him and how? This is what the doctor says we have to do, I told him. Nate said they can come arrest us if they want, but he's not sending his son away to some state institution. He rolled over and would not say more. I could tell he wasn't asleep, just angry. After a long while, I heard his breath even out. I lay there staring at the outline of the window, asking God to help me.

October 12, 1945
Andy's third birthday. We had a cake with candles and Rachel and the boys sang "Happy Birthday." It brought tears to my eyes, seeing them there in a circle around him in the high chair, telling him to blow out the candles. Of course Andy could not understand, though he banged his fist on the tray and laughed. Junior blew out the candles for him, and they all clapped, which made Andy laugh more. He loves clapping. It is so hard to see Andy growing up. He looks like any three year old, though he's small, but in every other way he has remained at the level of a little more than a one year old. I know I should be grateful that he is healthy, but it is hard to remember these things when I look at him and then look at the other children. I can't stop myself from thinking how Andy should be, how he could be, if only… Stupid, I know. I pray to stop thinking things I should not think.

October 26, 1945
Some of the summer people have contacted Nate to do work on their houses before the cold sets in. What a weight has been lifted, for everyone on the island. We know the worst now—Pete Giberson killed in action, fighting the Japanese on some island no one had ever heard of up

by Alaska. We are not constantly waiting for bad news. I did not know how much the war was a constant presence until it was over. Rachel and the boys are so glad to have their father back. Have I been too hard on Nate? Perhaps. When things are good, as they are now, it's easy to forget the bad times.

November 5, 1945
Still no frost. I have planted a second crop of lettuce, and the tomatoes I put in late still have a few green ones. It is wonderful to have a salad so late. How much these small things mean—good food, and the children playing and laughing out in the yard. It is as if a death sentence has been removed from all of us. We walk around with amazed expressions on our faces, unable to believe our luck. We have survived. Everyone on the island seems touched by this sense of wonder that we have made it, except, of course, the Gibersons. I find it hard to look Mrs. Giberson in the eye when I meet her down at the store. I know this is cowardice and a terrible lack of charity on my part, but her pain is too hard to bear. She will never be the same. How cruel it is. Lydia Giberson has gone off to college. Mrs. Giberson says she doesn't think Lydia will ever return to the island, not to live here, at least. It's too hard for her, having lost her twin brother. They were inseparable, you know, Mrs. Giberson said when I asked about Lydia the other day. I felt a terrible sense of guilt. Here I am full of happiness and relief when others have lost so much. There is no way to make sense of it.

November 13, 1945
I did not speak to Nate about sending Andy to the state school again until last night. I wanted him to think about it, as I have. I wanted us to discuss it in some real way. By now he can see what it is like to care for Andy, how much is involved. We were getting into bed, and I asked him

if he had thought more about it. "Yes," he said. "I will not send my son away to be taken care of by other people." I tried to talk with him. It would not be easy, and it's not something I take lightly, I said, but we have to think of the other children, too. What is it doing to them? I could not bring myself to say what I dread most, that I will spend the rest of my life taking care of Andy, never free of having a child. "I won't do it," Nate said. He grabbed the pillow and the extra blanket in the closet and went out to the couch. In the morning, he glared at me over the table at breakfast, as if I were some horrible, unfeeling person. As usual, he acts as if the decision is his alone to make. But it is not his alone. I am the one who does everything for Andy—changes his diapers, feeds him, wipes his nose three hundred times a day, rocks him when he cries. It is not right that Nate has the final say, not when the whole burden of taking care of Andy falls on me and will fall on me for years to come.

November 15, 1945

After a day of tense, guarded exchanges, Nate is speaking to me again. I can see that he believes it is settled, that he believes he has won. There will be no more talk about sending Andy to the state school, his leveling look seems to say. He claims no one on the mainland is going to bother to interfere with us over here. They are not going to come and physically take Andy away, and if they try, he says he will shoot them. Now that it is settled, in his mind at least, he moves on. He does not want to go back to the old patterns of constant fighting, constant pushing each other away, he seems to be telling me. Fine. I do not want to go back to that, either. After our long separation, I feel we have a chance to start over. We feel like old friends now, like two people who have known each other forever. Romance does not mean what it once did, but that is all right. Being friendly, being companions, counts for more than it used to. Maybe, I sometimes think, it is even enough. I will let go of talking about sending Andy to the state school. I will be a good, quiet wife.

December 6, 1945
A letter from Father Slade at last. I put off writing to him about Andy, though I have wanted to ask him for advice. As much as I felt uncertain, even recoiled from the idea at first, I am determined to convince Nate that we have no choice but to send Andy to the state school. Now I have Father Slade's response. It is not what I expected. I felt the reproach in this letter when I first read it, and it brought tears to my eyes. Does he think I don't love Andy? Of course I love him, which is why I believe the state school is the best solution. There he can be cared for by people who understand his condition. It is easy for Father Slade to suggest looking for other options, but I don't know what they could be.

Dear Phoebe,

I was so glad to hear from you and to know that your life is settling back into something like a routine again. I was glad, also, that you shared your concerns about Andy. There is a family here in the church who has a feeble minded daughter. They were about to send her to the state school when they met another family whose child has had such a bad experience there. They have formed a group to try to find some other way to care for these children and train them. I know it is complicated, but I would urge you to ask questions about the state school and whether there are other possibilities. These families have opened my eyes to the needs of these children, which are not always met in the big institutions. Maybe your state school is different, but I would do some investigating if I were you. I have always believed that children are a gift from God—all children. I would be sorry to see you send Andy to the state school and then find later that you regret doing this. I am sure you have prayed about this. You must have faith and trust in a wisdom that is greater than any we can know here on earth. I understand that you question why God has given you this difficulty to bear, but ours is not to question but to love. I hope and pray that you will be guided by love, the love that Christ showed us in his great sacrifice. I am keeping you in my prayers, as always. Do send me your thoughts. It means so much to get your letters and to be reminded of Snow.

With all my affection, and continued prayers,

Daniel

December 27, 1945

Nate cut down a tree, and we decorated it on Christmas Eve. Even Andy seemed to understand that something special was happening. On Christmas night, we had the party at the Improvement Center. Since Andy was born, I have not gone to the party. I let the children go by themselves and stayed home with the baby. This year Nate insisted. We were all going, the whole family. I held Andy on my lap the whole time, and he was mostly quiet. He only made those strange moaning sounds a few times, and with all the noise in the room, people did not seem to notice. They were polite. People came up and talked to me and simply ignored Andy. This is what they do, they pretend he isn't there, pretend they can't see him. I don't blame them. I would do the same thing if I were in their shoes. Still, I was glad I went to the party. It felt like an ordinary Christmas, like Christmas the way we remember it, before the war, though the exchange of gifts, the happy greetings, seemed tentative, as if we were testing out this new freedom and didn't quite believe it. Mrs. Brovelli made her Christmas cookies for the first time in four years. There's enough sugar at last. And coffee! And real butter. How luxurious these things seem, but soon we will take it all for granted again.

January 8, 1946

Sad news. Mrs. Cunningham is leaving the island. She will go to live with her daughter in Connecticut. The Coast Guard is automating the lighthouse. There is no need for a keeper anymore. Even if we did still have a keeper, we would have had to find someone else. Ethan Cunningham is married now and living in New York with his wife. What everyone said about him was true—he was not meant for life on an island. Certainly he was not meant to be a lighthouse keeper. I will miss Mrs. Cunningham. Weeks passed sometimes when I didn't see her, but simply the knowledge that she was here on Snow made a difference. She was the one person I truly counted as a friend. She was the one person who fussed over Andy and treated him like a normal baby.

January 17, 1946

I have been going to Our Lady during the day, when the children are off at school, and Nate is clamming or working on some project with Silas Mitchell. It's terribly cold in the church, but I can pray with much greater concentration there than at home. I take Andy with me and sit him on a blanket on the floor, beneath the statue of the Virgin. I know that she understands I want only what is best for Andy and the rest of us. I pray for an answer. Lord, show me what is best for my child. In the church, it all seems simple and clear—the help they could give Andy at the state school that we can't give him here—but once I go home, the doubts creep over me again, and I wonder how I will ever convince Nate. We have not spoken of it again, and I will not be the one to bring it up. But sometimes I see Nate looking at me in that way of his, as if he is try-ing to catch me thinking about it. It does seem that he can read my mind. I guess this happens when you live with someone for years, but I find it terribly annoying. Then there are those other times, of course, when he doesn't understand the most basic things about what I am thinking and feeling, even when I spell it out for him in capital letters. How hopeless we are at understanding each other, and how difficult it is to know another person.

January 23, 1946
Cold days and cold nights. It was just 15 degrees when we woke this morning. I seem to have far less tolerance for the cold than I used to. Maybe it's just that I don't remember winters in the past. Am I getting old? What a strange thought. Of course, thirty-six is hardly "old." But I feel if not older then different, at least. I get tired more easily than I used to, and when I look in the mirror, I am surprised. Who is that woman with a lined face? I ask myself. Who is that woman with a pudgy neck? It's ridiculous, but I see now that I really believed that I would never change, that I would remain that thin girl who went running to meet Nate in the park in Barton forever. I know I am just as vain as the next woman, though I like to pretend I am not. I can't help thinking that it's Andy who has aged me more than anything else. The days seem to consist of one long struggle to get him to eat and to keep his nose clear and to make sure he's wearing clean clothes and clean diapers. The only time I have to myself is when he sleeps, and it never seems long enough. I find myself fantasizing about horrible things, like giving him some drug that will make him sleep all day, just for once. God forgive me.

February 4, 1946
I have been sitting here while Andy is asleep trying to write to Father Slade. I have not answered his letter yet. This is the longest I have ever taken to respond to him, but every time I look at his last letter, I feel his reproach, and I don't know how I can respond. I almost threw that letter away, instead of saving it here with the others. I didn't want to read it again. Everyone else thinks they know what is best for me when they

don't. Andy is crying again—enough of this.

March 12, 1946

I took Andy over to see the doctor yesterday. The children were in school, and Nate was there when they got home. Captain Tony was running an extra ferry yesterday to bring a load of wood over, so I did not have to spend the night. I wish Nate had gone with me. Then he could have heard what the doctor said. Andy is growing the way you would expect for a mongoloid, but the doctor thinks his hearing is impaired. This is common. Of course it will be harder to teach him to talk, if he can, in fact, learn to talk. So far he makes only his moans and garbled sounds, though Rachel and the boys were all talking by his age. I can't help making such comparisons. When the doctor finished the examination, he said that the nurse would give me the papers for the state school on the way out. I could not bring myself to tell him that Nate is against it. I simply nodded and carried Andy out to the waiting room, suddenly aware of how heavy he is in my arms.

March 16, 1946

The piano tuner came over today. Every year I imagine that he will go directly to Our Lady of Snow without stopping at my house, but then he knocks on the door. "How's that piano?" he said when I opened the door. "In need of a little attention," I said. He laughed and replied he was sure that was the case. I made him a cup of tea when he was finished, and we sat at the table with Andy in the high chair, banging his fists on the tray and making his repertoire of noises. Then Mr. Gould went over to tune the piano at the church. Nate thinks that Saint Joseph's pays to have my piano tuned, too, so I can practice the Sunday hymns at home. This is what I have told him. But I know that it is Father Slade. He sends the money every year so that Mr. Gould will tune my piano, too. I could not help thinking as I watched Mr. Gould at his work that he is a messenger of sorts, a tangible link to Father Slade. How strange that someone you never see can remain so real and present in your life. It's been eight years now since we have seen each other.

April 9, 1946
The Cheavings sent a car over on the ferry yesterday, with instructions for Nate to give it a tune-up and leave it in the lot by the dock, ready for them when they arrive in May. This is just one of many projects. All the summer people suddenly want something—houses painted, bathrooms installed. There is money again, even here on the island. It seems like a miracle after the years of the war, and the years before that, when we made do with so little. Nate comes home these days and hands me a ten dollar bill to do the shopping. He doesn't even ask what I've spent it on or look for the change. Mrs. Daggett has the store stocked, and the summer people haven't arrived yet. It's the most substantial sign of the change in the times, to walk into the store and see the shelves full. I confess the sight almost made me cry the other day.

May 13, 1946
The piano sounds wonderful, now that it is tuned again, but I have no time to play. I sat down the other afternoon and the moment I touched the keys, Andy began howling in that horrible way of his. I am so undone by that sound that I picked him up immediately and paced the room with him, trying to distract him from whatever it was that set him off. It is a relief when Rachel comes home from school. She is better with him than any of the rest of us. She has such patience. He hardly ever howls like that with her, which I find frustrating and upsetting. I am his mother after all. But then I am grateful that someone can get him to be quiet for a few minutes. Rachel has managed to teach him a few words, giving him

a cookie if he talks clearly enough that you can make out something. I get so impatient and crazy when I am alone with him, and I don't have time for these things. She will sit with him for hours. I should simply thank God for this.

May 21, 1946
I wrote to the doctor a couple of weeks ago and explained that Nate was against sending Andy to the home. I asked the doctor if he could write to Nate and tell him the things he has told me. The letter arrived yesterday. I left it on the table where Nate would see it when he came in. He read it as soon as he came home and before I could speak to him, left the house. He did not return for supper. It was only later, after the children were in bed, that I heard him outside. I feared the worst, that he had gone off with Silas Mitchell, but there was no sign of being drunk when he came through the door, with the doctor's letter in his hand. "You put him up to this," he said. I tried to explain that I just wanted him to know what the doctor has said. "I told you I will not send my son away," Nate said. We stood on either side of the table, staring at each other in that awful way, neither of us backing down or giving in. I have done that time and again. I have let Nate say what is right and what is best for us, when it was not how I felt. I have let him have his way, let him tell me what to do. But this time I am determined. This is not his decision to make for me. I said nothing else, but he could see in my face that I was not done with this. He slept on the couch again and has not spoken to me all day.

May 24, 1946
I have spent the last two days putting in the garden. Andy loves the warm days and sits on a blanket beside me while I work, playing with his blocks, until he spots Rachel coming home and jumps up. At times like these, I forget for a moment. He's a child like any other child. But the

other times come too quickly, when he suddenly begins howling and hurls his food across the room, refusing to eat it. Then he stares at me when I try to make him understand what he has done and that he cannot do it again. It's that dumb look, that lack of understanding, that drives me to madness. By this age, I could reason with my other children, I could teach them.

Nate and I have gone back to being wary friends. We do not speak of Andy. It seems that Nate tries hard not to draw any attention to Andy. He keeps jumping up and grabbing him when Andy is about to howl. So we go on, and the days close over our last fight, as if it had never happened. But it did happen, and neither of us has forgotten.

August 19, 1946
Summer has flown by. No time for anything but the garden and the children and Sundays at church and cleaning the summer people's houses. Nate is as busy as ever, like the time after the hurricane. It is a tremendous relief to think that we will be able to make it through the winter without skimping and worrying and going into debt at the store. Brandon also sent me some money a few weeks ago and the statement for the savings account he set up. I tell Nate about the money Brandon sends, but I have not told him about the savings account. That money is for Rachel and the boys' education, so they can go to college.

Rachel and Phil and Junior are so happy during these summer days. The boys go off fishing and clamming, and Rachel now has babysitting jobs. She is so grown up, so graceful and beautiful. I look at her sometimes, and I am astonished to think that she is my daughter. She has the loveliest hair which I braid for her in the mornings—so thick and shiny. Everyone says she will be a beauty when she grows up. Yes, but she is bright, too. She is constantly asking questions, constantly wanting to know more. I find myself imagining already the day when she will leave the island and go off to better things. For she will leave. I will make sure that she gets an education, that she can do whatever she wants.

September 8, 1946
Another visit to the doctor. Andy has gained weight, and the sounds he makes are clearer now, though Rachel seems to be the only one who can really understand him. The doctor explained that by the age of five, Andy should be ready for toilet training. We could wait to send him to the state school until after he is trained, or we could send him before then. I came back on the ferry, trying to think how I will convince Nate. If I have to simply take Andy myself, I will. Who's to stop me from getting on the ferry with Andy one morning and taking the bus to Providence? But I know this is wrong. I can't do it without Nate. Andy was completely quiet on the ferry. I think it was the wind. He kept rubbing his face and gazing around with his big eyes, as if he was trying to see what was touching him. It was such a relief to have him quiet. I imagined staying on the ferry for days, riding back and forth in blissful silence.

September 24, 1946
A letter from Father Slade. I had almost given up hope and convinced myself that I would never hear from him again. My hand actually shook as I opened the envelope. He thinks I am a cruel and selfish woman. Maybe he is right.

> Dear Phoebe,
>
> You must forgive my long silence. There are so many things to do in a day, but that is a poor excuse. I have thought of you and prayed for you often. I hope the summer passed happily for you and your family. I am sure it is good to have Nate home and life back to something like normal. We didn't know how long

the war was or how hard until it was over. Not that those of us who stayed here at home and made do without butter have much to complain about. Whatever sacrifices we made are nothing compared to the men who fought over there. I still feel that I should thank each one of them personally. So shake Nate's hand for me and tell him how very grateful I am to him and all the other veterans. You know there have been times when I questioned whether I had made the right choice in life in becoming a priest. I felt this keenly during the war. Sure, I told myself, children still need to be taught, and the church needs to be there for people, perhaps now more than ever. But if I were not a priest, I would have gone overseas, too. I did not want people to think that I used the priesthood to shirk my responsibility. Then I realized this was vanity. What I really cared about was what other people thought. This is not the first time that sort of vanity has been my downfall. Why am I telling you this? Because it has occurred to me that it may be the same sort of vanity that has prompted you to go along with the plans to send Andy to the state school. I have not written in a long time. You may have already made the arrangements for Andy. If that is so, I do not want to intrude. But as I have prayed about this, I have felt strongly that I should raise this question with you. I can imagine it's impossible for you not to feel that Andy is somehow a reflection of you, seeing as he is your child. Of course it is not easy to have a child like Andy, who is not what you hoped for. I am suggesting, however, that you try to move beyond such impulses that come down to a sort of vanity in the end. I would not say this to you if I had not struggled with the same impulses myself. How many times I have thought first about how I will be viewed by others, instead of paying attention to what really matters, which is what lies in my heart. I do believe that God speaks to each of us, and if we listen long enough and hard enough, and pay attention not to what the outer world tells us but to that inner prompting, we will discover God's will. My prayer for you is that you do this, that you listen long and hard, and ask what God would want for Andy and his life. If I have taken liberties in saying all this, forgive me. It has been a repeated theme in my prayers, and I did not feel I could keep it from you. These words come with my deepest affection and respect for you.

In Christ's love,

Daniel

October 9, 1946

I have not even wanted to open these pages since getting the letter from Father Slade. What he wrote has followed me around for weeks. At first I felt that of course he was right. I was being vain and weak and stupid. Father Slade knows better than I do, I told myself. He has that vision and wisdom. He has thought and prayed about these things with far greater strength than I have. But then I began to see it differently. I was praying at the church, saying the rosary. I looked up at the Blessed Virgin Mary, and I saw that look in the statue's eyes, a look of forgiveness and compassion and understanding. For a moment, I was not kneeling before a statue but before an actual presence. Her eyes were suddenly alive. I felt as if she was speaking to me, as if she were about to bend over and place her hand on my shoulder. She was telling me that I am Andy's mother, and that as his mother, I am the one most able to decide what he needs. Nate is not his mother. Father Slade is not his mother. They do not change his diapers and wipe the food from his face. I felt suddenly angry, thinking of Father Slade so very far away, presuming to tell me what is best for my son. How does he know? How can he have any idea how it feels to care for Andy day after day, knowing that I am no good at this? The Blessed Virgin understood. Her look told me that I am the mother, I am the one who should decide. Her look told me that she did not judge me.

October 18, 1946

Andy is four years old. Rachel made a great fuss over his birthday. She wanted to invite the whole island, but I refused. There's no telling how Andy would behave. He's not used to being around other people. It might scare him. Rachel spent all afternoon making a chocolate cake, and she got Nate to help her with some wooden train cars. They've been working on them ever since the summer. Nate carved them out of wood and put on little wheels, then Rachel painted them. Now Andy wants to do nothing but slide them back and forth across the floor, making a great racket. How I wish every day could be like his birthday, with Nate and the children paying so much attention to Andy. But every day is not like that. The rest of the time it is just me, alone here in the house for hours, wrestling Andy in and out of his clothes, trying to feed him, trying to quiet him when he gets agitated. It is impossible to explain how exhausting it is to take care of a child like this.

November 7, 1946

I feel a despair greater than any I have known in the past. I have to force myself to go to Andy in the morning, to lift him from the crib and lay him on the towel to be changed. Rachel and the boys can get off to school with little help from me. This is a good thing, as Andy requires all my attention and energy. It's the same way when they all come home from school. I want to sit down with them the way I used to, to hear about whatever has happened that day, but Andy sets up his howling the minute I turn away from him. Sometimes I think he fully understands what he is doing, that he is being intentionally demanding, not allowing me to pay attention to anyone or anything else. I say the Hail Mary continuously.

December 11, 1946

Why is it that Nate and I always seem to be at cross purposes? These days he is constantly cheerful. He tosses a football around with the boys and tells jokes and makes them laugh at supper. He sits beside Rachel while she does her homework and asks her to explain it to him. He even makes Andy laugh, tossing him in the air until he makes this crazy sound. He's become the most attentive father, and when he's not out in the shed working on a car or fixing something, he's working here in the house, painting the bathroom at last and repairing the posts on the porch. He strikes me as maddeningly happy in my current mood. It's as if he has become this way on purpose, to taunt me. I know this is a ridiculous idea, but it does seem that the worse my mood is, the happier he becomes. I start each day by saying the rosary. I can't think how else to shake this gloom that hangs over me. The prayers help a little. I feel more ready to face the rest of the day, though there are times when they barely make a difference. I know I should not write such words. Prayer always makes a difference. Yes, I believe this, but sometimes I feel like Job, shouting into the void.

December 20, 1946

Today I received a Christmas card from Father Slade. It was worse than not hearing from him at all. A pretty scene of the holy family at the manger. Inside a printed message with his signature. Nothing else. I have not written to him, and I will not write to him. There is no way he can understand me. He has not even tried to understand. This is more upsetting than any of the rest of it, to think that he did not trust me enough, that he could not give me the benefit of the doubt about Andy. Somehow I am going through the motions of getting ready for Christmas. Nate went to the mainland two weeks ago and got real store-bought presents for the kids. He's like a child himself. He can't wait to give them the presents. I am trying to join in the general sense of merriment, but my heart is not in it this year.

January 16, 1947

I have decided to wait until March, when Andy will be nearly four and a half. I will say nothing between now and then. I will hold my tongue, as I have so many times before. Sometimes it amazes me that Nate and I live in the same house. How can he not see what it is like for me to take care of Andy along with everything else—cooking, cleaning, washing and mending all our clothes, making sure that Rachel and the boys are clean and dressed and ready for school. But he does not see. He is blissfully oblivious. As long as he has what he wants, he does not notice what goes on with the rest of us. We might as well be living on opposite sides of the world.

February 10, 1947

I don't have the will or the desire to write here anymore. If I have any moments to myself, I know I should spend them in prayer. How easy it is to lose a sense of God's presence. It frightens me sometimes, how quickly the prayers go stale and flat in my mind. On Sundays, when I stand at the altar, it all seems so potent and real. God is undeniably there. I feel that sense of guidance and forgiveness. I know God understands how I struggle. But back home, the rest of the week, I am not so certain. I must pray harder. I must make time for praying and reading the Bible a regular part of each day.

March 6, 1947

I waited to speak to Nate until the children were in bed, and he was done reading the newspaper. I showed him the last letter from the doctor. All the arrangements have been made with the state school. Andy is old enough that the move will not be too disruptive, the doctor says, and if we wait any longer, we will have to think about toilet training, which I cannot face. I told Nate that if he did not agree, I would take Andy over myself. I am not waiting for his permission any longer. I tried to make him see what it is like to take care of Andy, how it all falls on me. He simply stared at me. He did not say anything at all. We got into bed and lay there not touching or speaking. After a long time, I heard his breathing even out in sleep.

March 7, 1947

Nate came in from the shed at lunch time and said, "I'm not going to fight you anymore." So it is settled. I am going through Andy's clothes and getting everything ready. Nate will take him over next week, when the boys and Rachel are in school. It will be best this way. I see no point in alarming Rachel and Phil and Junior and having some prolonged goodbye. We will be going to visit Andy soon enough. It is not as if he is leaving the family. We can even bring him back for visits if we like. I feel at peace finally, knowing he will have the care he needs, the care I cannot give him.

Chapter Thirty-two

Rachel sat at the kitchen table in her house and turned the last page. There was nothing else, just the final brief entry. She watched the water sweeping over the rocks through the window and tried to remember the day when she arrived home from school to discover that Andy was gone. Her mother turned slowly as Rachel and Phil and Junior came banging through the door. They saw that her eyes were puffy and red. She told them that Nate had taken Andy to the state school. In Rachel's memory there had been other words, words of regret and grief, and her mother's tears and her own, followed by Rachel running out of the house and up the hill to the woods. She had wandered the paths in the center of the island, surrounded by the still presence of the trees. In the woods disbelief and revulsion, anger and sorrow, had taken shape inside her. At the heart of this response was her father and what he had done.

She returned to find the family seated at the table, about to eat. Rachel would not look at her father or speak to him, not that night or for days to come. She tried to remember more, but she could not retrieve anything beyond these isolated moments that had remained fixed in her mind for years. She saw her mother standing at the sink. She saw herself walking the path in the woods. She saw her father seated at the table. There was no explanation in this collection of moments for her belief that sending Andy away had been her father's doing from start to finish. Certainly her mother had never told her about the doctor or revealed that she had pushed Nate to take this step. It had been presented as an act handed down and executed by her father.

There was only one explanation, but she did not want to accept it. Her mother had planted the idea and then fed it, like a slow burning fire, and her father let her go on thinking that he was the demon responsible for sending Andy away, though he could have told her the truth, blaming Phoebe and the doctor and the state. That he had not done this was as surprising and strange as the knowledge that Phoebe was the one who wanted Andy to go.

Rachel went to the stove and put water on to boil. Through the window, she saw cars turning up Bay Avenue, leaving Our Lady. She watched the cars pull away and wondered how one went about rearranging and rewriting one's own past. She did not see how she could fit the past she knew into the altered landscape that confronted her now. They were all different people—her mother, her father, even she herself. They had been playing badly assigned roles, but these roles had come to define them. There was no telling who they truly were.

The tea kettle began to whistle, startling her. Rachel took the kettle from the burner and reached for a cup on the shelf, moving mechanically through the familiar motions. The steam rose as she poured water into the cup, warming her face. She considered returning the last diary to her father's house before he came home, but she no longer cared if he knew that she had read them. She had gone straight to his house from the ferry that morning, found the place empty, and taken the last volume back to her house. She had managed to get off the ferry without seeing or speaking to Brock or Alice, and when she went up to her father's, Nick's jeep was not there, parked at the side of the road. This was a relief. She did not want to see or speak to anyone.

Absently dunking the tea bag, she took the milk from the refrigerator and added some to the cup. She wished she knew why her mother had stopped keeping a diary or had destroyed other volumes if they existed. Rachel was left with only bits and pieces, hints and clues. If she could read the rest of the story, in her mother's own words, she might be able to make sense of it.

She heard Eddie's truck before she saw it through the window, coming from the direction of the church. Maybe he would go past without stopping. She went on half-hoping for this until he pulled over in front of her house, shut off the engine, and stepped from the cab.

"Come in," she called when he knocked.

Eddie was dressed in his Sunday clothes, a pair of clean khaki pants and a plaid button-down shirt. He wore a wool jacket, open down the front, over the shirt. He stepped through the door as he always did, suddenly taking up a lot of room. "You got stuck on the mainland, huh?"

Rachel nodded.

"Alice was really fuming this time. She says she's going to pull Guido's contract, but I think that's just a threat. There ain't exactly ferry operators standing in line. So you got fitted for the bridesmaid dress?"

"Yes," Rachel answered, surprised to be reminded of her reason for going to Barton.

"I'm sorry Nick didn't go."

"I thought he was going to get on the ferry. I really did, up until the last minute, when Guido pulled up the gangplank. I guess he's made up his mind. He didn't especially want to go to college to start with." She glanced out the window and then turned back toward Eddie. "I have to ask you something. Do you know how my mother died?"

Eddie shot her a quick look. "What do you mean?"

"I saw Father Slade yesterday. He said the death certificate read suicide. Did you know this?"

Eddie nodded yes.

"And you didn't tell me."

"Your father made me promise."

Rachel felt an overwhelming sense of rage. "How could you lie to me about something like that?"

"I didn't lie to you, Rachel. I just didn't tell you."

She gazed at him for a long moment, before she could bring herself to ask him what had happened.

He took a deep breath and said, "She took some pills, something the doctor gave her. Nate said she wasn't trying to kill herself. It was an accident."

"So why did the death certificate say suicide?"

"The coroner said it had to be intentional, an overdose like that, but nobody believed him. It was a mistake, an accident. I told Nate he should tell you, but he didn't listen to me. He wanted to have a Catholic burial. The only way to pull off the burial here on the island was to make sure nobody else knew."

"What did he think, that I was going to report Father Slade to the Catholic church?"

"He didn't want you to have to go through that, knowing the truth."

"So you knew, Father Slade knew, and who else?"

"Alice and Brock, Gina and Joe, a few other people."

"The whole island."

"Brock was the one who found her, so you know, word got around. He went to deliver some groceries."

Rachel had heard all she wanted to hear. She wished now that Eddie would simply disappear and leave her to stare out the window.

"I'm sorry, Rachel."

She pushed her hair away from her face and shrugged. She could not look at him. "Apparently Father Slade wasn't in on the conspiracy."

"It wasn't exactly a conspiracy. And if it was, it wasn't a bad one."

Eddie crossed the floor and wrapped his arms around her. She pressed her face against the scratchy wool of his jacket, biting back tears. He ran his fingers through her hair.

"Hey," he said at last, cupping his hand beneath her chin and tilting her face toward his. "Nobody meant to lie to you."

"I know."

"Every one of us felt responsible. It's been eating at us ever since. We thought maybe we could make it better for you." He wiped the tears from her eyes, brushing his fingertips over her cheek, and hugged her again.

She kept her face pressed to his jacket, crying silently.

"Rachel? If you're going to be mad at anybody, be mad at me, okay?"

She nodded. Her ran his hand over her hair again and pulled away. "I'm supposed to have dinner at Gina and Joe's. Why don't you come?"

"No. Not right now."

"I'll stop by later then, okay?" He pressed her to his chest, holding her close, and turned to the door.

She wanted to say something as she watched him go, but the capacity for speech seemed to have left her. He latched the door quietly and took off in the truck.

Watching him go off down the road, she thought of what the islanders had done. They had lied, yes, but they had done so to protect her. Even Gina and Joe had participated in the fiction that allowed for a Catholic Mass and burial. She had underestimated them, imagining that their Catholic faith represented little more than a set of rule-bound habits.

Rachel glanced at the school folders spread on the table. They would have to wait. She took her jacket from the peg and let herself out of the house. The wind blew off the water, making her hair swirl around her face. She pushed the tangled strands away from her eyes and went down the road, past the lighthouse and the inn. At Our Lady of Snow she turned up the hill.

The door to the church was unlocked. Rachel slipped inside and went up the aisle, taking a seat in the first row, in front of the statue of the Blessed Virgin. She could not bring herself to pray. No, the time for prayer was past. What she wanted was a conversation. "Why didn't you try to stop her?" she whispered.

The statue looked down with large eyes that struck Rachel suddenly as unbearably sad. They seemed to be saying that of course the Blessed Virgin Mary had tried to stop her, all of heaven had tried to stop her, but that was the thing about human beings. You could not stop them from doing the heartbreaking things they did.

Behind her, Rachel heard the door click open. She turned to see her father walking up the aisle. He walked the way he always did, with a slow gait that was somewhere between a saunter and a shuffle. When he reached the front row, he said, "I guess Guido got that old tub of a ferry running finally. We wondered what happened to you."

"I stayed at the Priscilla Alden."

Nate placed his hand on top of his head, feeling for the battered baseball cap. He removed the hat and held it by the brim. "Eddie said you found out about your mother."

Rachel stared at him. His weathered face appeared more shrunken than ever. "You should have told me the truth."

"I didn't see any sense in it. You were torn up enough as it was."

"Did it ever occur to you that I had a right to know?"

"I didn't want you to remember her that way. I didn't want anybody to remember her that way." Nate's tone dropped on these words. "I swear she didn't know what she was doing. She was feeling blue, worse than usual, and she just…took too many of those pills. She didn't know what would happen. I wish she had killed me instead. I wish that every day.

That stupid doctor. He said the pills would cheer her up. He didn't say they could kill you if you took too many."

"Did she leave a letter?"

"No. She just left the diaries."

"Where?"

"Sitting on the table."

"All of them?"

Nate nodded.

"So that was her letter—the diaries?"

"I don't know. I don't think she meant it like that."

Her father could explain it any way he wanted, but it seemed clear to Rachel that her mother had left the diaries there knowing they might be her last words.

"Why did you want me to read them?" she asked.

Nate shifted his weight from one foot to the other. "I thought if you found out how she died, maybe you wouldn't blame me. And I wanted you to know it wasn't me that sent Andy away. I never wanted Andy to go to that place. I hated everything about it."

He looked small standing there, grasping the hat, his shoulders folded in toward each other. For a moment, all traces of the bully were gone, and she saw the boy he must have once been. As angry and confused as she felt, Rachel recognized that there was something larger at work in her father's words and actions, which called for a different response. There were times when he had been a selfish, unfeeling person who had made everyone around him miserable, but he was not made of pure evil or pure good. Rachel wanted to turn to the statue of the Blessed Virgin and scream at her, to lie down and beat her fists on the floor. It was so much easier, and safer, to split the world into good and bad.

"I tried to treat your mother right these last years," Nate said. "I tried to make up for the hard times."

Rachel felt the tears sliding down her cheeks. Nate went pawing through his pockets and produced a rumpled napkin, which he handed to her. She took it and patted her eyes. After a moment, he sat down beside her. She could not remember ever being with her father in the church before. He had not even come to her brothers' baptisms. Now they sat facing the altar as though they were waiting for Mass to begin. She could only think that this would amuse and please her mother.

"I know that you did," Rachel said finally. She could not bring herself to say the words with much volume, and she could not bring herself to say more than that.

They sat in silence for a few minutes, until Nate cleared his throat and said, "Gina sent a plate of food over for you. It's back at the house. Pork roast and potatoes."

"Sunday dinner?"

"Sunday dinner."

Getting to her feet, Rachel waited while Nate settled the hat back in place, pulled low over his forehead, so his eyes were just visible, and slowly rose from the pew. Together they turned and walked out of the church.

Chapter Thirty-three

Rachel sat on the floor, surrounded by boxes, sorting through piles of paper and books. It was hard to imagine she had accumulated so much in just nine months. The shades rattled in the breeze that came through the open window. Though it was late in the day, her feet were bare and she wore shorts, and the air that moved through the room was warm and laced with the smell of salt. The mud flats gleamed in the last of the sunlight beyond the rocks. There would be time this summer to go clamming and to ride a bike out to Gooseneck Cove at sunset, but today she had other things to do.

Threading through the cardboard boxes that littered the floor, she went to the kitchen cupboards and began stacking plates and mugs on the counter. Many of the summer people had already come over for a weekend at least, and down the road the cottages waited for the true start of summer, boards removed from the windows and curtains framing the glass. Rachel wrapped the dishes in newspaper and placed them in a box. She would live with her father until after the ceremony. There was no sense in causing a scandal by moving over to Eddie's before they had made it legal. Rachel did not want to upstage Babs' wedding, which would come first. The wedding she and Eddie had planned for July did not involve bridesmaid's dresses and matching shoes. It would be a civil ceremony, conducted by a justice of the peace. Father Slade was arranging for an annulment of Rachel's first marriage, which could take up to a year. When that was finalized, he would bless the marriage at Our Lady of Snow, and it would be recognized by the church. The Brovellis could not be happier.

Rachel moved on to the mugs, lining them in a row on top of the wrapped plates, and then turned to the other cupboard. She had stored up more food than she would have imagined, cans of soup and jars of peanut butter and boxes of macaroni and cheese. She set it all on the counter, deciding what to keep and what to throw away. She was almost finished with clearing out the last cupboard when she glanced at her watch and saw that it was twenty minutes to ferry time. She pulled on socks and sneakers and hurried out of the house.

The sun fell slantwise over the tops of the trees, and the bay stretched to the horizon in the waning light, so startling in its beauty that Rachel stopped for a moment at the side of the road. It did not seem fair that Nick was leaving on such a glorious evening. She gazed across the water at the outline of the mainland, before going on, stirring up the dust as she walked along.

She could see the crowd assembled at the dock as she approached. Nick stood in the center, a duffel bag at his feet. In the distance, the ferry moved slowly toward the island. Rachel had dreaded this day, and now she dreaded saying goodbye. Nick received the notice to report for his Army physical just after graduation. He had gone to the mainland two days later and, as everyone expected, passed the physical. Now he was off to Fort Dix for basic training. He would catch the bus for New Jersey that night, when he reached Barton. It was a foregone conclusion that he would be sent to Vietnam. Yet as she spotted various people in the group milling around Nick, Rachel felt a surge of hope. He would be all right. She had to believe this.

Descending the path, she came alongside the porch, where George Tibbits sat facing the water with that quiet, expectant air. Miss Weeden was perched beside him, her purse cradled in her lap. Rachel called out hello and went on to the group at the foot of the dock. Alice stood next to Nick, her arm linked through his. Nick accepted the good wishes of Joe Brovelli and then his uncle, Will. The men slapped him on the back and pumped his free hand, as though, Rachel thought, they were sending him off to a football game.

"Nick," she said, stepping forward as the men fell back.

He shook her hand and replied, "Miss Shattuck."

She wished he would not call her that, but she knew he was right. She remained Miss Shattuck, though he was no longer her student.

"I'll write you," she said.

"That would be nice." His eyes were steady, conveying no emotion.

The ferry's horn sounded, and Alice started anxiously. Rachel took Nick's hand again, squeezed it, and moved away with the others. Crossing the parking lot, she leaned against one of the old cars. Alice wrapped her arms around her son and held him while Brock stood awkwardly off to the side, staring at the ferry easing alongside the dock. Lizzie and Ellen, skipping back and forth in front of their brother, paused to tug at his shirt.

Guido had just lowered the gangplank when Eddie and Nate came down the hill in Eddie's truck. They pulled up next to the store and jumped out, crossing the parking lot together. They both shook Nick's hand and exchanged a few words, before making a quick retreat, leaving Nick with his parents. Nate climbed the porch steps and took a seat beside Miss Weeden and George Tibbits. Eddie spotted Rachel and came to stand next to her.

Neither of them spoke. They watched as Brock gave his son a rough hug, and Alice clutched Nick's hand. Eddie put his arm around Rachel, pulling her close.

Down below, Nick hoisted the duffel bag to his shoulder and went up the gangplank. Standing at the railing, he waved as the ferry pulled away from the dock. The islanders raised their hands in a silent goodbye and watched as the ferry swung slowly out into the channel, sounding the horn one last time.

Acknowledgments

I would like to thank the New Hampshire State Council on the Arts and the National Endowment for the Arts for support that aided in the completion of this book. I am more grateful than I can say to Sandell Morse, Debbie Hodge, Jim Vescovi, and Brian Rogers, my first readers, for their invaluable suggestions and encouragement. Ilya Kaminsky deserves special thanks for reading multiple drafts, always being there in a writing emergency, and asking me to see and see again. For their assistance with research, I am indebted to Terry Whiting, Lewis Towler, Leela and David Towler Kausch, Ben Dwyer, Paul Nichols, Josephine Hughes, Hildred Crill, Bruce Loeckler, Mimi and Steve White, and Peg Custer. I am grateful to Deborah Schneider for her enthusiastic support, which has made publication a reality, and to Patrick Walsh, my editor, for helping to shape this work with his patient guidance. David Poindexter, my publisher, is a shining light in the publishing world—thank you, David, and thank you to all the good people at MacAdam/Cage, especially Melanie Mitchell, Tasha Kepler, Julie Burton, John Gray, and Aoise Stratford. Josie Avery made this book possible with her generous sharing of a place she loved. Her untimely death was a great loss, especially to those in the developmentally disabled community, whom she championed throughout her life. She will be remembered for the difference she made to so many people in so many ways. Finally, a heart full of love and thanks to Jim Sparrell, the most wonderful reader and research assistant, not to mention partner in cycling and life.

SOUTH KINGSTOWN PUBLIC LIBRARY

2143 00222 8492

AUG   2005

LIBRARY SURPLUS / WITHDRAWN

FIC   Towler, Katherine,
TOW   1956—

Evening ferry.

KINGSTON FREE LIBRARY
2605 Kingstown Rd., Kingston, RI 02881
401-783-8254